TEARS & CRUOR

BLOOD, BLOOM, & WATER BOOK FOUR

AMY MCNULTY

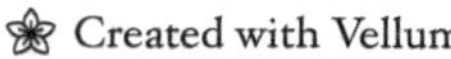 Created with Vellum

---

CHAPTER ONE

IVY

"Look! It's the Bean, love. We have to stop at the Bean. I haven't seen it up close for yonks."

Orin's curly, brown hair bobbed, its green specks catching the light in the last of the overcast sun. He skipped a step as we made our way from the Lake Michigan shoreline toward downtown Chicago, cresting over the last of the zigzagging path through Lake Shore Park. Though his scarf was dirty and loose around his neck and his forest green sweater—a perfect complement to his medium brown complexion—was all the defense he had against the frosty air without his coat, he didn't seem too disturbed by the cold. Some distance above his head, faint green balls of light hovered, moving this way and that like out-of-season butterflies in the stark November air.

The crowd of onlookers grew larger the farther we got from the lake, the curious glances growing in number as our group neared.

Autumn burst to life as we started to see what Orin was talking about: the shiny, reflective, oblong art installation near the road. She dropped my hand, but I caught it again. "Don't you dare."

"Dare what?" she snapped, with far too much conviction in

her deep brown eyes for a child of only eight. Her pale nose wrinkled as she fluffed her long, dark hair over one shoulder, and it kept floating behind her. Wind slapped like little daggers across my cheeks. Autumn's rainbow scarf and bright pink coat, her green leggings and brown faux fur boots were not enough to keep her warm in this biting wind.

"You're not going anywhere with Orin," I answered, gripping her hand hard through her pink woolen mitten. "How did you even get here? Where does Mom think you are?"

"At a friend's," she said without an ounce of guilt.

Orin was at the Bean now, his faery green lights zipping and reflecting off it like sparkling Christmas lights. I exchanged a look with Dean Horne, two steps behind me, not thinking about the awkwardness of the situation in which we found ourselves after what had just happened.

But even if I was newly crowned the vampire champion, it wasn't like I was entirely new to the game. I'd been the merfolk champion for weeks before this. Before today.

I didn't think Orin and the faefolk should have been parading around in front of tourists like flying little people with wings was an everyday thing.

Then again, it was nearing Thanksgiving and Christmas decorations were out in full force around the city, and it was hard to make out the details of a little figure inside each orb of light. Maybe they'd be brushed off as decorated drones.

My head throbbed and I closed my eyes for a second as I rubbed my forehead. Autumn took advantage of the momentary lapse of vigilantism and slid out of her mitten, running at full force after her faery prince.

The thousands-of-years-old charming creep.

"Hey!" I shouted after her, but Dean put a gentle but firm hand on my shoulder to stop me from giving chase.

"She's his champion," he said, as if simply reporting the fact that there was a thirty-minute wait to get some of Chicago's famous deep dish pizza.

"She's *my baby sister*." I whipped around to get out of his grip.

His face fell, his lips in a thin line. I could see myself reflected in his large, dark sunglasses, which hung out by a temple from the front pocket of his woolen trench coat—the puffy blue down coat, the dark hair pulled back, the pale face, the narrow nose, even the watery blue eyes, and the anger flashing in them. As the sun crested over the horizon, Dean took the opportunity to tuck his sunglasses more fully into his pocket, his unnatural sapphire eyes practically sparkling with the knowledge that he wouldn't need them to protect his strangely sensitive eyes for the rest of the night. With the 1940s-style trilby hat atop his medium brown hair and the stiff way he held himself, he looked like a film noir detective brought to life, minus a few years of living a grizzled, hard existence. Oh, he'd *lived* them—he had to have been born in the 1920s or 1930s—but those years didn't reflect in his late-teenage face. Unnaturally pallid, ashen face. Blink and you might wonder if you were staring at a handsome corpse.

"We need to have a chat," he said brusquely.

"You think?" Pacing, I watched Autumn over by the Bean, jumping up to brush her fingers upward against a floating green light. People were starting to notice, pointing out the lights and whispering amongst themselves, but frankly, I had other things to worry about.

"It's *all right*," said a familiar voice from somewhere to my right. I turned to take in the group approaching behind us. The one who'd spoken was Journey Slowe, one of the star students at Union High, my old school, and my step-sister's best friend.

My enemy's best friend.

Journey was one of the hangers-on of the vampires.

Whom I supposed were no longer my enemies and now were on my side in this war. This pointless war.

She was comforting Dante Johnson, another student at Union High—Journey's cousin, I thought, though I didn't know him that well. He looked a lot like her, from his dark brown skin to a similar curve of the nose.

He was legit in the middle of a panic attack, rambling something under his breath as his cousin tried to comfort him. He accidentally pushed her hand away as he freaked out.

"There were *mermaids* in the water. In Lake Michigan. In that water that's cold-as-a-witch's—"

"D!" Journey shouted, tugging down on a knit hat that flattened her long, black hair. Her expression scrunched up—in anger or concern, or both. The air turned to mist as she exhaled, rubbing her arms through her dark coat.

Her cousin stopped. He wasn't wearing enough to keep warm in this weather, though the choice looked intentional, his oversized black coat the only protection against the bite of the cold, his buzz-cut hair exposed to the frigid air. He gripped Journey by both shoulders. She had an extra coat wrapped over one arm, tucked against her, two purses dangling from her elbow. "There. Were. Flying. Gremlins. Journey." He enunciated each word.

"Faefolk," said one of the vampires—I didn't know all of their names yet. When I'd become the champion of water, I'd kind of hightailed it out of the hallowed halls of Union High that the vampires had infiltrated. This one, like all of them, was strikingly good-looking. And unhealthily pallid. As he removed his sunglasses from his face, his eyes shone like Dean's. He was wearing a 1940s-style suit similar to Dean's, his dark hair practically pasted into perfection beneath his hat. All the vampires dressed like they were stuck in a time that had long passed them by.

Some small way of clinging to the era they'd come from, I supposed.

"I don't think he cares much about the little details," said another vampire. This one I recognized. Devam Kapoor. Though he was dressed in a zoot suit, too, he wasn't supposed to be a relic from the first half of the twentieth century. He'd hung out with my friends and me all the time. He'd started dating Journey earlier this school year, and that apparently had led him down a path of no return. Though from the way Journey sneered at him just then, I couldn't say for sure if they were still an item.

Devam's medium brown complexion was now sallow, and though his shining blue eyes made him seem even more handsome and put together than before, there was a coldness about him that reached me even a few feet away. He slipped an arm around Dante, his other hand in his pocket, and said something like, "Let me get you up to speed," before I snapped my attention back to check on my sister.

"She's fine," said Dean, reading my mind. But vampires didn't do that—did they? Merfolk sort of could, but you had to be touching someone skin-to-skin to get access to their memories.

Autumn was posing for a photo in front of the Bean, one arm bent at her hip, and I found my feet moving, ready to slug Orin, acting like some older brother or babysitter, laughing as he snapped her photo with his phone.

Dean caught me by the wrist this time. Man, this guy was handsy.

Though I couldn't tell you why my heart sank to my stomach as I gazed at his face just then.

I swallowed and pushed through the tingling feeling reaching up to my head. I wasn't boy crazy. A handsome face wasn't enough to make me lose sight of what was going on here.

"Don't think I've forgotten that you've turned my classmates to vampires one by one." I stepped back, out of his reach. A jogger moved past just then and whirled her head back as she passed, but I didn't care if she'd heard.

"Two," he said. "We've turned two."

"Oh, okay, then. It's a two-for-one special on creating the undead after Halloween, so I guess I forgive you." I crossed my arms tightly over my chest.

"My aunt turned Mr. Kapoor," said Dean. If I didn't know

better, a look of guilt might have flashed over his features as he looked over his shoulder at the victim in question. "But Miss Kelly... That was Ember. It was an accident."

My mouth opened to retort, but the meaning of his words caught up with me. *Ember herself* had done this? My step-sister had turned Raelynn Kelly, one of my best friends' girlfriend, into a walking undead? I'd known all along she'd been in it to win it, but that was low even for her.

And she'd had the gall to warn *me* about the merfolk and how if they won this battle between species, they planned to flood the entire world? I never would have helped them even one iota if I'd known that at the start, and the only reason I'd stuck with them afterward had been because of my sister, manipulated into becoming the champion of bloom. I didn't trust Ember not to hurt her—or worse—to win this conflict and now she... Now *she* had willingly joined the side of the supernatural creatures aiming to flood the world?

She was starting to make the idea of literally beating her into submission in this war easier and easier. If I hadn't been plagued with guilt at the idea of doing so at the start, things could have been much different by now.

This could all have been over, one way or another.

I swallowed. "What do you want?"

Dean looked startled, as if he'd never heard the question before. Maybe he hadn't. "What do *I* want?"

"If you win this thing." I shrugged. "Just so you know, I'm not actually in this to help *you*. But I want to make extra sure I'm not helping usher in the undead zombie apocalypse in case I accidentally win."

"'Accidentally'?" Were those clamped lips a sign of his amusement?

"You know what I mean. No more lies, no more games..." A lump grew heavy in my throat. "I'm not like *her*, you know. I'm not in this for an epic romance."

"I can tell." The arch of the brow. The shine in his piercingly bright eye. Definite amusement.

I glared at him despite the irritating effect his smolder had on my ability to stand on legs that weren't wobbling.

"All right," he said, raising his hands in surrender. He glanced over his shoulder at a curvaceous, ashen vampire blonde a few feet away who looked like a vintage pin-up girl, though with a bit more material hugging her hips. Was he checking to see if she was listening? "We want vampires to propagate, I'll be honest," he said in hushed tones. "But just our coven. Only with volunteers."

"Volunteers, huh? Is that how you usually operate?" The mist gathering in front of my lips reminded me that Dean and his vampire friends didn't have that—warm breath coming in contact with cold air, that little indication that they were alive. "You told me Minnie convinced *you* to become like her, but what about the rest?"

Dean tore his eyes away from the blonde and nodded, the slightest tip of a fang protruding to dig into his bottom lip. "We all volunteered. Miss Kelly and Mr. Kapoor, too."

"You said Raelynn turned on *accident*—"

"But she was ready and willing, believe me," said Dean, straightening and slipping a hand into his pocket. "I've never seen an eager beaver with such moxie. It's just... We weren't supposed to grow our family before this whole thing was over."

"Then why weren't you punished for it?"

"The faery prince seemed... amused."

That reminded me to check back on Autumn. The crowd milling about the Bean was taking pictures in the reflected streetlight, children jumping up and watching their warped reflection do the same in the shiny sculpture.

But there were no sparkling green lights like fireflies dancing above their heads. No Orin. No Autumn.

I swore so loudly, everyone around me—vampires, Journey and Dante, strangers alike—stared at me as if I'd started floating three feet off the ground.

That reminded me—faefolk and their wings. I looked up.

The flock of green lights was higher now, headed west, far

above the Chicago streets. There was one larger blob among them.

As champion of bloom, apparently, my sister could hitch-hike a ride through the sky.

How they'd pulled *that* off without anyone noticing, I'd kick myself for never knowing.

CHAPTER TWO

EMBER

We drove for over an hour before I dozed off, my weary eyes no longer able to put up a fight. It was odd that they gave up then, as Calder had just said softly, "We're almost there." But with my head against his shoulder—my hair still damp, the bandage on his arm just inches from my finger—I breathed in his salty, fishy lake aroma, thinking about how warm and comforting that scent was.

I'd never known a lake's fishy odor to be comforting.

I awoke to the scent of something sizzling, a medley of pungent onions and something akin to creamy stew. It was dark in the RV where I still sat—alone now, a blue tartan blanket draped over me from shoulders to feet. I peeked below it and found I was wearing an unfamiliar puffy, purple jacket. The window was cracked open nearby, and though it was cold and dark now, I was grateful for the fresh air. It carried with it the smell of food, the warmth of a campfire, the smoke reminding me of nights spent camping all those years ago with Dad on the rare occasion he'd gotten my half-brother, Daryl, and me together. Of nights when Mom would charcoal grill us dinner in the backyard. Of—

My right hand sparked, then seemed to crackle, the brief flash of red and warmth overtaken by the blue chill of ice. The fire power of the champion of blood erased by the ice power of the champion of water.

Warmth erased by chill. So odd, considering it was the merfolk who were alive and warm, the vampires who were cold and undead.

But the merfolk were one with water, and the vampires' venom burned like fire.

I shivered at the memory of it.

"Brr." The door leading outside opened. My eyes adjusted to the moonlight illuminating the cabin and the approaching figure climbing up the few steps came into focus. Calder rubbed his arms, a black sweater over his tanned musculature, his thick, blond hair no longer wet, but messy in appearance. "You're up. I wanted to see if you were hungry." His emerald eyes focused on my powered-up hand as he approached, the icicles forming along the creamy white flesh, making me look even paler, almost as pale as Dean and—

The power snapped out of my hand, leaving just the faintest lingering touch of the chill.

"What time is it?" I asked, suddenly all business. It was the best way to quash the hurt cutting across my heart. "Where are we?"

Calder slid onto the cushioned bench seat beside me and took my hand in his. The warmth soothed the numbness, and there was a moment where something deep and primal flowed between us, and I had my definitive answer as to why the warm merfolk's champion fought with ice. The water, of course, and ice was the best way to make it a weapon.

The vampires fought from a place of blood and ashes, and they called forth the flame.

The merfolk wanted the water to encase everything, and wrap it all in its loving embrace.

For a second, Calder's and my warm breaths mixing in the chill of the RV, it all made sense to me.

Ending it all. Wrapping the world in ice—in water— making it a safe place for Calder and his people.

But just for a second.

Calder and I... We had a plan.

"Are you all right?" he asked, leaning in closer.

"No," I admitted quietly. Outside, someone laughed, a feminine, melodious sound that was closer to a song.

There were dozens of merfolk out there—more than had met up with us at the edge of Lake Michigan during our retreat from the faery attack. Wherever we were, this was it—the merfolk's new home base in light of their home being destroyed by the faeries.

Faeries who'd used flames to burn down a fortress. The tool of the vampires. And now with both sisters as their champions, the two species seemed more poised than ever to work together against me—at least until I was defeated... or dead.

But I couldn't let that happen. Calder and I weren't going to flood the world if we got Ivy and Autumn to surrender. We just had to make them see. We could undo Raelynn's and Devam's vampirism. Save my dad. Maybe, somehow, bring back Calder's...

I wasn't sure about that one. Calder's dad was dead. Not a vampire, but *dead*. Long before I'd been a part of any of this, years ago. But Calder, strong yet vulnerable, bulky yet somehow so fragile, he *needed* that hope to strive for.

"I'm here for you," he said. I fell against his shoulder again, rubbing my cheek against the soft cashmere of his sweater.

"To answer your questions," he said after a beat, "we're just outside of town. At Simmons RV Park. We have enough funds to rent out the place for the whole family. Considering we're in construction, we could be working on a new permanent home, but..."

He left the rest unsaid. *The rest of his family doesn't see a need for a permanent home if they intend for the world to be flooded any day now.*

"And it's 8:00," he added.

I pulled my head back. "Still Saturday?"

"Still Saturday." Chuckling, he planted a kiss atop my white-blonde head and I felt my cheeks flushing.

He couldn't blame me for wondering if I'd slept a day plus. It had been a long, long, *long* day.

Adrenaline shot through my system as I realized I was outside of *my* town, not back in Chicago with the Slowes like I was supposed to be. What would Journey think? Would she cover for me? How? There was no way Lacey, her mom, would buy any excuse she had for me not coming back to the hotel at the convention center where her dad was attending a culinary expo. She'd call my mom before Journey had even finished two sentences.

And would she even try to lie for me? What about Dante? He was part of this now. Would the vampires take him back with them to their coven, turn him, too?

My breaths were growing shallower as my blood pressure rose. I patted the coat that wasn't my own, looking for a phone that wasn't there—probably lost somewhere in the harbor, destroyed, or tucked back in my coat in Navy Pier. Yeah, it had to be there. I'd taken my coat off in the Crystal Gardens at Navy Pier before...

Before I'd first turned into a mermaid.

Not that it did me a lick of good to know that.

"Let's eat," said Calder, rubbing a hand over my back. "I know you're overwhelmed and probably trying to figure out what you're going to do now, but we have time. No one knows we're here yet. We've put miles and miles between us and the bloodsuckers' and pixies' last known location. You'll think better with some food in you." He nudged my shoulder. "You've gotten quite a workout. Not a bad swimmer for a first-timer."

My heart slowed as I took deep breaths and tried to ground myself in the moment. He was right. My stomach was practically caving in on itself, and though part of me was too nauseated to eat, most of me knew that I was getting nowhere, that this throbbing headache wasn't going to free my mind to think, until I settled down and ate. It gave me something to focus on, anyway.

Calder stood and extended a hand to help me up, then he picked up the discarded blanket I'd left behind on the sofa and draped it over my shoulders like a cape. "It's cold out there."

He led me outside, and I flinched as a burst of chilled air hit me in the face. Calder slid an arm around me and hugged me closer to him as he led us toward the nearest of several campfires.

The singsong echo of laughter and murmuring went virtually silent as we approached, the only remaining movement the bubbling of the half-eaten stew, or the merfolk who darted their gazes away from me or rubbed their metal bowls with their fingers.

But not Nerida. Calder's mother, Queen of the Merfolk, stood and flicked her long, auburn hair behind her back, her gauzy aquamarine dress not at all suited for the weather.

"Good evening, sleepyhead," she said, clearly biting on the inside of her cheek. "Come. Join us."

I looked to Calder, almost as if asking for permission. He swallowed perceptively but guided me toward a log with the smallest amount of space, choosing to stand behind me with a protective gentle grip on my blanket-covered shoulders. An older man with gray-and-blond hair, his tanned face flush in the camp light, shifted aside uneasily, clutching his bowl to his chest as if I'd steal it from him. He was the one who'd driven our RV, I thought.

"Introductions all around," called Nerida, clasping her hands together. Everyone at our campfire averted their eyes, the nearby groups of disparate merfolk silent even some distance away. "Come on now," she said. "This is *good* news, my people. Ember Goodwin here is the stronger choice for champion. By far." Her faltering smile there at the end didn't instill as much confidence in me as her words might otherwise have. "Now let's put the past behind us and look to the future."

I had to agree, even though there was no avoiding the sour

feeling in my stomach at the aura of uneasiness I'd brought to this circle. And if they ever picked up on the fact that the future I had in mind wouldn't match their own, well...

"I'm Queen Nerida, as you no doubt know, leader of the merfolk. This here is my brother-in-law, Calder's uncle, Beck." She gestured to the man who'd driven the RV and grumpily made some space for me.

Then she went around the fire, though there were only about a third of the merfolk present at this one.

"Rialta and Arno," she said, pointing to a Latinix couple probably in their forties. The woman was the spitting image of the teenager beside her—dark brown eyes, wavy, dark hair, a lean but curvaceous physique, and the same petite, straight nose—only perhaps with a line or two of white in her hair, a wrinkle or two on her face. "Their daughter, Cascade," Nerida continued, and I flinched when Cascade's eyes met mine.

Sure, we'd swum together in Chicago, but we'd also been on two sides of a number of skirmishes when I'd been champion of blood.

The same could be true of anyone here.

"Arno's brother, Dathan," Nerida said, nodding next at a tall and bulky man lingering behind the row of merfolk on logs, sparing only a second to glance my way as he paced around the perimeter. A guard.

"His son, Bay," Nerida continued, pointing to the strikingly handsome Latino teen beside Cascade. He had that kind of windswept hair that looked perfect messy, his muscular physique practically popping out from under a purple-and-gold Central High letterman jacket. He'd put his bowl down and was holding hands with the teen in a matching jacket next to him, a ghastly pale redhead with freckles and strong cheekbones. He was almost as muscular as the merman beside him, but he was perhaps a tad lankier.

"Llyr," Nerida continued, "and his twin sister, Laguna."

The redhaired, pale mermaid beside Llyr reminded me of a heavily freckled Ariel. She was hard to forget after the siren call she'd used in the waters of Lake Michigan to get those pesky faeries off us. At the moment, she was ignoring her food bowl, instead poking at the bottom of the fire with a long twig, pulling it back and waving it lazily before her, as if to watch the embers dance.

Nerida continued the introduction—Llyr and Laguna's parents, endless friends and relations, all making me wonder if merfolk only ever coupled with other merfolk and how the gene pool must have been dwindling by now—until at last Nerida went silent. Her hands clasped together in front of her, she looked at me expectantly.

"Ember," I said, my name catching on my throat. Calder squeezed my shoulder then moved around the log to scoop some of the stew into a bowl from a stack on a small table beside the fire. "Nice to meet you," I added when no one else seemed to have anything to say.

Thanking Calder as he held the bowl and a spoon out to me, I focused on eating.

Eventually, the merfolk began speaking again, moving around the campfire, Llyr gathering everyone's bowls and pointedly ignoring me, though I wasn't finished regardless.

As his uncle vacated the spot beside me, Calder slipped in, his own bowl cooling in his hands.

"They'll get friendlier," he said, loud enough for a passing Cascade to hear. She turned her head forward and kept walking, guiding Laguna by the arm as the redhaired mermaid stared relentlessly at me. "They're all just a little... worn."

"It wasn't the vampires who burned down your manor," I pointed out.

Nerida's head snapped in my direction, the soft note of her voice reaching over the fire. Her face was illuminated in the night by the flames in a fiery orange. "But it was the vampires who assaulted our home first."

"I think it was the *merfolk* who set a trap. You know what they say. Vampires don't go anywhere they're not invited." I hadn't found that to be true, to be certain, but I was at the end of my rope and the food had settled heavily in my stomach, my insides too upset to digest it at all gently.

"Mom," started Calder, but he stopped, and I could see why. Nerida looked as if she'd been born of the flames, the flush over her cheeks practically scorching her skin.

Nerida took a deep breath, steeling herself to speak more, then clamped her lips together tightly. "Never mind. That's the past. We're looking to the future. Even if the bloodsuckers were the first to cross a line—"

"The vampires are relatively new to this," I said, not sure why I was defending them. I was tired of everyone's warped point of view, tired of just being a pawn in this game.

Calder took the half-empty bowl from my hand and set it down beside his on the ground, slipping an arm around me. "Ember, listen—"

"No, *you* listen." My voice rose in pitch. The merfolk who'd begun to retreat toward RVs and tents all stopped moving, looking my way. Arno and Rialta, along with a number of other merfolk, were surrounding a large pile of white jug-like containers with long, black tubes sticking out of them—weed sprayers? But what lawn did they care about anymore? Seeing me staring at them, they went back to loading them out of a parked car trunk into an RV. Nerida stepped closer, Beck and Dathan at her flank like consummate soldiers.

"Do you have *any idea* what the vampires have taken from us?" Nerida snarled.

"Your prince?" I ventured, glancing around the clearing. There was some whisper of confusion on all the faces within earshot, and I wondered how much they even knew themselves.

"You mean our *king*," said Nerida, clenching a shaking fist at her side. It was a very unbecoming look on a woman so ephemeral. "My grandfather. They killed him."

"Minnie fell in love with him and tried to make him a vampire merman," I spat, though I just had Dean's words to go off of. "It didn't take. He died. It was an accident."

Nerida stepped closer in a flash, her gauzy dress kicking up wind that made the fire flicker. "If you believe that, you're a fool who's been as manipulated by them as he was."

I stood, ignoring Calder's urgent tug on my hand to get me to stand down. Face to face with his mother, I found myself half a head shorter, but I didn't feel at all subdued. "Dean, the vampire prince, was your grandfather's brother," I said loudly. I kept my eyes locked on Nerida, so I couldn't be sure how the other merfolk were taking it, but judging by the quiet gasp and subtle murmurs, it was clearly news to at least some of them.

Even Calder's grip went loose on my hand then. We'd talked about this before. He hadn't seemed to believe me, but he also hadn't cared.

Maybe seeing his mom's reaction just now confirmed what he'd thought impossible.

Nerida, on the other hand, wasn't the least bit surprised by the news.

"He may not have retained any of his merman ability, but he's still one of you," I continued. "Perhaps if you recognized that, you wouldn't have to be at each other's throats. You wouldn't have to fight like this. What's wrong with just letting things lie? With—"

"Hush." The word from Nerida's mouth was spoken like venom. "A walking dead is no family member of ours, just a lingering husk, a shadow of what once was." Those words were too similar to what Calder had said when I'd told him about the relationship—*dead is dead*. "And if you don't understand what we're trying to achieve here, maybe you don't belong with us."

"Mom," said Calder, jumping to his feet, ready to slip in between us if the fisticuffs started breaking out.

Nerida glanced at her son, then turned on her heel. "Get your champion in order," she said, her lips curling back to reveal glimmering white teeth. I could almost picture the venom and fangs on them—she was not so different from the vampires she loathed so much. "Or everyone you've ever loved is doomed."

She whirled away from the fire and toward the RV I'd ridden on the way here.

Beck and Dathan gave me the onceover before following, and as I looked around the campground, I found face after face transfixed my way, snapping away like a wave and looking elsewhere whenever my gaze met theirs.

"Ember, cool it," said Calder under his breath. "We can't accomplish anything if your army doesn't trust you."

"I don't need an *army*," I retorted. "*I'm* the champion. I'm the proxy for this battle—and don't you forget it." I rounded on him and poked him in the chest. "I'm not a pawn, Calder." My words choked in my throat, my steely resolve melting. "I'm not someone you can just use and throw away," I said much quieter, my voice shaking.

"I know," Calder said softly, slipping his hands on either side of my face. His eyes met mine and I felt my muscles grow weak, all the adrenaline keeping me angry slipping from my grasp.

Calder's phone buzzed from his jeans pocket and he ignored it, but it was the disturbance I needed to break out of this trance in which he'd held me.

He seemed so genuine, but I'd been here before.

"You should get that," I said quietly. The camp was back to movement around us, merfolk putting out fires and retiring for the night, leaving only the fire nearest us blazing.

"I don't know anyone who'd call me who isn't here," said Calder. "I'm sure it's just spam," he added, but he pulled the phone out of his pocket anyway. "Yeah, I don't know this number—"

My eyes flickered to his phone screen lazily. It was cracked but functional, newly encased in some kind of bulky outer shell with bits of rubber around it. Maybe it was waterproof protection. Looking at the screen again, my heart went sluggish.

"That's my mom!"

CHAPTER THREE

IVY

I liked to think I was all for safe driving, but this chalky, dirty-blond vampire was driving like the grandpa he ought to have been in years.

"We've long since put Chicago behind us," I barked. "Can you pick up the pace a little?"

Dean leaned forward and waved a hand at the driver in the rearview mirror, as if brushing off my order.

It wasn't *his* sister who was floating—actually *floating*—off into the sunset to who-knew-where. The first place to start looking was going to be that irksome faery's cabin. If I didn't find them there, I was going to use my newfound fire ability to light up some old books at The Hollow Tree. I'd make sure the bookstore cat was safe first, of course.

But maybe that would get his attention.

Though I'd hate to punish some innocent tomes for his transgressions.

"Relax, kid," said Dean, with all the charm and smugness of Bugs Bunny in one of those ancient cartoons making fun of the stars of the day. Humphrey Bogart and *Casablanca* and all that stuff. "We're almost there."

I crossed my legs in the backseat of the car and just stewed. Trains leaving Chicago to the suburbs this time of night were scarce, so Dean had had to call in one of his friends back home to bring a car to pick us up, and the rest of the vampires who'd accompanied their former champion to the Windy City were going to wait and take the 9:30 train and deal with the vehicle they'd left at the parking lot. Journey and Dante had parted from us somewhere at the Bean. I hadn't had the wherewithal to touch base with them before they'd left.

They just no longer were part of the group.

Then *this* vampire, one who'd already been in Chicago with us, had insisted on driving us back after the mint green vintage vehicle had squealed to a rough stop on the street in front of Ogilvie Station. *"I don't like the idea of Herbert driving this baby a second longer than he has to,"* he'd said, cradling the hood of the shiny vehicle with all the affection of a mother with a child. *"I'll treat her right."*

One of *those* guys.

I recognized the newcomer called Herbert—tall, broad-shouldered, and bulky—from battles, too. He'd shrugged and offered to stay behind, but the car-loving vampire had already sat behind the driver's seat without another word. The pin-up girl vampire had seemed a bit irritated then but hadn't said a word, and she hadn't moved to join us at the car, either. It was weird co-existing with them enough to notice anything like that, but that was the least of my problems just then.

Hours and hours had passed since Autumn had flown away.

No one seemed to be in a hurry but me.

I'd reluctantly had a croissant at the station while cursing the intermittent train schedule, but my stomach was still rumbling.

"You hungry?" asked Dean.

"Don't worry about me." My words were sharper than I'd intended them to be.

Staring out the window, I let the lights of the buildings and homes we passed hypnotize me for a moment.

"He won't harm her," said Dean in a soothing voice.

I was about to tear him a new one when I looked over to him. Leaning slightly in my direction, his eyes narrowed and his eyebrows pulled together as if there were nothing more in the world he'd rather do than hear what I had to say.

As if he genuinely just wanted to comfort me.

I relented a little, leaning back into the sleek leather of the seat. "I think he's done plenty of harm," I pointed out. "Just by dragging her into this."

The quiet melody of the stereo's big band music permeated the wave of silence that hung between us. The other words I was thinking went unsaid. He was almost as bad as Orin. He'd just manipulated an older, dumber girl into being his champion.

I wouldn't have sealed the deal with Calder if Dean hadn't sealed it with Ember first.

"Why Ember?" I asked quietly. I didn't know why I cared. "The first time, I mean. Was it all about her connection with that house being stronger than mine?"

"That was part of it." The quirk of his lip was the definition of sheepish. "I also thought she'd be easier to convince."

"Than me?" My eyebrows shot up so high, they practically cracked the skin in my forehead.

Dean simply shrugged.

"You mean easier to manipulate," I added.

"That's a bum rap. I didn't intend to manipulate anybody." He sighed. I didn't know vampires had air in their lungs that they could use to sigh. "I suppose that's why I lost her so easily."

"Because you *didn't* manipulate her?" I could feel the superiority oozing through my veins.

"Because I refused to keep lying to her." He dug through the open fold of his jacket to pull out a coin he held between his thumb and two fingers. "She seemed a little khaki wacky. She wanted some romantic hero—I tried to be that for her."

The sound coming from the driver's seat was something akin to a snort, with a little more venom injected into it.

The coin turned over in Dean's hand. It didn't look particularly special. A half dollar or something, some coin I'd probably seen all of once or twice in my life. "You're just kids to me, Ivy. I missed my opportunity to find a partner of my own to join me in this life long ago."

"You mean a teen in the 1940s when you were actually this young?" I met the driver vampire's eyes in the mirror and didn't shirk at his gaze. "So why didn't you?" I hadn't failed to notice that more than one of his kind seemed paired up. Including this lunkhead driving us and that pretty blonde we'd left behind in Chicago. At least, that was what I'd have guessed based on how he'd had his arm around her at times and how annoyed she'd been when we'd left without her.

Which gave me plenty of evidence for what kind of shoddy boyfriend this car lover was.

"He didn't have the stomach for it," the driver answered. "His idea of *romance* is setting a broken bird free from her chance at eternal life." He chuckled.

Dean's jaw twitched just slightly.

"Excuse me, and you are?" I asked.

"Leopold," the driver answered gruffly.

"Okay, *Leopold*, but what I mean is—what's your position in the hierarchy exactly?"

"The hierarchy?" he spat back at me. "What kind of dizzy dame—"

"Watch your mouth," I said. "The world has changed, even if you've fought tooth and nail not to notice that." The oxymoron of old timey music playing from a station on Sirius XM wasn't lost on me, but still—he'd used the modern technology and still had *chosen* the old music.

"Blondie was more of a lady," Leopold muttered under his breath.

"*Excuse me?*" I started, practically jumping forward to grab his seat's headrest.

"Okay, enough, point noted." Dean slid a hand on my

shoulder and gently directed me back into my seat. "Leo, shut your trap and treat our new champion with respect."

"You got it, *boss*," he sneered, taking an exit off the highway just a little too sharply.

I jostled sideways, bumping smack into Dean. One of his hands was fisted, likely holding on tightly to that coin of his, but he managed to take hold of me, as if about to yank me toward him to embrace him.

He didn't, though. Against the waist seatbelt, the position strained me, though my heart fluttered far too rapidly for my liking as he guided me back to my seat.

I needed a cold shower. And a nap. I could deal with this— whatever *this* was—in the morning.

If it weren't for needing to find my sister.

"Heading to your Pop's?" Dean confirmed, leaning back into his own seat and rolling the coin between his fingers.

"Yeah," I said, sighing. "Mom thinks Autumn's at a sleepover, so I don't want to worry her prematurely. If she can manage to worry at all about her elementary-school-aged daughter after Orin's brainwashing."

Orin had the ability to *convince* people of just about anything. It was how I'd gotten my dad and step-mom to not fight me on the fact that I wasn't going to be spending half the week with them back when I'd wanted to stay as far away from Ember as possible.

Now that my sister was a part of this, though, all bets were off.

No need to make Ember more comfortable in her only home than she needed to be. I had my mom's to retreat to if things got ugly.

Besides, Orin's cabin was in the woods behind Dad's new house. It was a place to start.

With a hot breath that tickled my lips as it exited, I dug into my coat pocket and pulled out my phone, scrolling through the contacts and dialing *Dad*.

He picked up on the third ring, and I put it on speaker.

"Hey, sport. Everything okay?"

Parental instincts always got them wondering if any unplanned contact meant that something was entirely wrong. And though it was, I couldn't actually tell him that.

"Just wondering if I can spend the night at your place," I said.

He'd tell me if Autumn was there. It was a Mom night technically, but it wasn't as if they'd never switched. Even before Orin had become my parents' long-lost "good friend," whose word was law.

"Of course!" said Dad. "Is something wrong?"

So no Autumn then.

Great.

"No, it's just... I haven't been spending a lot of time with you lately," I offered lamely. "I talked to Mom about going back to the split custody and she's fine with it."

There was a pause on Dad's end of the line and I could almost *sense* the gears turning in his head, how part of him had to be wondering why I'd asked to stay at Mom's and transfer to Central High at all, searching for some fight we'd never had, some reason why he'd just given up and let it happen without complaint.

"I'd love to see you, kiddo," said Dad, clearing his throat. "Ember's in Chicago, so it's just Noelle and me..."

I winced, hoping I wasn't interrupting something I didn't want to think about, but I heard a muffled voice, Dad going softer as he explained to his wife what I was asking.

"If you're busy, I can come back tomorrow—" I offered.

"No, no," said Dad, jumping in to interrupt me. "It's a bit late and we're just watching a movie"—I sighed in relief—"but of course you're welcome."

"Cool," I said. "I'm about twenty minutes away."

"Say, while I have you, what do you think about Thanksgiving here this year?"

To tell the truth, I'd almost forgotten about the holiday entirely. I exchanged a look with Dean, who was simply gazing at me out of the corner of his eye with idle curiosity. What did vampires have for Thanksgiving? The turkey's blood?

"Sure," I said, doing the mental math and realizing Thanksgiving was only five days away. "Though I'd feel bad about leaving Mom alone."

"Since when have we ever not invited your mother?" said Dad, exasperated. "Even if I'm remarried now... She's family. We're asking everyone. Even boyfriends."

Dean tugged slightly at his collar as the buzzing sound of Noelle's indistinguishable words echoed in the background.

"Well, your mother—Noelle—thinks perhaps right now isn't the best time to extend an invitation to the boyfriends. Is there something I ought to know?" There was a slight tremble in his voice as his volume rose. Dad wasn't the worst kind of "don't you date my daughter" type, but I was certain he wouldn't stand idly by if he knew that any of us had gotten hurt.

"Nope," I said stiffly. Staring at Dean, I got a great idea. "In fact, I'd love to invite my new boyfriend."

Dean arched an eyebrow at that.

"*New* boyfriend?" Dad asked. "You're done with that Calder?"

"Yup," I said succinctly and without regret. I'd been fond of him once, but after what I'd learned his family intended to do, there was no love lost there. "In fact, Ember appears to be dating him."

"Ember is... *What?*" Dad passed the news on to Noelle, who got closer to the phone, her voice a little more discernable.

"Ivy, are you with Dean now?" she asked.

So Ember had filled her in on the idea? Or her mothering instincts had picked up on the feud between Ember and me?

I didn't care.

I wanted this holiday to be as awkward as possible for the new foolish, flighty champion of water and her two-timing romantic hero.

"Yup," I answered. "Both literally at the moment and in the sense that we're now a pair." Grinning at Dean, my lips went so wide, it was if I were a beauty contestant and my teeth were coated with Vaseline. If vampires could flush, he might have shown some color to his complexion, but he shirked just slightly at my gaze regardless, the coin dancing between his fingers as he stared straight ahead.

"Well, I... I don't know about that kind of drama at our dinner table," said Noelle softly. "I know it's not our business, but—"

"Ask Ember," I said. "I'm sure she'll be fine with it. We're working out all the *bad blood* between us."

Noelle audibly sighed and Dad got back on the phone. "We'll talk about it over the next few days. Two more or fewer mouths to feed won't make much of a difference, I don't think."

"Okay," I said, trying to fight off the joyous splurge of adrenaline spiking through my system. No more hiding. Ember was going to help me get my sister out of this once and for all or she was going to stop standing in my way. However that might be achieved. "Do you think... Do you think I should ask Autumn to come over tonight, too?" I prodded, making doubly sure Dad thought she was over at Mom's or with a friend.

"She already stopped by," he said nonchalantly. On a non-Dad night? And he'd failed to mention this? There was something off about the tone of his voice. It rung just slightly mechanical. "She's sleeping over at her friend's house in the woods."

"*What*?" Had he *heard* the words that had slipped out of his mouth?

"She stopped in to pack a bag," Noelle added, like she hadn't just sent her youngest step-daughter off with what *she* knew to be an adult man. An ancient adult man, but the twenty or so she thought him to be was bad enough.

"Dad, I don't think that's a good idea—" I started.

Dean spoke up for the first time since I'd started the call.

"Maybe we can swing by the cabin and tell Autumn goodnight before I go home?"

"Dean?" asked Dad. The mechanical quality of his voice was slipping, the incredulity sliding back in.

"We'll do that," I said before Dad could harangue Dean for long. "I'll bring her back inside. Orin's cabin is far too chilly on a November night for a kid. She could come down with a cold."

"A cold...?" asked Dad, and there it was again. His confusion. The nonsense was winning out, but his confusion was plain.

"See you in a bit." I hung up.

Dean's lips clamped tightly together as he gazed at me, but as he opened them to speak, he couldn't stop himself from smiling.

"So I'm your new boyfriend?"

He'd placed importance on entirely the wrong thing there.

But I hadn't yet had that cold shower, so my ridiculous heart beat a few too many times at his ham-fisted attempt at flirting.

CHAPTER FOUR

EMBER

Rather than answering it himself, Calder handed the phone to me.

I supposed that only made sense. I just wasn't able to deal with the conversation to come yet. Too bad for me.

"Mom?" I said after I hit the *accept* button and put the call on speaker. The word caught in my throat.

"*Ember*," said Mom. Somehow, there was anger and relief all mixed up into one word. "I only *thought* you might answer, but—"

"How did you know Calder's number?"

"*That's* what you're worried about?" Mom sighed audibly, then murmured something to someone speaking beside her— Easton, my step-dad, probably. "Easton has it," Mom said abruptly into the phone. "He got it from Glory, who got it from Ivy, since the kid was dating their daughter. But never mind that, what are you doing away from the Slowes? You're supposed to be in Chicago with them. Lacey called me a few minutes ago to say that Journey and Dante came back to the hotel without you, but *with your jacket and phone*, offering half-hearted excuses that you'd gone off with a *new boyfriend*."

"And you knew that was Calder?" Okay, so that wasn't really the point Mom was stuck on, but anything to distract her. If my parents were getting savvier about the odd behavior going on around them, I'd need to be smarter—or somehow convince Orin to lend me a hand.

But I didn't know how likely he was to be "amused" by covering for Ivy or me anymore now that he had quite a bit of skin in the game.

The little pinpricks on my flesh reminded me that I couldn't very well just stroll into his cabin or bookstore anymore without expecting a fight.

"Ivy told us about the swapping boyfriends thing." She had? What was her play there? Mom's voice was clipped. "But that's beside the point. You're a high school senior—"

"I'm eighteen," I pointed out. I had one of those first-week-of-school birthdays. An occasion that had been rather subdued this year with Mom caught up in her whirlwind romance. I hadn't cared at the time, but considering everything else that had happened since, I was starting to get irritated at every little thing that had blown up my world entirely.

"You're *a senior in high school*," Mom reiterated. "Still under *my* roof. And legal adult or not, just leaving mid-trip like that was plain rude, Ember. What's the matter with you lately? I raised you to be better than that."

The hot tears simmering at the corners of my eyes must have been visible to Calder, as he slid an arm around my shoulder and squeezed.

"I'm sorry I'm such a disappointment," I said, my voice hoarse. "Maybe now that you've added three and a half other people to the family, you'll have better backups."

"*Ember!*"

A muffled voice in the background made Mom pause.

Another long, tired breath escaped her lips before she spoke again. "We can talk about this in person. I love you—I still think you were rude, both to the Slowes and to me for not telling us about your *change in plans*, but I just want to know that you're safe."

"I am," I said.

"And are you being *safe?*" Mom added. The question seemed ripped through gritted teeth.

"Am I...? I guess...?"

Calder dropped his hand off my shoulder to rapidly wave his fingers across his throat, signaling to cut out whatever I was about to say.

"Oh!" I said, picking up on what Mom must have assumed a teenager would do when running off with a *boyfriend* at night. My neck, cheeks, and ears felt impossibly hot. "Oh. No, we're not—I mean, I would be if we were, but it hasn't gotten to that," I said. All but voicing the "yet." I winced.

That really *wasn't* the first thing on my mind.

"Okay," said Mom in a clipped tone. "Because I know you had your birth control shot, but it takes a few weeks before you're really out of the woods. And condoms also protect against STDs."

"*Mom*," I said.

Calder choked on a chuckle he'd clearly been trying to stuff down.

"I was half-worried when I took you to the doctor, she was going to tell us you were pregnant with Dean's kid already."

"*Mom!*"

Calder's whole body was shaking. He stumbled and had to lean against a blue pickup truck a few paces back. I recognized it—from more than one skirmish—as his own.

There was more murmuring on the other side of the line and Easton got closer to the phone. "So where are you?" he asked without preamble.

I looked around. The river led to Standing Springs Park somewhere in the western direction. The boundless woods hugged the edge of the waterway that somewhere connected to the woods Calder's family technically owned that also lined up against our backyard.

"In town," was all I said.

"Then come home," he said. "Your mom and I can continue this discussion when you get here."

"No, I—" I struggled to think of what to say. I didn't want to go home just then. I knew I'd *have to* at some point, but I didn't want to be anywhere I might run into one of the stepsisters who'd more than once actually skirted the line of attempting to *murder* me.

Calder clutched his stomach, stumbling around as pebbles crunched beneath his feet. My heart sped up as I panicked at the idea of him appearing so sick, but he straightened up quickly and mimed coughing, then he pretended to blow his nose.

Oh. I was sick.

"I didn't feel well," I said quickly. "I was out with Journey and Dante"—I winced at the thought of how I'd left things, of how I'd now dragged even Dante into this, but at least I knew they were okay—"and I got really sick again. Calder was there, and he offered to take me home."

Calder mimed a fainting spell and I had to bite my lip a moment to keep from laughing. "I got too sick on the way back and we had to pull over. I'm at a motel."

Calder's face blanched and he pointed to the RV in which we'd ridden here, at the lingering merfolk a number of yards away.

"With his family," I finished. "He and his family were in Chicago for the weekend, too."

"Hmm." Mom's voice came back over the phone line. "And they cut their trip short to take you back?"

"It was a day trap," I added quickly, no pantomime from Calder necessary.

He nodded and shoved his hands into his jeans pockets.

"Can I speak to his mother?" Mom started. "You could have let me know earlier—"

"I didn't want to worry you. Unnecessarily. Or talk about the whole... Dean and Calder thing."

"You mean how you girls swapped boyfriends?" Easton added. "In my day, we just called that *playing the field*—"

"Not helping," Mom added.

"Nerida was driving," I said quickly, remembering Mom's other request. "So she went to bed first. In fact, if we keep talking, I'm afraid we're going to wake her."

"Hmm," was all Mom had to say.

"Come on, Noelle. She *is* technically an adult," said Easton.

Mom sighed. "I know that. But it's still *rude* to not tell people when plans change. To up and leave without your phone so I couldn't even contact you."

"Yet you managed to find a way." It slipped out of my lips before I'd thought better of it.

Calder started laughing again, his green eyes sparkling as he leaned back against the passenger's side door of his truck.

"It simply slipped my mind," I said quickly, to cover it up. "I *really* didn't feel well, Mom."

"Maybe you should go to the hospital?" she asked. "You nearly drowned just last month—"

"I'm *fine*, Mom. I mean, I will be. I just need to rest."

Sighing for the ages one last time, Mom relented. "Come home tomorrow," she said. "First thing."

"As soon as I wake up," I promised. It was a lie, but an easy enough lie to cover up. If I were sick, who was to say I couldn't sleep until 3:00?

"Goodnight, kiddo," said Easton, the chipper, dorky stepdad once more. "Oh, and while you have your new boyfriend, ask him whether or not he has Thanksgiving plans."

Calder and I exchanged a look. He shrugged, more of a "Why would I when my family wants the world to end?" type of shrug than an indication he didn't know.

"Why?" I asked.

"Because we're having Thanksgiving at our house," said Mom, brokering no argument. "And *someone* got it into his mind that we should invite these two boyfriends who've swept our daughters off their feet *multiple times* in the past few months."

"Ivy will be there?" I asked. My blood was running cold—

then hot. Unnaturally, venom-like hot. The phone dug into my palm as I gripped it harder.

"Of course," said Easton. "We're inviting Glory, too. And Tom if he's interested."

Mom snorted.

Tom was my dad. Who lived with the vampires. Who had never cared much about me to begin with, and who now stood on the opposite side of the line in this supernatural proxy war.

"Ivy probably wants to be with her friends," I said lamely, fishing for some sense that this wasn't happening.

I doubted they'd let Autumn out of the meal unless Orin brainwashed them into it. Which seemed a real possibility.

"No, she's already told us she's coming," Mom said. "With Dean, I think."

Yes, Ivy's new "boyfriend." Maybe he actually *would* date her. I was just a stupid kid to him, but she... She'd always turned his head. I'd just been too oblivious to really take note of it.

I hadn't *wanted* to take note of it.

Calder was before me, slipping the phone gently from my fingers. I realized with a start that frost had been building up along the edges of the phone case, the ice forming in my palm cracking and melting almost as soon as it solidified.

"I'd love to come," said Calder plainly, as plainly as if this really were *just a dinner*, as if he really were *just a boyfriend*. "Thank you so much, Mr. Sheppard and Ms. Goodwin-Sheppard."

He'd gotten the names right. Somehow, despite it all, that made a warm, fuzzy feeling blossom in my belly.

"Right. Calder," said Mom, almost as if just remembering this was his phone. "Okay, then," she said, her voice strained. "We'll see you both there. But we'll see you both tomorrow first," she added, her tone carrying with it some kind of underlying threat.

"Goodnight, Mom," I said, reaching over with my left hand

to push the *end call* button on Calder's screen. I was starting to get the ice under control, but my right hand still felt weird.

"Well, that went well, considering," said Calder, slipping the phone into his pocket.

"Yeah..." A small sigh escaped my lips.

We stood there awkwardly a moment.

"Hey," he said at last, hitching a thumb over his shoulder in the direction of his truck. "Do you want to head to a motel? You *did* tell your parents that was where we were."

The offer shouldn't have made me so excited. Shouldn't have caused a jittery feeling to travel up and down my body, from my head to my toes.

"But, uh, I don't mean..." Calder bit his lip and swallowed, shoving his hands into his pockets roughly as if to stop himself from stumbling. "I don't even *have* a condom." His face flushed. "Not saying I need to go and get one, either. I mean, of course I *would* if we needed one. Which we won't. Tonight. Or maybe ever. That's up to—I mean, it's way, way too early and we've got other things going on. Much more important things." He let out a deep breath and scrunched his nose up. "Am-Am I totally making this worse?"

I laughed. Really, really laughed, the sound echoing out into the night air and drawing the stares of the last few merfolk milling about by the tents and RVs.

At least if we messed this up and the world was entirely flooded, if I managed to eke through it all as a permanent mermaid, I'd know that there was no chance I had to worry about a human-transmitted STD.

CHAPTER FIVE

IVY

Though Leopold pulled into Dad's driveway, I decided to forgo the stop inside entirely. The curtains on the living room window were pulled back and Dad had his arm around Noelle in front of the TV. As I passed, I blew warm air into the palms of my hands, which, even with my gloves, were starting to grow numb. My parents looked so cozy in there.

Cozy was a luxury I couldn't afford anymore.

"You sure you want to do this alone?" Dean asked as he caught up with me. I knew he could teleport—or pause time, I guessed was what he was technically doing, which just made it seem as if he jumped from one place to the next in the blink of an eye—but he didn't need to in order to catch up to my pace, with those long, sturdy legs of his.

Another superfluous detail I most definitely didn't need to take note of right now.

"Yes, but apparently, I'm *not* doing this alone since you're here." I glared at him over my shoulder as I shoved my hands into my pockets.

"Perhaps we should head inside so you can grab a hat—"

"I'm fine," I lied. I just... didn't have it in me to play this game with my parents before I dragged Autumn back in there.

"It would give me time to summon more of the vampires."

I whirled on him, almost knocking into the bench at the back of the yard. "This isn't some part of your *war*. I'm just going to go get my sister. If I turn up with a battalion, those little flying butterflies might start assaulting us from above like they did the merfolk."

"It'd just be a precaution." Dean began slipping out of his coat. It was dipping into the 30s outside at night, and of course he didn't so much as tremble. "I think they'd be open to joining us to defeat the fishfolk first, but I'd just feel better about your safety if we had greater numbers." He wrapped the coat around my shoulders like a giant cloak over my puffy jacket.

I settled into the warmth, then sighed as I thought wretchedly of the time not so long ago that Calder had offered me his coat in the very same woods we were currently standing near.

It was too cold to give into my instincts to bat it away, though. What did Dean need it for? I shoved my arms into the sleeves and turned on my heel, heading for the treeline.

Leopold's car drove slowly down the street some distance away, almost as if canvassing the area, checking to make sure we really didn't want him at our side for this.

Like I'd trust that goon anywhere near my little sister. He'd punch her lights out without batting an eye.

As I slipped through the forest, the leaves snapped like twigs beneath my feet, their rigid, chip-like brittle texture the result of one too many frosts. I walked and walked, heading toward the river, figuring I could hug it and find my way there. The ground was uneven, the dirt almost painfully solid beneath my soles. A small branch got tangled in my hair, pulling it out of its holder and making me yelp.

"Let me," said Dean, the film noir hero just going for a stroll in the woods in the middle of a cold, November night.

Reluctantly, I let my numbing hands fall and slipped them back into the warm, lined pockets of Dean's coat as he took hold of the caught strand of my hair in bare, pale hands. With finesse, he managed to free the strands *and* leave the branch intact, letting it bounce back up and gazing up at it as if setting a caged bird free.

"Thanks," I muttered, finger-combing my hair to better cover my ears.

"Should I lend you my hat, too?" He smirked.

"I don't need to catch vampire lice, so no thank you."

He gave me a wide-eyed look that turned my snappy insult into the ridiculous comment it was. Barking out a laugh, I leaned back against the trunk of the tree that had assailed me. "So how'd your 'mom'—or 'aunt,' was it?—take the news?" Back at the station, he'd been on the phone to Minnie, the vampire coven leader, when I'd been trying to gulp down that croissant. Out of my range of hearing, he'd paced at the other end of the food court, grim-lipped all the while, and a few of the other vampires had joined him to listen to what she'd had to say. The sight of all those 1940 cosplayers huddled around a smartphone had reminded me that these lost-in-time vampires were nothing more than smoke and mirrors, only as devoted to their aesthetic as far as they could stretch it.

"That we lost the champion with the stronger tie to this consummate grounds or that apparently, according to you, I'm suffering from a form of parasite that feeds on other parasites?"

"That *I'm* your new champion," I said, fighting back the fluttering feeling in my stomach. He could dish it out as well as I did, though I ought to have expected that compared to Calder. This guy had had *decades* more practice. "I'm sure you spun it somehow that this was all for the best and didn't mention the small point that as soon as I get Autumn out of this, I'm out?"

"She wants to meet you," he said simply, the slightest tips of a pair of elongated fangs poking out between his lips as he spoke.

"Sure," I said, pushing myself off the tree. "If I find time between saving my sister from an immortal psycho and dodging my step-sister's watery assaults."

My ears strained to pick up the sound of the river.

"Shall I lead the way?" Dean gestured in the direction opposite where I was heading.

Shifting my shoulders up, I buried my chin into his coat a little better. "I don't suppose you would have told me at some point I was heading in the wrong direction if the tree hadn't forcibly stopped me?"

"I would have," he answered succinctly. Out of his pocket, he withdrew a coin and flicked into the air, catching it in his palm without looking to see if he'd tossed heads or tails. "But then you would have told me how you didn't need my help, so I figured it best to wait until you asked."

"And yet you couldn't help yourself from offering after all." I gestured for him to go ahead of me. "Thanks," I ground out between gritted teeth.

"Was that a sincere *thank you?*" he called out from in front of me.

"It's as close to one as you're liable to get."

We walked on in silence for a bit, the only sounds the shuddering echo of a coyote's howls ringing out across the night air, the twitch of other little forest creatures rushing through the frozen foliage to get out of our way.

"So... How'd you screw it up with Ember?" I asked, more to distract myself from the thought of becoming some scavenger's next meal after I froze to death than anything else. "Because she seemed enamored. Calder was *not* that suave. Not even close."

He so hadn't been my type, now that I could look at it with a little more distance. The whole intends-to-destroy-the-world last-nail-in-the-coffin aside, he'd been fresh-faced. Cute. A coward, really. I supposed that might have indicated some guilt on his part about the whole world-ending thing. But he wasn't forgiven.

I'd decided to be his champion because I'd felt sorry for him. And yet he'd been lying to me the whole time.

"I told you," said Dean. "I wasn't in love with her."

"You couldn't pretend you were a little longer?" I stumbled just slightly on a pile of brush, and Dean whipped around to slide an arm behind my back.

"Whoa, Romeo," I said, standing straight. "I'm capable of recovering from a minor stumble, thanks."

Dean let go, his mouth a grim line in the sparkle of the moonlight that shone through the lattice of trees overhead. His penetrating, unnaturally blue eyes were so strong in the darkness, I felt like they were about to hypnotize me, like an old school Dracula trick of his.

Shaking my head, I averted my gaze to the ground. "Like that. Seems to me Ember's the type of girl who'd eat all that up."

"*That?*" asked Dean, pivoting back to lead the way.

"That chivalry. The way you carry yourself, that striking attire."

"Thank you," said Dean without a trace of irony.

"Yeah, well, just so you know, dressing like it's a costume party every day doesn't make you the boy every girl wants to be with. You may fool some, but the rest of us take a look and are like, '*That* guy has issues. Or he's full of himself. Or both.'"

"I'm not *exactly* sure what you mean, but I guess you're telling me that in this time, my duds mark me as an old geezer."

"Have you seen *Twilight*?" I asked. He didn't respond. Orin probably would have said *yes*, the geek that he was. "Anyway, it's got a vampire boy from the 1910s or something. He didn't go around dressed in a bowler hat carrying a walking stick."

"I'm not sure that's an accurate encapsulation of the 1910s—"

"You're missing the point."

Dean turned around, those blue eyes actually making me lean back. "So if I wanted to seduce *you*, you'd prefer I dress in modern attire? I'd do almost anything for my champion, but not that." His nose actually wrinkled. "This is..." He brushed some small debris off the front of his suit. "This is who I am."

Only he didn't actually sound so sure of himself with that last bit.

I opened my mouth and shut it closed. Then opened it again. No need to comment on his personal issues. *"Hypothetically*, yes, I just meant that dressing like a modern teen wouldn't make you stand out so much. But what you're doing worked on Ember." I picked up my feet and passed by him, determined to keep going, even if I wasn't sure exactly how to get where we were going. "For a time. But I guess your surface charm could only go so far."

"She didn't like that I told you about my origins before I told her."

That made me pause. I raised an eyebrow. "You told me first? Why?"

"I needed you to see..." He cleared his throat. "I don't know. It just came out."

"You wanted me to trust you."

"I didn't want you to be my enemy."

"But someone had to be. You had your champion."

Dean shrugged. "And she didn't want to end you, either. We just wanted you to drop out."

"Then you couldn't get your wish," I said.

"Of having more vampires?" He shook his head. "We don't need some magic wish to get that done. We just needed to convince Orin to let it happen."

"Which you did."

"He was in one of his moods, I suppose." He tilted his head one way and then the other. "It's not enough for Minnie—she wants free reign—but it's plenty for me."

I studied his profile as he caught up to me. "You don't want the merfolk to be your enemies, do you?"

"I don't know any of them," he said curtly. "Everyone I know died out."

"Calder is your *nephew*."

"Great-great-nephew. And Nerida my great-niece, but... I

don't know them. I've never known them as anything but fish-folk who want to end me."

I supposed that was true.

"But you must miss... *it*," I said, my toes tingling at the memories swimming to the surface. "Being a merman. Swimming beneath the waters, breathing through your gills." My hand went to my neck, where gills had once grown as necessary, skin now scarred by the puncture of Ember's two retracting incisors.

I scowled.

"Minnie wanted to create a vampire merman," he said matter-of-factly. "A symbol of peace between our people."

"But the merfolk wouldn't accept you as just a plain old vampire, apparently."

"The merfolk have a very narrow definition of what's *acceptable* to them," he said quietly. He froze and I looked up, trying to figure out what had made him cease his movements. An enticing scent carried on the air, like animal flesh and blood and...

Blood.

My insides grew hot.

Shifting aside the last few branches covering our line of sight in front of us, Dean revealed the cabin in the woods that Orin called home.

And floating all around it, up and down and side to side like a laser light show, were all those little green balls of light.

CHAPTER SIX

EMBER

About twenty minutes after we'd departed the camp, Calder pulled his pickup truck into the parking lot of a motel just outside of town. I knew if we'd kept heading down that road, we'd have passed Journey's family diner, likely closed this weekend just because her dad never trusted the staff to run the place well enough on their own. Journey and I often laughed about that, how her dad could be a bit of a control freak when it came to his family diner.

I wondered if I'd ever be doing homework there while enjoying fries and a malt again, Journey getting pulled away every twenty minutes or so to help out in the back. Mr. Slowe would insist time and again that I sit back down—"You're a customer"—and not help out. I'd often help out when his back was turned anyway.

I wondered if Journey and I would ever even be friends again.

I had to believe we would. If not somehow before all this was over, then once it was done, once she understood why I'd crossed sides.

She'd only ever been associated with the vampires because of me to begin with.

"This okay?" Calder asked.

I nodded. I'd often been by this motel but of course had never had a need for it.

It wasn't rundown and junky—it seemed like the owners took great pride in the place. The sign by the road boasted Free Wi-Fi, cable TV, and an indoor pool, a must in the colder months if a facility was going to have a pool at all.

Calder shut off the engine and started heading inside, pulling his wallet out of his back pocket as he exited the car.

"Don't you have to be eighteen to get a room?" I asked.

He froze. As a junior, he couldn't be more than seventeen.

"Are you sixteen or seventeen?" I asked, realizing I'd never considered asking.

"A few months shy of seventeen," he muttered.

So *sixteen*.

And I was a legal adult. I swallowed. I knew there was some kind of law allowing an adult to date a minor if you were both still in school or one was fewer than three years older than the other, but that didn't stop the brief urge to flee that took over my body, the thickness in my throat rising to the surface. "I'm eighteen. I could..." I stopped myself. My wallet was back in my purse, presumably with Journey. With my ID.

Calder shook his head. "Just wait here. I have something for such occasions."

He slipped an official-looking ID from California out of his wallet and showed it to me.

"'Brad Collins. Twenty-one,'" I read off the card. The picture matched Calder and his baby-faced good looks. My eyebrow arched. "*Brad?*"

He took it back from me, his cheeks flushing. "I thought you were going to chastise me for having it in the first place."

I fluffed my hair over my shoulder and looked out the window. There weren't many other cars here, and the neon "vacancy" sign kept flickering. "It's bad for your brain to drink underage."

"I don't drink," he said, lingering by the door a moment longer. "My family all have these."

"They all have IDs saying they're Brad Collins, age twenty-one, from California?" I asked, shooting him an amused glare.

"No." He ruffled the back of his head, the mist escaping his mouth as he chuckled rising into the night air. "We all have fake IDs," he said in a quiet tone. "In case... In case we ever need to run."

Like they were right now. But they hadn't run far. Before I could ask more, he said simply, "Just stay here a sec," and shut the door after him.

Despite the approaching late hour, the cat nap I'd taken on the RV kept me wired, the thought of everything that had happened today—what a long, long day—coursing through my very veins.

The clink of sleet hitting the windshield snapped me back to the present moment.

The driver's door opened and I let out a little scream.

"Sorry!" said Calder. In his hand, he held a card key. His other arm covered the top of his blond head, though the sleet was distractingly sticking to his eyelashes. "I got us a room."

I would have grabbed for my bags, but I didn't have any. Even Calder had packed light, putting everything he needed into one backpack, promising me he'd taken an extra toothbrush and a pair of pajamas I could use for the night.

A little rain didn't used to bother me, but the second a drop fell on top of my scalp, I was overwhelmed by a sudden feeling of *need*, the scent of salt somehow lingering overhead no matter how I turned and stumbled out of the vehicle.

Calder, the backpack on his back, slipped in beside me and straightened me up. I hadn't realized I'd been practically on the pavement, my knees going week, and my legs drawn together.

"Come on," he said, the sleet like teardrops down his cheeks. "Just think of being *dry* and let's go."

"Easier said than done," I muttered, but I let him pull me to the door as I fought against focusing on the sensation of my damp, borrowed jacket clinging to my skin.

We got inside with Calder's keycard and took a moment just inside the door to shake ourselves out on the worn, muddied black mat covering the red carpet.

"It looks brutal out there."

Letting out a little yelp, I whipped around to see an older man with a bucket of ice in one hand. He scratched at the stubble on his plump pink cheek, his checkered shirt opened to reveal a plain white undershirt tucked into his worn and oily jeans. His gaze was focused beyond us, out the glass of the door, to the sleet pelting down across the pavement beyond.

I was so glad we hadn't been caught outside in that for long.

"Yup," said Calder curtly, his arm still around me, studying the guy who looked like a trucker or a hunter crashing someplace for the night. Maybe he was checking for signs of vampirism.

I supposed we *were* in the middle of a battle to the death.

Not that *I'd* be the one resorting to that.

"Kind of young to be here by yourselves," said the guy, examining us more closely.

"We're eighteen—" I said at the same time Calder said, "Our parents know where we are."

The man's dark eyes practically sparkled as he chuckled under his breath and shuffled away. "No judgement, kids. Just an observation."

I stuck my tongue out at his back and turned to Calder, his face echoing mine as we both burst into laughter.

"Come on," he said as the creepy stranger thankfully went into a room down the hall. Calder took my hand and led me to one of the rooms, a sign at the end of the hallway just beyond our door pointing out that the pool was one direction, the lobby the other.

We stepped inside. It was small and though tidy, there was

a sense of mustiness that permeated the air, the bedding and furnishing almost faded from layer after layer of dust that had been wiped away over time.

But right then, I was exhausted enough not to care.

I sat on the edge of one of the two full beds Calder had arranged for us, not even caring that my damp clothing would get the bedding wet as I lay back on it.

Calder put his backpack down on the table nearby and started shuffling through it.

"'Our parents know where we are'?" I repeated back to him. "You're not skilled at lying, are you?"

"It wasn't a lie," he said, clearing his throat. "Not entirely. We told your parents we were at a motel, and I left word with Bay when I was packing to pass along to my mother." He shrugged.

I sat up on one elbow. "Your mom would be okay with us coming to a hotel alone together?"

"Yeah." He put down a carefully folded pile of clothes and a couple of unopened packages of toothbrushes. "Merfolk often mate young."

A tingling sensation shot up from my core so fast, I had to lie back down to keep from tumbling over. "Does *everyone* think I'm sleeping with the boy I just started 'dating' today?"

"Your parents don't know the ins and outs of how it happened," Calder said quietly. "And my mom is thinking beyond this world. Big picture. An heir for a merfolk kingdom unlike any other there's ever been."

I let out a dry laugh. Of course. There'd be no worries about high school pregnancy because there wouldn't be a high school in her version of the future. There wouldn't be any judgement because there'd be *no one left to judge* me. Including my own family.

Rolling over, I tucked my knees up to my chest.

"So we're dating?" he asked. The room went painfully silent.

I rolled back toward him. "Do you not want to be?"

His eyes tore away from mine the moment I met his gaze, his eyelashes fluttering. He was holding something red in his hand and practically wringing the life out of it. "You know I do. But you only want to be with me because I agreed to help you. Bring the undead back to life. Put an end to the fighting."

"The undead..." I thought about what he was saying.

He stiffened visibly. "The vampires."

"And your dad?"

"He's gone," he said quietly. "I get that. I wouldn't know how to wish for him and for an end to the fighting at the same time." I picked at the stiff comforter as we both went silent a moment. "Is it true, then, what you told me?" he continued after a beat.

I sat up. "Is what true?"

"That the bloodsucking—that *Dean* is my mom's uncle."

"Great-uncle," I said flatly. "Your grandpa's brother. Orin confirmed it, if you can believe anything he says." I shrugged. I didn't really want to think about Dean right then.

"My mom... She knew."

"Seemed to."

"But she never told me."

"Would you have still battled him?" I brushed a strand of hair behind my ear. "'Dead is dead,' you once told me."

One of his shoulders bobbed just slightly. "I didn't really believe it then. But family is family, you know? It's too late now, isn't it? But I can't say what I would have done had Mom told me long ago. Maybe Mom felt the same way and that's why she never brought it up. Maybe she was worried I'd chicken out. Unreliable Calder." He looked sad when he flashed me a tepid smile. "I kind of look like him, now that I think about it. Him mixed with my dad..." He got choked up and I wished I could reach over and hug him.

But now that he'd said it, I couldn't get the few similarities between him and Dean out of my head. The shape of their faces, the sweep of their hair. I shuddered. I thought we could use a change in subject, admittedly a far less important one, but something I needed to get off my chest. "You don't know *how long* I wanted a boyfriend."

"You had one."

"I had the *shadow of one*." I sighed. "I've never been good around guys. I just get nervous and besides, there's school and so much else to worry about." I threaded my fingers together. They were still a bit cold and clammy from the sleet. "But I wanted a boyfriend. Sweet and funny and handsome—someone who cared about *me*."

He moved closer to the edge of the bed, the red cloth at his side as he reached his other hand out to brush away some of the hair sticking to my forehead. "You're so beautiful," he said. "And smart. And witty. You could have had any guy at school."

I chuckled. "Nice of them all to let me know that."

The air hung heavily between us, my heart pounding too hard in my chest.

Calder cleared his throat and took a step back, tossing the red fabric at my lap. Confused, I picked it up to gaze at it. It was a bikini top. I blanched.

"The pool closes at ten," he explained, but then he pulled a long, little piece of metal that reminded me of an oversized bobby pin out of his pocket. "Which makes it the perfect location to get some practice in if you're up for it."

I looked at the giant red numbers on the room's clock. 10:15.

So that was what the swimsuit top was for.

"Um, you didn't give me a bottom?" I pointed out.

He tapped one of his thighs. "Yes, I did," he said, grinning. "When I made you my champion."

———

Since I couldn't slither the motel hallways with a tail—at least I hoped I could avoid ever crawling on my belly—there was still a need for *something* to cover my bottom half. I settled on pajama bottoms and a towel from the bathroom to use as a transition into the water.

The transition of going from naked legs to mermaid tail in front of Calder was all that consumed my thoughts, even as I watched him legit breaking and entering into the pool room in front of me.

We were here with his illegal ID. I had a mass of supernatural creatures out to get me, I'd disappointed my mother—I had other things to worry about.

Like being naked in front of a boy I'd been "dating" for all of one day.

Not to mention he'd probably gotten a look back in Lake Michigan anyway.

In the dim, filtered light let in via the few panes of glass that overlooked the brightly lit hallway, Calder peeled off his shirt and flung it on one of the plastic lounge chairs by the poolside, along with his lockpick. He'd left the pool lights themselves off, so as not to draw the attention of any passerby. Shaking his head and running a hand through his spiky blond hair, Calder rolled his shoulders and stretched his arms over his head like an athlete. I realized I was just staring with my mouth agape at the plane of muscles that had no business being on a teenage boy's abdomen when his fingers slid into the elastic of his pants and stopped.

"Maybe you should wait and look again once I'm already in the water." He rubbed at the back of his neck and turned around.

Kicking off my borrowed boots, I shuffled to the opposite end of the pool and tossed the towel down on a lounge chair. The chair was torn in a few places, an old, round burn mark making me wonder if it had been here since smoking at a public poolside had been a thing. I kept my back to Calder and took my pajama top off. Beneath, I was wearing the red bikini top he'd given me, having already changed in the motel room's bathroom. And beneath the pajama pants, I was wearing... Absolutely nothing.

I hesitated at the elastic of the waist, just as he had. There was a splash behind me—not so loud as to alert the staff, but loud enough that it snapped me out of my fugue state.

"I'm facing the other way," he said. "Tell me when you're in the water and I can look."

I started pulling down on the pants but hesitated, staring over my shoulder. He was in the deep end of the pool some distance away, his back to me, a sheen of water droplets along his solid back muscles making him look like some kind of god emerged from the depths.

Sighing, I shook the thought out of my head and ripped the pants off quickly, wrapping the towel around my lower half like a makeshift skirt. The coarse material scratched against my bare skin, but I wouldn't let it slip from me if my life depended on it.

Still, it made for an awkward descent into the shallow end, down the ladder. My toes curled on reflex as they slipped below.

"Are you in yet?" asked Calder. True to his word, he didn't turn around.

I strode forward toward the deep end, each movement like walking against settling cement. "Yeah. You can look."

The water temperature was just right after the sleet that had assailed us outside, like a lukewarm bath that in another situation, in a private, smaller setting, might have lulled me off to sleep.

The skin over Calder's pectoral muscles seemed to harden as his eyes lit up and he looked my way. Then he frowned.

"You're still human."

I stared down at my bare legs and my scratchy towel skirt. "Yup."

Was it supposed to be instantaneous? That seemed inconvenient. I *did* need to shower again at some point.

Calder swam to the line demarking the deep from the shallow, his serpent-like movements as he slithered through the water fascinating to behold.

The faintest tip of translucent scales poked up from the water's surface right before he rested before me—like an angel, were it not for the water obviously holding him upright. Below the shimmer of the water, his blue tail kept him afloat.

"Hold your legs together," he said, then he held both his hands out toward me.

To take hold of them both—or even one—I'd have to let go of the towel, expose myself.

Gazing into the sheen of his verdant eyes, I trusted him.

The towel fell from my hips, and I took no note of where it ended up as I put my hands in Calder's. They were wet but warm, the unexpected softness of his palms sending shivers up my arms and down my spine.

"Legs," he said, the ghost of a smile dancing over his lips.

"Right." I snapped my legs together.

"When you turned before, your life was in danger—twice," he said, for all the world the master instructor in Mermaid Transformation 101. "But you shouldn't need that burst of adrenaline to change."

With my heart about to thump right out of my skin, I wondered if another kind of adrenaline shot could be responsible for my transformation today.

He closed his eyes, and I followed suit, though I kept peeking at him every few seconds, taking in the mellow tan of his skin, the smooth chin with only the faintest hint of stubble.

"To transform, we simply need to *feel* the water, either literally or in our minds," he continued. "Being in here will make it easier for you—perhaps too easy once you get used to it—but the littlest drop of water from the sky could be enough to change you if you're ready for it."

"That would have been a pain," I said. "If I'd have turned in that sleet storm out there, then come face to face with that nosy guy while I was flopping on the ground."

Calder opened his eyes just a little. "It could happen.

That's why I have to teach you both how to turn it on and turn it off. Ivy never quite perfected it."

My heart sank at the sound of her name on his lips.

"But I have a feeling *you* will." He pulled my hands toward him. "Now focus."

I closed my eyes.

"*Feel* the water, the way it caresses your skin."

I did, trying to calm my beating heart. His skin was still on mine, his breath so close, I could practically inhale the salt and fresh air that radiated off him even in this dinky place, but I focused instead on my legs, all the way down to the very tips of my toes. I shuffled the feet together, one big toe crossing over the other. There was something I couldn't quite name, something almost pulling my limbs together as I focused more and more on the feel of the water against my bare skin.

"The water caresses you," he said, and for a moment, at the sound of his voice, I felt almost as if there were an arm there, wrapping around my legs. A strong, muscled arm. "The water is home." His hands dunked mine below the water's surface. "I'm here, the water is here, and you're a part of it."

My eyes snapped open as a burst of electricity shot up my legs, from my toes to my waist. Gone was the separation below, and in its place was unity, a sense of wholeness.

My fins—my *fins*—scraped against the concrete surface of the pool's bottom, sending an uncomfortable shiver down my back.

They were red. I knew that from when they'd appeared in Lake Michigan, but to see my red tail here, my pale red fins— they were eye-catching. Unnatural for a fish, at least one far from the tropics, I would assume. I'd never seen another merperson with a red tail. All of them had had blue—including Ivy.

"Come on," said Calder, beaming. He dropped one hand to tug me to his side. In the deep end of the pool, my tail flapped freely. There was no sense of danger, no feeling of loss over the fact that there was no floor below me. This was how it was meant to be.

"You've got it!" Dropping my hand, he swam ahead of me. "Though that's only half of what you can do." He dipped below the water entirely.

He didn't come up—not after thirty seconds, after a minute, after two. I was floating there, just getting used to the gentle sway of my tail, watching as a shadow moved across the dark depths of the deep end.

Some voices carried like insect buzzes over from the direction of the windows overlooking the hallway.

Without thinking, I dove under.

The voices vanished, replaced by what I could only describe as the heartbeat of the water itself. Calder swam up to me, his fins flicking at my own. My eyes adjusted almost immediately to the dark, and the small, private world beneath the water's surface seemed as bright as the sunniest afternoon.

"Say something," he said, his voice not quite normal but clear as day nonetheless, tinged with the notes of a beautiful song.

My fingers shifted to my neck, where there were new folds in the skin, flaps that shifted slightly at my touch as if they were alive.

"Gills," he explained. "Don't poke them too much."

No sooner had he finished warning me, did my nail catch on some of the tender flesh beneath the surface and I let out a little yelp.

"That hurt." The words bubbled out of my throat and hung across the water's thick, heavy surface. My voice echoed in my head like an opera singer's.

I laughed, the sound transforming into something that could only be described as pure, unadulterated beauty.

Calder's laughter joined mine, a bass to my soprano, the sound dancing everywhere around us.

Before I could think twice about it, I flapped my tail

toward him, the two of us circling the suddenly far too limited space of the deep end of the pool in tandem, round and round.

"Try to keep up," Calder said, sprinting off faster. The flap of his tail sent a wave of warm water right into my face.

Rather than getting angry, I simply found myself up for the challenge. Flipping my fins with a strength I'd never expected to find in my lower body, I surged forward, flapping and flapping to bring Calder back to my side.

CHAPTER SEVEN

IVY

I didn't hesitate, just pushed aside the last of the brush and brambles and skidded over the dirt and leaves surrounding Orin's cabin before pounding on the door with a clenched, hard fist. The green lights flickered around me—I may have brushed past one, and I felt a slight pinch on my cheek—but they weren't what I was focused on. I pounded again.

Before anyone could answer inside, the air grew moist with precipitation as a sheen of sleet started flicking down on my head. I flinched, thinking the water might turn me into a mermaid, then I remembered that wasn't a concern for me anymore.

Why, then, did my legs tingle as the sleet coated my hair, got stuck on my eyelashes?

A faint scent of something *burning* assaulted my nostrils, and when I turned around, I found Dean beside me, smoking —literally releasing smoke from every bit of exposed skin pore —the moisture causing him to sizzle a red, smoky steam.

The vampires were allergic to water.

He stumbled as he caught up with me, shirking under the meager protection of his hat, his body seemingly weighed down by the mere sprinkle of icy rain.

I flung myself out of his oversized coat like it was on fire and hurled it over his head, offering him as much protection as I could.

He managed to lift his head just enough to look at me, those unnervingly alluring blue eyes widening just slightly with a silent plea.

Swearing under my breath, I knocked harder, then decided to just go ahead and try what I'd seen on TV, ready to ram against the door with my shoulder.

Only the door opened as I leaned in, and I found myself ramming straight into the svelte but sturdy chest of the faery man I'd come to pummel anyway.

"Ack!" he said as we crashed together with a *thud*.

But I didn't let up, so we both fell together to the ground, an open book Orin had been carrying in his hand clattering to the dirt floor of the cabin as I threw all my weight on top of him.

Dean lurched in behind me, throwing his wet coat and hat to the floor and stumbling to the roaring fire, over which roasted a shank of ham and bubbling stew of some kind. He practically collapsed against one of the rocking chairs there, one hand gripping the back of the tree-like wood with moss and vines crawling up its surface. Red smoke still poured from Dean's pores, though it was diminishing now the more time he spent near the fire.

"Hey!" said a far too familiar voice in a child's register. "Don't cough all over our dinner."

He wasn't the one *coughing*. He didn't breathe. His skin was merely steaming up the entire cramped cabin, hitting the back of my throat about the same time it seemed to hit Orin's, the two of us starting to hack up a lung, the movement jostling the tortoiseshell glasses on Orin's face.

There was more coughing than expected. The familiar little cat-like hack of Autumn's fits, and a couple more unfamiliar—at least one higher in tone and another deeper in register, the entire cabin turning into a symphony of phlegm.

"The windows!" sputtered Orin. "Open the windows!"

The front door was still open, the red mist escaping out through that way, but it wasn't enough.

Orin moved to get off and I put my weight into my hand, pushing down on his shoulder, no longer caring to shelter my nose and mouth from the smoke. The coughs got worse as the smoke assailed my mouth.

"Harming the..." Orin kept coughing, then he groaned. "Harming the—"

"Referee is a game-ending penalty," I sputtered through the knives catching in my throat. I wasn't watching anyone else, but someone got one window open and then another, a bulky form leaning across Orin's small bed. "See if I *care*," I muttered.

The air was cleaner now, the pattering of the sleet outside filling the cabin as the last of the red smoke dissipated, Dean slipping out of his suit jacket from his position on the floor and loosening the tie at his collar, as if he even needed more air.

Orin wrinkled his nose in Dean's direction. "Call me barmy, but they do have these things called *weather apps* on phones now. I know you're stuck in the last century, but if you want to know when to avoid heading outside so you don't light up like a smoke bomb, it might help. Just saying. Unless that was an intentional attack. If so, well done. But you got the wrong target. Champion versus champion, newly christened champion of blood. It's all right," he added to someone behind me —little flowing green balls of light, I saw for the second I spared the open door a glance. "Head back out. We're all right. Just knackered." He coughed a few more times.

I narrowed my eyes at him and then remembered what I was here for—even more than my rising urge to smack some sense into him.

Autumn. She sat in the rocking chair Dean hadn't been leaning against, still in the same outfit I'd seen her in in Chicago, minus the jacket and scarf and mittens, which had been discarded atop the green comforter of the small bed a short distance behind her.

But at the back of that chair, clutching the two stick-like pegs at top of the mossy-covered surface, was a woman I'd never seen before, a man joining her and Autumn near the stone fireplace.

They were stunning, the both of them—but severe, too, like they knew they were superior to everyone around them and they wouldn't let anyone forget that. The man was only half a head taller than the woman—they were both unnaturally tall and svelte, almost like woodland elves stepping out of a picture book.

They shared a medium brown skin tone with Orin, both with the thick and curly brown hair he had as well, though the man's was clipped so short as to make the green highlights found in all of their hair seem almost like the wandering, mesmerizing path left by a rake through a Zen garden.

She had high, plump cheekbones, almost like a cherub, and he had a long, straight nose that ended in a perfectly symmetrical bulbous tip. Their eyes were both green mixed with brown, like a sheen of murkiness lurking beneath the surface of a mossy pool of water.

And the clothes they wore—earth tones of brown and verdant green, an almost leather-like velvety material. They were form-fitting, showing off their long, lean bodies that would easily be at home on a gymnast's mat.

I must have been staring too long because Orin managed to get free from beneath me, gently shoving me aside so he could crawl out from under me.

"No offense, love. I can tell you're beautiful. But I'm not like most men looking for a snog from a pretty face."

If that had been a joke, I wasn't laughing.

He winced as he sat up and pulled his legs to his chest. "Step too far? I know you're technically a kid, but you're all kids to me. Besides, I'm not into romance. Well, reading about it—watching it, all right. But me in the leading man role? I'll pass, ta."

I grumbled as I stood on shaking feet. "I didn't ask and I don't care," I said. "Being aromantic or asexual doesn't mean you can't possibly be a creep."

He cocked his head then, his posture softening, as if thinking about what I'd said. His eyes lit up and he nodded. "Well, that joke went a bit pear-shaped. I'm sorry," he said. "Won't happen again."

"So glad for that," I muttered, crossing the small space to get to Autumn's side. "Now stop hanging around my little sister like a creep." Bending ever-so-slightly, I rested a hand briefly on Dean's shoulder as I passed him, my eyes connecting with his to see if he was okay. He offered me a faint, forced smile and looked away, the firelight flickering as a reflection in his vibrant blue irises. Something was still wrong, but I had my sister to worry about.

I grabbed her by the arm, but the woman dug her own hands into Autumn's shoulders. "The champion of bloom is not going anywhere." She spoke with an English accent, far more prim than Orin's own cockney-style speech.

"Oh, I think she *is*," I said, not intimidated by the woman's glare in the least.

"Stop," muttered Autumn, rolling her shoulder to get me to drop her arm. She let the woman's hand rest undisturbed on her other shoulder. "We're about to have dinner."

"Yes," said Orin, "perhaps I should make some introductions."

"I know who they are," said Dean, his voice somehow scratchy despite the fact that he hadn't been coughing from his smoke attack.

"Well, I don't." The noisy, sleek material of my puffy coat punctuated my point as I crossed my arms over my chest.

Orin held up a hand after tucking his reading glasses into his shirt pocket, the other hand cradling the book I'd knocked to the ground against his side. "And before you say you don't care, at least let me get it out there. My parents." He cleared his throat, like the descriptor had gotten clogged up in there and had been difficult for him to pass. "Oberon and Titania."

My back stiffened despite my determination to remain uninterested. "You just got those names from Shakespeare." I was no dean's list student, but I wasn't stupid. And I *had* worked at a bookstore for a time. At *Orin's* bookstore for a time.

"Or Shakespeare got the names from them," Orin said on a rush of hot air escaping his lips. He shoved his free hand into his pocket and rolled up on the balls of his feet, stretching his legs awkwardly.

"King and Queen of the Fae," said the woman, her tone brokering no argument. As if I would bother.

"I thought you said your family didn't take on human forms," I said to the traitorous faery.

"I said they didn't *care to* take on human forms," he muttered. "Or something of that nature." He flashed a dazzling, entirely false grin at his rigid parents. "I'm chuffed they changed their minds and decided to move into my cozy, cramped getaway from the bustle of the rest of the world—"

"If you had done your job properly, there would have been no need for a single other fae to come here." Oberon spoke with a deep baritone voice that would have sent normal children crying even when simply commenting on the weather.

A chill ran over me at that moment, whether from Oberon's intensity or the cold, moist air seeping into the cabin, or both.

Orin must have seen it on my face because he squeezed himself around me and past his father to slide the worn book onto the over-stacked bookshelf that for all practical purposes would have had no business in such a small living space. He leaned on the bed to close the window, then he moved to close the door and the sole other window in the cabin, near the small wooden table and its sole wooden chair.

"Don't anyone help or anything." Orin grunted as the last window closed.

The cabin grew flush with heat almost immediately, some of the tension creeping up my back loosening in the glow of the firelight.

Oberon and Titania didn't move at all.

"Those are the rest of the faefolk outside?" I asked, gesturing to the glass of the window through which a shimmering ball of green light glowed.

"Are you trying to get a count?" asked Titania, her upturned nose rising.

"I'm not here to fight you." I checked on Dean to make sure he agreed with me, but he was lost, mesmerized by the firelight. I stared at my right hand then, remembering how it could now burst into flames, a fire I could fling at any part of this wooden cottage, which would go up like kindling. I clenched the fist. "I'm here for my sister."

Autumn scoffed. "I don't want to go." She pointed toward the roasting ham and Titania finally moved, slipping around the rocking chairs to stir a ladle into the soup. In those short few moments, as the hard line of her mouth softened somewhat, she resembled a caring mother, a parent cheerfully making some food for her son's friends.

I snatched Autumn by the arm again. "I don't care. We're going."

"Come *on!*" said Autumn, sinking into the chair and becoming dead weight. "Dad knows where I am—"

"Because you had your prince *trick him* into thinking it was okay." I whirled on Orin. He raised both hands in surrender.

"It's just dinner and a sleepover—with my family here. My *whole* family." He gestured to the window, to the sparkling green lights outside. "My parents thought it best to watch over her, get to know her a little better—"

"So you can convince her to murder her family for some nefarious goal I can only begin to guess at? Yeah, no thanks. And next time, take a cab instead of dangling my little sister fifty feet in the air." Standing in front of Autumn, I wrapped my arms around her torso, picking her up entirely. She was much heavier than she'd been the last time I'd done this—years before—and this time, instead of jumping into the embrace of her beloved big sister, she was fighting me, squirming and kicking out her bare, dirty feet.

"We're going!" I said. Dean snapped back to the moment and took that as his cue to stand. He reached for his jacket and then his coat but hesitated, and I noticed the latter was still damp.

Rising above the crackling of the fire, the patter of the sleet against the windows reminded me. Dean was stuck.

But he could handle himself. I didn't owe him anything, not really. He was one of the people who'd dragged my family into this mess.

"I'll come back for you," I offered lamely, not sure I could make it here without him to guide me.

He just shook his head, his bright blue eyes somehow growing dull and glossy. "Don't worry about me. Get your sister out."

"You're not going anywhere with our champion." Oberon appeared before me in a flash, almost as if he'd relied on a vampire's trick of pausing time, though I realized I'd seen him move like a blur out of the corner of my eyes.

I gripped my squirming sister's back tighter, wondering what the faefolk's powers were—being able to shrink and fly was an obvious one, but there had to be more. My mind cycled through everything I knew about Orin: wind powers, I thought, and the ability to command—

Another pretty "up there" swear word escaped my lips. My feet were frozen to the ground. The faery king had told me I wasn't taking Autumn anywhere, and my feet were complying.

Like a cloying fly buzzing around the decomposing mess of my brain just then, the *urge* to do as he commanded was seeping into my consciousness.

I fought back, a burning sensation breaking out from my

heart, its fire spreading like poison—like venom—throughout the rest of my body.

"Leave me alone!" Autumn shouted right into my ear. "Just go home!"

The venom snapped back—straight to the heart, like prey fleeing from its predator.

The confusing haze hung over my mind, weighing me down, down, down.

My grip loosened on Autumn and she slipped to the dirt floor at my feet. Without a word, I stepped around her and flung open the cabin door.

CHAPTER EIGHT

EMBER

It was hard to sleep after an evening like that one. My heart pounded hard in my chest—the first time I'd felt so *alive*, so *happy*, in as long as I could remember.

The shower I'd taken afterward had been a little more difficult now that I knew what it was like to be a mermaid, to swim for the fun of it and not just when fleeing for my life. Calder had been such a good teacher, talking me through growing my legs back as we'd idled on those plastic lounge chairs, that I thought I had it down.

Being wet and thinking of how glorious it felt to be a mermaid—thinking of *Calder* particularly—that made my tail come out.

Being dry and thinking of dryness, of coming back to the cold reality of the human world, that would change me or keep me human, even if wet.

Trying not to think of Calder.

That was harder than it sounded.

Calder's easy breaths rose and fell in the bed next to mine, his breathing as a human less magical than it had been underwater, but no less alluring. His steady inhales and exhales were hypnotizing, almost lulling me to sleep.

But then I would remember it was just me and him in this

room, and I thought of our time together in the pool, and my heart raced like crazy.

Snatching Calder's phone off the nightstand between us—he'd said I could use it if I needed it before he'd gone to bed—I rolled over and woke up the scratched screen.

He didn't use a passcode. There weren't many apps on his home screen, and I didn't want to pry, so I brought up the browser and started searching for whatever crossed my mind.

A new swimsuit. Wherever Calder had gotten the bikini top, it was from someone with a smaller cup size than my own, so it'd been a little snug. Besides, it was plain and a bit too... revealing.

I flushed at the idea of being *revealing* around Calder. I hadn't had *anything* on below the waist.

With just a few clicks down the rabbit hole, I was looking at vintage-style swimsuits. Calder had gotten one thing right: the color. There was an adorable red tank top style top with white trim and a little white bow at the bottom that would have gone perfectly with the wardrobe I'd built up during my time with the vampires.

My stomach went sour. Was it stupid for me to want this exact swimsuit, considering?

No. The vampires were a part of my past. Blame it on midnight loopiness or the jittery feeling in my stomach, but I logged into Mom's Prime account and had it lined up to be sent to my house in just two days. Well, tomorrow, technically. I really needed to sleep already.

Sighing, I rolled over, just about to let go of the phone to give sleeping the old college try when it buzzed in my hand. The first few lines of a text appeared across the screen.

I was going to ignore it, my grip growing looser, when I saw the name.

Ivy.

My breath stopped.

I swiped at the message.

We have a problem, it read. *The faefolk are too strong.*

So why was she discussing this with her *ex*? Thoughts of Dean going to Ivy and talking to her without me swam to the surface.

Was there no one I could be with who didn't have a secret dialogue with my step-sister behind my back?

I must have made some sound because Calder's voice permeated the darkness. "What is it?" he asked. "A message?"

"Yeah," I muttered, sliding the phone across the nightstand toward him.

He picked it up and frowned. "Maybe we should see what she wants."

"Why is she texting *you*?" I glanced at the glowing red clock. "At midnight? The day we supposedly switched sides?"

Calder's face pinched as he rubbed some alertness back into his eyes. "Ember, I have no idea. Maybe she wants what we want. A peaceful end to things. She *did* reiterate over and over to me after she got mad at me that she was only in this for her little sister."

The skin on my arm started itching unnervingly, unyieldingly. I shot up, tossing the motel blankets off me, eager to dispel the gnawing sense of guilt growing inside me.

I shouldn't have assumed this was going to be some dark, dirty secret. Just because *Dean* had met with her behind my back...

Calder had met with *me* behind Ivy's back. But, as he'd said, she'd clearly been over him at the time.

"Call her," I said, straightening. "And see what she wants."

Sighing, Calder pushed aside the motel blankets and kicked his legs off the side of his bed, too, clicking the switch on the small desk lamp. He was sleeping only in boxer briefs, and despite the fact that I'd seen more of his exposed chest than his covered upper torso today, the sight of it on his bleary-eyed, fresh-from-sleep body just made my core do loop-de-loops.

"Don't tell her I'm with you," I said as he began sliding his finger across the screen.

He froze and raised an eyebrow.

"Okay, she might figure out I would be," I said, scrambling to explain myself, "but I mean, you can make it seem like you snuck away and I'm out of earshot."

"I'm not that good at deception," he said plainly.

I believed him. I'd had enough of doubting him and thinking maybe he was out to just use me like Dean had been.

We had a plan.

And Calder *cared* about me.

"Just try," I said. "Feel her out. I'll jump in if I think I ought to."

Grunting and worrying at his bottom lip, Calder finished tapping at his screen and then must have hit *speaker* before putting it down on the table between us because I could hear it ring.

Calder was an open book when it came to me.

There was a lightness in my limbs, a sudden feeling of weightlessness, as I regarded his profile.

"Hello?" Beyond Ivy's voice was something that sounded like beans tumbling—the ongoing sleet falling outside. She was outdoors? At this time of night?

Calder started speaking, but the word caught in his throat. He tried again. "What's up?"

Ivy scoffed. "What's up is I'm stuck in the middle of this forsaken woods you own behind my dad's house with no clue how to get back to civilization, my sister has the ability to *command* people to do things just like that flighty faery prince does, his *parents* just stepped out of a Shakespearean sonnet and won't let her out of their sights, and my vampire prince is stuck in their cabin until this relentless sleet finally lets up. *That's* what's up."

Calder exchanged a look with me, as if looking for some kind of advice on how to handle it. I mouthed, *"And you called me?"*

"And you called me?" Calder echoed out loud.

"Yes, genius, I called you. Because I figured you were somewhere near Ember. I tried her phone first and it went straight to voice mail."

"It *is* past midnight," he said.

I pinched the scratchy sheet between two fingers. She'd tried *me* first?

Really?

After everything?

"What do you want from me?" I mouthed to Calder.

"What do you want from Ember?" Calder posed out loud. I'd meant him, not me, but that was close enough. "Are you looking for some way to end this?"

"I want to save my sister," Ivy explained plainly. "She's Ember's family, too."

I would have put an end to this ages ago. *I* wasn't the little brat who'd tried to kill anyone, who'd almost knocked my pregnant mother down the stairs, accident or not.

I crossed one leg over the other fiercely. "Why do you need me?" I said out loud, blowing my cover.

It was clear she wasn't interested in some secret liaison with my boyfriend, anyway.

"That's what I thought," Ivy said sharply. She took a deep breath, almost as if to calm herself. "Autumn commanded me to leave her alone. To leave the cabin she was in."

"And she hasn't commanded me, you're saying." I thought about it. If Autumn had those kind of powers that Orin had used to convince our parents that Ivy's switch-up in custody arrangement was all right, that Autumn spending so much time with what they thought was a young adult man was no big deal, what was to stop her from commanding me to surrender?

"No," I said flatly.

"*No?*" Ivy spat back at me.

I exchanged a look with Calder, who nodded. "I can't go without a plan. If she had these powers, why didn't she command us to do anything earlier? All she's been using is her vine powers."

"I don't know!" Ivy was clearly exasperated. "As far as I

know, Mr. and Mrs. Faery Rulers didn't show their faces until that disaster back in Chicago, so maybe they're coaching her on how to use the extent of her abilities."

"Which are?" I asked, as alert and ready as I'd ever be. I needed to know this to win.

There was clearly no talking sense into an eight-year-old.

"The vines, the commands—I don't know, I've seen Orin use wind powers before. And the shrinking and flying? Who's to say she can't do that? They carried her back here, but—"

"Carried?" I asked.

Ivy was silent a bit. "They picked her up and it looked like she floated home."

That was unsettling. But at least it made me think she more likely than not couldn't fly or shrink herself. At least not yet.

Calder ran a hand over his face and then crossed his arms tightly over his smooth pectoral muscles.

The patter of sleet seemed to grow louder then, and now that I knew where she was, I could picture it assailing the half-shed tree branches above her. "So you're just going to leave me stranded? In a sleet storm? In the woods? And let my sister slip more and more into their clutches?"

"Do you want to surrender to me?" I snapped.

"*No!*" She seemed offended I'd even ask.

"Then there's no point in me helping you."

"*No point?* Ember, our parents are *married*. They're going to have a baby together, we'll be connected by blood—"

The word 'blood' on her lips lit a fire somewhere deep inside me, the faint echo of that familiar drag of venom pumping out through my thundering heart.

"I doubt you'll die in the woods behind our house," I said plainly. "If you're not interested in surrendering to me, we have nothing to talk about."

"Ember, you—"

"Thanks for the intel on Autumn," I said, snatching Calder's phone off the desk and hitting *end*.

As soon as I did, the fiery feeling spreading throughout my body retreated and I felt like I might throw up.

"You're not messing around," Calder said. He nodded just slightly, a grin slowly growing on his face. Then his face fell. "But we didn't even explain *why* it was so important we win."

"She wouldn't believe me," I said, settling his phone back down. "She'd probably accuse me of being so lovestruck, I was all in on the flood-the-world concept."

"Are you?" he asked plainly. "Lovestruck?" he added, the word catching a little in his throat. He chuckled and rubbed the back of his head.

"Goodnight," I said, trying to keep my own mouth from curling upward. I flicked the nightstand light off and rolled over, giving him my back. "Maybe," I said softly.

The rustling of sheets indicating Calder was going back to bed stopped abruptly. "Did I just hear 'maybe'?"

"*Goodnight*," I emphasized. But there was something fluttery spreading throughout my body, a sense of euphoric joy I had no business experiencing in light of everything going on.

———

We pulled into my driveway about 11:00. I was truly very sleepy. But I'd forgotten about motel check-out times when I'd guessed I'd be sleeping in today. Besides, better to rip the bandage off and get it over with.

"You sure you don't want me to go in with you?" Calder reached across the console of his pickup truck and squeezed my hand.

"I am." I scanned the driveway for any sign of Ivy having made it successfully back to the house, but it wasn't like she had a car to begin with, so I didn't know what I was looking for.

I'd *had* a car that was now somewhere in a junkyard thanks to that little brat and her vines.

"I don't think it'll help matters any to have you there," I

said, thinking of what my mom seemed to think might have been going on last night.

"It would if there are other princes there. If your *step-sisters* are there."

"I'll call you," I said simply, then I scratched my cheek. "When I get my phone back, anyway."

Calder took that hand he'd been squeezing and placed a kiss on the top of my knuckles.

He was an athletic teen from my own timeline, so to speak, a rugged guy who didn't dress up but somehow looked gorgeous without even trying.

The move seemed so old-fashioned, so much more at home with Dean and his stuck-in-the-past way of undead living.

But it made my heart melt. Far more than it ever had with Dean.

"Thank you," I said simply. "Thank you for giving me the push I needed..." I left the rest unsaid.

"Thank you for believing in me," he said simply.

And then I tore myself away, wearing a cobbled-together borrowed outfit and nothing to carry away. I felt naked without my purse, without a single thing of my own weighing me down.

Naked and free.

I tried the front door, but it was locked, so I had to ring the doorbell.

I waved at Calder and his pickup backed up, the engine a bit loud for a quiet neighborhood in the morning.

Easton appeared out from the kitchen, pattering over on bare feet, an open robe settling crookedly over a plain white shirt and striped flannel pants.

"And she lives," he said by way of greeting as he opened the door, a mug of steaming coffee in his other hand. His brown-and-gray hair stuck up at all angles and his ruddy cheeks were a mess of fine, subtle lines and dark stubble.

He had no idea how not far off he was with that statement.

I gave him a polite smile and headed for the stairs.

"Hold it," Easton said. "So what's up, sport? You feeling better? You've got to wait for your mother before you vanish behind a locked door upstairs."

I clutched the staircase bannister awkwardly. "Where is she?"

"Getting bakery with the girls."

The girls. So Ivy had made it out of the woods and was now on an outing with Autumn?

Yes, that had been *such* an emergency last night.

"I'll wait upstairs—" I started, but just then I could hear Mom pulling into the driveway.

My hand clutched the wood harder. *Rip off the bandage*, I repeated to myself. *Just rip it right off.*

I was starting to regret sending Calder away. I couldn't even call him without my phone.

Easton seemed oblivious to my distress. "Hey, so, did your mom tell you Ivy has a campus visit this weekend?"

"Huh? No." I wondered if Ivy would even care to go at this point.

"We're leaving Friday, right after Thanksgiving, and we should be back by Monday." He took a loud slurp of his coffee. A car door opened outside, that little obnoxious bell going off to indicate Mom had left her keys in the ignition or her headlights on or something. "Noelle thought since Glory and Autumn are already coming along, maybe we should just make a little weekend getaway of it. We have a bed and breakfast booked, nice little place a bit out of the way but still along the lake there. I called, and they had a cancellation, so we're booking the whole thing. Want to come?"

"Where?" I snapped my head back toward Easton. What nonsense was my mom planning for me behind my back? I was already enrolled in college via early admission.

"Fowles U," he said. "I don't know how Ivy feels about it, it's just one of her 'maybes,' but Glory and I went there and it's got a gorgeous campus. Especially this time of year. Just an hour west of here. Real quiet community, college town. I bet you'll like it, even if you already know where you're going. Could just be a nice weekend family fall getaway."

"Yeah, sure," I said, the repeated sounds of car doors slamming outside causing a sweat to break out down my back. I'd agree to anything just then. Who knew what life would be like tomorrow at this rate, let alone at the end of the week.

Muffled sounds of conversation carried through the air, one high-pitched voice particularly loud, though I couldn't make out what she was saying. Figures hovered beyond the glass of the front door and Easton opened it for the rest of our family.

Autumn burst through, my mom with a box of bakery in her hands behind her, and Ivy staring blankly ahead, two more boxes of bakery in her own. Ivy looked rough, damp—like she hadn't slept a wink. Mom looked bright and cheery, but she was still in her pajamas with her coat tossed on top.

"Oh! *You're* back," said Autumn, the smile vanishing off her face.

My mom laughed. "Don't sound so disappointed, honey. Here. Take the donuts. I need to have a chat with Ember." She sounded far less cheerful now.

"Let her be," said Autumn, and there was something strange crackling through the air just then, something I couldn't put a finger on. "Don't consider her in trouble." She stuck her tongue out at me. "Thank me for getting you out of a grounding."

"Thank you for getting me out of a grounding." The words were out of me before I could blink, my hands at my throat.

"Right, then, let's you and your dad and me go eat all these yummies," said Mom without blinking. She turned around and grabbed the two other boxes of pastries out of Ivy's hands without a word, heading to the kitchen without even taking her shoes and coat off.

Ivy hardly reacted, except to narrow her eyes straight at me.

CHAPTER NINE

IVY

I could see Ember right in front of me, sense my anger toward her, but there was this fogginess over my mind.

With the echo of Autumn's voice from the kitchen, the fogginess retreated.

"You can talk to me now," Autumn had said when she'd come across me in the forest. "Just do as I say."

What she'd wanted was three boxes full of donuts and other sweets for breakfast, and when she'd told Noelle this the moment we'd walked through the front door together, Noelle had dropped the pan of eggs she'd been scrambling and gotten her coat to go buy some.

Things pushed deep inside came back floating to the surface—important things, like how Autumn had used her mind control powers on me and left me a husk of a person until we'd fulfilled her wish for enough pastry to rot her entire mouth.

"Hey, hon, I hardly saw you a second before you were all off to get some breakfast." Dad sipped from a mug beside the staircase, and with a start like a cold splash of water against my face, I realized Ember wasn't there alone.

I was cold and damp and the door was open to a warm, if

dangerous, home. Sighing, I stepped inside and brushed past Dad and Ember, looking around.

"You look a little worse for wear," said Dad. "No shower in that cabin?"

"What cabin?" asked Ember.

I gave her *a look*. As if she needed to ask. Autumn must have told him I'd spent the night there with her.

But no, that wasn't where I'd been all night, and Ember darn well knew that.

"I'm tired," I said plainly to Dad. "And I do need a shower." I sniffled, and I hoped I wasn't about to come down with pneumonia because of a night wandering in the woods.

Rubbing my temples, I picked through a blur of memories. Autumn had known the way home without Orin's help, at least as far as I could tell. There had been a bouncing green light just over her shoulder if I shut my eyes tightly and tried to get the haze of a memory to clear, but I couldn't tell if it had simply been a trick of the morning light trickling through the lattice of trees overhead.

One thing I knew wasn't in those memories, though.
Dean.

I cursed internally and patted my jacket pocket. My phone was still there, thankfully. I pushed aside some messages from Paisley, who was still concerned about Lyric, two best friends I'd barely spent time with since this had all begun. I didn't know how to tell Paisley that Lyric's girlfriend, Raelynn, was a vampire now and that probably accounted for most of the stress in their relationship.

I needed to meet up with the vampires and put my foot down about my friends.

Raelynn and Devam may have been lost causes, but they were turning another high school student into a vampire over my dead body.

I chuckled darkly under my breath at the literal interpretation of that I was leaving myself open to.

My head hurt and I was so tired.

I went about searching to see if I'd thought to have gotten Dean's number, but I hadn't.

I did see a number that might help me. Raelynn herself. Not that we'd ever been especially close.

A hand floated out over my phone screen. "Now hold on a second. You just got home. You can at least greet your old man with a good morning."

I looked up and Dad smiled. Sighing, I slapped my phone down on the table next to the coat rack and peeled the soggy thing off. It was stuffed with down and was not acclimating well to its new status as a wet rag.

Ember still hovered beside us on the bottom stair, looking as fresh as a daisy. So glad her retreat through the chilly waters of Lake Michigan had gone so well.

"Morning, Dad. Can I please take a shower and crash into bed?" I snatched the phone off the table. Let them all think I'd spend the day sleeping in my room. Even Ember couldn't bring herself to stab me in my sleep, could she?

Oblivious to the violent bent of my thoughts, Dad took one final gulp from his mug before speaking again. "I was just talking to Ember about the school visit this weekend. After Thanksgiving."

"Huh?" My mind buzzed.

"Fowles University. This weekend. Your mom, Autumn—I'm inviting Noelle and Ember, too. I cleared it with your mom. Due to a cancellation at the bed and breakfast, we've got the whole thing booked now."

"Great." I headed for the staircase, staring pointedly at Ember as I passed her. "I'm sure Ember is so excited about it."

She swallowed visibly and looked away, but I kept walking up.

"Of course, *the real question* is if Autumn feels like going," I said, knowing how strange my little sister dictating a college visit trip would sound to my dad's ears. That was all for Ember. For the self-centered lovestruck idiot who'd brushed off my strained cries for a temporary truce.

"Of course she wants to go," said Dad. "Like it'd even be up to her if she didn't."

"You'd be surprised," I muttered, heading up and straight for my room.

———

One warm, warm shower and a change into dry clothes later, I sat on my bed, my bedroom door locked, my ears straining to hear the sounds of the household. My chin sunk into the thick collar of my black-striped blue sweater dress, the ultra-thin thermal top and leggings completing the outfit and adding several more buffers against the cold, in addition to my woolen socks and loose '80s-style leg warmers. My slightly damp dark hair was loosely tied into a bun atop my head and I'd skipped the makeup. Now that I was warm and relatively safe, it was time to find out what had happened to my pretend vampire boyfriend.

Actual vampire. Pretend boyfriend.

Autumn giggled somewhere in the distance as some kind of big shuffling came from Ember's room, like she was moving furniture. Good. I hoped she was moving a dresser behind her door with no plans to ever remove it.

I dialed Raelynn. I knew she was diving headfirst into the whole vampire thing, but even vampires stuck in the previous century used smartphones.

She answered after a few rings.

"Ivy?" she asked. "Ivy Sheppard? What is this I hear about *you* being the new vampire princess?"

I winced. "Not a princess," I said. "A champion."

"Yeah, yeah." She laughed, the sound an echo of what it had once been like. Facsimile of her actual teenage laughter. An imitation from a wailing corpse. "I just figured. Everyone calls Dean the 'prince,' so his champion has to be his 'princess.'"

"And then we'll ride off into the sunset, the blood of our

enemies dripping down our cheeks." My nails dug into my comforter, the chipped blue of my polish in serious need of some maintenance. "About the *prince*. We got separated last night during the sleet storm. He got stuck. You seen him?"

"Stuck? Stuck where? To tell the truth, I've been kind of *out of it* all weekend." She paused and I swore I could hear her slurp. "Getting used to feeding, and let me tell you, there's *nothing* better." She groaned.

She was hardly the same shirking honors student who'd clashed with Lyric, the toned athlete who took charge in any relationship, but who had loved her passionately nonetheless.

"Rae?" I asked. "Rae, are you listening? Is Lyric there?"

How long would it be before she turned my friend?

There was some murmuring on the other end of the line and then the voice changed.

Feminine and high-pitched, but somehow still sultry. "Your friend Lyric has been permanently disinvited from our manor, but my nephew is here," said Minnie, Dean's "aunt" and the vampire queen. "As are our new allies."

"Allies." It didn't come out as a question. More a statement of disbelief.

I knew exactly whom she meant. Whom else could she be referring to?

"Oberon and Titania," Minnie clarified unnecessarily. "As well as Orin."

"Don't *trust* them!" I sputtered. "I don't care if blood came from bloom, there's still only going to be one *winner*, and I can tell you, they don't think it'll be you."

There was a telltale sudden halt of the furniture moving in Ember's room, and I realized I'd spoken a bit too loudly.

I sighed. "But Dean's all right?"

"Yes," she clipped. "Why wouldn't he be?"

"I don't know," I said. "I was forced by my own sister's whims to leave him behind in a cabin with our enemies in the middle of a hailstorm."

"Allies," said Minnie curtly.

Sure. "Can I speak to him?"

"You should really come here," said Minnie. "Introduce yourself to the coven. You've hardly been our champion twenty-four hours and you're already trying to squirrel my nephew away on some private lovers' getaway."

"Whoa, you are *way* jumping to conclusions," I muttered. "He's just the only one of you I know. Look, I have a goal here: to get my sister out of this game."

"In which case, you should be happy we're forming an alliance. At least for now." A little hissing sound escaped her lips. "Do not speak to me as if were a little girl, child. *Of course* I know there can be only one winner."

"I want her *out of the game*, not going up against merfolk."

Minnie had nothing to say to that.

"Okay," I relented. "But I don't have a car. So send someone to come get me. And Autumn."

I wasn't sure I should leave her here with Ember, even if Autumn could go tell her to jump in a lake.

Though to a mermaid, that wasn't really the threat I'd meant it to be when I'd first thought that in my mind.

"Give us fifteen, sugar," said Minnie, her voice dripping with falsity.

———

I slipped on an older woolen coat that just barely still fit me. It was brown, worn, and dull, and so not my style, but my winter coat had congealed into an unfixable mess.

Autumn hummed as she slid her feet into her faux fur UGG boots. I hadn't been sure if she'd *want to* go alone with me and I had zero strategy for convincing her since she could so easily command me, but fortunately, she seemed aware of the situation and eager to go. She'd taken her own shower and put on a new outfit: pink cheetah sweatpants and a solid purple sweatshirt with a pony design on it. She was somehow more fashionably coordinated than usual.

Ember hadn't poked her head out of her room to see us off. The back of my neck prickled at the idea of her maybe climbing down her window and disappearing to who-knew-where.

"We hardly get to see you these days," said Noelle. "Either of you. I wish you'd stay for dinner."

"*Noelle*," said Autumn, letting out a groan. "Let us go have dinner at the Hornes'."

"Of course," Noelle said, brightening.

"Have fun, kids." Dad ruffled Autumn's hair and then retreated to the living room, where some sports game was blasting. He cheered in tandem with the crowd, not sparing a moment to think about where he was sending his daughters off to.

Though I supposed in his point of view, I was taking my sister to my boyfriend's house for dinner. For some reason.

"Don't forget to have Dean ask if any of his family will be joining us on Thursday." Noelle's hand moved from where it was resting on her belly and gestured to the dining room. "We have a lot of space, but I need to know how many mouths to feed."

I didn't think vampires ate turkey, but admittedly, I hadn't spent much time with any yet.

"I'm sure his family has plans," I said, helping Autumn into her puffy coat. "But I'll ask," I lied.

The last thing I wanted was a house full of vampires on Thanksgiving—I supposed unless Ember was bringing a house full of fish.

The slight squeal of a brake sounded outside.

"That's our ride," I said, sparing one more glance up the stairs. Ember had gone suspiciously quiet after all that furniture arranging.

"Okay, girls, have fun," said Noelle.

Autumn was already halfway down the driveway, headed toward a restored shiny red classic car that looked far more prehistoric than anything Dean had ever ridden around in.

At the driver's seat was Minnie herself, her bright red hair tucked into a driving scarf, her eyes bedecked with cats-eye sunglasses, even on this overcast day.

I froze on the porch as I shut the door behind me. I hadn't expected the coven leader herself to show up to get me.

No one was next to her in the seat and I could just barely make out a form in the back from where I stood.

As I neared—Autumn already at the front of the car, following some instructions from Minnie to bump the seat up to leave room to crawl in the back—it became clearer the guy in a disheveled suit, his trilby hat askew, his glasses more pasted on than resting properly, was none other than Dean. I'd never seen his hair slightly mussed instead of perfectly greased into place, but it was clear even from the bit visible under his hat that he was not in a good mood.

Almost like he'd had a hangover, but I doubted if he drank alcohol it had any such effect on him.

Autumn started climbing in beside him, but I tugged on her arm. "You ride shotgun."

Once we were all settled and wearing our flimsy cross-waist seatbelts, Minnie pulled off onto the road, and I stared at Dean. He gave no response. Not even the slightest movement of his shoulders to indicate he was breathing.

Which of course he wasn't, I reminded myself.

"Welcome, girls," said Minnie. "It's *so nice* to see you." Her white-gloved hand adjusted the rearview mirror to center the reflection of her sunglasses. "I told Dean he couldn't just *name a new champion* and fail to bring her to see me."

I glanced to Dean again, but he didn't say a word.

"I'm sorry," I said to him—not her. "I didn't mean to leave you, but Autumn's order made it so I couldn't—"

Autumn fiddled with the radio dial. This car really was accurate old school, no Sirius radio to be found—not even a CD player or tape deck. Some contemporary, upbeat pop song blasted out and she leaned back. In the reflection of the mirror, Minnie's plump, red lips pinched.

"How are you doing?" I asked Dean. "You look like you're in pain. Can you feel pain?"

That got his attention. His head turned slightly. "Would it matter if I could?"

Someone was getting all Nietzsche on me for daring to ask a relatively simple question. "I told you I'm in this for Autumn," I muttered under my breath. The music ought to have been loud enough to cover me, but Minnie's grip on the steering wheel grew tighter regardless. Sighing, I sat back in the seat and dared to close my eyes. Utterly exhausted, I shivered. The thin, retractable top did little to keep the interior warm, but I supposed the vampires' inability to feel *anything* made it so that wouldn't matter.

"Can we go to McDonald's?" Autumn shouted over the radio as the song transitioned into a punky beat I vaguely recognized as a 1980s tune.

Minnie whapped the dial on the radio until a classic melody played by a symphony orchestra filled the air. "We have a chef at home for all the bloodbags, darling."

"I'm *not* a bloodbag," snapped Autumn. Her brows knitted together as she turned to face Minnie and I *knew* that look.

I didn't say anything to interfere, though. I was too exhausted and Autumn was safe in front of me, so too bad for anyone else who got in her way.

"Of course you're not, darling," said Minnie, nonplussed. "But you don't want to fill your flora-filled veins with that junk, do you? My chefs make nutritious meals."

"'Nutritious' means 'gross.'" Autumn pouted. *"Take me to McDonald's right now."*

Minnie's hands clenched the steering wheel harder, but she didn't make any sudden moves. "That won't work on me."

I perked up. Interesting to know.

"Take me to McDonald's right now!" Autumn clearly didn't believe her. "Take me!" She kicked out one of her legs, then growled and unhooked her seatbelt, turning around to look at me.

"Autumn, get back in your seat—"

"Make her take me to McDonald's!" she said, looking at both Dean and me.

I stilled. That sense of confusion hung vaguely in the air, and my heart echoed louder in my brain.

"Faery magic doesn't work on the undead, kid," said Dean matter-of-factly. So he *could* speak. "It has its origins and hopes and dreams, and there are none of those for walking corpses. So save your breath."

I didn't have time to wince too hard over Dean's sudden emo phase because my heart was slowing, a burning sensation spreading outward from my chest, slowly, slowly, rolling up my arms and down my legs all the way down to my toes.

Autumn was not moved. She focused entirely on me. "Make. Her. Take. Me. To. McDonald's."

My arms flung outward without my consent, toward Minnie to drag the steering wheel in the direction of the nearest McDonald's, traffic and safety be damned, but my seat-belt caught me tightly against my waist

"Blood. The venom pumps. The thirst calls," said Dean, as if reciting an ancient curse without the slightest bit of guilt or interest.

But his words did *something* to me. Made me picture blood. Focus on that burning inside me—the venom.

My gums stung as my incisors seemed to lengthen, sharpen, poking my bottom lip, the taste of my own blood hitting my tongue like the sweetest cake, the juiciest steak—the best thing I'd tasted in my entire life.

My eyes burned, so I shut them and focused instead on my insides. Gone was the heartbeat, gone was the rhythm of my breath. Both were replaced with silence. Stillness. But beneath it all moved some kind of fiery life force, an ever-present burning. The venom in my veins.

That was what gave the vampires their false sense of life.

It sounded like someone popped open a glove compartment and rifled around. Then something hit my lap, all while

Autumn was shouting, her demand to go to McDonald's far beyond toddler tantrum levels at this point.

"Put them on," said Minnie smoothly, and I felt for what had landed in my lap.

Sunglasses.

I slipped them over my eyes and then opened my eyelids at last. These were dark—the darkest shades I'd ever worn. The world around us looked painted in night as we pulled up to a familiar manor down a rather crowded street. These vampires were no recluses.

Autumn was pouting, her arms crossed over her chest as we came to a stop behind a Horne Moving Co. truck parked in the driveway. For a second, I wondered if the vampires were on the move like the merfolk were, but then I remembered these undead had a moving business. The first time I'd met this wretched vampire beside me, he'd been carrying heavy boxes of my family's stuff into Noelle's home with ease.

Autumn shouted, "Stay away from me!" as she pushed open the car door and pattered up the driveway.

I felt nothing. No sense of confusion. No haze in my brain.

Autumn ran up the Hornes' front steps, where she was greeted by Orin as he stepped out of the front door.

He got this look on his face as she spoke rapidly, like one got when humoring a little kid and listening to them tell an exaggerated or embellished story, and he nodded, holding the door for her and gesturing inside.

He nodded toward the car and I looked away.

"Well, that's one way to beat faery magic," I said, running a shuddering finger over the back of my ice-cold hand. "An advantage merfolk definitely don't have." I didn't mention the fact that I'd warned Calder and Ember of Autumn's newfound trick. I didn't think Minnie would take that well.

Flexing my right palm, I brought warmth to it, but the red of the fire quickly sputtered into a purple mist, almost as if ice had doused the flame.

Strange.

"You have twenty minutes," said Minnie, shutting the car off and readjusting the rearview mirror to use as a vanity. Puffing her headscarf, she stepped out of the vehicle. "Then I expect you inside to join us. We have the next stage of a war to plan."

Her point was punctuated by the sound of her heels on the cold driveway.

CHAPTER TEN

EMBER

I couldn't tell exactly what Ivy was yelling about on her phone, but I didn't think she was just calling one of her school friends and catching up with everything she'd missed since transferring.

You didn't get *that* kind of annoyed unless lives were at stake.

I did make out the words "Don't trust them," and my heart sank. That made me think that the vampires were part of an alliance—against Ivy's wishes. Though Orin had warned us of this, with the whole blood-came-from-bloom business.

The vampires and faeries were going to team up to take the merfolk down before they turned on each other.

And here Ivy had been worried about her sister's mind-control powers posing a problem for *her*.

I couldn't let that happen. I was the only one I trusted to make the right wish—and that meant the merfolk had to stay in this until the end.

Changed into my own clothes—my *own* clothes, a burgundy ribbed sweater and a pair of jeggings—I began tossing all the vintage attire I'd been stockpiling in my closet with the help of Dean's "aunts" on the top of my bed. Artemis, my white-with-black-spots cat, opened one eye blearily at me from my pillow as a sweater just about missed the tip of his tail. Staring at the clothes for a bit, I realized how dumb that was—I was thinking *breakup* mode, and I didn't have time to wallow in my sorrows. There was more going on here than just my love life.

Ivy's voice grew louder and I went back to pushing my dresser in front of the door. It wouldn't hold for long if either Sheppard sister decided to burst in here, but it'd slow them down enough that I could make a run for it through the window if need be. Arty's eyes grew wide at the sound, his posture rigid, showing he was ready to flee at the first sign of trouble.

I sympathized.

I couldn't think until I was sure she couldn't burst in here and blast me with her ice—er, fire.

Groaning, I lay back on my bed and scratched Arty's chin, calming him, one of the hangers with a 40s-style dress attached to it poking me in the butt. I was still so mixed up. I was ice—she was fire.

I was mermaid, she was vampire.

But none of that mattered. I just wanted this all to end.

Right. I sat up straight. I had meant to catch up with schoolwork. With the days I'd been missing lately, I was woefully behind.

It felt like a stupid thing to be focusing on just then, even if it ought to have been the *only* thing I had to worry about. If Mom had never remarried. If the vampires and merfolk hadn't formed an uneasy truce to make sure she had, resulting in two selfish step-sisters.

I strode across the room and rummaged through my backpack, removing everything I'd need to write an English paper due before Thanksgiving break. My laptop was in need of a charge, so it was a little slow to boot up, even after I figured out the problem and plugged it in. I sat there at my desk, my hands folded across my lap, just deep breathing. In and out.

I knew I ought to have told Calder what I'd overheard, but was it so much to ask for *one* normal day?

I wasn't preparing for the world to end. I had to believe I'd win and there'd be a future—for everyone, even if it wasn't the future they wanted.

The mumble of Ivy's voice grew stern, almost as if she were trying to keep things quiet. I popped open Google Docs to start writing my paper and found a message from Joe, the jock who loved to bother me for help with all his English essays.

Do you know who represents "pride" and who represents "prejudice"?

He was basically asking me to outline the whole essay for him. Sighing, I typed back, *Did you read the book?* And got to work.

I was finished with my intro and first paragraph, running my finger over a page in the text I wanted to get a quote from, when footfalls exploded upstairs, Ivy shouting something at Autumn to get ready. Tense, I grew still.

I did. Joe's responding message appeared on the screen. *But I kept falling asleep. So I may have missed some things.*

More mumbled discussion, a door shutting. I wrote some more. About half an hour later, two sets of feet pounded down the stairs.

I strained to listen. My parents' voices carried up the stairs, though I couldn't pinpoint what they were saying.

Then the front door slammed and a few moments later, a vehicle—a familiar engine a little too loud to be a modern one—peeled away. My room didn't overlook the street, so I couldn't have looked if I'd wanted to.

On shaky legs, I went to my window overlooking the backyard. I couldn't say what I was looking for. Some sign that the faefolk were migrating from the woods behind my home? I rubbed my temples. It was a miracle for a few short moments I'd been able to focus on schoolwork at all. How would I even be able to sleep in this house, feeling pinned in on all sides by the enemy?

Dean used to sneak into my room without my parents knowing. Not for anything scandalous or romantic, but just to watch over me. I'd confused it for at least a little romantic chivalry for a time, but now I simply saw its practicality. Could I convince Calder to do the same?

What could a merman do to guard me in my water-free room?

My laptop pinged with another message, and before I read it, I was overtaken by a surge of determination. I quickly typed out the rest of the essay, ran it through spellcheck, and didn't bother with a second read. My "normal" life was lucky it had gotten that much out of me. I dragged it into the digital drop box and turned it in.

Stretching my arms up over my head, I realized it was already late afternoon as my stomach grumbled. Out of bored curiosity more than anything, I clicked on the message.

Never mind. Slowe is helping me.

Journey? She was supposed to be in Chicago. I glanced at the clock. I supposed she could have been back by now. And working on her essay, just as I was.

I found her name in my message inbox and typed a greeting to her. My finger hovered over the mousepad a minute before I decided to send.

She didn't respond.

I typed in Joe's box instead. *Is she helping you online?*

Joe responded almost right away. *We're at the library.*

Journey wasn't about to let her trip and the disaster of yesterday's little skirmish at the beach deter her from getting her 4.0, either, I could see.

You know her cousin, Johnson? Joe wrote. *He's here, too. And he's like tripping or something.*

Tripping? I typed back. Dante wasn't the kind of guy to do anything like that.

I don't know. He's acting weird. Slowe keeps leaving the computers to go talk to him and he's cradling his head in his hands.

Is Ivy there? I asked. *Or a little girl who looks like her?*

Ivy Sheppard? He wrote back.

No, Poison Ivy, I started to type back, but I deleted it, a growl depending in my throat. *Is there ANYONE who looks weird? Dresses in vintage fashion like Dean?*

Your boyfriend?

My ex-boyfriend.

Wrong thing to get him to focus on. *Did you just spill some tea? Go, girl!* Joe was entirely obnoxious. *So Miss Goodwin is officially on the market again?*

I'm seeing someone else, I wrote back hastily.

Joe took a minute more to respond, and there were spots forming at the very edge of my vision.

He finally wrote back. *It can't be Poole, can it?*

You're not answering my question. Are Journey and Dante there alone?

I guess? Joe wrote. *She's coming back. Do you want me to ask?*

NO!

Okay...?

Just don't mention me, I wrote back.

He was probably messaging me something more, but I was already halfway across the room to grab my phone out of its charger—only to remember that my phone wasn't in its charger. Journey had it. Or her mom did.

I went to work pushing aside the dresser I'd dragged across the door. The noise this time proved too much for Artemis, and he crawled under my bed. As I opened the door, Mom was coming up the stairs.

"What is going on up here?" she asked. "I heard you dragging furniture around before and I thought you were just going through one of your redecorating phases, but shouldn't you be resting?" Her gaze narrowed into the gap leading into my room. She could probably make out the dresser totally out of place and sticking halfway into the room. "If you were so sick yesterday—"

"I'm doing a lot better," I said. "Mom, can you take me to the library? I need to do some research for this essay."

Mom's lips pinched. "I came up to tell you I just got a text from Lacey. They're back. Journey will give you your phone tomorrow at school—"

"She's at the library, too," I said. I clicked my heels together. "Please let me go? I need to apologize to her."

Mom let out a deep breath. "Okay. Just give me a minute to get ready."

I took a few minutes to do the same.

<hr>

"What time should I expect you to be finished?" Mom looked around at the parking lot, which was only half as crowded as it might have been on a typical day. Sunday was always less crowded and the library closed early. I checked the time on Mom's car. It closed in just half an hour, actually.

"I'll get a ride," I said. Between Journey, Joe, and Joe's ability to call Calder—I didn't have his number memorized—I'd find a way. "We might continue the study session at the Slowes' diner or something once the library closes."

That ought to buy me more time if I needed it.

"All right," said Mom, studying me warily as I climbed out and slung my backpack over my shoulder. My first instinct was that she *knew* all about the merfolk, the vampires—but then I realized she was probably just worried because I'd been "sick" and acting strange for weeks on end.

"Thanks, Mom." I shut the door behind me slowly, a pang of guilt weighing me down for just a moment.

As the automatic doors to the library parted ways for me and a blast of warm air assailed my face, I stepped inside and looked around warily. A middle-aged librarian glanced up briefly and went back to her work.

My heart practically stopped at the shrill shriek of a little girl, but the head of thick, black hair that ran past me just then didn't belong to Autumn.

A mom apologized for her daughter cutting me off and mouthed, "Shh" to the little girl running amuck.

Ember Goodwin, legal adult scared stiff of her little step-sister. I was seeing her everywhere.

"Hey! Goodwin!"

A few other patrons looked toward the row of computers at the back, at Joe, who waved his arm over his head, oblivious to the whole try-to-be-quiet-at-libraries thing.

I made my way toward him.

He had a big grin on his thin lips. The dimples that appeared kind of made his light brown skin pop. If his messy brown hair hadn't made it clear he hadn't bothered with today, the baggy sports team sweatshirt, the plaid pajama pants, and the flip-flops—when it was a high of forty today—with no coat in sight would have made that all the more clearer.

My eyes scanned around for Journey and Dante. There was a computer next to Joe's around which a stack of Jane Austen books was piled and a coat I recognized immediately to be Journey's.

"She took her cousin outside," said Joe, picking a pencil up off an almost-blank piece of lined paper sitting beside a pristine copy of *Pride and Prejudice*. There was about a paragraph typed in a doc on his screen. He was trying, apparently, but was lost now that his makeshift tutor had up and disappeared. Her essay was in full flux, several pages in.

"So, like, Slowe was telling me both Elizabeth and Darby have moments of pride and prejudice," said Joe. An older man looked up from his screen on the other side of the computer cluster and frowned.

"Darcy," I corrected, sliding out of my backpack and sitting down in Journey's vacated seat. I let my bag fall to the floor.

"And that it doesn't have to do with racism?" Joe asked hopefully, as if waiting to be corrected.

"No," I said, shaking my head. "Are you sure you were awake for *any* of it?"

He scratched his head. "Gimme a break. You know I can't read well."

Sighing, I read over what Joe had written so far and stopped myself from correcting the obvious grammar mistakes and typos. "Keep going with that," I said. "You know, there's a movie and a TV series..." I felt like an awful tutor. But I just wasn't in the mood for Joe being Joe *today*.

"I know," he said. "I fell asleep during the movie, too."

Growling, I snatched Joe's almost-blank piece of paper and pencil from him. Leave it to Joe to find one of the most romantic pieces of literature written by one of the cleverest authors *boring*. I wrote down one basic point of both Elizabeth and Darcy demonstrating pride and prejudice, not bothering to tell him where to find the quotes to support his argument. It would have to do.

"Thanks," he said with a grin as I handed his stuff back. "You're all right, Goodwin."

I scowled at him and he raised his hands up a little in surrender. "More than all right. Amazing." He smirked.

"Maybe someday you'll return the favor," I said, not expecting him to do so at all.

"Hey, I told you about Poole's major crush on you, didn't I?" Joe ran his pencil around one of the holes in the paper. "And look how that turned out."

I didn't bother confirming the bit of gossip he seemed to be eager to get his hands on. I was too focused over my shoulder, waiting for Journey's return.

"So are you going to transfer to Central like Sheppard did to be with your boy?"

The thought hadn't even occurred to me. I'd just kept doing my schoolwork, but yeah, the vampires had infiltrated Union High—Dean as a student, Minnie as principal, and a few others who passed for adults as various staff.

But unlike Ivy, I had no excuse to transfer.

"No," I said plainly, feeling like for once lately, I had my head screwed right on my shoulders. "No need."

Because maybe this could all be over by Thanksgiving. Somehow. Something buzzed from the backpack dangling off the back of Journey's chair, and I was going to let it be, but it was followed by a familiar ring tone—Taylor Swift's "You Need to Calm Down."

"That's my phone," I said under my breath as I unzipped Journey's backpack. My purse was at the bottom. I transferred it into my own backpack and took out my phone, zipping Journey's backpack back up for her.

"Smart, staying put," said Joe, apparently oblivious to me rummaging around in my friend's belongings. "Your man can't be your whole life, you know?"

The number appearing on the screen was unfamiliar, probably just a scammer. I dismissed it and entered my passcode, taking the opportunity to scroll through my messages. There were a number of missed calls from Mom from the night before.

"Why don't you just help yourself then?"

Jumping in place, I looked up. Journey hovered over the chair, one of her braids a little out of place, her cheeks somewhat windburned from the cold outside.

"Journey," I croaked. I froze. I'd come here to see her and now I had no idea what to say.

She gave me this heavy-lidded look I knew she reserved for the clueless and the idiotic, one she'd never directed my way.

Getting out of her seat, I shook my phone at her. "I heard it ring. I'm surprised you had it on you—I'm surprised you're here at all." I gestured around the library. Though I was speaking in a hushed tone, the older man who'd given Joe the stink eye for speaking too loudly was directing that glare at me.

"What?" said Journey, nonplussed as she slipped into her vacated chair. "Doing homework? Some of us have plans for the future."

Yeah, going to Bradview with me. That had been our plan

now for ages. No need to even gamble on getting a random roommate.

That was all set in stone. Vampires and merfolk be darned. Right?

Journey was giving me the cold shoulder so perceptibly, Joe whistled. "Something happen in smart girl paradise?"

Frowning, I picked up my backpack and shifted it over my shoulder, clutching my phone in my hand. There were random books in the bag since I'd figured Mom would wonder if I asked to go do research without bringing anything.

"Mind your own business and get back to work," Journey snapped, leaning over to look at Joe's computer. Her gaze drifted over the notebook paper with my handwriting on it and she frowned at me. "You can't *do* an assignment for someone."

"I didn't," I said defensively.

"You gave him the whole structure."

"He still has to write it out. And find evidence."

"Ladies, ladies—no need to fight over me." He grinned.

We both united to give him *the look* at that comment.

"Can we talk?" I asked, ignoring Joe.

An announcement came overhead that the library was going to close in ten minutes and for patrons to please make their way to the front desk to check out any materials.

The old man at the computers sighed and stood, shuffling into a coat while muttering under his breath, then walking away.

I looked around for Journey's cousin. "Where's Dante?"

"In my car," said Journey, all business at the computer, saving her work and then starting to pack up the books and notes she'd piled around her work station. "I didn't think I could easily explain his *state* any more to Mom or Dad or Uncle and Auntie, so I thought it best to try to get some work done here while he has time to calm down."

Over her shoulder, Joe made some kind of gesture to me and nodded. Right. He thought Dante was high or something.

"His state?" I asked.

Journey whirled on me and stood, slipping into her jacket.

She didn't say anything. Joe sighed and saved his work, folding his piece of paper and shoving it inside his book. "I really wanted to finish today," he grumbled.

My heart was racing. Dante was upset about what he'd seen, I was sure, but what had the vampires I'd left them with made of that?

I grabbed for Journey's hand, ignoring her surprised shout of "Hey!" and closing my eyes.

I didn't know exactly how the merfolk mind-reading thing worked, but from Calder's little crash course in fighting as a mermaid, I'd gotten the idea that it involved skin-to-skin contact and a pressing *urge* to know the answer.

Instead of hearing Journey's thoughts like I expected, I *saw* things. From her eyes.

Idling around a shiny, silver object as the sun set, a spattering of people around us. Flashes of green light permeated the air, and a chill breeze slapped my face.

Chicago. The art installation—Cloud Gate.

Wheezing caught my attention and I turned. Dante. He was hyperventilating but gritting his teeth, clearly trying to work through it and not seem affected. The sweat that dotted his brow said otherwise.

"Dante, I can explain—"

"No, cuz, you can't." He took another deep breath, in and out. Then, seeming to give up, he flicked both hands at his head as if to pantomime how his mind had exploded. "Am I high? Is this what being high is like?"

He turned pointedly to stare at the group of cosplay, pallid monsters. They looked like they were milling about, getting ready for a 1940s photo shoot. My heart—Journey's heart—clenched at the sight of Devam, and I looked at the ground. Laughter rang out in the distance, and I looked up in time to see Ivy with Dean, Autumn running after Orin.

"Why aren't you flipping out?" Dante asked. "Don't tell me you knew about this." He jumped back suddenly. "Are you one of them?"

My hands—Journey's hands—went to the faint outline of scars at my neck. "No." It sort of felt like a lie. "But I knew. I've known for weeks."

Dante muttered a string of curses under his breath.

Before I could say anything more, Devam was here. At our side. "Hey, Johnson," he said to my cousin. Ignoring me—Journey. As usual. He draped an arm around his neck. "I take it you have questions. Let me get you up to speed."

He guided Dante down the crosswalk a little, putting some distance between them and Ember's step-sisters. I went after them.

Dante reacted, albeit delayed, to being jostled around, wiggling out of Devam's grip and pushing him back as if the touch burnt him. Maybe it had frozen him. Vampires were cold. So cold. So inhuman.

Behind a small cluster of trees in the park that kept us out of view of passersby, Devam held his pallid brown hands up in surrender. "Don't flip your wig, bud."

A sharp breath escaped through my clenched teeth. "You *didn't* grow up in the '40s."

Devam looked my way, acknowledging me for the first time in what felt like forever. "Did you change your mind yet, doll?"

"Don't call me that," I said, crossing my arms. The two purses I was carrying and the extra coat squished a little painfully against my chest. "And no."

"Shame," said Devam, leaning toward me and inhaling. Vampires didn't need to breathe. "You smell so... succulent."

"Okay, you are really creeping me out, dude." Dante took a step back, then hesitated, moving between me and Devam. "Keep your creepy pale self away from my cousin."

I put a hand on his arm. "Dante, it's okay—"

Devam shrugged and leaned forward. "Maybe I can give you *a* taste then."

I—Journey—shrieked as Devam grabbed Dante by both shoulders, opening his mouth wide, exposing those gleaming fangs. And then he sunk his teeth in.

I jumped, back to the moment, back in my own body. Dante's blood had been drunk—though a first, single bite wouldn't have been enough to change him.

Not unless the vampire hadn't known what he'd been doing.

"Is Dante—?" I started.

The lights overhead flickered.

"The library is now closed," said a voice over the speaker. "Please make your way to the front entrance."

"Journey," I said. Getting his first taste of venom would explain any high-like behavior Dante was exhibiting. Journey's eyes watered.

I wondered if she was doing her best to keep Dante away from the Hornes. To keep him from becoming like her ex-boyfriend.

"Thanks for the help, ladies," said Joe, shuffling away. "See you in class. Hope you two intelligent beauties find a way to patch things up."

I glowered after him but then turned back to my friend.

"We have to go," was all she said, brushing past me.

I followed, funneling in with the rest of the patrons as the librarians gestured for us to leave. "Have a nice evening," one said, a bright smile on her dark red lips.

A muffled scream filtered in through the layers of glass leading to the parking lot.

Everyone turned to see what it was.

Journey was the first to act, shoving past the people in front of her and rushing toward the door.

"Wait!" I cried out, my hand growing cold, the ice forming more on instinct than anything.

I shoved past the other people, too, including the harried mom and that little girl. The mom yanked her daughter back to her.

There, in the middle of the parking lot, Joe was on his butt on the pavement, his book beside him.

And hovering over him was Dante.

IVY

Dean leaned an elbow against the car door and stared out the window toward the vampire manor. He didn't say anything for a full minute. So I cleared my throat and spoke first. "Working with the fae?"

He shrugged. "The thinking is we take out the enemy first—"

"Ember," I pointed out. "We take out my step-sister. The girl you mooned over for weeks."

"I've told you I wasn't *mooning* over anyone."

"Okay, but *that* aside, then what? You honestly think I'll beat my own sister into submission?"

He picked at his lips with his thumb but otherwise didn't move.

"Because you know Autumn is more gung-ho about this at the moment. She might not have qualms about beating *me*, but I'd hesitate to fight back." I let out a deep breath, realizing I hadn't been actually breathing. The utter cold of my lungs hit the air, but it didn't bother me at all.

I was a vampire.

The only thing that really bothered me right then was thirst.

"If Ember is out of the picture, my *only* concern is getting my sister away from this mess." *Breathe in, breathe out.* With a fiery flash, my heart started pumping again, the fire in my veins softening.

"You've made that abundantly clear."

"Then why team up with *them*?"

Dean spoke softly. "Do you think I care about winning?"

"*Yes.* Don't you all? What else is the point of all of this?"

Sighing, though I knew he had no need for it, Dean faced forward, rummaging in his pocket and pulling out his shiny, silver coin, which he held between the fingers of both hands. "I agreed with Minnie that this would be a good idea—for *you.* More chances to be with your sister, more chances to convince her to drop out, right?" The coin tumbled heads over tails as he moved it between his fingertips.

"Oh," I said. "But I take it Minnie is looking at this more as a real thing, a chance for help in taking out one enemy rather than focusing on two at once?"

Dean's eyebrows arched and he nodded, as if that were obvious. "If you don't convince Minnie you care about this, then, well, I can't help you."

"Well, aren't you a genuine Prince Charming?" I huffed. My breath was cold now—but far less chilly. And this time, I felt it. The air on my exposed nose, the chill in this unheated vehicle idling in a driveway as the sun went down. I was becoming human again.

"Ivy, I'm tired."

"I didn't think vampires could get tired. Do you sleep?"

The coin stopped fumbling between his fingers. "I'm getting tired of *life.*"

I shifted uncomfortably, unbuckling my seatbelt once it dug into my hip bone. "You're not *that* old. Even without"—I gestured at him, as if that said it all—"you might still be alive."

"And about to become one of the few centenarians in the world." He flicked the coin up and slammed it against the back of one hand. "In which case, I'd probably still be tired. Ready to move on."

"With elderly children, middle-aged grandkids, and great-grandkids probably a bit older than me to see you off," I pointed out.

That didn't seem to help any. He pulled his hand away. The coin showed *heads*. I didn't know what he'd been flipping for, though. Letting out another deep breath, he slipped the change back into his pocket.

"Sorry. That was insensitive of me," I said after a beat. "You have a gift. It sucks it comes with some major downsides, maybe, but it is what it is and—"

"I don't care if we lose," he said, cutting me off. One of his incisors poked out and pierced his bottom lip. "No, that's not right. I'd feel bad about some of my family dying—and those new kids, they don't deserve their lives cut so short. But for most of us... We've had enough time."

"So you're saying... you want Autumn to win?" I shook my head. "I trust the faefolk to use the consummate magic for good about as much as I trust a three-legged cow to beat a cheetah in a race across the desert."

Dean startled and stared at me. Then his lips quirked into a grin. "You have a way with words."

I brushed that off with a wave of my hand. "My point stands."

"I just don't care if we lose."

"Well, that's the same thing, buster." Ugh. Spending time with this old man was seeping into my vocabulary. "If you don't keep on your toes and hope for the vampires to win, then the world is literally screwed." I couldn't believe *I* was the one saying this. I didn't care about winning. But if I just dropped out, would these supernatural troublemakers just leave us all alone? Would they start it all over again the next time someone moved into Dad and Noelle's house? Noelle was pregnant, and they weren't above using children... Though I hoped they'd give the poor kid at least a few years to learn to walk before they roped them into this.

It was my turn to sigh. "Unless you're hiding something from me? What do the vampires really want if they win?"

"More vampires," he said succinctly. "That's the truth. Expanding our family, but in a controlled way. Too many unsupervised vampires would mean too many opportunities for our kind to be exposed. Too many vampires means too few people to feed *on*."

"And you don't *have to* kill someone to feed on them." I swallowed.

"No," he said. "But turning someone into a vampire is practically murder."

"Hardly." I scoffed and gave him a onceover. Dang, he made the afterlife look good.

"It is." He picked at a thread on the back of the seat in front of him.

"Since you're talking to me right now and have maintained your good looks for the past seven decades, I'd have to disagree," I said. The way he was picking at that thread really annoyed me. I reached out and put my hand atop his to stop the fidgeting, fighting through the initial shock of his skin so clammy and cold.

"The vampires winning sounds like the best of three options," I said.

"You don't even know what the faefolk want."

I tilted my head at him, as if to say, "Really?"

"I'd be fine with vampires not existing anymore," he said quietly. "I waited so long for this, for the battle to begin in earnest, and it's just... It feels awful, Ivy. Fighting my former kin. Breaking up a family and using kids—"

"Ember and I aren't kids," I said. "Maybe to an old man like you, but you need to at least start thinking of us as equals."

He pulled his hand down away from the back of the seat and looked at me. The sun was just an orange glow on the horizon, so he didn't panic when his sunglasses slipped down the bridge and the very top of his unnaturally blue eyes shone back at me.

"I mean it," I said. "I think you might feel a little better about this if you didn't view us as playthings to be protected."

He flipped his hand over to put his smooth, marble palm against my rougher one and squeezed. "You don't want to hurt anyone."

"I *don't*, but we're long past the point where that's been a concern." I took a deep breath. "But you're right. I need to decide to win, not just to get out of this as fast as possible. I need to *win* as fast as possible and I won't accept hurting Autumn or Ember—if the latter can be helped." I muttered that last part under my breath. "We need a plan, Dean. I need your head in the game. I need your help."

"I can do that." His lips pinched, but there was no stopping the slight smile that was breaking out onto his face. "For you. I owe you girls at least that much."

I tapped a heel against the floor of the vehicle. "Did I just have to convince the vampire prince not to give up on living?"

"You did," he said, using his free hand to slip his glasses off entirely and drop them in his coat breast pocket. "Though just long enough to see you get your life back."

A sense of heaviness pervaded my limbs.

He chuckled and ran a thumb over the back of my hand. "Don't let my life be on your conscience, doll. I'm old. I may not look it, but I feel it in my brittle bones."

I had to bite back a smarmy comment about his old age because I was distracted then by his eyes. So close to me, they sent a shiver down my body from head to toe.

Dean misinterpreted the cause. "Let's get inside. We keep it warm in the winter for our bloodbags."

"Your *volunteers*," I corrected. But before he could let go, I pulled his hand back. "Can I ask you something?"

"Anything."

My heart almost stilled, but I fought off that rising venom, that sense of losing control.

"Why blue?" I asked. "I'd think maybe you had blue eyes... *before*... and they just got brighter, but you all have them."

"Blue eyes not your thing?" Those same irises were practically twinkling now with mischief.

I chuckled despite myself. And didn't answer. "That's not what I meant. Vampires have red eyes, typically."

"Yeah, in *pictures*." He laughed. "And we can't go out in the sun and we don't have reflections in the mirror and—"

"So it's just the blood," I said, brushing the rest of his spiel off. "Drinking blood and living forever without aging. That's the *only* thing people got right."

"Vampires as you know them in fiction derived from stories about Vlad the Impaler, an evil man who tortured countless people and probably drank their blood. But that didn't make him a vampire. Just a human. A monster."

"And your kind didn't exist in the real world until the 1940s...?" I asked. "Why?"

"Ask the fae that." He nodded toward the house. "Minnie has existed for long before that, but she was the only one."

"I doubt that," I said. "Doesn't seem like she would just... wait for company."

"She was asleep," he said, then he briefly went on to explain how the chaos and bloodshed of World War I in Europe had woken her, how she'd made her way back here, to the site of a love lost, to a changed world—to the consummate lands where she'd fought for bloom once before, a twisted creation of their own venom.

"And that answers your other question," he said. I almost forgot what he meant.

Shifting out of his overcoat and then his suit jacket—wrinkled, I noticed, for the first time since I'd known him—he rolled up the sleeve of his long-sleeved crisp, white shirt and stared down at his inner wrist.

Then with a hiss, he brought the arm up to his mouth and sunk his teeth into it.

I flinched, my back hitting the car door behind me.

He pulled his arm back and wiped some blue—blue?—

smudge off of his pert, red lips. Then he held his wrist out above his head.

A trickle of blue slipped down his skin.

"The venom," he explained. "The fiery, poisonous thing that keeps us alive even after we're already dead—it's blue." He shrugged as he rolled his sleeve back down, not seeming to care that he was tinging the white fabric with blue dots, though the wound had begun sealing up almost immediately. "So I guess it affects the color of our eyes somehow. Reflecting the life force within us."

Blue reminded me of the water, of merfolk, with their blue fins. I stared down at the small bit of my sweater dress that poked through the top button of my old, big coat. Blue was a color I was drawn to. Vampires had always been red—blood and fire, Ember's color of choice—in my mind.

But in that moment, like a symbiotic life force in my veins, I could *feel* the venom. A separate entity. But part of me now— just one small part of me.

"Ivy," said Dean, breaking into the brimming sensation, snapping me back to the moment. "What would you think if... If we win, we make our own wish?"

"What do you mean?"

"Instead of wishing for the proliferation of vampires, instead of just letting the merfolk and faefolk disappear..." He left the rest unsaid.

"We could wish them all out of existence?"

"Well..." He tugged at the collar at his shirt. "We could wish them all human."

Human. "Then if the vampires win, and the merfolk and faeries are supposed to disappear—"

"There won't be any merfolk and faefolk *to* disappear."

I chuckled. Then the laughter grew stronger. "You make it sound so simple." Rubbing a hand over my eyes, I couldn't believe we'd all wasted so much time fighting—for this simple solution.

"Simple, it's not." He hooked a thumb toward the manor.

"We can't let anyone know our plans. None of these geezers will agree to turn human, I promise you."

He had a point.

"But you do? Agree to become human, I mean?"

"One more run at a life as a human seems a fair shake to me, considering I've overstayed my welcome on this bright blue ball in the universe." His bright eyes shone then, almost like the thought gave him hope.

Hmm.

"Okay. But to be the one to make a wish, that means I have to win. I need a crash course in everything vampire," I said.

Dean smiled and opened his door. "Let's start by introducing you to the family."

With a blink, his door was shut and he was on my side of the car, opening the door and extending a hand down toward me. "And then we can practice that little maneuver if you're ready."

Oh, I was *ready*. I took his hand and used his support to get out of the car.

With the hope of this ending with no blood on my hands, I was *so* ready now. Fireballs, time pause, getting by without taking breaths—throw the vampire book at me.

But if there was something Ember's time as the vampires' champion had taught me, the one thing I was *not* learning was the taste of someone else's blood.

CHAPTER TWELVE

EMBER

"Dante!" Journey screamed as she rushed him, wrapping both arms around him and nuzzling her face against his broad shoulder, as if trying to *will* him to calm down with a simple act of love.

I scrambled after her, my head pounding, my vision going a bit black. I helped Joe up to his feet and turned around to the lingering patrons, the library staff who had stepped out, a phone in one of their hands.

Probably ready to call the police.

"We're fine," I said sternly. "It's fine. We'll be on our way. Please, he's just sick."

Most people headed on to their cars, that mother covering her daughter's eyes as she skirted as far away as possible. The librarian with the phone stepped back toward the door, but he still dialed something, bringing the phone up to his ear.

"We have to get out of here," I whispered in a hush toward Journey and Dante.

"You can come to my place," Joe offered, straightening his baggy, worn sweatshirt and then bending to snatch back up his book.

I realized with a start as he tugged that I was still holding his hand. His bare hand on mine. When I thought to wonder what he'd been doing, why he wasn't that upset about Dante knocking him on the pavement, the scene popped into my head.

"Hey, Johnson, you okay? Slowe said she left you in her car. You don't look so good, bro."

I—Joe—approached Dante, who was pacing relentlessly back and forth in the parking lot, both hands on his head, mumbling under his breath. Nearby, the old guy who'd been using the computers near us muttered and shook his head as he climbed into his vehicle.

"Bro, bro," I said. "Let's go by the cars, okay? Wait for your cousin—"

"Leave me alone!" Dante shouted, shoving me—Joe—to the ground.

That explained that.

Dante still had his hands atop his head in the present moment, but they lowered as he stared at me. "Ember?" His anxiety seemed to be smoothed over with subtle confusion.

"Let's go," said Journey, stepping back to grab him by the arm and tug him toward her car.

Dante's head snapped sideways as he looked at me over his shoulder, even as he allowed himself to be dragged away. "She's okay?"

"I *told you* she was," answered Journey.

I felt my own hand get tugged out of the way just as a car went past where we'd been standing. Right. I was still holding Joe's hand. I dropped it and straightened myself.

"Look, I know some guys—I mean, well... It's not my first time trying to ride out someone's high," said Joe, running a hand through his dark hair. His teeth were chattering a little as his warm breath hit the air. He really needed to wear a coat. "And my parents are gone for days at a time. You guys can crash at my place."

Journey frowned, chewing her lip. "Okay."

"*Okay?*" I asked.

"Do you have a better idea?" she asked, her voice sharp. "I don't want my family or yours to think Dante is tweaking or something. And I'm not going *there*." She could only mean the Horne Manor. "It would just make him worse."

"Besides, you're not on their side anymore, right?" I asked, to be sure.

"I'm not on *anyone*'s side," she spat. She turned to Joe, who looked befuddled. But he often did. "Lead the way and I'll follow you."

"Ember," said Dante, cocking his head. "Do you mind explaining—" He cut himself off, his hands going to his throat, his eyes going wide again.

He was not adapting well to a single shot of venom.

"Okay," I agreed. "But I'm calling Calder."

Journey let out a huff and directed her cousin to her car.

Oh. I needed a ride.

I backed up out of the way as Journey started up her vehicle. "Where do you live?" I asked Joe, my phone already in my hand.

Joe rattled off an address and I typed it into a text message to Calder.

"But I can give you a lift," he said, scratching his head again.

I thought about it. The library was closed now and if that staff member was calling the police...

"Okay," I said, sending off instructions for Calder to meet me there. I added that it wasn't an emergency, but I'd met up with Journey to get my phone back and we had an issue.

Joe's smile could have rivaled the Joker's. "Maybe you could help me finish this thing?" He tapped his book.

Shaking my head, I let out a deep breath. "Fine."

I supposed it was the least I could do, considering—and the best idea I had of distracting him from the details of everything that was really going on.

If Dante was any indication, the fewer people who learned about it, the better.

Joe lived in a small ranch house near the Interstate, its yard a bit overgrown and cluttered with fallen orange and yellow leaves, the sound of the passing traffic flying by on the highway nearby impossible to avoid entirely even once we'd shut the door behind us.

Joe moved forward past Journey and Dante to quickly toss some blankets, a pair of pants, and a bunch of worn, threadbare pillows off his three-seater couch. It was brown and mottled in places.

"Let him lie down," he said, gesturing toward the sofa. Journey guided Dante toward it, and Dante just focused on his breathing, his eyes barely leaving me, no matter how he was positioned.

Journey sat down beside the couch in a leather recliner that didn't really have any room to recline with the scratched and ring-stained coffee table in front of it. But she hovered at the edge of it anyway, her coat still on, in no mood for reclining. I took my own coat off and hung it over my arm, my phone still clutched in my hand in case Calder had trouble finding us.

Joe slipped down a hallway and into the kitchen. "He needs some juice," he said. "I think it's juice—well, it can't hurt. Do you ladies want anything?"

"No," said Journey quickly. "Thank you," she added, her shoulders loosening somewhat.

"No, thanks." I strolled over toward the couch and sat in a hard folding chair that had been dragged to the other side of the coffee table.

Journey and I stared at one another, neither of us speaking.

Joe shuffled back in and handed Dante the glass full of orange juice. The thirsty man shifted up to lean on his forearms and guzzled it down as if it were the blood or venom he so desperately sought.

Joe chuckled as he took the glass back from him. "Easy there. Man, you've clearly got the munchies. Let me see if I can find some chips. Or pickles. Those are always good."

He strolled off. He spoke as if from experience.

My shoulders bobbed, more to myself than anything. So I wouldn't have ever expected to go to Joe Cruz's house before all of this. But a sometimes-marijuana user who otherwise treated me quite nicely, even if he *was* always using me for his homework help, was the least objectionable company I'd found myself in lately.

Except for Journey. I couldn't forget that I'd dragged her—and Dante now—into this mess.

"I'm sorry," I said. "I'm sorry Dante got involved in this—that you ever did."

Journey's lips grew thin. "If apologies could undo the past..."

"What do you want me to say?" I threw my hands up. "I didn't ask to be part of this, either."

"Yeah, well, there's no *reason* I need to be and yet—"

"Girls, girls, hold up." Dante took another deep breath and sat up. He looked almost back to normal, though his eyes were red-rimmed. "Back up," he said, making a rotating motion in the air with both hands. "Explain to me why I'm not hallucinating. And why I feel so..." He squeezed nothing in the air. "Angry. Unsatisfied."

I took a deep breath and looked over my shoulder. Someone—presumably Joe—made some noise down the hallway, and a toilet flushed.

"Vampires, mermaids, and faeries are real," I said succinctly. "And they're fighting to wipe out the other species."

Putting two index fingers to his lips and leaning his elbows on his thighs, Dante nodded, not saying anything.

"But while they do exchange blows—and *kidnap* hostages," added Journey, her irritation as plain as day, "it's supposed to come down to a battle of champions."

"A proxy battle," said Dante, nodding, as if it all made sense.

"The champions are my step-sisters and me," I explained. "And I used to be with the vampires, and Ivy with the merfolk, but what you stumbled on—was the two of us swapping sides."

"And even though I've been hanging out with the vampires in *support* of my friend and to try to pry my boyfriend away from them, now my best friend is working for the enemy," added Journey. She tossed her hands up. "Who wanted to *flood the world* and drown us all, last I knew."

"That's not going to happen," I said sharply. "I promise."

"Just like Devam wasn't *in danger* of becoming a vampire." A vein at the side of Journey's forehead seemed to become engorged.

Dante blew out a breath and leaned back into the couch. "I knew something was up with that creepy hipster." He gazed at me. "You were dating a vampire, too."

"An older one than Devam," I said, clearing my throat. "And now I'm with a merman."

He winced. My mouth opened and shut, and I wondered not for the first time if I'd had had a chance with Dante—more than the pity dances he'd offered me when I'd gone stag to Homecoming the years before this one—if Journey was right that her cousin had had a crush on me.

Because I used to have a crush on him, too. And I felt so, so terrible I'd dragged him into this.

That Orin and Dean and Ivy and Calder and all of *them* had dragged him into this, really.

I checked my phone screen again, but there were no more messages from Calder besides the one that said he was on his way.

"And what happened to me?" Dante rubbed his neck. There was a small, circular Band-Aid beneath his fingers. "What did that bas—"

"Language," said Journey, speaking over him.

He glared at her. "What did that *gentleman* do to me?"

"He bit you," I said, and Journey seemed surprised I knew exactly what had happened, though it would have been a good guess regardless. Still, I didn't want to keep secrets from her if I could help it. "I read your mind back at the library. Saw what happened back in Chicago after I... left."

"So I'm a vampire?" he asked the question entirely seriously.

"*No,*" said Journey sternly as I said, "Not yet."

Journey's brows arched.

"Or ever," I added. "Stay away from the vampires—from Dean, the principal, the school nurse, the janitor, my mom's secretary, Devam, Raelynn Kelly—anyone who looks like they're on their way to a costume party—and it should pass. Journey was bitten once and she managed not to succumb to the temptation to offer her blood again."

Journey chewed on her lip. She didn't add that *I* had been the one to bite her.

Dante chuckled and shook his head. "Stay away from—is there an entire vampire *community*? We have *high school* vampires now? Like some after-school club?" There was some noise down the hall and Dante lowered his voice. "That *blood condition* going around that made Raelynn and Devam look so sickly?"

"Yeah," I said. "That. And... And it was my fault."

Dante stared at me but didn't ask what I would have in his position—what I'd done that would make me feel it had all been my fault.

Maybe it was enough for him just to know, to understand I'd do *whatever* it took to undo my mistakes.

"So I need more than one bite to become a vampire?"

Journey and I nodded.

"A number of bites," said Journey.

"Usually," I added, wincing. All it really took was one vampire who didn't know what she was doing. I took a deep breath. "Journey, I switched sides because Calder and I have a plan—to fix things."

"Fix things?" she echoed. The twist of her lips told me she doubted that.

"Here we are," said Joe, his voice upbeat and chipper. In one hand, he had a bag of potato chips he tossed in Dante's direction—and Dante had the reflexes to catch it. In the other, he cradled a somewhat chunky laptop, which he put down on the coffee table as he took a seat beside Dante on the couch. He opened up its lid and pressed a button, and it echoed out with the chime of an older version of Windows. He looked over the room, at the way all of our gazes were stuck on our feet. Dante held the bag of chips unopened.

"What'd I miss?" Joe asked.

The doorbell rang then, helping us escape the problem of how to answer.

Joe sighed and got to his feet the same time I did.

"It's probably Calder," I pointed out.

"Either that or someone looking to save our souls, but it's a bit late in the day for that."

I couldn't tell him that if Calder and I got to put our plan into action, maybe, in some respects, we were both right. Only Calder and I had more than just everyone's souls to save.

CHAPTER THIRTEEN

IVY

I strolled out of the administration office of Union High the Tuesday before Thanksgiving, my head held high at how smoothly the process had gone.

Paisley squealed and did a little bouncy dance as I exited, her short frame only coming up to my shoulder as she gave me a hug, her light brown ponytail bouncing. "Our Ivy is back! We have her back!"

Lyric, tall and svelte and firm, stood straighter from where she'd been leaning against a nearby row of lockers. "You transferred to our rival school for about a month and then came back. That might be a record." She tossed her startlingly straight medium-length blonde hair over her shoulder and then went back to clutching her tablet and books with both hands.

"It just didn't feel right," I explained as we headed down the hall. Grey, Paisley's boyfriend, was nowhere in sight for once, which meant the baseball team that usually accompanied him everywhere was also conspicuously absent. I didn't mind, though. Those boys always had their heads in the game, and I was playing something of a much more harrowing variety.

Like a prickle on the back of my neck, I felt the janitor—Herbert, I'd learned his name was—before I saw him looking at me. Handsome and rugged in his janitor's overalls, he was, like every vampire, startlingly pale and wearing sunglasses inside in the semi-darkened hallway.

Lyric flashed a wide smile at him and stood even straighter, like a model down a runway.

"Stop," said Paisley, elbowing Lyric even as she kept an arm looped through mine. "You've barely broken up with Raelynn. And you know you're going to get back together."

"I don't know about that." Lyric frowned and ran her fingers over the side of her neck. There weren't visible traces of a bite, but she'd been in and out of the Horne Manor over the past few weeks, trying to get Raelynn back. Raelynn, more focused on her new transition than anything, had gone through different phases of wanting Lyric to forget her and wanting Lyric to join her.

One of the things I'd steadfastly put my foot down about was that *no one* was going to become a vampire until this was all over. I just hadn't mentioned that once this was all over, no one would ever become a vampire again.

And my friends weren't allowed to set foot in that place.

As far as Lyric knew, Raelynn had changed after her "blood condition" had "almost" killed her, and she was now way, way, way into something that smelled vaguely like a cult.

Which meant Lyric couldn't just get up and get over that and walk away.

I sighed. Raelynn and Lyric had always been on-again, off-again. But breaking up over typical misunderstandings didn't leave the scarring that a breakup like this one would.

The warning bell rang overhead and the crowd in front of us shifted, moving from lingering around to striding in every which direction with purpose. Paisley and I were headed to bio, but Lyric had statistics. She sighed and gave us a mock salute. "Welcome back to the hallowed halls of Union High," she said sarcastically as she took a few steps backward. "May I recommend you refrain from switching schools to chase tail in the future. Less paperwork and make-up homework that way." She spun on her heel before I could respond.

Fact was, I had no other way to explain my brief stunt transferring to Central High, where Calder and his merfolk "family" were all students and alumni. And I quite literally had grown a tail—a mermaid one—during my time there. So she wasn't that far off.

"Don't take it personally," said Paisley under her breath. "She has just been *in a mood* the past few weeks."

"Love hurts," I said, though I knew my "breakup" with Calder has been nothing like Lyric and Raelynn's.

"But speaking of, *you* moved on rather quickly." She slowed our collective pace and nodded toward the end of the hall.

Dean approached, his sunglasses lowered slightly in our direction. He looked decidedly casual for him, by which I meant he had on pleated brown slacks and a gray-and-black striped vest sweater over a crisp, white dress shirt.

If that was him "not caring," I'd have to introduce him to the concept of jersey pants and hoodies.

"I thought I'd have to rein Lyric in after her breakup, but dang, girl, when did you and Calder even split up? And stealing your step-sister's boyfriend? Harsh." She playfully slapped me with the book she held in her free hand.

"Yeah, yeah," I mumbled. Yet my intense desire to play it off didn't quite work that smoothly. My heart thumped louder as Dean narrowed in on us, making a beeline toward the same open classroom we were headed to.

He wasn't in this class with me. Or at least he hadn't been before I'd transferred.

Dean seemed to understand my unspoken question, and from the small stack of books—no tablet—in his hand, he produced a sheet of paper. "New schedule," he explained. "I aced out of most of my previous classes."

"Sexy *and* smart," said Paisley with a whistle.

Both Dean and I stared at her, and her rosy cheeks reddened even further.

She took her arm out of mine and, cringing, slipped inside the classroom.

I idled outside it a moment, trying not to stare at him because his far-too-pallid form did a number on my insides it had no business doing.

"You aced out?" I asked.

He shrugged. "I got a PhD once. And then a master's in another subject entirely. Then I realized I was never going to do anything useful with any of it, so I dropped out."

"And went back to high school," I said, amused. "You're living an actual recurring nightmare for most people."

"Don't I know it," he whispered quietly.

That *hadn't* been what I'd meant.

Mr. Goldman cleared his throat in an overly obnoxious tone. "Inside, please." He pushed his spectacles up his nose, his graying slightly-too-long hair only on the sides of his head shifting with the movement.

"I'm transferring back in," I said, reaching into my notebook for the piece of paper. "And I'm transferring in," Dean added, showing him the same paper.

Mr. Goldman sighed and snatched them both without looking at them. "Yes, I know. And your cousin, too," he added to Dean. "Now get inside already."

"*Cousin?*" I mouthed to Dean.

He nodded.

Last I knew, Dean had been the only other "student" from the vampires, unless you counted Raelynn and Devam. All the others had probably been too bored at the prospect of repeating high school to bother.

Paisley had saved two seats beside her in the very back, and I rushed to slip in beside her, ignoring the murmurs and stares of the rest of the class. They were quickly diverted by Dean behind me regardless, but Dean left me utterly dumbfounded when he slipped into an empty seat in the front row, near the door.

Maybe he thought it the best place to protect me should any merfolk get any bright ideas and attack during the day.

Ember was still going here. And the vampires hadn't heard hide nor hair from Journey and Dante since Chicago. Even though Devam had admitted to biting Dante.

But still, Dean sitting so far away when there was an empty seat right here beside me stung.

It shouldn't have, but it did.

"He must not want to be distracted during class," Paisley offered quietly, knocking my arm with her elbow.

I smiled fleetingly and stared at my notebook's cover on my desk, picking at a piece of the cardboard around the top of the holes.

The gasps and whispers drew my attention back up again.

"Yes, yes, we have new—and returning—students in this class," said Mr. Goldman, bringing down a projection screen as he fired up his Mac. "But we also have limited time and a lot of subjects to cover." He stared pointedly at me. "We can't wait for anyone to catch up." A projector overhead connected to his computer turned on, and a figure stepped into the spotlight.

Dark blonde, thick hair, coiffed into a 1940s style with the curly rolls around her hairline and bumper bangs. A pink sweater with puffy shoulders and sleeves, though as tight as if painted on across her torso, her chest like bullets in an angular bra. Swishing as she moved was a pleated burgundy skirt over black tights with a single line up the back of each calf and a pair of white high heels with black toes.

Zelda. Dean had introduced me. She also worked as the secretary at their moving company, he'd said.

"Excuse me," she said, her steely, black eyes lowering as her heels clattered down the aisle and she made her way to the open seat beside me. She had a string of pearls around her neck, I noticed, as she slipped inside the seat, one leg carefully crossed over the other.

I looked down at my own outfit—baggy off-the-shoulder black sweater with bits of fabric poking out all over and a blue tank top underneath. Ripped jeans and a pair of black boots. My hair sloppily sticking out of a bun. I'd sunk into my desk, my legs extended outward to the point where I rested my toes on the rack beneath the desk in front of mine. We were like Bert and Ernie, uptight and relaxed, tidy and slovenly.

She wore the dark contacts instead of the glasses, but the effect was just as jarring as her nightmarish eyes bore into my soul and Mr. Goldman started droning on about energy and the chemistry of life. Never mind that the laws were being proven wrong with two vampires sitting right under his nose.

"Hi, Ivy," Zelda said quietly, her tone no less upbeat for the soft way she spoke. "I saw you practicing the other day."

Paisley looked on, curious, but said nothing.

Practicing my vampire skills in the Hornes' backyard after our little tête-à-tête with the fae.

"I wondered if we might partner up," she said, barely perceptible. "I owe Dean a favor."

———

Paisley, Zelda, and I hovered over the microscope, taking turns looking inside and labeling the different parts of the bacteria that inhabited our slides.

A few tables ahead of me, Dean worked with two of the basketball team boys I didn't know that well, his gaze only occasionally heading in my direction.

"This looks like a cartoon," remarked Paisley with her forehead against the microscope. "Hey, what if we make like a model out of JELL-O instead of just writing it all down on this diagram?"

"Where are you going to get JELL-O?" I asked.

"At home. Like for extra credit. Do you think Mr. Goldman will go for it?" She didn't wait for an answer, instead placing her forehead back against the microscope. "Alan would love this stuff. Oh, he'd probably eat the model I made, though."

She was talking about her kid brother, who was just a bit older than Autumn.

Paisley scribbled something down on her illustration. Zelda's was all filled out in impeccable cursive penmanship. A felt-tipped pen still rested in her hand as she crossed her legs atop the stool she sat on, resting her chin on her palm and staring out the window.

I looked behind me to make sure there weren't merfolk doing synchronized swimming in a makeshift toddler pool in the school's backyard, but the yard was pointedly empty, a strong gust of wind kicking up a pile of leaves someone had so carefully raked together.

"I'm going to go to the bathroom," Paisley announced suddenly, tossing her pencil down and scooting back on her stool. "And I'll ask about the JELL-O. If I make one for Alan, too, he'll probably leave it alone."

"'Kay," I managed, not sure Mr. Goldman, who sat in front of his laptop wholly focused on the screen, his brows drawn together, would smile kindly on an elementary-school-level project for extra credit.

I took a turn at the microscope, adjusting the focus to watch the little creature flop around. It was hard to believe that this little alien-like thing could have power over creatures so much bigger than it.

I wondered what a vampire's venom would look like under such scrutiny. What made it blue?

"Has Dean told you anything about me?" Zelda asked. It was the first time she'd spoken since her introduction. I supposed talkative Paisley made that easy for her to get away with.

We were at the back of the classroom and everyone else buzzed with their own conversations. I didn't think anyone would overhear us. "No." Like a prickle at the back of his neck, Dean turned then and nodded.

I smiled back and pretended to look away for a second,

leaving Dean to look through his microscope via sunglasses. The boys with him watched him curiously, almost as if hoping to get a glance of his eyes without the sunglasses. No such luck.

"What would happen if you didn't wear protective lenses during the day?" I asked. I leaned back against a small slit of wall between two windows and gestured behind me. "It's fall. It's usually pretty overcast."

"That doesn't matter," explained Zelda. "Any sunlight burns our eyes."

I tried to think back to the fights I'd had with them before. They'd all been pretty good about keeping their sunglasses on —or contacts, which would have been harder to knock out regardless—but there may have been a time or two where some background vampire or another had been screaming as steam poured out of their skin. But maybe that was just when they were covered with water.

"It's funny you should ask that, about the eyes." Zelda stared down at her paper, running her pen cap over the empty space. "Dean tried to get me out of there. Before I turned. And his punishment for that was to stand out in the sunlight without protection for hours. He was blind for weeks."

Blind? So that was why they flinched from the sun? I wondered why their blue-venom-filled eyes couldn't handle even the slightest bit of natural light.

But I had to back up. She'd said something a little more worrying. "You were being kept against your will?"

"No," said Zelda quickly. Her shoulder bobbed a little. "Well, I mean, I had nowhere else to go." Her perfectly-round mouth puckered into an "o," and if she'd had breath in her lungs, she probably would have let one out. "I only had Leo, and he was a full-fledged vampire by then."

"Then why was Dean punished?"

"Well, he *did* get me as far as the driveway," she explained. "And then we were caught. And I had a change of heart to my little brief change of heart. I had nowhere to go without Leo. And it wasn't that I was *afraid* of becoming a vampire." She said the other word so softly, I almost couldn't hear it myself. Then she laid her pen down and stretched first one arm, and then the other overhead. "I just... I got scared. Of death, I suppose." A flittering smile danced over her lips. "But then, I should have seen from the start that becoming a vampire was the one way to avoid that."

Our conversation dropped for a short while, as other students in the class continued laughing, continued sharing what they'd discovered in the microscope. Continued living—when the three of us who were at least part-time vampires were sullen and quiet, hardly noticeable at all, but for the two of them being so gorgeous and dressed to stand out.

Maybe that was how they left their mark a little. They may have only dipped their toes into the world of the rest of us, but they sure as heck were intent on making an impression when they did.

"You said you owed him, though?" I asked, the question popping to the forefront of my mind.

Zelda's small smile fell. "I've always felt bad about what happened. I should have told him *no* right from the start. Then he wouldn't have been punished like that."

"Or if you hadn't gotten caught, you would have run off to live a normal life."

"Which would have been over by now most likely." Zelda's eyes grew heavy-lidded, her smoky eyeshadow popping against that deathly white skin. "No, I would have come back. I might have wandered around for a while, but I would have come back. Leopold would have found me and taken me home."

That name again. I didn't like that one. Not that I'd actually pictured myself *liking* any of them. But he was especially stuck in the old days. He looked like a teenager and he treated me like a little girl. With *far* more condescension than Dean ever had.

"So you owe him," I said, tapping my fingers against the elbow of my opposite arm. "You didn't think to make it up to him at any point between then and now?"

Paisley walked back into the classroom then, but instead of heading straight back to her lab partners, she went over to Mr. Goldman, trying to get his attention. Mr. Goldman didn't even flinch, his eyes still glazed over as he stared at his laptop.

"He's never needed anything from me before," she said. "He... changed somehow. A little. After that. What softness was in him got hidden away beneath layers of charm and stone." She uncrossed her legs as she stared at Dean, who was filling out his paper with a measured slowness to his pen's movements, his free hand in his pocket as he leaned against the counter.

"We stopped creating new vampires after me—for a while," Zelda continued.

Mr. Goldman, with a sigh heard clearly across the room, turned in his chair to give Paisley his full attention. I couldn't hear everything she said to him, but she was gesticulating wildly, pantomiming circular and oblong shapes.

"That faery prince asked us to stop, and Minnie—reluctantly—complied. We lived for years just sampling our blood-bags, never taking one away to join us for more than a year or two." Her flippant remark about stealing human beings from their lives for a sizable portion of it didn't fail to register with me—but she *was* one of them, so what did I expect? She didn't notice my reaction. "So I don't think his conscience was ever tempted to rouse again. Not for ages and ages, at least."

"Until this," I said. Mr. Goldman was shaking his head and Paisley's expression fell. "Until Ember and me."

"He wants what's best for you. And of course I want to win —we *have* to win." Her dark, dark eyes seemed to somehow grow even darker at that. "But I'll do whatever I can to make sure you girls are all safe. If you want your sisters to surrender rather than get beaten into submission or..." She left the word "killed" unsaid. "You have my word you can come to me. Not the others, but Dean and me. We'll do whatever you think necessary for a most favorable outcome."

Her gaze shifted back to the window as Paisley walked back over to us, clearly dejected. Outside, re-raking the fallen leaves, was that startlingly handsome vampire janitor, Herbert. Beside him was a new janitor in matching overalls. Leopold.

"Thanks," I said quietly as Paisley rejoined us. "I may need to take you up on that."

"JELL-O is a no-go." Paisley slumped forward and dragged her arms at her sides as she sat back on her stool. "Mr. Goldman doesn't have an ounce of creativity in his body."

I chuckled. "We can still make JELL-O sometime soon regardless." I nudged her arm with mine and slipped in beside her, our cheeks practically pressing as we both vied to look in the microscope. "If you're not sick of it after Thanksgiving."

"Where are you having it this year?" asked Paisley, taking another turn peering down the lens.

"Dad's. And Mom's invited." I leaned back, checking to see what Zelda thought of that. Dean and I had decided to keep it to just him and me there for Thanksgiving, but if Zelda could be trusted to watch herself...

The bell rang overhead and the classroom grew even rowdier as students packed up their things and started shuffling toward Mr. Goldman's desk with their papers in hands.

"All right, all right," said Mr. Goldman. "Since school is a half day tomorrow, I won't be seeing you. Make sure your diagrams are turned in before you leave and enjoy your turkey or tofurkey as applicable. Or JELL-O casseroles." He pointed a look at Paisley.

Paisley and I stared at one another and started giggling. I nodded to Zelda and Dean as I made my way up and handed Mr. Goldman my diagram, exiting the classroom with one of my best friends as if nothing at all were the matter. As if I just had a normal life with my normal friend.

In the hallway, I almost slammed into Ember.

Though her long, almost-white blonde hair was down in a simple unaccented fashion, she had on a willowy red plaid box coat that looked more at home in Dean and Zelda's favorite decade. The top two buttons were undone, revealing a simple sweater and a pair of jeans I supposed weren't part of the whole "1940s vampire" getup.

Still, I felt a burning sensation in my chest at the idea of her trying to look even *at all* like she still had venom running through her veins.

Even if—perhaps, if that purple, mutated ice-fire attack back in Chicago had been any indication—perhaps she did.

"Ivy," she said simply, nodding and sticking her nose in the air. She had a backpack dangling from one hand. Her eyes went wide as she gazed over my shoulder and she picked up her feet, rushing down the hall and toward the front door of the school.

She was headed home half a day early.

I'd almost forgotten I might run into her here. Almost.

I'd barely been to Dad's since Sunday. I'd been too busy practicing. I'd only gone home to sleep. I could have just gone to Mom's, but I had to keep an eye on Autumn. Dean had snuck in to guard me at night the two nights I'd spent there this week so far before I switched over to Mom's for the latter half of the week.

There'd been no incidents, but Dean had thought that might have been because Ember had *known* he could sneak in. He'd apparently done it for her to protect her from *me*. As if I'd clobber her in her sleep or something.

"I guess she didn't transfer," Dean said over my shoulder.

Of course. He was standing there with Zelda; their mere presence had sent Ember scurrying.

Paisley laughed. "You're joking, right? Change schools because you dumped her? I don't think even *I* would do that, and Grey and I have been together since we could walk practically."

I forced myself to chuckle and held my head high. This was

vampire turf and my enemy was headed off it. I had nothing at all to worry about before Thanksgiving.

And I had a few more days to practice all the vampire fighting techniques to be ready for what was sure to be a holiday like I'd never experienced before.

CHAPTER FOURTEEN

EMBER

Thanksgiving dinner—the whole everything-from-scratch shebang—began at 6 A.M. promptly every year.

Or so Mom told me as I attempted to rub the sleep from my heavy eyes for the fiftieth time since waking. This was the first time Mom had made a true Thanksgiving dinner since I'd been a toddler—certainly the first time I could remember.

We usually went out to eat. Just the two of us.

Now the extra dining room chairs were at the top of the basement steps, the door leading downstairs still open as Easton made trips up and down to grab them. He let out an exaggerated sigh of exhaustion as he leaned against the top batch, a cloud of dust going flying into the air from setting them down.

"Are we inviting the whole town?" he joked. Behind him, the newly painted walls along the staircase reminded me with a sharp pang that just a month ago, Ivy had left some damage there with her ice powers. My parents had chalked it up to a leaking pipe the experts could never quite pinpoint the origin of.

"I don't think I defrosted this right." Mom swore under her breath. She'd already dressed up for the afternoon, her stiff, perfect blonde hair not even moving as she bustled around the kitchen. She'd just thrown an apron on top of her silky peach blouse and black dress pants.

Easton dropped the dad jokes and leaned over her shoulder as I stood before the sink, letting the cold water rush over the fresh green beans.

"It looks fine, honey." He grabbed the brush she was using for basting. "We have plenty of time to cook it."

Easton was an old hat at Thanksgiving dinners, apparently. Celebrating with his ex and his daughters was nothing new.

I couldn't even remember the last time I'd seen my dad on a holiday.

Slowly shuffling the beans around, my palm tickled with a prick of energy as my hand kept getting pelted by the cold water.

I wondered what my dad—vampire bloodbag—thought of me now. Knowing how deep he was into the whole vampire lifestyle, I was likely enemy number one in his eyes.

At this point, I couldn't care less. As long as I had Calder...

My legs snapped together, my pink track suit fighting to tear, to meld sinew with sinew and form scales.

My phone buzzed from the counter, snapping me out of the moment. With a rush, I flicked off the cold water and dried my hand on a towel beside the sink before grabbing for the phone.

Easton kept instructing Mom on how he usually cooked the turkey, and rather than get annoyed by anyone telling her what to do like she usually would be, she laughed. Easton had started doing voices and wriggling the poor dead turkey's leg.

"Let me give you a hand," Easton said in a high-pitched Mickey Mouse-type voice.

Mom crackled and bent over, patting her stomach and the baby inside.

I had to step into the hallway to get away from the display.

My older brother, Daryl, from Dad's first marriage, had

wished me a happy Thanksgiving and said he hoped I could maybe come to his and Irene's next year. They wanted to do something special for their first year as a married couple. I was so surprised by the invitation that I thanked him and said I'd definitely think about it.

I'd probably only seen him fewer than ten times in my whole life. I couldn't imagine traveling several states away to sit amidst strangers, including my dad's first wife, whom from everything I gathered didn't think highly of me, as if I were the one who'd stolen her husband away.

Like I needed more family drama in my life.

Still. He'd made the offer.

That counted for something in this messed-up family of mine.

Of course, then he asked if I'd heard from Dad yet.

No, I lied. If it all went according to plan, I'd have ended this war and made vampires humans again long before Daryl's wedding next summer. Dad would have no choice but to snap back to reality.

Another message I'd missed was from Journey saying her family might swing by after they ate their own dinner.

Dante is doing better, she wrote.

He hadn't been to school all week, citing the flu.

I'd been going long enough to get all my assignments, ducking out of the way whenever I saw a vampire, and cutting class to head home early.

Maybe this time next week it'd all be over.

I wasn't going to transfer for the few days before Thanksgiving. I couldn't even if I wanted to—I'd seen neither hide nor hair of Orin, and if what I'd overheard last weekend was right, Ivy had more or less confirmed blood and bloom were teaming up.

I couldn't mind trick my way to a more convenient life.

So glad staying away from the Hornes did the trick, I wrote back.

One less problem for me to worry about. And if it all hit the fan, there was one more person who at least knew what was going on now.

A text from Calder popped up. *We're almost there.*

Letting out a breath of relief, I slipped the phone into my jersey pocket and went back inside the kitchen.

I had just about got the green bean casserole prepped and ready for the oven later on—ignoring Mom and Easton's flirting and snickering—when the doorbell rang.

It was only 8 A.M., but I'd wanted Calder here early. Long before Ivy and Autumn—on a "Mom" day and spending the morning at her townhouse—would show up.

"I'll get it," I said quickly, wiping my hands again.

"But who would it be so early?" Mom asked down the hallway.

"I asked Calder to come help with the prep," I called over my shoulder.

Mom mumbled something in response, but I didn't hear it.

Just seeing his form through the frosty glass sent my heart into overdrive.

I unlocked and opened the door. Calder stood there, behind him the two teen mermaids I'd met before, though I'd spent virtually no time with the other merfolk since the escape from Chicago.

Calder had assured me his mom was okay with that, as long as I checked in with him every day.

"Come in," I said, struggling against the lump in my throat to smile. I'd known he'd be bringing backup. Supposedly, there were to be others just down the block, a mere moment away.

If Ivy and Autumn were to be at this dinner, who knew what tricks they had up their sleeves.

But this was *my* house and I wasn't going to be scared away.

"You remember Laguna and Cascade," he said, and I nodded, their names coming back to me. Cascade's dark brows narrowed on me as she crossed her arms and jutted her chin out at me in minimal acknowledgement. She had on dark jeans but a puffy blue blouse in a halfhearted attempt to dress up, her thick, black hair framing her perfectly-oval face. Beneath that blouse, her bra was dark and highly noticeable—perhaps a bikini top, though I hadn't known the true-blue mermaids to care much about nudity. Laguna, the redhead whom I'd be unlikely to forget due to her siren call in the waters of Lake Michigan, wore a seafoam green loose, BoHo dress mismatched with a dark brown open cardigan sweater and what appeared to be a large shard of a smooth green rock that dangled from her neck. Her hair was wild, messy, but it complemented her look well.

Calder shut the door behind Laguna, as she was too busy staring at a piece of wall art depicting a Hawaiian beach to bother.

Then he smiled broadly at me, his tan face lighting up. He had on a pale blue dress shirt, the top two buttons undone, the sleeves folded up and back to reveal his wrists, and a pair of pleated khakis, just a little wrinkled, like he'd had to dig the pants out of some forgotten closet before coming over.

Still, he looked handsome enough to turn heads.

And here I stood in a track suit. I stared down and noticed a sprinkle of breading from the onions snagged on a patch of the fabric.

"So how can we help?" Calder asked as I went to brush it off.

Laughter bubbled out from the kitchen. "Well, Easton got sidetracked when trying to bring the extra chairs into the table." I gestured to the dining room beside us. Easton had also brought up the table's extra leaves, and the thing stretched practically as far as the length of the room.

I led them into the kitchen and the open basement door.

At the top of the stairs, beside the stack of chairs, Artemis, my cat, froze mid-grooming his little head, his tongue stuck out and his front paw dangling in front of his face.

"Hi, kids," said Easton, the oven rack clattering as he loaded the turkey inside.

Mom smiled from where she was peeling sweet potatoes at the kitchen island. "That's so sweet of you to offer to help out," she said. "But won't your parents miss you today?"

"*Mom,* their house burnt down," I reminded her.

The peeler she was holding clattered to the cutting board. "What? I—" She bit her lip. "The place off 17th?"

"Yes, Ms. Goodwin-Sheppard," said Calder, clearing his throat. "We, ah... That is, my family lives differently. All pooled together into one house. We're at a campground now. Most of us are eating there today."

"You should have told me! You could have invited everyone!"

Calder offered a faltering smile. "I don't think everyone would have fit..."

Laguna was over by the chairs now, crouched down, the balls of her feet lifted into the air. Arty backed up and headed down to the second stair, his eyes glinting as he peered up and watched her cautiously.

She stuck her hand out toward him and he slowly, slowly made his way over to sniff it.

Huh. He hadn't liked the vampires at all.

He arched his back into her touch now, and she ran a hand along his cheeks and down along his back to the base of his tail.

My heart grew cold all of a sudden when I realized cats wouldn't survive a flooded world, and as far as I knew, Laguna wasn't opposed to the merfolk's plan.

"We appreciate you having us here," said Cascade sharply, not sounding the least bit grateful. She yanked a chair off the pile, sending Arty scurrying back down the stairs with the sudden movement, his claws clicking across the hard surface.

Laguna stood and followed Cascade's lead, struggling to drag the next chair off. Calder jumped up to assist her before she buried herself under the thing.

"If any of you want breakfast, we have plenty of pastries." Mom frowned as she looked at the multiple boxes stacked on the corner of one of the counters. "They're a few days old, but... I don't know why we bought so many."

I did. Autumn had demanded she buy them—and then had lost interest in eating the prized bounty.

Easton headed back toward the stairs. "Let me bring the rest of the decorations up. Calder, might a strapping young man like yourself lend me a hand?"

Wincing, Calder reached for my hand and squeezed it before letting go.

Despite the cheerful façade on Easton's face, I didn't trust him one bit, either. Calder *had* been "dating" Easton's firstborn daughter until just last week, as far as my step-dad knew.

Artemis' shining eyes vanished as the cat scrambled back down before Easton could step on him—he must have silently, like a little predator, skulked back up to watch us.

Mom went back to mashing potatoes, looking up as Cascade and Laguna reappeared in the room to grab another set of chairs. "Do either of you enjoy cooking?" she asked.

Laguna wandered over to the greasy boxes of pastries and removed a Danish.

"Ember could use some help prepping the potatoes. Or would you rather work on the sweet potato casserole?" Mom let out a breath before kind of wobbling on her feet, clutching her stomach.

"Mom?" I appeared at her side to support her in a flash.

"I'm fine," she said, not dismissively or unkindly. "Just a little morning sickness..." She brushed her arm against the back of her head.

"Why don't you go rest?" I said, looking around. "You two took care of the turkey. Everything else, I can do."

Cascade crossed the room then and snatched a chocolate croissant out of the top pastry box. Her lips downturned as she bit into the dry, flaky thing. Laguna displayed no such emotion as she munched on her frosted treat.

Easton was talking, though I couldn't make out the words over the stomp of his feet up the stairs. "Mr. Turkey Giblets," he said as he ascended the stairs with a giant, open cardboard box in both hands, Calder with a similar one behind him.

There was tinsel and all sorts of pilgrim paraphernalia hanging out of Easton's box. Including a terribly drawn hand-shaped picture of a turkey, crinkled and yellowing with age.

"Ivy wanted to throw him out years ago, but I held on to it. I'm going to hang it up today and see if she notices. First drawing she made specifically for me." Easton put the box down atop the empty kitchen table and pulled out a horrible turkey drawing. He frowned and "Mr. Turkey Giblets" slipped from his hand. "What's wrong, hon?"

"Morning sickness," I answered at the same time Mom did.

"I told her to rest," I said. "It's way early—and we're almost done here. It's too early to put the rest of this in the oven, even."

Easton took my place at Mom's side and I stepped back to let him. "Let me get you upstairs," he said to his wife. Over his shoulder, he looked at the lot of us. "I'll be back down in a few minutes to see if you need help with anything."

The four of us stood there blankly until we'd heard my parents ascend the stairs.

Cascade put her bitten-into croissant back atop the box and slapped her hands together, as if to wipe the stickiness away. "Calder said you wanted to discuss something with us today."

Calder slipped his arm behind my back. On Sunday, when we'd left Joe's and come up with the idea, he'd sworn the other teens would be the best people to tell first. Without telling them our true end game. We needed their help to win—then it would be up to me to make the wish that would change everything.

I just had to make them think that *changing everything* meant drowning the world.

"I'm guessing nothing too big will happen today," I said, slipping my arm behind Calder's back and squeezing him in turn. They needed to think that Calder was my everything—that I'd be willing to give everything up for him. It wasn't hard to pretend. He was important to me; it was just that so was everyone else I loved, too. "We asked you here to be prepared in case it does," I explained, "but with too many guests, a cramped living space, and Autumn apparently being a fan of the holiday, according to her dad—I just don't see it delving into chaos."

"Too bad," said Cascade, gripping the edge of the counter behind her as if she hoped to crush it with her bare hand.

"Hear her out," said Calder, motioning for her to calm down.

I took a deep breath.

Journey had helped me devise this plan in Joe's driveway after we'd all thanked him for his hospitality.

She believed me that I wanted to undo vampirism—without eradicating them. Turn them into humans with a wish and then there'd be no vampires to disappear after they lost the war, right?

The faefolk—well, they weren't exactly human to begin with. I could deal with them disappearing. I shuddered at the memory of their sharp little twig swords.

Journey had offered to spy on the vampires if I needed her to.

But I didn't want her anywhere near that place. Didn't trust them to keep her and Dante safe.

Besides, I didn't need a spy to know Ivy and Autumn were going to be planning something together—and soon.

"Ivy is visiting a college this weekend," I explained. "And the whole family is tagging along. I looked up the place"—I slipped away from Calder a moment to pick up my phone and bring up the campus map—"and there's a manmade lake that runs along the campus and practically the whole town." I tapped on the screen to enlarge it, showing both Cascade and

Laguna at once. "We're renting a bed and breakfast here—the entire bed and breakfast. So..."

I looked to Calder for confirmation and he nodded. "We thought we'd end it. This weekend. It's supposed to be mostly empty because of the college kids going home for Thanksgiving, with only a skeleton staff and a few students who couldn't go back still there to show Ivy and her family around. The town is small, remote—*full* of water. The bed and breakfast is pretty isolated, like you can see across the lake to the university, but there aren't other houses right next door or anything. We already suspect Ivy and Autumn have something in mind for this trip." My lips pinched tightly together as I passed my phone to Cascade so she could get a better look. "And yet I'm going anyway. Calder said he was going to pretend he has a campus visit, too—albeit a year early. They have a great swim team," I added. Then I let out a deep breath. For a second there, I felt like I was actually giving Calder some college advice. But they had to think I assumed it would all be over long before Calder had a chance to send in college applications.

"There's an RV park a mile over from where you're staying, too," said Cascade thoughtfully. She passed the phone to Laguna, who was practically leaning on her arm to get a better look. "You haven't presented this to the family," she said, over my head to Calder.

"I wanted to know what you thought of it first." Calder ran a hand over the back of his head. "You know my mom makes Ember feel uncomfortable—we just thought, well, let's get this over with, and this time next week, we'll all be breathing out of our gills full-time." He side-hugged me again, resting his cheek atop my head. "What better way for her to accept the princess once and for all? We can get married in a grotto church in the warmest tropical waters of the sea."

I knew it was just a part of our charade, but something grew tight inside me at the idea of becoming Calder's bride. I knew I was far too young. My ideal marriage was not as a half-fish.

But... But there was something about the idea, molded another way, that didn't feel wrong.

Cascade and Laguna exchanged a look and Laguna actually spoke. "I want to live in the tropics," she said quietly. "I'm... cold."

It was only the consummate lands keeping the last of the world's merfolk stuck here in the Midwest, in the murky rivers and lakes, in the cold for half the year.

Cascade sighed. "Let me run it past Bay and Llyr. And then the family." Her eyes narrowed. "You better talk to your mom tonight."

"I will," Calder said. "But you're right—if we're going to do this, we need to make plans."

He stepped back from me and pulled his own phone out of his back pocket. "I could use your support," he said.

Cascade let out a harsh breath and followed Laguna and Calder out of the room, Laguna dropping my phone in my extended hand as she finished off her days-old pastry.

I heard them exit out the front door as they went to make their calls.

I got back to work finishing up Mom's sweet potato casserole, and a few minutes later, Easton clomped down the stairs, poking his head in the kitchen to begin rifling through his box of decorations again.

"Where are your friends?" he asked.

"Outside. Calling their family." I tossed the last of the peeled and chopped sweet potatoes into a pot with water. Now we just had to mash them before putting them in a glass dish to bake and sprinkling them with mini marshmallows. I couldn't forget the peanut butter and maple syrup to add to the potato mixture, either.

The front door opened again, and my heart stilled as the stovetop went to work, heat rising slowly from the pot. Ivy and

Autumn and their mom weren't due until it was time to eat, so I wasn't sure why I was so anxious.

But something in the air felt wrong. My hand stilled on the stirring spoon.

"Thought I'd show up early. See if I could lend a hand." The cockney English accent filled the air.

Orin.

"Hey, bud," said Easton as he turned around to greet our intruder with a smile on his face.

Of course. Easton was still brainwashed into thinking this was the beloved twenty-year-old local business owner family friend whom he trusted implicitly with his elementary-school-aged daughter.

I whirled around, my back to the oven, then jumped forward with a little gasp as I found it uncomfortably warm on my backside.

"I see you weren't expecting me." Orin stuffed his hands into his coat pockets. He looked fashionably casual somehow, his hair wild and his gray coat opened to reveal a green sweater and a pair of khaki slacks.

"You're always welcome," said Eaton cheerfully, passing one of the boxes of decorations toward Orin. Orin lagged a second and moved quickly to accept it, as if being told to *actually help* when he'd come to offer his *help* hadn't at all been what *he'd* expected.

"Where's Calder?" I asked bluntly.

He shrugged. "I didn't see him."

Easton walked past Orin with the other box of decorations, leaving Orin and me alone.

"But I *may* have flown in through the window." He smiled.

"Of course." I moved to go after Easton, away from this pompous jerk.

With a crash, the box Orin had been holding clattered to the floor and he was at my side.

"Wait," said Orin. "Let's have a chat."

I couldn't move. It wasn't that I didn't want to, but I couldn't...

With horror, I shifted my eyeballs, the only thing that seemed free to move, to stare at him.

He'd just used his powers on me. A prince attacking a champion.

Calder stepped into the kitchen, Cascade and Laguna right behind him.

"Hey!" snapped Calder. "Get away from her!"

Orin stepped back, his hands up in the air. "No harm, no foul. I just thought I'd have a word..." His eyes narrowed at the mermaids behind Calder. "Before anyone else got here. You don't have to wait for me if you don't want to," he said to me quickly.

Calder stepped between Orin and me, and I felt almost like a *release* slip over me. My mind still buzzed with a strange sense of being invaded.

"Orin?" called Easton from down the hallway. "Is everything all right?"

Of course he'd ask if *he* was all right after hearing all that commotion.

"Just peachy," said Orin, and with a wink, he vanished. No, not vanished—turned into a little green flying ball of light.

Before we could even react, it flew off, out the kitchen and out of sight.

"Oh, did Orin have to go?" asked Easton, disappointed as he walked back into the kitchen. He bent down to grab the box Orin had dropped carelessly, picking up Mr. Turkey Giblets and the other decorations that had escaped in the tumble.

Calder sent me a look as if to ask if I was okay and I nodded. Then he helped my step-dad pick up the box's contents and got to decorating.

Leaning up against the counter, I stared at the heap of uncooked food all around us. Cascade and Laguna didn't move, their stances ready to fight even when the threat was gone.

We only had a few more hours until everyone else was due to arrive.

The pot full of water and sweet potatoes started bubbling, a sharp burning scent hitting the air, and I scrambled to get back to work.

Once this was over, who knew if Autumn and Ivy would forgive me for winning, even if I didn't flood the world like they expected.

If this was our only Thanksgiving as a somewhat united family, then at least it was going to have good food.

CHAPTER FIFTEEN

IVY

"Do you think Dad put out Mr. Turkey Giblets?" Autumn danced in front of me on the sidewalk leading to Dad and Noelle's driveway. "*I'm made of paper so no one can eat me*," she added, in a poor imitation of Dad being the embarrassing parent he often was, always making a big deal out of a stupid drawing I'd done when I'd been, like, three.

"Probably," I said. "Unless it finally got lost in the move."

Mom huffed up the pavement behind us and I turned to take the store-bought pie box off the top of the casserole dish she'd insisted on carrying herself with two oven mitts.

Mom had gotten a discount off the pie from work, no doubt, but she'd still insisted on making something this morning to bring along. It was a little burnt at the edges, but that crispy quality actually added some nice flavor to the potatoes in my opinion.

"Thank you, dear," Mom said. Her face—lined with the earliest stages of wrinkles that made her seem tired—lit up as she looked up at me in the few inches I had over her. She had the same long, dark brown hair as Autumn and me, though hers was tinged with silver. Her eyes were brown, like Autumn's, her figure plumper than it had been years before— the divorce, amicable though it may have been, and struggling with stressful hours at the job she'd had to take afterward seemed to have worn her down more than it had the likes of Dad and Noelle.

Still, side by side, my mom and step-mom, it'd be obvious to any that Dad was attracted to head-turning beauty.

At the front porch, I turned, facing the street, waiting for my own startlingly gorgeous "boyfriend" to show.

I'd been on high alert since we'd pulled up. I'd taken note of the empty blue pickup truck I knew to belong to Calder—and though the streets were lined with unfamiliar vehicles over to people's houses for the holiday, there were more than a couple I could have sworn I'd seen parked at the merfolk mansion before it had burnt down during an assault from my new *allies*.

But it wasn't as if I were foolish enough to think they wouldn't show. I'd just hoped I'd have my own entourage in place before I got here.

Autumn kept ringing the doorbell, and before long, Dad answered it, bracing himself for Autumn to jump on him and wrap her legs around him. He stumbled and made an *oofing* sound that could have been genuine or could have been him teasing her for getting so big or could have started that way and then gone on to genuine discomfort over time.

Dad directed Autumn to slide to the ground and kissed the top of her head. "Hey, kiddo. Don't you think you've grown big enough yet?"

I could have spoken the predictable words along with him.

He reached out to tap Mom on the shoulder, being careful to avoid the hot casserole dish she had in her hands. "Glory, you look lovely, as always."

Mom smiled and blinked rapidly, her eyes filling up with tears slightly. She had on a puffy down-filled purple winter coat, but beneath I knew she'd put on a nicer sweater and a pair of black slacks she generally saved for the holidays.

"Let's let you put that down. This way. Hi, sport," he said

to me over his shoulder as he guided Mom to the dining room. "You look stunning."

Offering Dad a flittering smile, I sighed, splitting off from him to bring the pie to the kitchen. As I passed the living room, I peered in to see the TV on with one of those fireplace videos next to an actual crackling fireplace. Autumn tossed her coat on the sofa and swirled around, and for a second, I thought I saw floating green baubles around her, but when I paused to look closer, I figured it had just been a trick of the light. I went ahead to the kitchen, taking note of the mixture of Thanksgiving and Christmas decorations found peppering the hallway. There was even a sprig of fake mistletoe hanging over the entryway to the kitchen.

Murmuring voices went quiet as I appeared. Ember—dressed in a navy blue pair of slacks and a red cardigan sweater that reminded me too much of the 1940s style the vampires favored—turned her gaze on me, tossing some of her too-blonde hair over her shoulder. On one side of her head was a blue shell-shaped hair ornament tying her golden locks back into a side-ponytail.

Beside her were Calder, Laguna, and Cascade, looking for all the world like a bunch of normal high schoolers come over dressed up for a Thanksgiving dinner. Except for their faces. There was no avoiding the hard lines of their expressions. Even Laguna managed to radiate anger in my direction, and I'd never seen her angry at anything.

"Ivy," said Ember stiffly, straightening some dishes on the kitchen island that clearly weren't in need of straightening.

"Hey," I managed, adding my mom's store-bought pie box to the small space I found beside the two homemade pies cooling off on racks.

I slipped out of my coat to reveal the 1940s sweetheart neckline dress in blue I'd borrowed from the ladies at the Horne Manor. They'd told me blue was my color. That it made my eyes pop.

The effect on Ember was immediate. She turned her back

toward me as Calder took a careful step around the island. "Where's Dean?" he asked abruptly.

"On his way," I said, though he hadn't checked in with me in a while.

"We already had a visit from another prince," said Cascade sternly.

That was news to me. The faeries had agreed to take the backseat this holiday. Autumn hadn't wanted it ruined. And besides, they needed to prepare for this weekend.

Swallowing, I shrugged. "I didn't invite him."

"But Mom and Easton definitely did." Ember frowned. "Old family friend Orin."

"He got to my mom, too," I said defensively. Two out of those three parents were *mine*.

Ember snatched a roll from under a cloth napkin covering a basket. "He said he wanted to talk to me. Alone."

I tucked my coat over my arm. Now that was news to me. Today was supposed to be hands off unless the merfolk started something. Which would be hard to do in a house some ways away from the nearest lake and river. But we'd been crafty enough when I'd been a mermaid.

"What'd he want?" I asked, grabbing my own roll as Ember dug into hers.

"He didn't get a chance to ask. Seeing as how he's more your friend than mine, I thought maybe you could tell me."

I opened my mouth and then shut it. She could think I was keeping something from her or not. I really didn't care.

Dad walked into the kitchen then, humming, "I'll Be Home for Christmas."

"Doesn't this smell delicious." He gripped both of my shoulders. "Ember and her friends have been so helpful since early this morning. Come see how we decorated the dining room." He nodded at Ember. "Maybe we can start bringing everything out to the table?"

As soon as we were in the hallway, Dad leaned in and asked under his breath, "Is this okay? Being with the ex-boyfriend?"

"Dad, you invite your *ex-wife* to your house for the holidays."

"That's different. We're family."

"If you say so."

Mom was in the dining room, speaking with Noelle, who seemed to sparkle with some kind of rosy glow, dressed like the perfect mother in a stock photo for the holidays. The room was full of decorations—probably Noelle's and Dad's melded together as only half seemed familiar. Garlands streamed atop the windows, paper cut-outs on the walls. There were even thin strands of silver tinsel atop the red-and-green tablecloth that lined the elongated dining room table.

"Ivy!" said Noelle warmly. She had a mug in her hand that steamed with the heat of her beverage. "You look lovely."

Someone bumped into me and I jumped, stepping aside to let Ember and her train of merfolk bring in the first of the dishes and lay them on pre-arranged hot plates.

"*Hey, Ivy,*" said Dad in his ridiculous high-pitched voice. "*It's Mr. Turkey Giblets.*"

I slowly turned, the effort to move my neck like swimming upstream, to see Dad shaking my worn and ugly turkey drawing in front of my face.

Ember snorted once she'd let go of her dish and I rolled my eyes.

"Yeah, thanks, Dad, for that." Sighing, I brushed past him and went to hang up my coat on the rack near the front door.

The doorbell rang and before I could even turn to see who it was, I was facing Dean and Zelda in the entryway.

"We saw it was you, so we let ourselves in." Dean smiled and took the coat from my hands that I was about to hang.

I let him finish the task I was perfectly capable of finishing myself and smiled. Threading my fingers together, I nodded at Zelda. "Thanks for the dress."

The two of them looked amazing, not a hair out of place. Zelda's vintage wrap dress was a deep burgundy that matched her lipstick perfectly. Dean's suit was a dark gray, his tie a matching color. He hung his gray trilby hat on the rack beside my coat.

"Ember's *guests* have been here since this morning." The words left a hollow discomfort in my throat.

"Yeah, we saw a few along the way. Enjoying their Thanksgiving from their cold parked cars." Zelda laughed, a tittering sound that reminded me with a wince of Minnie.

"She also claimed Orin stopped by and wanted to speak to her alone, but they didn't get the opportunity." That got no reaction. Was I the only one concerned? "And you're a hundred percent sure we can trust the faefolk?" I offered.

Zelda and Dean exchanged a look.

"We don't know them," admitted Zelda.

"Only Minnie does. And what she says goes." He seemed almost pained to say that.

Before we could say anything more, Noelle popped out into the hall. "Ah. Dean. And...?"

"Zelda." The blonde bombshell introduced herself. "Dean's cousin." She had *that* lie ready to go.

Noelle shook Zelda's proffered hand. "Oh! The more, the merrier. I asked Yvonne what your family was doing for the holiday, and she said you were having a *grand feast*."

I winced at her descriptor. I did *not* need to know what was going on there, though getting everyone ready and full of energy for the weekend ahead put plenty of ideas in my head.

"It is," said Zelda quietly, "though truth be told, I can't eat much." She rested a hand on her stomach. "Allergies, you understand. So I thought I'd accompany my cousin here."

Noelle frowned. "Hmm, well, let's see if we can scrounge something up for you."

Noelle and Zelda took off down the hallway into the kitchen and I leaned over to whisper to Dean, "What about Ember's dad?" The soft aura of coldness that seemed to emanate off him collided with my cheek like a gentle slap, and I swallowed darkly.

"Probably later," Dean said. "Minnie offered him a taste first."

Offered him the chance for *her* to take a taste of *him*, most likely.

Shuddering, I walked slowly toward the dining room, where Dad was speaking loudly to Mom, Autumn running circles around Ember and the merfolk in attendance. They all stuck to the walls, frowning anytime my sister passed by.

I caught her by the shoulders. "Let's sit down," I said, directing her to a chair beside me.

Dean slipped in on my other side, and the four enemies moved as one to sit in spots directly across from us.

"Mrs. Sheppard found us some cranberry juice, cousin." Zelda waltzed in with two wine glasses filled with bright red liquid just about halfway up. My heart skipped a beat as I had to push down the idea that it was blood. She slid in beside Dean, across from Cascade, and put the glass in front of him.

"Ms. Goodwin-Sheppard, dear," Noelle corrected her as she stood at the end of the table. Dad scrambled to pull out the chair for her before retreating to the other end, Mom shuffling quietly to sit in the free seat beside Autumn, near Dad.

Vampires and merfolk aside, it was a little weird not to have Mom on the opposite end of a Thanksgiving table.

Not that we'd had one this big since we used to get together with aunts and uncles and cousins for the day before we'd all radiated out to our own celebrations about a decade ago.

Noelle held her hand out to Cascade on one side and Zelda on the other, almost as if offering to broker a peace between the two. Cascade's scowl seemed permanently etched into her features. Zelda took the dismissive and haughty approach, looking anywhere but straight across from her. But they both took Noelle's hands, everyone following suit with their neighbors.

"Oh!" said Noelle, dropping Zelda's hand. "You're freezing, dear."

Zelda laughed, a little tittering sound. "Sorry about that. Poor circulation."

Cascade mumbled something indecipherable but clearly harsh under her breath.

My own hand in Dean's grew chillier by the second, but there wasn't an ounce of instinct in me to pull away.

My skin tingled against his, and the feeling spread contentedly throughout my body.

Why? I wanted to know. I could not be so stupid as to be attracted to an undead grandpa.

Better prepared for the cold touch of Zelda's skin, Noelle took it up again.

"Would anyone like to start?" Dad asked. "And tell the room what you're thankful for?"

I stared straight ahead at Ember, trying to get a feel for any tricks she might have had up her sleeve. But for all intents and purposes, this felt like the calm before the storm.

She had to know we had plans for this coming weekend. She looked too self-assured not to.

"I'm *so thankful* for my new family," said Ember. Her tone made it so she could almost be taken seriously if you weren't looking for a reason not to. The way her gaze skirted over Autumn and me was a clear reason not to.

Dad took it literally, though. "That's beautiful, Ember. I'm so happy to have added you and your mother into my life. And that new little darling to come." He jutted his chin across the long table toward his wife.

Mom spoke up next, her face a little flush. "I'm grateful for my daughters. For my work. And for good friends."

"I'm grateful for my daughters as well," said Noelle. "For my wonderful husband, and for my girls to be getting along well enough to invite all of these friends. And for some of those friends to help with this beautiful bounty before us!"

"I'm thankful for turkey," said Autumn abruptly, making

the adults in the room laugh. "And Mr. Turkey Giblets!" she added, and Dad did a turkey call in his Mickey Mouse voice, making Autumn burst into laughter along with her parents.

Ember rolled her eyes.

Somehow that irritated me more than Autumn's flippant remark.

My fingers dug hard into Dean's palm. "I'm thankful for all of that," I said. "But most of all, I'm thankful to be able to know a good idea from a bad, and for the empathy to put others before myself."

Ember scoffed, and Noelle's eyebrows arched.

She cleared her throat. "That's lovely, dear. Guests? Do any of you have anything to be thankful for?"

Merfolk and vampires alike stared anywhere but across the way at their enemies.

"Song," Laguna said softly after a moment of silence. "Beautiful creatures. Warm waters. And wonderful melodies."

"Beautiful," said Mom, smiling broadly at her across the table.

Laguna's ears went red and she looked away.

Yeah, look away from the humans you want to drown.

"My family," said Cascade then. "They're the only thing that really matters to me."

My grip on Dean's hand grew tighter and he offered a squeeze back.

"My family as well," said Zelda. "Though I find this world has so much to offer, so much to be grateful for..." She left the rest unsaid.

That just left the princes.

"I'm thankful for the people who believe in me." Dean turned to face me, giving me a smile. I didn't imagine Ember bristling.

"And I'm thankful to the Goodwins and Sheppards for inviting us here," said Calder quickly. "For this feast—for those of us who can enjoy it anyway." He stared pointedly at the goblets of juice on top of Zelda's and Dean's plates.

"Amen," said Dad, and everyone murmured their echoes of the word.

Standing, Dad picked up a casserole dish, handing it off to Mom, then another to Laguna, who ignored him until Calder reached across her to take the dish from him. Then Dad went to work cutting the turkey. "Everyone, let me know if you want white or dark meat."

People chimed in with their preferences, and Autumn greedily declared, "Both!"

"Zelda? Dean?" Noelle asked as they quickly passed the casserole dish I handed them on to her. "You don't want anything but juice? Dean, you, too?"

"I'd rather not be ill and ruin your dinner," said Dean. "But thank you, Mrs. Goodwin-Sheppard."

"Ms.," Ember corrected him.

He rounded on her for the first time since he'd sat down but said nothing more.

"If you're sure." Noelle didn't seem sure at all. Perhaps she wondered if the Hornes were contagious. They were—just not how she supposed.

Once everyone had their plates piled high with food—everyone other than Dean and Zelda, who still just had their red juice in the middle of wide, empty plates—we dug in, Autumn swinging her feet beneath the table, the toes of her cat-design-socked feet scuffling against the floorboard.

Cascade wouldn't stop glaring at Zelda and Dean, but Zelda just leaned back in her seat, crossing her legs delicately and sipping from her glass like a woman with many, many more years of sophistication than her dewy-eyed youthful appearance suggested.

The parents kept up the conversation mostly, Autumn frequently jumping in, as if this were all nothing out of the ordinary. Ember and Calder chimed in on occasion, Dean and Zelda only speaking when spoken to. Laguna pushed food around on her plate, sniffing a piece of turkey she'd stabbed with her fork, and then putting it back down. She did clear her plate of mashed potatoes.

"So, Ivy, you excited about tomorrow?" Dad asked. He leaned over toward Laguna, who ignored him completely. "We're going on a big family trip tomorrow. Ivy's looking at a college."

"Fowles University, right?" said Calder, piping up. "Ember told me." He nudged her playfully with his shoulder then, and Ember could hardly contain the smile breaking out on her face. "My mom wants me to go there, too. Got us a tour this weekend."

"Oh?" said Noelle, putting her fork down gently on the delicate china I'd never seen in use before today. She looked to me, though she kept speaking to Calder. "You plan to be there this weekend, too? I don't know if you'll have time to spend with my daughter. This is a family trip, you understand."

When I didn't flinch, Noelle turned to her own flesh and blood to see how she'd react to her straightforward if mild-mannered proclamation. No boyfriends this weekend.

Right.

"No, that's fine." Calder slipped an arm around Ember and leaned back in his chair. "I'm going with family, too."

At that, three phones went off at once, Calder, Cascade, and Laguna all looking down and pulling phones out of their pockets—or in Laguna's case, strangely, her boot.

"No phones at the table, please, kids," Dad said.

"Easton, it's fine." Noelle's eyes went wide. "They're the... Their house burnt down and maybe their family needs them."

Just then, the doorbell rang.

"Let me," said Dean, hopping to his feet so quickly, I thought he might have used his vampire ability. He gestured for Noelle, who'd backed up from the table, to sit. "Since you're all eating."

"Oh," said Noelle. "Thank you, dear. It's probably the Slowes. They were going to try to stop by for dessert after their own dinner."

But from the utter silence echoing out in the hallway as the door opened, it didn't seem likely it was a group of family friends just here for a normal celebration.

Dean's footfalls were joined by another pair, slow and steady, the boots heavy.

And then Dean reappeared, Ember's dad beside him. Shorter than Dean by just a smidge, he nonetheless looked almost as suave, his golden-gray hair slicked back, his suit somewhat out of fashion.

Ember shot to her feet, her chair wobbling behind her. Calder caught it, saving it from crashing to the ground.

"Tom?" asked Noelle. She looked a little green. "You never responded to our invite. I thought—"

"Sorry about that," said Mr. Goodwin, though he didn't look sorry at all. He ran a hand through his stiff hair. "Thought I'd drop by. I was in town. Hey, hon," he said to Ember.

Her lips quivering, she fled from the room, tears already staining her cheeks in the short moment she passed me by.

CHAPTER SIXTEEN

EMBER

I bolted up the stairs into my room and turned around to slam the door behind me, but I stopped when I discovered I was about to slam it into Calder's face.

He put a hand on the edge of the door. "Em," he said softly.

All the tension in my body dissipated, my shoulders relaxing as I stepped back and let him come inside.

He shut the door behind him.

I hadn't turned on my bedroom lights, but with a *click*, the automatic timer on the year-round white Christmas lights hung over my bedframe flicked on, bathing us in a mixture of dying sunlight filtered through my curtains and soft artificial light.

"This doesn't change anything," Calder said after a moment of silence. "We're going to save him—"

"I know," I said, falling against his chest. His arms encircled me, clutching together against the small of my back. "It's just... His face. Did you see? He looked at me with such hatred. Like being a vampire was more important to him than..."

"Addiction changes people," Calder said when I wouldn't finish my sentence.

"But that's just it." I let out a deep breath and maneuvered out of Calder's warm embrace. "He's always been like that. Whatever he was into was always more important than his family." I slipped down at the edge of my bed.

Calder sat beside me. "I'm sorry."

I leaned against his shoulder in a half-hug.

We sat like that in silence for a while.

A soft knock came at the door.

"Ember? Honey?" It was Mom. "Do you want to talk? We're about to have dessert—"

I didn't realize I was crying until just that moment. Silently. Tears simply streaming down my cheeks. "Okay. Just give me a minute."

Mom cleared her throat. "I don't know exactly what happened between you and your father—recently, anyway— but I asked him if he might take some dessert to go. Journey's on her way. Lacey just texted me."

"Okay," I said. I didn't know what else to say.

Mom walked away and Calder stood, extending a hand down to me.

"Could I just have a minute?" I wiped at my cheeks. "I need to wash up."

Calder nodded, and once he'd shut the door behind him, I got up from the bed and walked around my room, slowly, swinging each leg in front of the other.

A quick flash of light startled me, though it was so quick, I couldn't say for sure whether or not I'd imagined it. I raced to the window at the back of my room, shoving aside the curtain.

Swinging wildly through the air like a moth to a light, a little green ball of light swayed back and forth in front of my window—and dangling from it was a pie.

My first instinct was to open the window and grab for it.

A foolish instinct, considering the only thing it could be.

"Oh! Careful!" said a quiet voice in my ear. It had a cockney lilt, and it was only somewhat as tinny as one would expect, considering the faery's size. "It might still be hot."

It was. Yowling softly, I dropped the aluminum foil onto a pile of dirty laundry poking out of my hamper.

"Well, I hope *that*'s still edible. You don't strike me as the type to get your clothes overly sweaty at least."

Fully-formed, Orin sat on my open windowsill, his feet dangling inside my room.

I sucked on my fingers, then remembering what I could do—what I *needed* to do in the face of a threat—I summoned ice to my hand and pressed my right hand toward my left, instantly cooling the lightly burned fingertips. "What are you *doing*?" I hissed.

"Bringing fire-baked chestnut pie," he said, jumping inside and straightening his dress shirt. "Thought about ringing the doorbell, but then everyone and their mother—quite literally—would know I was here again and I wanted to talk to you first."

"But how'd you know I'd be *here*?"

"We've got eyes everywhere." He tapped the side of his temple. "Plus, we knew Minnie was going to send your pot and pan over to mess with your head."

"My what?"

"Your dad," he explained.

Okay... I shuffled backward toward the door. "Then say it. Whatever it is you have to tell me."

"Well..." Orin ran a hand through his hair, the curls bouncing with the movement. "It's not so much anything you couldn't have already guessed—we're all going on this trip this weekend. Figure a little distance from the consummate lands might make for clearer heads and we can end this once and for all."

My back hit the door, my icy hand reaching behind me to grab for the knob. "And you want me to surrender?"

"That *would* be helpful," said Orin. "But I'm afraid if I convinced you to do so, that would be taking the biscuit on my part, prince or referee or no."

His continuously incomprehensible slang aside, I swallowed. *Convinced?* Like he'd *convinced* my parents that he was their friend, like—

Turning around, I opened the door, about to call for help.

"But *we* do have another task for you," said Orin at my side, whispering in my ear.

The door opened.

Autumn looked up at me and smiled brightly.

She opened her mouth and spoke.

————

"You're hardly eating," Journey said, sucking on her fork to get the very last bits of the sweet potato pie her mom and dad had brought over.

We were in the living room, near both a roaring, real fire and a yule log crackling on the TV. Easton had thought it was clever somehow. I didn't get Dad humor.

I put the slice of chestnut pie I'd only had a bite of on the coffee table. I'd felt strange eating it—a little sick. My head seemed to float on a cloud and for the life of me, I couldn't remember anyone bringing the pie. We definitely hadn't made it.

Calder finished his giant slice of sweet potato pie and put his empty plate beside mine. "I'll eat it if you don't want it."

I nodded at him and he scooped it up, even using the fork I'd left behind on the plate to eat it.

"How's Dante?" I asked Journey. Across the hall, Mom, Lacey, and Glory laughed about something in the dining room as Easton and Mr. Slowe debated hotly over football teams and which of their favorites had the better chance of winning.

"Better," she said, the corner of her lip twitching just slightly. "Keeping him away from them—from temptation— was key, I think."

The vampires had trickled out to the front porch, Cascade and Laguna hovering around the entryway, neither enjoying any dessert, Cascade clearly tense as she watched the others' every movement.

"You're so strong to be able to resist that yourself. The venom inside me..." I trailed off as my heart squeezed tightly. Its beat echoed loudly in my ear, reminding me of what it was like to have the venom flow through my veins.

"I was only there for you and Devam," said Journey quietly. "You're somewhere else now. And Devam is dead to me." She winced. "No pun intended."

"He won't be for long," I said. Down the hallway, Autumn's little singsong voice carried through the air. "Not that you have to forgive him, but... I'll undo the damage I caused."

"*We*," said Calder softly. He leaned his head toward the hallway, where the mermaids were standing guard. "We'll undo it all."

I nodded solemnly.

Autumn did a little dance as she came into view, swirling around with some green tinsel above her head.

"Well, aren't you talented," said Lacey as she nearly got bumped into during Autumn's dizzy spell.

My head swam a little just watching her. I knew I had to keep an eye on her, even though there weren't any faefolk here that I could see—not since Orin's strange visit this morning. When he'd claimed he'd wanted to speak to me alone and...

Bending forward, I cradled my forehead. It pounded, and my insides felt all jumbled up, like my heart was straining to pump venom when it needed to forget that. I was a mermaid now, not a vampire.

"Ember?"

The sound of my name came from more than one direction. I snapped back to the moment, finding both Journey and Calder studying me, concern etched on their features.

"Yes?" I blinked maybe a few too many times.

"We were just..." Journey bit her lip and her gaze got stuck over my shoulder out the front window.

Zelda was leaning against the bannister, staring inside without blinking.

Dad had left before I'd gotten downstairs again, though I had no doubt he lingered somewhere nearby.

Journey spoke softer. "I just wanted to know if Dante and I should drive over to Fowles University this weekend."

"No!" I said, so sternly I scared even myself. I let out a breath. "It's not that I don't appreciate the sentiment, but you've done more than enough. Stay safe."

"If we could spare someone, I'd keep them back to watch you," said Calder quietly. "But they... They won't see much point in guarding anyone, considering."

Considering they all thought I was about to flood the world. I should have been more than ready to make a few sacrifices along the way, then, no need to worry about hostages.

I grimaced, my fingers digging into the stiff suede of the couch.

"Lock your doors," I said, quieter, my own gaze meeting Zelda's, the slight shape of Dean's shoulder coming into view beside her. "Stay safe and stay out of it." Ivy paced in front of the window and Dean stepped into view, leaning over to whisper in her ear. Her face reddened, and I didn't think it was just from the cold.

"This will all be over soon," I added.

CHAPTER SEVENTEEN

IVY

I smoothed out the material of my blue 1940s-style shirtwaist dress. The hidden metal clasps down the front had been a little loose, the material just a little musty, but it was surprisingly comfortable. Since it had short sleeves, I was lucky it was one of those weird Midwest days where a warm front had pushed aside the chilly air and now fifty degrees felt like eighty after a string of days near and below freezing. There was still a bit of a bite in the air, though, as a gust of wind nearly sent my blue pillbox hat flying off my head, despite the bobby pins I'd used to keep it in place.

It wasn't my ideal outfit, but I thought I rocked it, with my long, dark hair down, a little added curl for bounce. Dean had noticed my dress on Thanksgiving had seemed to unsettle Ember, how she hadn't exactly tossed out the clothes his coven had lent to her, how she'd seemed to think the 1940s vampire fashion was "her" thing. So, since my dad had insisted I'd "look nice" for my day of college tour, I'd co-opted it and embraced my part in this bloodsucking vintage empire. I shivered as another blast of wind worked its way through the warm air and grabbed my puffy blue coat out of the trunk of Dad's Jeep. It had never dried properly, so it hung heavily with clumps here and there over my body.

Mom leaned on the front of her decade-old sedan as she texted someone from work. She'd claimed Black Friday off a year ago, anticipating this trip, and yet they'd still tried to get her to come in to work.

They were still pestering her about it.

The trunk behind me opened. "I wish your mother could have gotten a better job. Her talents are wasted in retail." Dad scratched a freshly shaven cheek as he tossed his and Noelle's weekend bags inside. "This threatening her job over not coming in during vacation time she arranged a year ago—"

I whirled on him. "They threatened her job?"

Dad winced. "I guess she didn't want you to worry about it."

I rolled my eyes.

"And you don't have to," Dad said. "I told her when we talked on the phone this morning that she *had* to come. Consequences be damned. And Noelle could always give her a job at her company if need be."

"I'm sure Mom would *love* to work for your new wife," I muttered. My parents got along ridiculously well, considering, but I'd always picked up on something just below the surface with Mom.

The divorce had been more Dad's doing than hers, I was sure of it. And Mom wasn't exactly living her best life. More like just scraping by.

I got that she had Dad all in on this parenting thing, and a lot of single moms didn't have that. But still...

The clomp of Noelle's heels rang out from the open garage, a business crossbody bag hung over her shoulder. "Ivy, don't you look beautiful." She gave me a quick hug. "You're going to nail the interview."

"It's just an exploratory visit," Dad said, motioning for her to "calm down" as if trying to rein her in from getting carried away. "No pressure."

"Please," I said. "You and Mom have been going on about how you loved your time there for so long—"

"Yes, but you're your own person with your own path in life," he said. That was an understatement. I doubted any of them had switched majors from waterworld annihilation to bloodsucking breeding like I had before even finishing my senior year of high school. "I just thought that considering you don't have any other specific interests in a college or a job right out of high school…"

Autumn practically waddled out from the garage, the bag she'd packed at Mom's now overstuffed with a variety of toys.

"Honey," said Dad, "I don't know if you need to bring the whole toy chest."

Autumn cradled the bag to her chest, the fluffy mane of a My Little Pony settling under her nose and over her mouth, like some bright pink nightmare of a child beard.

"Oh, let her bring them." Noelle playfully swatted Dad's shoulder. "It's not like we're going to be hurting for space with two vehicles." She looked down at the edge of the driveway, where Mom was parked and still typing on her phone. "Glory, you're taking my car, right?"

She was?

Mom looked up from her screen and frowned. "I don't know if I should."

"Nonsense." Noelle dug into her business bag and fished out a set of keys. "That way you won't have to worry about gas or wear and tear…"

Mom sighed as she stepped away from her car and stared at it. There were rust spots around the wheel wells, more than a few scratches along the side from carts at her store's parking lot.

"Besides, you'll be doing me a favor in case I need to leave early for some reason." Noelle handed her the keys. "Then you can ride back with Easton."

"Thank you," Mom said glumly, taking the keys from Noelle. She turned around to fish her bags out from the trunk of her car.

"You're *not* leaving early," said Dad as his wife walked back beside him. "You promised."

"I shouldn't have to," said Noelle, "but you never know when running a business." Noelle ran a business supply business, a description that made me fall asleep about halfway through. She'd explained it once by pointing out she'd gotten the Slowes great deals on everything from the napkin holders to the menus at their diner. It was more than I understood about Dad's work in consulting for managers and human resources, I supposed.

"You're closed for the holiday weekend!" Dad protested. He sounded a bit whiny.

Noelle let her hand dance over his chest without a response as she headed back into the garage. "Ember!" she called into the door leading inside. "Ember, are you ready? The rest of us want to get on the road."

I stuffed my hands into the pockets of my puffy jacket and ground my feet into the pavement of the driveway.

It was ending this weekend. I wasn't fool enough to think that Ember didn't know that, either.

But she didn't have as many on her side. She didn't want to *save the entire world*.

Once she had surrendered, well, I'd work on getting Autumn to submit somehow. Dean and I had an idea for a wish... and even if it didn't go as planned, the vampires winning was the best of three bad options.

Plus, her mind control powers didn't work on me when I was ready for them.

Autumn opened the back door to Dad's Jeep and crawled inside.

"Honey," said Mom as she passed by with her bags. "I thought you were riding with me?"

Autumn pouted at her as she reached for the door to shut it. "I want to ride with Ember."

Everyone did a double-take when she said that.

But yeah, she was *not* causing Dad and pregnant Noelle to

get into an accident with some scheme of hers against Ember before we even got to our destination.

"I'll ride with Dad, too," I said, coming around to the other side of Dad's Jeep and sliding in beside Autumn.

Mom's chest hitched as the color drained from her face. Yikes. I hadn't met to hurt her feelings, it was just—well, I'd make it up to her next week once this was all over.

I'd make it up to her by saving the world and keeping her youngest child out of harm's way.

Dad laughed. "But if you're both in here, I don't know how Ember will fit—"

Noelle slipped her arm through Mom's, her bag jostling against the duffle bag Mom was struggling to carry. "She can ride in the front. And then I can drive my own car since Glory seemed a bit hesitant—it'll be perfect. Girl time and Daddy-Daughter time at the same time."

Dad stared blankly, blinking far too infrequently. "If you're sure..."

"I don't know how many times I have to tell you this, but I'm pregnant, not ill," Noelle said. "I feel loads better this morning." She was already at her car in the garage, taking the keys back from Mom and popping the back with a click.

"You look... nice."

I jumped in my seat. I hadn't shut the Jeep door yet and there was Ember, standing right beside me. I hadn't even noticed her leave the house.

She had a 1940s-style wool box coat over her outfit, a pair of dark pants sticking out at the bottom, but the rest of her attire remained a mystery. Her blindingly-blonde hair was down and thick with waves, her eyes covered with dark-lensed white-framed sunglasses that definitely looked like something vampires would wear.

Standing outside in the sunlight on a moderately warm day, she fanned her face and slipped her coat off, revealing a modern pink, ribbed pullover sweater to go along with the corduroy pants. So she wasn't overly committed to co-opting vampire fashion, then. But one of her bra straps—red and white fabric threaded together like a rope—poked out through the wide gap of her loose shawl collar. She noticed me staring at it and fixed the material over her shoulder to hide it. It had looked more like swimsuit material than a bra strap, now that I thought about it.

"Thanks," I mumbled after a beat, not really meaning it, and shutting the car door just as she opened the front passenger side.

"Should I go with my—*our* moms?" Ember asked. She looked over the Jeep at our moms gathering around Noelle's car, loading it up.

"No!" said Autumn. "You have to ride with Dad."

Dad stared down at Autumn. "Sister road trip?"

Autumn nodded as Dad shut her door. She turned to me as Dad took Ember's small suitcase from her. "*You* can ride with Mom and Noelle. I've got this."

"Yeah, that's exactly why I think I need to be here." I buckled in.

Ember got in before Dad, who touched base with Noelle and Mom for a minute. Clearing her throat, she settled her coat on her lap and reached behind her to put her own seatbelt on, then tested it by pushing hard against it, as if making sure we hadn't tampered with it.

Then she quietly pulled her phone out of her coat pocket and started typing on it.

I did the same. *We're pulling out of the driveway in just a few minutes*, I wrote to Dean.

Dad was in the car and we were backing up out of the driveway before Dean finished typing his reply. He kind of took to texting as if it were just the natural evolution of hand-written letters. *We are ready and standing by. Leopold, Zelda, and I are in Leo's car. Minnie and her team are hanging back, watching what that caravan of merfolk might be up to. They'll follow them if they all come.*

I looked up from the screen to watch my surroundings as

we headed toward the interstate. Autumn was humming and dragging her rubber-case tablet out of the backpack she'd brought with her.

We knew the merfolk couldn't swim all the way there. There was a humanmade pond on campus, but it didn't connect to any other sources of water. But that didn't mean they couldn't evade detection by swimming partway. It made sense that most of the vampire forces would hang back to keep an eye on them.

Besides, it helped having fewer of them around to hamper Dean and me. And Zelda. She seemed to be on our side, willing to help Dean and me keep both Autumn and Ember safe. If possible.

But then there was the problem of Leopold. Still, one vampire was manageable.

So long as it didn't turn into a whole bunch of them. Which it probably would, knowing that Ember likely had something up her sleeve.

Leaning sideways, I attempted to get a better look at whatever Ember was typing.

Dad was singing some song from his heyday and tapping the steering wheel with both hands. When we finally made it through town and safely pulled onto the interstate, he spared a glance around the car. "This isn't much of a sister road trip," he said. "Girls, get off your devices for two minutes."

Ember flipped her phone over screen-down on her lap just as I'd adjusted myself in an ideal position to get a peek at some of what she was writing.

"Autumn," said Dad.

I looked over and realized she'd put in her earbuds. I poked her arm and Autumn sighed, pulling just one earbud out of her ear. "Daddy, I'm watching something."

I checked her screen. An episode of *My Little Pony* was frozen. At least she wasn't texting faery soldiers about some plan I wasn't aware of.

After Thanksgiving dinner, Zelda, Dean, Mr. Goodwin, and

I had hung out on the front porch, Mr. Goodwin doing his best to keep out of sight since Noelle had asked him to leave after Ember had had her little dramatic episode.

"Minnie wanted to know if you changed your mind," said Mr. Goodwin, sliding out from behind a post and standing in front of some bushes that wrapped around the porch. In his 1940s attire, complete with slicked-back hair and a slightly receding hairline at the corners of his temples, he looked like a total sleaze—but one who, through means shady or otherwise questionable, must have done pretty well for himself. Though I knew it was just through Minnie's generosity. For a second, I felt sorry for Ember having this guy as her dad.

"About what?" I asked, peering around the post.

"Maybe you want to stir things up today." He shrugged. "Seems easier than moving the whole coven a few hours away for some show-down miles and miles from the consummate lands."

Dean tossed his coin in the air. "As soon as we get Ember to surrender, we'll be facing our own allies. Better to get the faefolk away from these trees." He waved in the direction of the woods behind the house. "We can fight well anywhere—at night especially. Remove the fishfolk from their water and the faefolk from their forest, and we've got the advantage."

Mr. Goodwin frowned. "There's a pond on the campus."

"One that's surrounded entirely with no little rivers for the merfolk to escape through." I glanced inside. Dad was talking to Mr. Slowe, Mom and Noelle with Mrs. Slowe. I knew in the living room Calder and Ember were sitting with Journey. Every few seconds, the figure of Cascade moving across the front door some distance away came into sight. I moved slightly to get out of lip-reading angle. "We've got this covered. We're not ruining today."

"The faefolk agreed to leave the holiday alone," Zelda added, moving to sit on the railing. She had a good line of sight for anything that went on inside the living room now. "And they agreed to the campus plan, which makes me think we still have to be on our toes."

"Of course." Dean tossed his coin one last time and caught it in his palm, tucking it inside his pocket without looking at it. "We're ready.

I'd asked Mom and Dad if it was all right if I stopped by the Hornes' home for their supposed big feast for a bit. The evening had gone rather uneventfully after that. As uneventful as practicing flame and time pause powers in the backyard while vampires were sucking on blood inside could be considered.

"Let's play a road trip game," said Dad, clicking the Jeep into cruise control.

"Dad, some of us are a bit old for—"

"I Spy!" said Autumn, ripping the other earbud out of her ear.

Sighing, I slipped back into my seat, watching the world go by under the overcast sky. Every time we passed by a store, a swarm of vehicles spilled out of the parking lot, other cars getting rather creative with where they were parked. Thankfully, the Interstate itself wasn't too bad. There was just a lot of shopper overflow onto the exit ramps.

"I spy with my little eye... something black!" Dad said.

"That sign!" guessed Autumn, pointing to a billboard warning about the hazards of vaping use.

"Nope," said Dad.

"The dashboard of the Jeep!" guessed Autumn again.

"Nope," answered Dad.

"Black Friday?" said Ember softly, hardly moving other than to shift her gaze out the window to the chaos below.

"Ding ding ding," said Dad.

"*Dad*," Autumn chastised. "That's not how it's played."

I checked my phone screen again. Paisley had sent a message about going shopping with her family. I wished her luck. I'd never thought I'd miss the stress of Black Friday shopping. It seemed so normal now... so quaint.

Several rounds of "I Spy" later, Autumn had taken her earbuds out of her tablet and was blasting a YouTube mix of Disney princess songs. Ember was sleeping—or at least pretending to—and didn't look at her phone once. I kept Dean updated, and they claimed they were shortly behind me, though I couldn't see their vehicle anywhere behind Noelle's. Despite my head growing a bit dizzy with the idea of the weekend ahead, I remembered to check in with Lyric. My text wishing her a happy Thanksgiving had been read but never responded to.

I knew she was still upset about Raelynn, but Dean had promised me his family would keep Lyric away from the house. She was most likely still just wallowing in her pain.

I wondered if she and Raelynn would make up if—*when*—I won this.

Because my wish—if I managed to make it—was going to make Raelynn and Devam human again.

"Daddy, I have to pee." Autumn shut off the screen on her tablet.

"Okay, pumpkin," said Dad. He took his eyes off the road to fiddle with the GPS on his mounted phone screen. "Oh, perfect timing. There's a rest stop just a few minutes ahead."

"But I have to pee *now*," said Autumn.

"Hey." I nudged her. "We're getting there. Settle down."

She fidgeted in her seat, yanking at the shoulder seatbelt to keep it away from her. "I can't help it. Daddy!"

"We're almost there." Dad readjusted the rearview mirror. "Ivy, why don't you text your mom and make sure they know about the change of plans?" I did as bidden, and Dad kept talking. "We can get some gas and snacks and drinks while we're at it."

"Don't mention drinks!" whined Autumn.

"Okay, okay," muttered Dad. "Did you go before we left?"

"*Yes!*" Autumn sighed.

Ember took in a sharp breath and rustled. Maybe she really

had been asleep the whole time. She stretched her arms overhead, twisting back and forth in her seat.

Autumn's legs bounced as we finally got off the exit ramp leading to the rest stop. Then she screamed.

The car swerved slightly and Dad's tone grew dark. "Autumn, you can't shout like that when I'm driving—"

Autumn growled. I was still trying to figure out why Autumn was so upset when I *felt* it.

Liquid sped into my thigh and I let out a little yelp, too. "*Autumn*! Did you wet yourself?"

Dad moaned.

"I did... *not*!" Autumn screamed, her face twisted in discomfort. "It was her!" She pointed to Ember.

Ember didn't reply, but a sense of iciness lingered in the air between my seat and Ember's. Her right arm on the armrest in the door flashed blue—or purple-ish even—for a moment.

How had she...? Had she humiliated my sister by coating her seat with ice that melted?

"Autumn, just stop." Dad massaged his temples as we pulled into the parking lot in front of the main rest stop building.

Autumn's hand grew bright green on the seat between us, a little pink flower growing out of her palm.

"Autumn—" I started.

The flower bloomed and out from inside glowed a green ball of light.

With a screech, Autumn flung her hand toward Ember and the little green light—a figure clear now to me within, its wings fluttering—went flying on a strong gust of wind toward Ember.

But the wind was so strong, the whole car went rushing forward.

CHAPTER EIGHTEEN

EMBER

Screaming. From my throat. From Easton's. Even from Ivy's behind me, but not from Autumn. Not anymore.

The Jeep went from rolling slowly into a parking spot to flying up over the curb, across the sidewalk—on which no one was walking, thank goodness—and right up onto the grass.

Then there was the prickling pinch at my cheek, at my mouth. A little wooden spear no bigger than a toothpick but wielded with the madness of a warrior's spike as the insect-like thing flew all around my face.

Unbuckling my seatbelt, I screamed again and unlocked the door, diving outside into the patch of grass as Easton slammed on the brakes.

"Ember!" he shouted, followed by a string of expletives the likes of which I'd never heard from him before.

I hit the ground hard, my ankle bending painfully as I tumbled onto my side. Then I thought to flick out my right hand and shoot some ice to make my landing a little softer. All that came out was this crinkly slush that splattered beneath me as my thigh slammed into the ground, soaking my side.

But I didn't have time to rest. Grunting, I rolled up onto my knees, sore but thankfully not in as much pain as I'd expected. But the green light divebombed at me, sliding across my cheek like a slice of a needle-thin knife.

I swatted at it. Mom's car slammed on its brakes in an empty parking spot a few feet away. Before the light could get any closer, I threw out my right arm in a broad arc, summoning the ice to my palm once more.

The ice encased the flittering green light like a snowball and it froze in the air, then fell to the ground.

Yes! Apparently, it was easier to defeat these flittering faery bugs than I'd thought.

"Ember, don't move. You might have broken something," said Easton. He was telling me not to move while he was tugging on my arm, helping me get to my feet.

"Ember!" Mom was there, too, at my side. "What happened?!" she asked Easton.

"I'm fine, I'm fine," I said, getting to my feet and brushing my pants off. "I just... I thought it was a wasp."

"A wasp?" Mom asked, incredulous. "So you *jumped* out of a moving vehicle?"

Easton looked over his shoulder. "Why would there be a wasp in November...?" A wave of panic washed over him. "Girls?"

I looked around. Autumn and Ivy were nowhere to be found.

"You need to get the car back into the lot," Mom said. She looked over her shoulder. The rest stop wasn't too crowded—it wasn't like it had a Black Friday sale. But there were other cars and a few curious faces looking over from an open van a few spots away.

"But the girls—"

"Had to go to the bathroom," I reminded him, the words slipping through clenched teeth.

"Easton, just... move the car. Before someone calls the police." Mom massaged her temples.

"Are you okay, Ember?" Glory hovered next to Mom's

running car a few feet behind her. "Easton, where are the girls?"

My palms grew sweaty. "I'll go check on them."

"Ember—" started Mom.

I did my best to smile. It must not have been entirely convincing since Mom leaned back away from me.

"I need to clean up anyway," I said, gesturing to my damp outfit. I found my soaked coat and sunglasses on the ground beside the open passenger's side door. Slipping the glasses into my pants pocket, I retrieved my phone from the floor of the car as I tossed the coat back inside.

My ankle just a tiny bit sore, I limped a little every time I favored the wrong leg. I heard something from Glory as I shuffled to the rest stop building about how it was strange that her girls would just run into the bathroom after an accident like that. Maybe one day they'd get a clue that something weird was going on here, but I supposed with Orin's mind control influence, that wasn't going to happen any time soon.

My head swam as I reached for the outer door, my ankle buckling under me as I stepped inside and leaned against a brick wall. A mural of a forest scene took up the entirety of wall across from me, laughing at me with small details like a unicorn just beyond the trees in an open meadow, a cluster of faeries peering around a bush.

Well, at least unicorns were still a myth. Unless someone proved to me otherwise.

My limbs shaking just a bit as I forced myself to breathe deeper, I brought my phone up to my face. My screen was cracked, a line vertically down the middle that broke off into little hairline fractures in every direction. I must have stepped on it in my haste to get out of the vehicle. The chuckle that escaped from my throat was more resigned than I ought to have felt at just eighteen years of life. I brought up Calder's contact and dialed him, bringing the phone screen to my ear. The jagged lines pinched just a little.

"Ember," he said by way of greeting. My name was tense on his tongue.

"Calder, I'm in trouble. Maybe." I switched the phone to my left hand and gripped my right one into a fist, letting it grow colder as my eyes roamed the open building and landed on the doors to the restrooms. Overhead, a rare autumn sliver of midday sunlight soaked through an atrium ceiling, bathing the open building—the fantasy mural—in light. There was a mermaid, complete with seashell bra, swimming far off in a little pond in the corner of the art.

"What happened?" he asked. "We're a mile away from the rest stop." I didn't ask how he knew; we'd agreed to install a Find-My-Friend app on each other's phones in anticipation of this weekend. And the plan had always been to hang back a bit and head in the same direction.

I explained about Autumn's little response to my lame impromptu attack, but give me a break, I couldn't bring myself to *hurt* her. Though she was making that more and more tempting every day.

"And I don't know where they are," I finished. "I guessed the bathroom if Autumn really had to go, but I'm..." My voice dropped. "I'm scared to check, Calder. I thought I could handle this, but two against one—and if Autumn's faeries are *with her...*"

"Almost there," said Calder. His voice seemed firm enough to give me the strength to stand a bit straighter against the wall. He'd always seemed like such a coward when he'd been on the opposite side, but now... Now it was like being with me, working toward *our* goal, not his mom's, was enough to give him the confidence he needed.

"Did you shake them?" I asked. We'd known the vampires were probably watching the RV camp. They'd been spotted parked down the road several miles for days now.

I could hear Calder shifting in his seat. "No," he answered. "But they've just sent one car after us. If all goes to plan, Mom is leading the rest of the RV motorcade around the long way after a bit. It'll buy us some time—most of the bloodsuckers should follow them instead. It's not like it's a surprise we're on our way—right there," he said speaking to someone else, whichever merperson was driving.

An insect—probably all in my head—worked its way up my spine as the door to the women's restroom opened and out stepped a stranger. Just a normal, short-haired person who didn't look at home in the 1940s or like they'd been part of the cast of a Tinkerbell meet-and-greet. They only spared a quick glance at me as they made their way out the front door.

"If they're following you that closely, though," I said once the open space was empty again, "they have to know what's in your truck bed."

"It's covered with a tarp," Calder said succinctly. "But sure, they can guess."

A familiar voice shouted, "There!" It sounded like Llyr, but I couldn't say for sure. I hadn't spent a lot of time getting to know Calder's family in the brief week I'd been their champion.

It'd been less than a week. Less than a week and here we were, trying to put an end to it. But we'd hoped it'd be on campus, near water, not here, not just off the interstate...

"Calder, we need to get out of here," I said. "The truck bed isn't going to save us. And there are witnesses and—"

"Hang the witnesses," snapped Calder. "A car just pulled out—most of the people are at the gas station, and that's some distance away. Ember, we can take them."

"*No*," I said. "There's Mom and Easton and his first wife." My voice caught in my throat.

I blinked.

There was something *moving* on that mural. I was sure of it. Unless I... I put my cold right hand to my forehead. I *was* feeling dizzy.

"Ember?" Calder's voice called through the phone.

The door to the restroom burst open and Autumn came running out, the hand dryer still audible as the door shut behind her. While my eyes darted that way, something fluttered out of the corner of my vision and I snapped back to find a flurry of green lights soaring out from where they'd hidden among the mural—straight at me.

My phone cluttered to the floor as a startled cry escaped my lips and my hand shot out in front of me. I drew on whatever inner power I had to stop them and out sputtered that crackling, purple slush, its pattern like flames encased in ice.

With a flash of green light and a roar that echoed out throughout the open atrium, a tiny fluttering object grew big, a faery queen complete with flower crown and earth-tone animal-skin-like attire growing from palm-sized to towering, lithe human-sized in a flash. She spun and slashed at my crackling purple icy flames, a stick sharpened to the point of deadliness headed straight for my head.

I ducked, my weak ankle caving somewhat as I rolled and slipped on my own crackling slush that still rained down from above.

"Champion versus champion," I gritted out, forcing myself to stand taller despite the pain shooting through my ankle. I slashed out again with my right hand, this time shaping that fiery purple ice into my own version of a sword, slamming the long edge of it against the woman's torso and sending her back against the brick wall. "Or was that ever really a rule?" I shouted, my voice carrying throughout the atrium. It echoed. "Or something you faefolk just made up in some plot to ensure your own victory?"

With a pop, Orin appeared out of a orb of green light, landing next to Autumn, who just stood back smugly, her arms crossed as she watched her little green orbs float about the open building. Sunlight danced over them, making them twinkle brighter.

"No, it's a rule," said Orin, scratching the side of his nose. He was wearing something more akin to what the other faefolk seemed to favor—not that I'd had enough time to really study the lot of them. His tunic was patched together, earth-tone, animalistic, almost like the dirt itself had been poured over his shape and caked into some sort of outfit. There was a round pouch dangling from his leafy belt, and in his brown-and-green hair were woven some vines and bits of ivory bellflowers. "But more for the final blow," he said, grinning. "Submission from one champion to the other and all that."

"You lousy little cheats."

The door behind me shot open, and I turned. Glory, walking at an average gait, was being practically mowed over by Calder, Llyr, and Bay.

Tears welled behind my eyes at the sight of them, my muscles growing weak.

"Ember!" shouted Calder. He and his mermen counterparts slid in position on either side of me.

"What is going on here?"

I'd almost forgotten about Glory.

"Autumn? What are you...? Where's your sister? Orin?" Glory's brow went from tense to slack, her eyes almost going glassy. "Orin, you're here." She smiled as she looked over at the tall faery woman I'd slammed into the brick wall. "And who's this? Your mother?"

The woman rubbed the back of her palm across her lips as she stood straight. "Titania," she offered, nodding.

Glory seemed to lack energy as she sleepily ambled past me. Bay flinched, his fists clenched at this side, but I put a hand on his arm to stop him. She was Autumn's mom, no skin off my nose if these people did something to her—but I didn't fight dirty like the Sheppard sisters did.

"Autumn, I wanted to check on you," she said dreamily, taking her daughter's hand. "Your dad said you wet yourself in the car."

Autumn's face darkened, a deep shade of red. "I did *not!*" Her eyes found me. "*She* did it and tried to make me seem like a little kid!"

I shrugged. "You *are* a kid. Now act like one and surrender." I stood straighter, the jolt of pain from my ankle searing up my leg as I dug my heels into the linoleum floor. "Or I make no promises about *anyone's* safety."

Okay, I *could* at least pretend to fight dirty like them.

But Ivy was nowhere in sight. If I could rough Autumn up just a little, get her to surrender—

My mind went hazy and I stumbled, my ankle collapsing in a sudden unbearable amount of pain. Calder swooped in and caught me, his heady scent of salt and lake water offering me comfort.

I needed to fight Autumn—

My head grew dizzy.

I wasn't going to hurt her if it could be avoided, but I needed to try—

My brain went blank.

I can't fight Autumn, I thought to myself. *I won't fight back*, I thought again.

And with a sudden clarity as my gaze rested on Glory's daydream-induced-like expression, I realized the same warm, fuzzy nothingness was spreading out from my brain down to every fiber of my limbs.

A flash of a memory.

"Hi!" said Autumn outside my bedroom door. "Happy Thanksgiving. You can't hurt me, okay? Do not hurt me. Ever. And forget I asked you this until you want to hurt me."

With a sudden realization that for one moment fought through the fogginess, I realized it was already too late for me, that I'd lost this fight the day before it had even truly begun.

CHAPTER NINETEEN

IVY

I kept pacing at the back entrance to the rest stop, staring over at the gas station a short distance away and taking stock of the number of people around, the potential for witnesses. It wasn't like the college campus would be entirely empty, either, even if most of the students had gone home for Thanksgiving break. There we'd find the humanmade lake to tempt the merfolk into laying it all out. But if we could take care of things here before they even had any advantage whatsoever...

If they'd even be tempted into showing their faces here, since the most water they could find was in the bathroom.

I checked my phone again. Autumn had insisted on drying her own pants in the bathroom without any witnesses. After that little show in the car, I knew she wasn't alone. That the faeries were a blooming blossom away. She was probably fine.

My phone buzzed with a text from Dean. *They're pulling into the rest stop.*

So they had been tempted. Calder along with Bay and Llyr at least. A small number of their army, but that was fine. They didn't have the advantage of water here.

The sun poked out from behind some clouds overhead and I squinted, holding a hand up to block the light.

Okay, we didn't have the advantage of darkness, either.

But Autumn would do well in the sunlight. She didn't even need to be near any plant life to get stronger. She could create her own.

Since no one was in hearing range, I jammed my finger on Dean's profile in my contacts and dialed it.

He picked up on the first ring. "Ivy?"

"Where are the rest of them?" I asked. I didn't have to explain who.

"Ernesto is keeping me abreast. The RVs have started up, but they're taking the back roads. We have little doubt as to where they're headed, but if the bulk of the coven can head them off before they dive into any water—"

"There won't be a reason for them to dive into any water until they get to the campus." I realized I'd been pacing so long, I was starting to feel a burn in my calf muscles. "Corral them in one location without any rivers for them to escape into, and we're set."

"Assuming there aren't any uncovered drainage gates connecting your manmade lake to the sewers," said Leopold, speaking up. Dean must have had me on speaker. The unpleasant vampire half-grunted, half-chuckled. "I could see the fishfolk slithering down in the sewers like crocodiles with their fins between their—well, they wouldn't have legs, would they?"

"Leo," admonished Zelda softly.

I didn't comment.

"We stick to the plan," added Dean after a beat. "We don't need to attack the lot of them, just Ember. The faeries are going to take care of the bed and breakfast. Once we arrive, it's just a matter of brainwashing Ember into submission and then... We'll deal with what comes next." *Fighting our allies.* "The mermen are there now. Pulling up in the truck and jumping out. Headed inside the building. Your folks are out here in the parking lot. Didn't even seem to notice them despite the hack job they did on parking in a rush. Oh, but where's your ma? Hmm."

"*Hmm?*" I repeated. "What do you mean, where's my mom?" With a jolt, a shattering-glass-like sound echoed out from behind me and I ran back to the back entrance, my pacing having taken me some distance away. Autumn and Ember were going at it.

I swore under my breath.

Dean kept talking. "Ivy, that tarp we mentioned on the back of the truck. When they parked so quickly, there was, I think, a splash—"

But I was already running inside, opening the exterior door with my free hand.

I stilled between the two layers of doors.

Mom had just walked in, her face going from confused and alarmed to almost... peaceful as she walked right between Autumn with Orin at her side. Ember stood across from them with the mermen. There was a spattering of green orbs all around, too.

Ember was outnumbered, and the only advantage she might have had right now was taking my mom hostage. But if I went in there now and really drove home the fact that she was losing this, she might be more apt to drag Mom into this... Desperate moves and all that.

"Ivy? What's going on? We're outside—"

"Stay there," I whispered harshly.

"But—"

"*Please*," I reiterated, plastering myself against the wall in the entryway, trying to stay out of sight even while I had a good shot. "Just get into position out there, a little out of sight. Autumn's got this. Ember might be surrendering and then..." I couldn't bring myself to say the rest. And then somehow we had to get my sister—my naïve, power-hungry little sister—to surrender, too.

I didn't fool myself into thinking she wouldn't try to get me to cave first. I just knew she'd *try* to avoid hurting me.

Like she was *trying* to avoid hurting Ember. Ember wasn't moving. Her face looked almost as dream-like as Mom's did in that moment.

Right. Autumn's mind control could work on Ember, even if it didn't work on vampires.

Bay bumped Llyr's arm and pointed my way. *Crap.* I'd been spotted.

Yanking open the door, I stepped inside, a rush of warm air blasting me from the air vent above.

Bay darted out, faster than he had any right to be on his human legs, swooping around Calder and Ember to reach for my mom.

My mouth open, a shout caught in my throat.

It was an endless moment before I realized I needed to fight, to do what only vampires could do.

I thought back to my practice sessions with Dean this past week. I'd successfully paused time, but not for long enough. Not in a stressful situation like this. I wasn't a natural at this like Ember had been. Closing my eyes, I summoned the venom to spread out from my heart.

Come on!

My heart thumped and slowed and then it stopped, the burning sensation making my appendages tingle.

Pause time, I ordered myself, speaking to the venom inside me.

Like someone was pulling them from my gums, my incisor teeth elongated with a pang. I hissed, and my eyes shuttered, the sunlight streaming through the glass ceiling above actually painful against my pupils. I fumbled in my coat pocket for the pair of sunglasses I'd thought to keep on my person for just such a moment, and when I slapped them over my face, I opened my eyes to find the world frozen.

A faint blue light tinged everything, like seeing my surroundings through an unpleasant camera filter. Bay with his arm out, reaching for my mom, Ember still looking forward with that dreamy look on her face, Calder trying to speak to her, his brow etched with concern. Autumn was grinning, oblivious to our mom being a target beside her, but Orin was looking straight at me.

It sent shudders down my spine.

No, I realized, he wasn't looking at me. He was looking at a ball of green light between me and my mom—one halfway to becoming a full-sized faery man. Oberon. His sharp stick spear was aimed right at Mom's head.

What the...? My feet picked up and I ran toward my mom, but it was too late, too much. The world breathed back to life and I was only halfway to her.

Oberon yanked Mom out of Bay's grasp just in time, but instead of whisking her off to safety, he held her like a hostage, the pointy end of his stick stuck just under her chin.

"Hey!" I shouted, finally getting Autumn's attention.

"Mom!" she said, her eyes bulging.

"It's all right, love," said Orin soothingly to his champion.

But it wasn't all right at all.

Titania floated across the room to join her husband, the other flying green lights hovering around them.

Ember seemed to snap out of it at that moment, watching the scene curiously, her hand glowing a wild purple color.

I looked down at my own hand. Through my sunglasses, it was difficult to tell, but my fist glowed a bright color, too.

"Come on," whispered Llyr in a quiet tone that nonetheless carried across the room. "We need to retreat."

Ember's eyes met mine as she looked at the faery-hostage scene. It wasn't *her* mom...

"Your dad is one of us!" I reminded her.

That didn't seem to do more than soften her brow just a little. So she wasn't close to him, but...

"Surrender to our champion now, mermaid!" shouted Oberon, his back to the wall. Did he even know that was *our* mom and not Ember's? There was a highly detailed mural behind him of a woods that made the faefolk fluttering in front of it look quite at home.

"Autumn?" Mom asked, a little bit of recognition clawing back onto her face. "Ivy? What's going on?" Her head moved slightly and the skin on her chin pricked the sharp stick, the blood almost impossible to see but likewise impossible for me to ignore as its tangy copper scent hit the air. My fangs demanded to be let free, my mouth gaping open in a snarl as another monstrous predator sound rumbled from my throat.

"Ivy?" called Dean's tinny voice from across the room. I'd dropped my phone near the door at some point.

"It's all right, Mrs. Sheppard," said Orin, holding both hands up in the air. "We're just rehearsing a play. You're standing in for Viola. Let us rehearse and don't say a word."

Mom's eyes went cloudy once more.

I glared at him, and he shrugged. "Okay, so maybe I'm crossing my Shakespearean references here." As if that were my point of contention.

Autumn tugged on Orin's shirt, her eyes pleading, but he totally, utterly ignored her.

Jerk.

Before I could blink, a bolt of ice shot out toward Orin, clipping him in the side. He'd turned his back to Ember in his bid to calm my mom down, and now she was hurling the might of her power from her right hand straight at him.

"Hey!" he snapped, having the audacity to look angry, his lip curling as he turned her way. "No hurting the referee—"

But now I'd sent my own power flying, shocked to find it as mutated as Ember's. Crinkling, melting, crystalizing ice, a slush of fire running the length of crackling frost sputtering from my fingertips. I hit Orin square in the abdomen.

He shrieked and floated upward just slightly, his hands moving as a rush of wind appeared out of nowhere, almost knocking me down. Before I could blink, the wind grew stronger, moving upward, smashing up against the glass ceiling overhead.

And shattering it.

Everyone screamed.

I paused time again, focusing.

Glass shards dangled precariously several feet above our heads.

Grunting, determined to make it all last, I stumbled forward. The front doors to the rest stop were open, Ember and Calder heading outside with Bay and Llyr at their heels. Dean, Zelda, and Leopold headed inside, each group turned to face one another mid-stride as they went in opposite directions. But rather than worrying about them right now...

I ran to push Autumn's wide-eyed form as far as my muscles would muster, the venom burning through my body in that moment so strongly, I could swear it was singeing my nostrils. Her frozen body slid back, just out of range of the glass. Then I ran toward Mom, snapping Oberon's stick spear in two with a strength I hadn't known I was capable of, before snatching Mom and dragging her into the nearby men's bathroom.

Then, as if I needed to let out a deep breath, I gasped, and the warped color seeped out of the air, the world returning to motion. I couldn't see it in here, but the sound of those glass shards falling against the linoleum floor was like a hail of daggers clattering to the ground all at once.

"Ivy?" asked Mom after she let out a startled cry. "What was that? Where's...?" She looked around and spotted the urinals. "We're in the men's bathroom."

"Stay here!" I shouted at her, praying she'd do as I said, and I ran back into the foyer.

"Ivy!" called Dean from by the door.

With a crackle across the air, I found myself whisked over to the door as well, a penetrating wind slapping against my cheek. Dean had used his own time pause, and since I hadn't been holding on to him when it had started, he'd moved me without me realizing, just as I'd moved my mom and Autumn.

I checked on my sister. Her face was reddening and she pounded a fist against the mural behind her. "What did you do?" she shouted, looking up at Orin hovering a few feet above her.

Good. Let her get angry at them. Let them try to smooth *that* away.

Orin popped back to full size. "Calm down, love. He wasn't *really* going to hurt her, were you, Dad?"

Oberon brushed some glass pieces off his arm, ignoring Orin entirely. Orin frowned.

"The merfolk are getting away," snapped Leopold, drawing my attention back to the other matter at hand.

"Fine. Let's deal with that before they take my dad hostage to boot."

I ran outside with them, Dean holding on to my wrist and bringing us in and out of time pauses to make our steps cover greater distance in less time. When I wasn't the one who needed to control the thing, it went smoothly, my focus wholly determined to get to Ember before they started up that truck and—

Bay was in the truck's driver's seat, but Calder and Llyr were ripping a tarp covering the back of the pickup truck aside. Ember, donning her white classic sunglasses, was crawling in through the opening they'd made, her legs snapped together, mid-transformation, her pants shredding around her. Her sweater had been flung off somewhere, revealing she was wearing a red vintage-style swimsuit top.

Dean gasped as the world moved back to life, his shaky hand on my wrist a subtle but undeniable sign he was straining himself with the few time pauses he'd executed in a row.

Ember finished her dive, the tips of her red fins poking out before her soaked head popped up beside it, Calder and Llyr heaving themselves up and into the bed of the truck with a mighty splash.

I chuckled dryly. I actually chuckled as the truck started up.

"They brought water along in the truck?" I asked out loud.

Zelda hissed beside me, Leopold letting out a roar as he put his all into shoulder-ramming the side of the truck.

But as his shoulder came into contact with the metal, Ember let out a shrieking wail, a sound at first so frightening that I found it penetrating into my bones. It was an echo of a sound I'd heard before.

A song. Beautiful beneath the waters, frightening above it. A siren call.

I found myself stepping toward the bed of the truck, a hand extended toward Ember.

"Ivy!" shouted Dean, wrapping his arms around me and pulling me back. "Don't listen to her."

Calder and Llyr exchanged a look and joined in Ember's chorus, their baritone and tenor voices adding a shrieking sour melody to Ember's soprano.

This wasn't just a siren call. It was a *death shriek*.

Zelda yelled and covered her ears as Leo stumbled and punched wildly, his fist aiming for Llyr's torso up above him in the truck but missing by yards.

The pickup truck squealed backward and then took off, heading toward the on-ramp leading to the interstate.

I stared numbly, my ears ringing from the aftermath of the song in the air. And then I laughed. Three merfolk sat upright in the back of a pickup truck headed to the interstate, water splashing out behind it like leaking oil.

"Ivy?"

I turned to find Dad, huffing as if he'd just jogged over. His brow wrinkled, his posture stooped, he stared off at the truck before it blended into interstate traffic, his mouth agape. "Did Ember just jump in the back of that pickup?"

A strange guffaw escaped my lips. Stumbling, my limbs weak from something—the time pause, the siren call—I leaned against Dean's chest and just laughed like I'd lost my marbles.

CHAPTER TWENTY

EMBER

The water in the truck bed, so cold when I'd first dived into it, now wrapped around me from head to fin like a warm, welcoming cocoon.

"Ember?" Calder's voice was clear, though changed to its underwater sonorous melody.

I opened my eyes just as the water splashed above us, the truck descending, probably taking us down an off-ramp. I couldn't say for sure. Calder, Llyr, and I hadn't sat up since we'd put the rest stop behind us.

My pants, still attached by the waistband though shredded down the legs, contained my phone in a pocket. It vibrated. The battered thing was hanging on for dear life. I should have invested in a waterproof case.

I couldn't bring myself to reach into the pocket and pull it out, to see if it still worked. It was too comfortable lying here on my back, floating in just a couple of feet of water. The only thing that would make this moment any better would be if I had room to stretch, to swim, to burrow into the depths of a body of water and its sweet, salty promise.

"She doesn't look good," said another voice. Not Calder. Had to be Llyr, but I was drifting, drifting into my cozy water cocoon.

"Ember?" A hand brushed against my cheek, my arm. "Her cuts. From the faery weapons? I think they might be poisoned."

I drifted off, the adrenaline of the battle long, long behind me.

———

Taking in a deep breath, I was met with the potent perfume of fresh roses.

I sat up in a flash, finding an unfamiliar, fluffy white comforter decorated in baroque floral patterns. A damp towel folded on my forehead fell to my lap. I was wearing a fluffy pink robe. I blushed when I looked between the layers to find nothing beneath.

"Oh, thank goodness," said a familiar but unexpected voice. "You seem better." Mom got up from a stiff-looking sofa chair adorned with a floral pattern similar to the one on the comforter.

"Mom?" I asked, aghast. I looked around. I was in a strange, cozy bedroom. On the nightstand beside me was a single red rose in a vase of water, my phone beside the vase. There was a couple of drops of water pearled on the cracked screen. "Where am I? How did I...?"

Mom put the back of her hand against my forehead. "Much better." She smiled and sat at the edge of the bed. "Mrs. Meriwether was right. All you needed was a little home remedy and your fever would be gone in an instant."

She gestured at a tray on another empty chair. There was a bowl there and a little bottle that held in it a vibrantly green liquid.

I'd never seen a "remedy" sold in "hello, I'm poison" colors.

"Mom," I said, "back up." My phone vibrated and I looked over to see nothing more than a garbled screen. Great. "I was at the rest stop—"

"And you had a little accident with the wasp. Jumping out

of the moving vehicle." Mom sighed. "And Easton driving up over the curb! Thank goodness that didn't happen on the road."

"And where are we now?" I looked around. Homely bedroom. Alien place.

"Our bed and breakfast for the weekend," she said. "Calder called to let us know he brought you here from the rest stop. Really, Ember, this is a family trip and I wish you'd have stuck with your family rather than meeting up with your boyfriend at the rest stop. I don't care if he's here to visit the school, too." Mom's pinched brows grew laxer as her eyes took on a far-off quality. "I was so mad, but... But you weren't feeling well and I was going to call an ambulance and..." She grew quiet, a dreamy expression growing over her face.

"And?"

"And Mrs. Meriwether said you'd be right as rain with her homemade remedy. Mrs. Meriwether is the proprietor of the bed and breakfast, you see. She and her husband." All tension slipped out of Mom's shoulders as she crossed one leg over the other and gripped her hands across her knee.

"And you... Gave me a homemade remedy a stranger offered up?"

Mom didn't even flinch.

With a start, I flung aside the bedding and jumped to my feet, wincing as my weight came down too hard on my injured ankle. I rolled up the robe sleeve and inspected my arm. There was a scratch, but it didn't look any worse than a cat scratch. No infection or purple marks on the skin, nothing that might have made the mermen panic over me.

Unless I'd actually been given the antidote.

How? *Why?*

"Ember, you have to rest."

"Where is everyone?" I asked. "The owners of this place, are they—"

"Easton went with Glory and Autumn and Ivy to check out the campus," Mom said, blinking rapidly as she reached to touch my arm. I stiffened instinctively and rolled my sleeve down. "Mrs. Meriwether offered to make the two of us dinner."

Jumping out of her grasp, I hobbled to the door. "And Calder?" Without my phone, there was no way to contact him.

"Calder's helping Mrs. Meriwether out," Mom said, like that wasn't at all strange. "His friends went ahead to join the rest of his family for the campus tour, he said."

That didn't sound right at all.

I twisted the door handle. It shook beneath my hand but didn't budge. I shook it harder. "We're locked in!"

"So no one will disturb us, of course." Mom stood up softly and wrapped an arm around me, trying to guide me back to the bed. My eyes darted around the room, looking for some confirmation that the owners of this bed and breakfast were members of the mind-controlling faefolk. There was that alien-looking "remedy." Evidence or not, though, what else could it be?

A small, open doorway led to a bathroom barely large enough to hold the clawfoot tub, the toilet, and the sink contained therein. Across the side of the tub hung my soaked clothes, the shredded pants, the water-logged sweater, and the retro red tank top swimsuit piece I'd ordered earlier in the week that I'd been wearing beneath my clothes this morning.

Mom didn't let me linger, directing me back to the bed. "You rest, dear. And then when Autumn and Ivy get back, we can... We can..." Mom's eyes went glazy again.

I bolted upright again, my ankle be damned. "Mom, can I use your phone?"

Mom blinked, the more familiar look of disappointment— her lips pulled tight into a slight grimace—sliding back onto her face. "I don't know what you did to break your phone like that. First your car, now your phone. Money doesn't grow on trees, honey."

"It smashed when I jumped out of the car," I said bluntly. "And my car breaking down—wasn't my fault."

Mom frowned. "I know. Though I don't know *how* vines managed to grow up like that around the engine."

"*Mom*," I barked. "Your phone. Please."

Mom shook her head. "Who do you need to call?"

"Calder."

"I told you Calder is downstairs, honey. Mrs. Meriwether told him to help with the food and he jumped to it like a polite boy does." She pushed me backward and grabbed for the comforter. "You rest some more until dinner," she said softly. "You can see him then."

Groaning, I let her think I'd relented and rolled over, facing my back toward her.

Those had to be faeries downstairs, and somehow they'd used their powers on Calder before he'd been able to fight back. He must not have known what to do after I'd passed out. Our plan *had* been to head for the bed and breakfast, waiting for the rest of the merfolk to show and get close enough to the humanmade lake edging up against the inn and the campus. So that was what he'd done. Maybe he'd asked his mom for advice. I wondered where the merfolk were now.

Just as Mom sat back down in her sofa chair, I flung the comforter back and padded over to the nearest window. Wincing at my sore ankle, I flung back the pale yellow curtains that had hung perfectly symmetrically until I'd messed with them.

"Ember, you shouldn't be walking around so much."

I gazed out at the late afternoon, the sun almost nearing the horizon. The backyard of the bed and breakfast housed a garden in hibernation, scores of white Styrofoam covers hiding what was most likely a spring and summertime array of plants. Mostly roses, if I'd have to guess. Arches over two ends of the garden were covered in withering brown vines from top to bottom.

And a number of yards behind the garden, as expected when we'd done our research, was a rocky slope that led straight to the contained body of water connected to the nearby college campus.

"Rest until dinner," Mom said softly.

I relented—for now—hobbling all the way back to the bed. I'd need my strength, and if my enemies were actually giving me this chance to recover it, then I'd take what I could get.

CHAPTER TWENTY-ONE

IVY

"Founded in 1878, Fowles University was actually originally located in a much smaller building seventeen miles south of here," continued the student giving us a tour. He'd introduced himself as Trung, an overly perky, broad-shouldered black-haired junior wearing red pajama pants and a gray "Fowles U" sweatshirt. "We moved here in 1907, after the city funded the creation of Lake Fowles." He gestured to the expansive body of water behind us, and my family turned as if on cue to take it in. It covered the entire shore of the campus and then some into the town beyond, the other side of it visible from where we stood, lining a park and fishing grounds. The fish, too, were added artificially, Trung had explained at one point. "981,685 gallons of water were pumped direct from Lake Michigan into trucks and brought here over a process that took months, even after the basin was dug. We Fowlies call it 'Fowl Lake' sometimes—not to be confused with 'Foul' with a 'u.' But because of the ducks that often rest here throughout the year." He gestured again, but there weren't currently any birds at all.

He didn't let us think over that point for too long.

"This way," he said, clapping his hands together. He clearly had a schedule to keep. I couldn't blame him. The air was getting noticeably colder—more appropriate for November—as the sun started descending on the horizon.

"Daddy, what's that?" Autumn called beside me as we passed a giant boulder conspicuously bolted in place at the edge of the lake.

Mom visibly reddened as Dad chuckled.

"That, little girl, is the Kissing Boulder," explained Trung. "Couples who vow to be together forever say a pledge and kiss in front of the boulder."

"Gross." Autumn's face wrinkled in the direction of the craggy boulder.

Trung leaned in. "Legend says the couple will be together for the rest of their lives."

"As friends, I guess," Mom muttered under her breath. That told me all I needed to know about the effectiveness of *that* superstition.

Dad didn't seem to have heard her; he was pretending to have a hard time catching up to Autumn, who was tugging him toward the nearest building. It was a dorm, what Trung had promised to be the last stop on the tour.

Tomorrow I'd have interviews—we'd been expecting them today, but we'd arrived just a little too late after the fiasco at the rest stop—and would be welcome to hang out with the few students who'd stayed behind over Thanksgiving break afterward.

I had a feeling I'd be slipping away to deal with some supernatural crises long before I'd ever have a shot at kissing anyone at the eyesore of a boulder.

"So what did you study here, Mrs. Sheppard?" Trung asked as we strolled toward the dormitory Dad and Autumn had already disappeared into.

"Ms.," Mom mumbled quietly. Then she cleared her throat. "History."

"Ah, my friend is a history major. She's planning to get her master's and become a professor."

The corner of Mom's lips quirked. "How nice."

"Mom works in retail," I blurted out.

Trung's face fell just a little, but he quickly recovered, plastering his broad smile into place. "We do boast a ninety-six percent placement rate."

"Of the people who actually respond to the placement survey," I added.

Mom's brow arched and she stopped just as we reached the glass doors.

"I had kids," she said. "And was a stay-at-home mom for a while."

I shrugged. "Just saying. You spent an awful lot on a degree from here that hasn't really come in handy."

"It's come in..." Mom's face was turning a bit purple, the crow's feet lining her eyes deepening for a moment before she took a deep breath.

A sting of guilt pierced through me. I'd meant to criticize the idea of having to go to college at all, not the way Mom's life had ended up. There was nothing *wrong* with how her life had ended up. It was just... Why did I even have to care about college right now? I didn't know if I'd make it that long.

"Your father is very successful in his field," Mom said.

Back to square one. I *had to* go to college, apparently.

"And *he* paid back all your college loans," I pointed out. Money was tight for her. And she could have gotten her job without a degree. Add student loans on top of penny pinching, and I didn't know how I'd cope in a similar situation.

"Is that what this is about? Honey, there are scholarships. And your father and Noelle can afford—"

"To send two people at once to private colleges? They're well off, Mom, but even that's a stretch."

Mom gulped. "It's my understanding your step-sister has a number of scholarships lined up. Besides, there's always work study, like what Trung is doing here." She nodded toward him. That smile on his face, even now as he watched Mom and I argue. I didn't think even with the prospect of money hanging over my head could I ever manage to produce such a thing, particularly about this college campus. "You can get a job at my store this summer. We can commute together. Or maybe your dad can help you get your license and a car by then."

"And if not, that's just more expenses to worry about. A summer job will pay for textbooks if I'm lucky. Mom, I'm *not* getting a scholarship to a place like this. My grades aren't *that* good."

"Okay, Miss Knows-It-All, then what *is* your plan?" Mom was right. I hated it when I got backed into a corner and knew I was wrong. She may not have been right about me having to go to this fancy college, but she was right that I had to have *some* plan.

Shrugging, I jammed my hands into my pockets. "I don't know. Get a summer job, like you said, for starters."

Mom looked a bit relieved at that.

"I'm sorry," I muttered quietly. Too quietly. It was this battle, all these supernatural things going on around me. They had me on edge and I couldn't even tell my mom *why* a pricey college was really the last thing on my mind about now.

"That's all right," said Mom softly. Her throat bobbed just a bit, and I knew I'd gone too far.

In my head, I cursed the merfolk and Ember, like they'd put all those words in my mouth.

Trung's head volleyed back and forth like he was watching a tennis match. "So what are you thinking about studying, Ivy?"

I rolled my head toward him, about to tell him, "Really?" when I clamped my mouth shut. Poor Trung didn't deserve my ire.

"I actually don't know."

"There are a lot of undeclareds freshman year," he said, his brain whirling through some predetermined script he must have memorized with just the right thing to say no matter what answer he was given. He held the door open and both Mom and I stepped past him, offering him our thanks. "We have advisors to help. And while working on general requirements, there's a ninety-seven percent chance you'll find the subject that speaks the most to you."

"Wow." Autumn's voice echoed over the open common room. With a loud squish, like the air being let out of a balloon, she flung herself on a worn, pleather sofa in front of a crackling fire. My hand tingled at the sight of the flames and I tucked it into my pocket as I scanned the building for any signs of anything out of place.

"This is the common area." Trung pointed out each asset as he went along. "We have books, movie nights on our big-screen TV, games... Down the hall here is the communal kitchen for those tired of simply microwaving their meals in the dorms—or who want to save a little money and avoid the cafeteria." He seemed especially pleased at adding that last piece of information. Tying it back to my objections over the cost of the place. "And we alternate floor by gender, allowing for the large shared restrooms, though of course we respect gender identity. You pick whichever floor makes you feel the most comfortable."

Dad overheard that and opened his mouth, no doubt to make some Dad joke wisecrack about students mixing for reasons other than gender identity, but Mom shot him a look that shut him up. Trung continued undeterred. "My friend, Ashley, is here and she's expecting us on the third floor. She can give you a look at one of the girls' dorms. It's typically two to a room, though the more credits you earn, the better your chances of securing a solo room if that interests you."

He headed toward an elevator next to the hallway leading to the communal kitchen.

Mom, Dad, and Autumn hopped to it, falling into line. My feet picked up slowly, shuffling toward the group as the elevator door slid open.

But I was careful to keep an eye out on my surroundings. Even if Ember was supposedly being kept under lock and key back at the bed and breakfast.

Which Orin's parents had managed to take over during our

drive over—probably because they'd been able to fly ahead. They'd mind-controlled the real owners before we'd gotten there, I'd have to assume. Wherever those people were, they weren't still at the bed and breakfast.

That had made for an *interesting* check-in, topped off by Orin convincing my parents that there was nothing at all weird going on, that it was totally fine he was there unexpectedly, and we needed to get back to what we'd come here for.

Through the glass doors, I saw three figures standing around the Kissing Boulder.

Recognizing the shape of those hats, I felt for my own atop my head. My vampire guardians.

I fished in my pocket for my phone, but there were no messages on the screen I had to worry about. Only a continuing thread of blissful nonsense from Paisley.

"Ivy?" called Mom. They were all waiting for me in the open elevator, Trung's hand conspicuously out to keep the doors from closing.

"Coming." I shoved the phone into my pocket and hurried after them, ready to get this tour over with, my mind so very far away from this shiny, too-perfect place. With all its high percentages, its boulder of lies, the debt it promised to weigh me down with. A veneer on a much more disappointing reality.

Just like the fluttering smile I etched onto my face.

———

"You guys go ahead. I'll hitch a ride with Dean."

Dad frowned, his attention caught halfway between Autumn running off to the car and Dean leaning against the Kissing Boulder a couple dozen yards away. Zelda and Leopold stood together with their hands entwined just beyond Dean, staring down at Lake Fowles.

"You could have told me he was coming—" Dad started.

Mom jogged after Autumn now, grabbing her by the upper

arm before she ran right out into the parking lot. Autumn spun on her, her brow furrowed, clearly annoyed.

"We've been over this," I said. Dad had already been annoyed to find my vampire "boyfriend" at the rest stop, but with Ember taking off on her own, he'd had more to worry about.

I tried to placate him again. "I didn't think we'd meet up along the way—just run into each other." It was sort of the truth. I hadn't *planned* on the whole rest stop fiasco. But apparently Autumn had. I gripped my right fist so hard in my pocket that I could feel myself carving indents in my palm with my nails.

I couldn't keep letting her be in charge. I needed to talk to Dean, get the update.

Dad sighed. "All right. But don't forget you have the interviews at eleven. It's really nice of them to come in on a Saturday during a holiday weekend—"

"I know." I nodded at him. "Dad, I've got this."

He rubbed an eyebrow, his posture stooped. "Your mom was telling me you're having second thoughts about college—"

"*Dad*. Can we talk about this later?"

He looked as if I'd slapped him, but he offered a fluttering smile. "Okay, kiddo. Have fun with your friends—but I expect you back at the b&b by eight."

"*Dad*." I pointed across the campus to a towering clock that had taken up ten minutes of Trung's campus spiel. It was already 7:50.

"Nine," Dad relented.

I quirked an eyebrow.

"Ten, and that's final."

"Okay."

We stared at each other awkwardly for a little bit and I wasn't even sure why.

Things used to be so much simpler with him. And now... All I seemed to care about was keeping an essential truth from him. He was supposed to protect Autumn—heck, he was supposed to protect *me*—but I knew I was the only one who could protect my sister.

I'd always been sheltering Autumn. She'd never really know the pain of her two parents having been together and then suddenly... not one day.

Dad leaned over and gave me a hug.

I patted him awkwardly on the back, biting my trembling lip to stave away the tears that were threatening to form.

"Whatever you choose to do, I'm proud of you," he said.

"Thanks." The word escaped my throat almost on reflex as I nuzzled my cheek against his shoulder.

Then we parted, and he was gone, taking Autumn with him and Mom. Hopefully, keeping Autumn from doing anything too stupid before I got back.

The wind, colder than the air, snapped against my cheeks as I shuffled over to Dean. He caught his coin mid-toss and shoved it back into his pocket as he stood.

"I don't think you're supposed to sit on the Kissing Boulder," I said dryly.

His bright blue eyes darted over his shoulder to gaze at the monstrosity of the stone. "Is that what it is? I thought it was just some rock they forgot to clean up."

"You had to take the tour," I explained. There were no signs to indicate there was anything special about this hunk of rock. Almost like it was a secret—a "secret" that the "Fowlies" readily told to anyone even thinking about adding a few dozen grand to the university's coffers.

"Let me guess." Dean ran a hand over the back of his neck. "Kiss on the boulder and you'll be in love forever."

I tilted my head, studying it. "I actually thought it was just near it, but yeah..." I laughed. "Maybe that's why my parents got divorced. They were supposed to climb up on top of the dang thing."

Someone let out a long, deep whistle and I bristled to see Leopold sneak up on us, Zelda trailing a few feet behind. "One of those wacky superstitions, huh?" He turned to Zelda.

"What do you think, bird? Want to give it a whirl? Kiss on the rock and our love will last forever?"

It could quite literally last that long for a couple of vampires... if things never changed.

Zelda slanted slightly away from him, her fingers running through a curl of her very stiff blonde hair. "Wacky superstitions," she repeated gently.

She didn't offer to kiss him regardless.

"So," I said, eager to change the subject, "what's the update on the bulk of the merfolk?"

"They parked at the RV park at the edge of town, as expected," said Dean. "But they haven't jumped into the lake yet."

"I *wish* we could tell them to just go jump in the lake," muttered Leopold.

I ignored him. "They haven't sent anyone else after Ember and Calder?"

"No. Ernesto and Ruby are watching the bed and breakfast. The two merboys who were with Calder and Ember never left. Seems Titania has them all brainwashed inside."

Hmm. I hadn't seen any of the merfolk, unless you counted Ember, when we'd stopped by. Ember had been sleeping, recovering from just a hint of faery poison—good to know those sticks they carried were sometimes coated in that, even if it had no effect on vampires, apparently—thanks to the faery's remedy.

She'd needed Autumn to be the one to make Ember submit, she'd explained. And Autumn hadn't poisoned Ember.

Still, now she was weaker...

My palms went clammy. Tonight could be the night. How were we going to get my parents out of the way? Maybe Orin would just tell them to stay in a room and ignore all the sounds outside of it.

"So what's the plan now?" Leopold asked, crossing his arms gruffly over his chest. "I'm getting awful tired of this strictly from dixie stuff. If you ask me, our coven is big enough and getting plenty bigger..." He pounded his fist into his palm. "Let's end this."

"That's the plan. But first, we try something." As I bobbed my head toward Dean, he nodded back.

"You're still shooting ice with your flames?" Dean asked me as the chaos at the rest stop wound down. Mom and Dad spoke in raised voices with Noelle, all in a tizzy over Ember's quick and unexplained retreat with her boyfriend. Leopold was leaning on his car, updating Minnie and the other vampires on the situation with his phone, a scowl etched on his features.

"Yeah..." Making sure none of my parents were looking, I showed him my palm. The flames crackled, steam sizzling in the air as ice met flame at the fire's center.

"Hmm," said Dean. He exchanged a look with Zelda. "What if...?"

"What if what?" I asked when he didn't finish his sentence.

He looked me straight in the eye. "What if there could be a vampire mermaid?"

Now, before we went back to confront a weakened Ember, was the time to test it.

Zelda didn't miss a beat as she swept in behind me to reach for the coat I was unzipping and stepping out of.

"Trying something, huh?" asked Leopold, giving me a far too appreciative look from head to toe. Gross. I didn't care if he was as handsome as the rest of them, he was so stuck in the past, he was incredibly off-putting.

"Yeah," I answered, brushing past him and not apologizing for slamming into his side.

"Ivy," said Dean, following after me, "maybe we shouldn't do this here. A bathtub—"

"Won't give me ample room to stretch," I said.

"But you won't sink to the bottom and drown, either." Dean's neck was stiff, his muscles strained to keep himself from grabbing me and stopping me, I could tell.

"I'll stick to the shore," I said. I was at the edge of Lake Fowles right now, the quiet stillness of the water so less inviting than the living, breathing lake back home had ever been.

My heart thumped so loud in my ear, it was all I could hear. It was slowing, and as it slowed, as the burning sensation rode out from my core and down through my body, something bristled at the back of my neck. A warning. *Stay away from that water.*

But that was foolish. I wasn't a full-time vampire. And besides, there was another part of me that felt the pull like a siren's call.

Remember the water, I thought to myself, closing my eyes. *Soothing. Home.*

And then, before anyone could insist I think twice, I walked in.

It was cold at first—so cold, so heavy. There was still time to turn around and walk back. The water merely lapped at my knees now.

"Ivy, maybe this isn't going to work," said Dean. But I didn't turn around. I didn't dare look at him and get a reminder of what I was now, what I could change into.

I'd practiced being a vampire all week. But I was part-mermaid, too. I knew that better than I knew the craving of blood.

Looking down, I realized my bare legs were oozing red steam. But it didn't hurt.

I kept walking forward.

The water was nearly to my pelvis now.

"Ivy!" called Zelda. "You're going too far. We can't reach you. We can't go after you—"

"What is this ditzy dame up to?" Leopold laughed. "It'd be rich if we lost our champion without an enemy in sight." He didn't seem that worried, though.

Not that I cared if he was. In fact, I welcomed his steadiness. Dean and Zelda were the ones responsible for my wavering confidence.

I could do this.

The red steam spread out now like a fluttering flower radiating outward from my legs into the water.

I stepped forward, my legs as heavy as metric-ton weights.

The cold, biting water came up to my waist now.

The steam hissed out from my skin.

No, I told it, biting sharp incisors I hadn't even noticed into my lip, tasting the blood seeping out and pushing back against the craving that blossomed in my belly. *No*, I told myself. *You are human. You are mermaid. You are vampire. The water. The salt. The venom. The prince.* In my mind flashed Dean and then I pushed an image of him aside. Calder. As a merman. The merfolk showing me their world.

I stopped my instinct to take a deep breath—I wouldn't need it as a vampire. As a mermaid. It was only as a human.

And right now, that was the one part of me that could take a rest.

I dove underwater and crunched up my legs to my chest. I could still stand and be half out of the water, but I wouldn't right now.

The steam grew so thick in the dark water, the fuzzy mist seeping all around me as my body grew heavy, heavy, slipping down to the bottom, the too-perfect pebbles coating the water bed.

But mermaids didn't sink. Humans didn't steam. I was all three. Vampire. Mermaid. Human.

My legs snapped together under my skirt, and with a garroting buckle, my body seized up. Skin melded into skin as scales grew down my legs and my feet twisted out, becoming opaque blue fins.

I took a deep inhale of air, reaching for the gills that should have appeared at the side of my neck, surprised to find none.

Surprised to find I wasn't breathing in any way.

I gasped. My incisor dug out of my lip, and as the underwater world around me came into crisp view, I saw the red steam retreat and a little drop of blood from my lip bubble out toward the surface.

The craving hit my stomach hard.

And I knew. Even without my skin oozing steam, I knew.

I was what Minnie had tried to achieve decades ago.

I was a mermaid vampire.

And yet, in the end, Minnie would regret ever trying to create one. For basically, decades and decades later, putting the idea in my head.

Because when this was all over, there wouldn't be vampires or mermaids.

And the world would just have to go on without its hidden magic.

CHAPTER TWENTY-TWO

EMBER

How I managed to drift off after realizing the predicament I was in, I couldn't say.

Perhaps faery poison was just *that* effective.

The quiet knock on the door roused me. My eyes blinked hard. Night had fallen. That sent me upright on the bed quicker than anything. What had happened in all those hours I'd wasted fast asleep?

"You put some clothes on," said Mom. "I'll get it."

"No, just wait for me." The idea of letting her get the door made me uneasy, but I *did* need to put something on. Flinging aside the plush comforter and silky bedsheets, I scrambled for the bathroom, slipping on my mostly-dry swimsuit tank top and wrapping myself back up in the robe. I didn't have time to find some not-shredded pants because I realized Mom had opened the door.

"Thank you, dear," she said.

Mom was grabbing a tray from a figure cloaked in the darkness of the hallway, visible steam pouring off of a bowl at the center of it, the rich aroma of veggie broth headed my way.

The lightly tanned, strong hand retreated as she took the tray.

"Calder!" I practically barreled down Mom to get past her before the door shut.

"Oh!" Mom called out at the sound of ceramic sliding along the wooden breakfast tray. Since there was no splash and clatter to the ground, I could only assume she'd managed to save the meal, but at that point, I couldn't have cared less.

I grabbed Calder by the wrist, and our eyes locked.

His looked a little dazed.

"*Calder*," I said again. "What are we doing here?"

He seemed to search for an answer, perhaps a beat too long, his brow furrowing just slightly.

"*Calder*." I squeezed his wrist tighter. "Where are Bay and Llyr?" As if I could trust these faeries had just *let them* leave.

Calder blinked. Behind me, there was a soft clank of Mom putting the tray down. "Ember, you are being entirely too high-strung. There's been something off with you for weeks—I knew that birth control shot seemed like too simple a solution. Now come back to bed and let's enjoy our supper."

Not letting go of Calder's wrist, I turned to find Mom at the plush chair beside the bed with the tray on it, dipping a spoon into one of the two bowls of soup.

Calder pulled himself out of my grip and I tumbled after him into the hall before he could try to shut the door behind me. A clang of keys drew my attention to his other hand, aimed at the keyhole of the bedroom door behind me.

"Really?" I asked. "What kind of bed and breakfast locks their guests in?"

With a flutter not unlike a pesky fly and an unsettling sharp hiss somewhat like a wasp, something brushed atop my head, rustling my hair. I swatted at it and missed, but the annoying insect let out a massive *pop*. With a mild but notice-able gust of wind, a full-sized chuckling Orin materialized into existence.

He grabbed the door knob and pulled the door shut behind me, jostling me as he ripped the key from Calder's hand and turned the lock. "I imagine it has to do with keeping nosy guests out of rooms undergoing renovations or otherwise out of use." The door locked with a click and he pulled the ring of keys back, tucking it into his button-up shirt pocket. "But it suits us just fine for keeping troublemakers or *hostages* out of the way now, doesn't it?"

"Ember?" Mom's voice was muffled through the thick, wooden door.

"*You*," I croaked, pounding a fist against his shoulder. He made a face as if I hurt him, but my knuckles stung more than his shoulder probably did. "Did you take over this place? Where is everyone?"

Orin looked at Calder as if he would defend him.

Punching him again in the other shoulder, I had to shake out my sore hand.

"Ow," said Orin, cradling his most recently assaulted side. "Watch it. Harming the referee is a losing penalty—"

"I'd like to see you kick me out." My voice was shaking. "I don't buy it. You were a participant in this thing all along. Who died and made *you* referee? You were lying all along."

A snarky smile danced on the corner of his lips. "Vampires and merfolk alike abide by the rules *I* set forth—"

"You mean, *our faekind* set forth."

Both Orin and I turned to see the figure silently and skillfully ascending the stairs. Calder remained still, looking forward blankly.

The queen of the fae, managing to look somehow like a free spirited, bohemian bed and breakfast owner in her flower-pattern and earth-tone wrinkly blouse and long, ruffled skirt—a bed and breakfast owner who carried herself with the regality of an empress.

"The vampires are our sires—they took our place in this game for so long. It only makes sense they listen to us." She threaded her hands together. "And as for the merfolk, well... The ones in this game are mere children. Infants. They don't remember how it all began, how it all changed. Not exactly."

"Then you could have taken advantage of their cluelessness

and won easily." I crossed my arms and leaned back, stumbling just slightly because of the weightlessness in my head.

"We had other concerns." She gazed over my head at her son, as if I were the mere fluttering annoying fly. "A planet to enjoy. Unlike the merfolk, we have no ambitions of wiping off the other's eco terrain entirely. Our Mother Earth thrives with bounteous oceans." She bared the tips of her teeth in a movement far too reminiscent of a vampire's. "Until *your kind* made it so both bloom and water faced crises of epic proportions."

Climate change. Okay, I may have left the TV on when I was in the other room on occasion or used a few too many single-use plastics, but the way she was glaring at me, it was as if she were accusing me of singlehandedly being responsible.

"So what do you want?" I asked, my unsteady voice betraying just how effective her intimidation was on me. "If you win this thing?" I grabbed Calder by the hand, seeking comfort in the warmth of his skin, even if his mind was clearly elsewhere.

"We won't flood the world if that's what you fear." She glanced to her son, who shirked backward, stuffing both hands into his pockets. "We will save it. By ridding it of humanity."

———

Clearing my throat, I scrubbed the pot in the bed and breakfast's kitchen sink. "So... I know Autumn and Ivy aren't back yet, but is having us do the dishes really a great use of the power you hold over us?"

Calder blankly accepted the pot as I finished with it, drying it with even strokes of the rose-adorned pristine white dish towel in his hand.

"You'd prefer we keep you tied to a chair?" Orin asked. He brushed some apparent lint off his pants and then fluffed his hair in the reflection of the double-decker ovens.

"*No.*" My stomach growled as I grabbed for my mother's soup bowl. They'd taken our dinner from my mom but had kept her locked up in that room, so I'd lost my appetite. "I just... don't get what's going on here."

No one was answering my questions. Mom was in Lalaland and Calder was practically catatonic, both likely victims of the faefolk's ability to command their victims. But I still retained use of my faculties. Why had no one ordered me?

So I thought, anyway. Last time Autumn had pulled that trick on me, I hadn't exactly been aware of it.

Though that instance had come with a sort of weightless brain fog. I wasn't sure I felt that now.

My nose itched as I dunked the bowl under the sudsy water, the handknit scrubber coarse against my fingers as I swept it over the porcelain. "So what's the plan?" I tried to sound casual, but my heart was pounding, my blood growing thick in my veins. "Brainwash Easton and Glory to stay out of the way and then brainwash me into surrendering? Then it's just a matter of taking Ivy out, I guess. If you can convince Autumn to kill her sister just before killing off everyone else in the world. Does she *know* about that, by the way?"

Orin stiffened just slightly.

It seemed I had hit a sore point.

"Of course not," I continued, rinsing the bowl with clean water from the faucet. My insides were burning now, but I fought to quiet it, ignoring the sense of rising... panic? It wasn't quite panic. It was familiar, though. "Autumn may be a malleable little girl, but I think even if you promise her she'll be a princess in a kingdom of faeries, she'd change her mind when you got to the part about how *no one else* will exist to be there with her."

Calder took the bowl from me like a robot without a soul.

My head pounded and I tried to hold back tears. Biting my lip, I fought to calm my inner turmoil. I was alone. So alone. Even though Calder was right here.

"I suppose *you* won't miss anything," I continued. My bowl was next, full nearly to the brim. The soup smelled sour, the contents cold. "Print books might last a few hundred years.

And maybe you can hook up some kind of faery power to run your iPhone for all your archived movies. Though perhaps you'll always wonder just where humanity could have gone with all of that. What kind of technology—and entertainment—you'll have missed out on when the most you'll have to enjoy from then on is the dance of all the worms under your feet."

Orin's voice seemed tense. "You know, people lived without TV—without books even—for hundreds of thousands of years."

"I'm sure you'll get used to going without, too. Not like you're a huge geek or anything." It was a cheap shot, but it was the only thing I knew for sure might bother him.

My nose tickled and then my lip pinched. *Blood.* I knew that sense, that sensation. The tang of blood permeated the air—and not just from my bottom lip. *That* was what had my heart racing, more so than my panic.

But I... I wasn't a vampire champion. Anymore.

"If you're trying to get under my skin, it isn't working." Orin launched himself up on the counter beside the small pile of dirty dishes I had left and my nose wrinkled as I looked him over.

"I disagree." I dumped the contents of my uneaten soup bowl down the sink.

Taking a deep, heady breath in, I searched for the scent. There was the sense of blood in the air—but it was off somehow. Almost too... *cold.*

My muscles tensing, I plunged the bowl into the sudsy water in the second sink. "*I* think you'd miss humanity very much."

Orin shifted his head back and forth, as if weighing a decision. "I think 'very much' might be a bit twee—"

"And *I* think," I continued, "you'll miss your peace and quiet. No one need bother you now, not unless you want them to. But a world with just faeries running the show? You, the prince? You'll be expected to do all sorts of princely duties. Even though you're far, far too old to do what your parents tell you." I stared him down. "Yet that doesn't seem to have stopped you from doing exactly what they say ever since they decided to come out of whatever faery tree they've been hanging out in the past however many years."

"Just shy of a thousand," Orin muttered. "But who's counting?"

Rinsing the bowl with less care than I would have had I really cared about this task, I shoved it at my poor Calder robot and darted across the kitchen, the scent of that cold, unnatural blood guiding my way.

"Hey!" Orin snapped, but I didn't stop.

Not until I headed down a small, dark hallway from which the scent was calling me and reached a door.

"What do you think you're doing?" Orin asked. "Do you want me to *command* you to get back in there?"

"Shh." I put my finger to my lips and hesitatingly, almost fearing to, put an ear to that door.

There were slithering sounds, so quiet, I wouldn't have heard them had there been anything else but a *tick, tick, tock* of a grandfather clock near the front door.

"Stay away from there." Orin's voice was quiet, tense, his hand gentle as he wrapped it around my arm and pulled me back.

My jaw set and I broke away. "Where are your parents? The other faeries?"

His mother had been the only one I'd seen since waking up here, and she'd been conspicuously absent since "suggesting" we clean the dishes after the soup she'd made for us.

No matter how hungry I was, I was glad I hadn't eaten any, though I worried about my mom and the baby even more now.

Orin took hold of my wrist and tugged me toward the kitchen, but I dug my heels into the runner rug.

"Where are Bay and Llyr?" I asked, my voice growing louder.

"Quiet, woman." Orin slapped a hand over my lips.

I chomped down, my vampire fangs somehow in my mouth

in that moment, the taste of his blood so, so sweet—like nectar, sweeter than any other blood I'd ever tasted.

It was enough almost to make the hunger drive me mad, to give in—

But no. I was a mermaid as much as a vampire. More than a vampire. And I needed to know.

In a flash, Orin cried out and drew his hand backward, his grip on my wrist gone. My fangs retracted and I bolted for the door, turning the handle and nearly tripping down the rickety wooden stairs I hadn't expected.

A blast of cold air hit my face, and with it that strong scent of cold, cold blood.

A myriad of green lights sparkled in the otherwise dark basement, bobbing up and down.

Orin swore as he stumbled down after me.

But it was too late. As I blinked, the image before me became clearer in the pale blue light.

They were *feeding*. Faeries were feeding, sucking something —blood, essence—straight out of flesh like hummingbirds with their nectar.

On the floor were two crumpled-up bodies, discarded, ignored—mere husks of people, their skin sagging on their bones.

And in two chairs—their skin sallow, their bodies halfway to the state of the ones below them—were Bay and Llyr, rope-like vines tied around them.

The shriek that escaped my throat tore at my insides like daggers.

CHAPTER TWENTY-THREE

IVY

Breathe in, breathe out.

It was a mantra I repeated to myself. To force water —and oxygen—through the gills sprouting at my neck. Because the longer I forgot to breathe, the more the vampire venom won out, the more my limbs and tail grew heavy with a sense of sinking.

There was a delicate balance to being a vampire mermaid. In a fight against water dwellers, it would certainly be something to have a little extra advantage.

Muffled voices reached me overhead, the surface of the humanmade lake acting like a barrier, an obstacle that made sure the message was lost in translation as it reached me.

It was no doubt Dean and Zelda and Leopold, concerned that I hadn't resurfaced. That was, at least Dean and Zelda might have been concerned.

Flipping my fins, I spun around. I'd tell them what I accomplished and get back to a little more practicing...

A deafening *splash* halted my swim, a large, round rock sinking to the lake floor in a sea of disturbed water bubbles.

What the...? I didn't have time to think too hard about it. There was another heavy *splash* of a rock a few feet away from the first one.

And then I heard it, the gentle, quiet humming of a song.

Twirling around, I came face-to-face with an approaching school of merfolk, Nerida in all her haughty glory at the helm, Calder's uncle, Beck, and Bay's dad, Dathan, flanking her on either side. Of the other people my age I'd ever interacted with, only Laguna and Cascade were in sight, hovering together at one end of the large group—which consisted, I thought, of virtually every merfolk there was.

Other than Calder himself—and Bay and Llyr.

I floated in place, flipping my fins, moving my arms this way and that to hover in place, my back toward the shore and my only backup the vampires who couldn't set a toe in these waters to defend me. They must have spotted the movement —vampire eyes were keen in the night—and thrown the rocks in to warn me.

But it had been too late.

"Now this a surprise." Nerida's voice, as soft and melodious as ever beneath the water's surface, carried across the too-still waters of this humanmade lake. "How are you...?" She gestured in front of her, needing virtually no movement to stay upright and in one place, other than the subtle, gentle bobbing of her fins.

"This doesn't mean I'm on your side," I said, deciding not to even bother with pretense. My voice was strange as it left my throat—an echo of the mermaid singsong sweetness, but something darker beneath the song, like I was singing, but it was a funeral hymn.

I wasn't the only one who noticed. Tinny, melancholic gasps rung out from the merfolk swimming behind Nerida.

The venom, weakened though it may be, that traveled through my veins tensed and grew stronger.

"*What* are you?" Nerida's voice had taken on a sharp edge, though it still never achieved the gravity of my own.

My own expression as a mermaid vampire.

"Stay back," I hissed, baring my fangs. Small dribbles of venom dripped off them, impossible to miss as they sizzled on contact with the water, breaking off into steam that trailed over my head.

Beck and Dathan didn't cower, though, breaking past Nerida to head my way.

"Stop!" Nerida shouted, stilling the two angry mermen.

"Where is my son?" Dathan snarled. "And the two other young mermen sent to guard our champion?"

I wondered if my face betrayed anything. I could easily guess where they were. Autumn and Orin had used their brain-washing technique to ambush them when they'd arrived at the bed and breakfast, taking them as hostages, along with Ember and Noelle, even if I'd only seen the latter two safely secured in one of the inn's bedrooms. Because Autumn hadn't been ready to end it yet. She'd wanted to see what a college campus was like. She'd wanted to enjoy our trip for just a little while. So we'd had our few hours of pretending my family was the same as it had once been, unfractured, whole—just a family out to see a college with her vampire guards trailing a few short steps behind.

"Didn't show up when you expected them to, did they?" I quite liked the thick, gothic song of my voice now.

As Cascade drew closer, the corner of her mouth twerked up. "And we managed to take your little group by surprise, didn't we? No warning from the bloodsucking spies you sent to stop us?"

Dathan's brow furrowed and he said something to her in Spanish, gesturing for her to stay back.

Anachronistic though they may have been, the vampires all carried smartphones. They were *supposed* to get updates as soon as the merfolk caravan left their trailers and descended into Lake Fowles by the RV park we figured they'd head to. Then again, this lake was relatively small compared to the bodies of water the merfolk were used to traversing. Dean could have gotten the call since I'd descended. They moved so quickly, they could have been across the lake when I'd been flexing my muscles and getting used to all the strange sensations.

"They can follow us all they like up there," said Beck. "Once we're down here, they can't reach us."

"Please," I said. "We've done this dance before—the vampires brought their diving suits." Well, the ones trailing the merfolk mostly—not Dean and Zelda and Leopold at that very moment, but they had them in the trunk of their car, so perhaps they were on their way to put them on now.

"Oh, you mean the ones my girls here snuck out of the camp to poke holes in before we dove in?" Nerida gestured to Cascade and Laguna. Laguna laughed under the water then, the beautiful sound so abrupt, it was almost unnerving.

"Laguna's song can bust locks," Cascade said, crossing her arms over her chest. "When sung quietly and concentrated in the right direction. You never knew that because you didn't stick around long enough to find out."

"They can get more," I said, my fangs grinding against my lower teeth.

"Yes, after they run to the nearest twenty-four-hour sporting goods store and back," said Nerida. "*After* they discover the issue, of course."

She turned her head, and as if on cue, something caught my eye off in the distance. At the other end of the lake—I was right, this distance was nothing for them all to swim, a mere couple of minutes' journey from one end to the next when a merperson was so inclined—and there far off was a mass of red steam sizzling skyward.

I clenched my fist at my side. "I don't need a diving suit."

Nerida turned back to me. "Apparently not. Somehow, Minnie's created the abomination she aimed for all along."

"She had nothing to do with this." My throat was somehow parched in this watery environment. "I don't work for her."

"Oh?" Nerida's chin jutted outward. "Not getting along well with your new master?"

"Maybe I'm not just aimlessly following what some *old hag* with a glittering, beautiful face wants anymore." I made sure she got my meaning, even if she was unfathomably younger than Minnie herself. "Maybe I have to wonder what's in it for the champion in all of this if she doesn't get to wish for what *she* wants."

"Power and life as a supernatural creature not enough for you?" interjected Beck. "Or wedding a prince?"

"Gee, that's a tough one." I made a show of weighing the options with both hands. "Becoming a princess or not eradicating everyone on the planet. I can see how that'd be so hard, considering *every* girl's childhood dream. I'm good, thanks."

Nerida tittered. "You mock us, but you know that simpleton little sister of yours would easily choose being a princess."

I swallowed. A huge part of me was afraid she wasn't wrong. "Bet you wish you'd wound up with her as champion, then. Would make world destruction that much easier."

"And have you stopped to consider what the fae want should they win?" she asked.

The answer was *no*. Because whatever it was, though it couldn't be worse than what the merfolk wanted, I wasn't going to like it.

And it wouldn't matter because I wouldn't let Autumn win.

"I imagine it's something I wouldn't like." I wasn't going to rise to her bait.

Nerida tittered. "Well, let's hope you never find out." She pointed a long, spindly finger at me and with the pinch of her face and her wild, auburn hair floating every which way above her head, I was struck by her resemblance to a sea witch.

Her voice was sweet but as cruel as a goddess'. "If she won't tell us where our missing boys are, then we have no choice but to take her hostage in exchange for them."

"You can't," I said, my gothic voice suddenly less intimidating with the slight waver that worked its way through it. "Only champions can harm champions." And I knew right where theirs was.

"Who said anything about *harming* you?" She pouted.

That seemed to be cue enough. Beck and Dathan shot forward in the water like a missile, Cascade and Laguna only slightly slower as the two groups pinned me on both sides.

Behind Nerida, a mass of merfolk stirred, at least half the entire group swarming to life, a song of melancholic rage carrying on the bubbles they kicked up. The fish Trung had mentioned being transplanted into this humanmade creation scattered out of the way at the sight of the invaders in their midst. It was like the welcome under Lake Fowles, only twisted, darker—a hazy dream become a vivid nightmare.

A scream reached my throat but came out as a sort of sickly wail.

Kicking my fins, I spun in place. I couldn't take that many alone and excuse me if I didn't trust Nerida's promise that they didn't intend to harm me.

Think, I told myself as Beck swam up beside me. *There has to be something. Something you can do that they can't. You're a hybrid, for Pete's sake!*

My dress weighed me down. Though my tail was free to move beneath the skirt, the soaked cloth clung to my skin like a funeral shroud and felt like it weighed a hundred pounds.

Cascade was at my other side just as something gripped me by the fin—*hard*—my tail yanked to a stop like someone had ripped my arm out of socket.

I cried out in pain as blackness speckled the corner of my vision. Pulled back mid-swim, I tumbled backward into the mass of figures, my head slamming against a hard chest. I struggled as Dathan's arm clamped across my throat, my fins still pinched in what I found to be Laguna's greedy fingers.

Laguna opened her mouth into a wide 'o' and the first few notes of a beautiful song erupted from her throat.

But at the same time, the piercing venom in my stilled heart filtered the truth, the manipulative core of the melody. The siren call that Laguna was so good at. Vampires had at least *a little* resistance at this sort of commandeering.

"Stop!" The command came out as more of a grunt as I struggled, the strong forearm threatening to crush my larynx.

But I didn't need to breathe.

My skin tingled, a hiss erupting and followed by blood-red steam.

I was heavier than ever in Dathan's and Laguna's grips, my weightiness bringing them down with me.

Laguna's song wavered a moment as the three of us tumbled to the lakebed together.

"Lift her up!" shouted Nerida from somewhere in the masses around me.

"She's too heavy!" said Dathan.

Beck, Cascade, and a dozen more merfolk followed after us, the lakebed not so deep, our sinking not so quick as to make it so they couldn't easily catch up with us.

But that wouldn't matter.

Laguna's nails loosened in my heavy fins. Dathan's hold slipped as I rolled, too much weight for his grip.

The steam reached their gills, their underwater coughs like sick, gurgling cats.

And in that moment, I drew on what little training I'd had with Dean—but all of it. I needed it to work.

Pause time, I said to the water. *Pause time*, I said to the power in my veins.

And I did.

Everything went silent, the merfolk frozen in varied positions, all tossing up arms and recoiling back from the frozen steam.

The water was still, but I could push through it, like flapping aside a gauzy curtain with each movement of my hand. I swam around the figures, weaving through, a path available to aid in my escape like some kind of divine providence.

My heart strained to keep it all so still, but I willed it to happen, pushing through the strange sensation of immobile water, making my way.

At the edge of the lake, I saw two figures in diving suits. Two men.

Dean and Leopold?

They had run back to the car to get them. Cascade and Laguna's little stealth technique hadn't reached the vehicle not trailing their caravan.

With a sudden and intense sense of relief, I let go, an unnaturally still fish before my face scrambling back to life and swimming far, far away from me.

My skin steamed and then stopped—stopped when I focused on the venom letting go, on the need to be a mermaid more than a vampire—but knowing I would always be both.

One of the forms gurgled. Dean. Since they had no need of the air, the vampires forwent their diving masks beneath the water's surface, replacing them with simple handkerchiefs over their noses and lips. It wasn't entirely enough to keep out the red steam.

Swimming toward him, I surprised myself by collapsing straight into his outstretched arms, my heart thundering, alive, beating, despite the sickly burn of venom gripping its edges.

He held me tightly, unable to say a word, his arms the only variety of comfort he could offer.

Somehow it was enough.

And I felt like an idiot in that moment when I realized... When I realized what I felt.

It was too soon. Too impossible. But in some small way I couldn't make sense of, Dean was like coming home.

Dean claimed a portion of my heart, and if things didn't go our way, he could soon be no more.

If this was what it felt like, despite all the common sense fighting for mastery over my heart, I'd never make fun of my friends and their romantic drama again.

Because it was impossible to stop this feeling. *Impossible.*

Pulling back just slightly, I pushed the handkerchief down over his lips and pressed my own to his, tasting the death on the red steam from his skin and not even caring.

It was cold, but it made me feel warm. My head went hot as a tingling sensation filled my body, from my arms down to the tips of my wounded fins.

Leopold gurgled beside us and I drew back, my eyes meeting Dean's through his diving goggles, the strong, sturdy ice-blue gaze in no way unsettling. His diving-gloved hand went to brush aside a stray strand of hair that had escaped out of my pillbox hat, askew but still bobby-pinned to my scalp, and his fingers grazed my cheek.

Leopold made noises again, moving faster and pointing.

We both turned.

The merfolk were closer, in danger of catching up any second.

But they had all stopped—their heads all turned as one to look above them overhead.

I followed Leopold's extended pointer finger up and saw it, too.

A swarm of something—bats, swallows, butterflies—tittered and dove and trembled overhead. The sound they made was frightening, like apex predators, inescapable even beneath the muffling effect of the water's surface.

"The fae!" shouted Nerida from the mass of merfolk some yards behind us.

The merfolk braced themselves, their arms covering their heads.

And then, instead of diving down deep, the mass of fluttering creatures drew together into a giant orb-like shape—and flew at a great speed away.

Away.

In the direction of the bed and breakfast I knew Orin to be keeping an eye on, where my family would be.

Where Autumn and Ember could be at this very moment, Autumn's curiosity about the college campus placated, one taking the other out of the fight.

CHAPTER TWENTY-FOUR

EMBER

In a flash, several of the small, bobbing lights became life-size figures, pale and dark variations of bare-footed people clad in Earthy attire right out of a Shakespearean Festival. Each and every one had lips that were painted haphazardly with what, I realized, could only be blood.

My hand found my mouth before I even realized that there was a part of me deep down that was yearning for a taste of it.

"What is she doing here?" the faery king asked, his jaw set.

Orin grabbed me by the arm. "Got lost looking for the john, I venture. Sorry about that. Won't happen again." He tugged me toward the stairs.

I rolled my arm and yanked it out of his grip. "You've killed them!" I said. "You... You can't—"

"And what, pray tell, do you think the vampires do to their victims?" The soft, feminine voice came from the stairs. The faux bed-and-breakfast matron lightly trailed a hand down the staircase as she descended. "I'm afraid we haven't introduced ourselves properly. I am Titania, as you may recall. This is Oberon." She nodded toward the faery I assumed to be Orin's father. "Well?"

"Well?" I echoed. My heart was in my throat.

"What do vampires do when they—or their champion—create new vampires?"

My stomach dropped. "That's... That's different. It's not *final* like..." I pointed to the dead bodies on the floor and had to turn around, a horrible retching coming out of my throat, though there was no food to eject.

"The taking of a life is the taking of a life," said Oberon simply with no affectation. "Vampires are our children, the venom in their veins from our flowers—"

Titania held up her hand to signal to her husband to cease speaking. All of the larger faeries stepped backward, lining the walls of this cramped and dank basement. There were still small ones fluttering about the room, casting off their greenish glow. One landed on Bay's neck and I realized with a start that he was moving just slightly, breathing in and out.

"Stay away from him!" I screamed, whipping my right arm toward the little ball of light and sending a sizzling, crackling purple flame that way. It sputtered between the prone forms of Bay and Llyr, just barely missing freezing—or singeing, my power couldn't decide if it wanted to be fire or ice—Llyr's flesh.

But it sent the remaining faery lights scattering, which was all I needed.

I ran toward the two mermen, standing between them. Holding my hand out in front of me, I dared anyone to take a step closer.

I couldn't spare a moment to check to see if Llyr even still had a chance.

"It's supposed to be champion versus champion," I said.

Titania sneered. "A mere agreement between us and the merfolk of long ago. To simplify matters. There is no divine punishment if the agreement is broken."

Orin looked at his feet. I wondered how much fun he'd had as *referee* of this nonsense, always scheming to dive in as a player in the match when it suited him.

"Champion needs to defeat champion to claim victory,"

added Oberon. He licked his lips. "But that doesn't mean we cannot have a few morsels along the way."

My legs faltered, wobbly. Beneath my robe, I felt bare, exposed—my vintage swim top now dry, but nothing else at all on. The dank, cold air of the basement clung to my exposed skin.

Spinning, I quickly aimed my power at the ropes keeping the mermen tied up. Fire or ice—or some crackling purple mixture—it would be enough to snap these ties made of thick vines.

I didn't count on it working *that* well. Both Bay and Llyr tumbled forward. I rushed to try to catch them, skidding on my bare knees beneath the robe and managing to only kind of prop them up beside me on the floor. Llyr's head rolled back, his mouth popping open, a moan escaping his lips that sent some relief through me.

I didn't know either of these mermen well, but they were Calder's friends. They were flesh and blood like me—supernatural, but not born so long ago as to be disbelieved. They still hadn't lived their lives yet.

"We fae can partake of the bounties of the wood as well as the essence of the flesh," said Titania. Her brown eyes sparkled. "Do you think your mother enjoyed our stew?"

I felt sick. "What did you feed her?"

"Nothing to worry about, child. I was merely teasing you. It was an organic meal we enjoy on occasion ourselves. It does make one... rather tired, though." She gestured to Orin and then the stairs. He took a beat too long to respond, causing her eyebrow to arch. He scrambled up the stairs.

Coward.

"She should be fast asleep in her guest room bed," Titania continued. "That way she won't have to witness any of this. You'd prefer it that way, wouldn't you?"

My blood ran cold. "Witness any of what...?"

Orin returned again, pushing Calder down in front of him,

but it came across as an overly clumsy show of power, considering Calder wasn't fighting at all.

"You mustn't forget about your prince as well," said Titania. "As soon as our champion returns, you'll surrender to her or we'll eat him right in front of you." She pointed out the bodies in the corner of the basement, then the limp forms of the mermen on either side of me. "You know of what we're capable."

"Ivy won't let you do that—" I cut myself short. Ivy was on the vampires' side now. She didn't care about Calder. She probably never had.

"If all goes as planned, the champion of blood won't be present," said Titania. "Though our window may be short."

Carefully, I guided first Bay and then Llyr to the ground, resting their heads against the cold, unforgiving concrete. I couldn't protect them all. Not alone. Where in the world were the merfolk when I needed them?

Not that their powers would do any good here.

The lake. If I could somehow get everyone to move out there—to the lake behind the bed and breakfast. But *how*?

"So, child," said Titania, sauntering over toward Calder, her fingertips dancing across his shoulder, "will you surrender to our champion?"

I gritted my teeth, my incisors retreating and descending in turn. I wanted to *bite* her, to drink her, but…

"You know I can't." My voice was hoarse. Titania's fingers trailed up to Calder's throat, her nails threatening to slash across the tender flesh of his skin. "If I surrender, they're as good as dead anyway."

"Yes, child, but *you* needn't be," said Oberon.

"For how long?" There was no water around us, no hope. And even if there were, the faeries could dive beneath the water's surface. "If you win, humanity is doomed."

"We thought perhaps you'd like to have time to say your farewells," said Titania. Her words carried no emotion. She leaned on Calder's shoulder and whispered something in his ear. His face conveyed no reaction. "But very well."

Calder launched himself toward me, as lifeless as a marionette. Though there was no obvious sense of menace in him, my instinct was to recoil. I crawled backward on the cold floor, shuffling between the two mermen's nearly lifeless forms until my back slammed against something hard—and warm. A hot water tank?

I let out a cry and recoiled, pitching myself straight into what I'd been trying to avoid. Calder's outstretched arms.

Instead of offering me an embrace, they wrapped around my throat and squeezed. His eyes were lifeless.

"Cal..." I managed to say between gasping breaths. I hit his forearm once, twice, three times, shifting to try to kick him in the stomach, my body too crammed against the wall and the giant, hot water tank to do anything.

The giant, hot tank...

Stars swum in my vision as my muscles weakened. I blinked and saw the leering faces of the faeries all around me, Orin's head hung, his normal sarcastic smile gone, as he leaned back against the wall behind the stairs. I blinked again. Calder, so cold, so heartless in front of me.

No, I thought. *He's not heartless—he's anything but.*

With a strangled cry dampened by the bruising flesh at my throat, I summoned the last of my strength to tilt my right arm back, to summon the ice to my hand—the crackling, purple ice that looked like frozen flame.

Titania's evil-sorceress-like laugh echoed throughout the basement. She probably found my efforts futile, misdirected.

But I shot out the crackling ice and it struck the hot water tank behind me, the metal ripping apart in what could only be described as an explosion. The water soared out—uncomfortably hot, but not burning, the sensation enough to get Calder to react. He blinked, his hands loosening at my throat. His mouth fell open and he recoiled, dropping his grip on my skin.

Gasping for breath, I let the last of the hot water assail me as I fought for air. On some sort of instinct, my tail grew, snapping my legs together. Dunking my neck under the stream, I filtered desperately needed oxygen through the gills at my throat.

Every breath stung, the gills that hadn't even been there before as bruised as the rest of my neck.

Something hot spread out from my core—my internal bleeding like a siren call to the venom still nestled somewhere deep in my heart.

Vampires could heal faster than humans—faster than mermaids.

I flopped onto my back like a fish plucked from a pond, the surge of hot water now reduced to a shallow puddle all around me. I wasn't the only one twitching so—Bay and Llyr had been revived with the splash of water, Calder's tail having ripped through the track pants he'd had on.

Around us, little orbs of green light flittered to and fro. The human-sized faefolk lifted their feet and examined their ankles in disgust, as if the shallow basement flooding merely inconvenienced them. Orin, now halfway up the stairs, was the only one with dry feet.

A small but steady stream of cooler water filtered out through the hole, the tank trying in vain to refill with water so long as the valve remained on.

Titania and Oberon laughed, the trickle of water from the tank behind me reduced to mere background noise.

"That would be so delightfully humorous were it not such a pathetic attempt," said Titania over the rush of the water.

Breathe in, breathe out, I told myself, shifting my neck so my gills were bombarded by the continuous stream of water. *Feel the water. Feel the venom spreading out from your core.* My heartbeat thundered in my ear, growing faster and faster.

"What happened?" sputtered Calder, looking around. He shifted out of his soggy windbreaker and crawled with his forearms toward me. "Ember, what did I—?"

"Feel the venom spread!" I spoke out loud, my voice cracking, my throat so sore.

My heartbeat stopped. I blinked and opened my eyes, everything so much sharper around me. The venom reached my throat and the pain, the scratchiness, and the discomfort faded away.

I stared down at my tail, flapping my fins in the shallow water.

But I was a vampire. Yet I was still a mermaid.

"Ember, your eyes…" Calder reached me again at last and brushed a strand of soggy, platinum hair out of my brow. "They're piercing blue."

His flesh so close to my face, the blood coursing through his veins…

I bit down on my lip, only flinching slightly when the incisors broke skin, my body shivering with delight at the taste of my own cold blood.

Somehow, I was a vampire mermaid, just like Minnie had tried to create all those years ago.

I leaned into Calder's arms, and he took my cold forehead against his warm neck. He hugged me tightly to him, my robe shifting off, revealing my vintage swim top. "I'm sorry," he said. "Whatever I did—whatever they made me do—I should have been stronger. I should have stopped it." His breath hiccupped. "I'm so sorry."

In that moment, with him accepting me even with my half-dead flesh in his warm, warm arms, I could have forgiven him for anything. But that—that had been *them*. The faefolk. Not him.

There was nothing to forgive.

Leaning back and meeting his eyes, I nodded. Bay and Llyr regrouped on either side of us, coming to their senses with the aid of the moisture hanging in the air, clearly groggy still, even if finally awake.

My eyes scanned the room, and I flinched at the sight of

the corpses in the corner. Washed up against the wall, wet now, thanks to me.

The room glowed green with faefolk. Small, human-sized... We were outnumbered. And this seemed just a small sample of the horde that had descended upon us in Lake Michigan.

From the stairway glowed a different set of colors—green, but blue and red as well.

Orin had pulled that wretched orb out from somewhere—his pouch, perhaps; he'd been known to keep it near him. He stared at it and then at me, as if trying to divine some explanation for my transformation in its jewel-like surface.

"Surrender," said Titania simply. "Or die."

"I choose neither," I said, my voice a horror that made even me flinch. Calder didn't recoil, though. He squeezed my shoulder harder.

The door opened and a small, almost indecipherable hum of a familiar Disney tune filled the dank air of the basement. The light from the bed and breakfast above filtered in down the dark basement.

"Where is everyone?" Autumn. As coy and mischievous as if she'd been playing a game of hide and seek.

"Champion," said Titania, a grin on her face. "You're back. Come here." She waded through the water with no more trouble than she'd have walking on a cloud of air to reach the bottom of the steps. "Let us end this, child."

Autumn skipped down the stairway. Orin backed up, slipping the orb back into his pouch as he let his champion pass.

Titania put a hand on her shoulder and helped her descend.

Autumn's nose wrinkled before she stepped down to the bottom step. "It's wet."

"Yes," said Oberon, adding a sour, false sweetness to his voice as well. "But it's not enough to cause any harm. Come see the flopping fish we've cornered for you."

Autumn peered around Titania, and with a nod of the queen's head, a swarm of green, floating lights buzzed at the corner of the room, blocking Autumn from seeing the corpses.

Calder's nails dug into my palm.

So Autumn didn't know how ruthless the faefolk could be. And yet the fate of humanity could depend on her.

"Autumn, get away from them!" I said. But my voice was so strange—like a song, but a sad one, a mourner consumed with revenge. "They're evil!"

Titania laughed perfectly evilly then, as if to accentuate my point. But Autumn had recoiled from *me*—leaned against the faery queen's chest at the sound of my voice.

"*She* is clearly the enemy, child. And like an evil witch, she won't surrender." Titania shifted closer to Autumn's ear, but what she said carried across the trickling water's echo in the room. "She's chosen death."

"Autumn, don't listen to her—" I started. But my voice made the girl recoil up another step.

"You can't!" I screamed.

But Autumn raised her hand, and the green light from her fist shone brighter than all the others in the darkness of the room. So bright, I had to cover my sensitive, vampire eyes with my forearm, blocking out what could very well be my final moment on this Earth.

CHAPTER TWENTY-FIVE

IVY

Soaked to the bone, I pushed forward on my wobbly, newly reformed legs, my blue dress weighing me down with every step. But I hadn't exactly packed a spare along with the scuba suits in the trunk of the car.

I shivered. After sunset, the slightly off-kilter warm fall day was now dreadfully cold. I could see my breath leaking from my nose and mouth.

Human again.

Dean tore off the hood of his diving suit, exposing his pallid face to the fresh air of night.

"What happened?" Zelda ran toward us, a smartphone in her hand. "Everyone else's suits were sabotaged—"

"I know," I said, breathless. My voice was my own again. "We've got to head to the bed and breakfast. My dad, mom, and Autumn are there—"

"And Ember and her mom, too," added Dean.

"Them, too." Noelle *was* carrying my future sibling.

Leopold was mostly out of his suit, shaking himself out like a dog. "Time to end this, then?"

That hadn't been my first thought, seeing the swarm of faefolk and the school of merfolk turn toward the inn. But he was right. This was it. The end.

I'd planned for it this weekend, and yet here it was and I felt so unprepared.

Zelda dangled the car keys in her hand and led us toward the driver's side door of the mint green car.

"Thanks, doll," said Leopold, snatching the keys from her hand just as she was about to open the door. Instead, he held the door behind that one open for her, a smarmy grin on his face like he was doing her a favor.

My eyebrow furrowed. Somehow, a dull sheen coating Zelda's sparkling blue eyes made her seem more lifeless than she ought to have been. Even if she *was* undead.

But it was hardly the time to say anything. Resigned, Zelda tucked her skirt under her legs and climbed in the backseat, her lips a thin line.

Dean collected his and Leopold's discarded diving suits and went round to the back, tossing them in the trunk before heading to join Leopold in the front. He stopped to open the door next to Zelda, but I already had it open and it just seemed awkward and strange.

Still, I smiled as we got into our respective seats.

Leopold started the car up and put it in gear. The tires squealing, we peeled out of the nearly empty parking lot of Fowles University and hit the dark road, lit only at the parking lot exit by a soft amber light overhead.

Turning, my wet dress squeaking harshly against the leather seat, I watched the university disappear behind us out the back window.

I wondered if it'd be the last time I ever saw something like that—a glimpse of a future that *could* be, whether it was the one that would make me the happiest or not.

"It seemed kind of nice," said Zelda softly. "Lots of girls my age went to university."

"Not you?" I asked, turning back around. Then I felt stupid. She'd probably turned in high school like the rest of them.

"Not me," she said quietly, but loud enough in the near-silent car to be heard.

"You're too gorgeous for school, doll," said Leopold, adjusting the rearview mirror to glance at his girlfriend. "I guess—if you cleaned up some—you, too, kid."

"Excuse me?" I had to fight back the urge to shoot him with a ball of flame.

"I meant it as a compliment."

"Leopold, just shut up and drive," said Dean, coming to my defense. If I didn't know better, I would have thought he'd sighed as he leaned an elbow on the armrest and looked out into the sleepy town. "And grow up already. You've only had seventy years."

Zelda giggled. It was sweet, without the tinge of sour that infected the somewhat similar laugh from Minnie.

It was infectious.

Despite it all, I laughed, too.

"What's so funny?" Leopold asked, no sense of humor in his tone. "You all in cahoots or something?"

But we kept laughing, practically all the way. It wasn't even that funny.

Then Dean made a shushing noise, bidding us to be quiet. We stopped. Overhead, that swarm-of-bees-like sound rung out throughout the night. I stared upward and blinked. Even with my dulled human eyes, I could make out the dark form of a swarm.

"Where did they all come from?" My voice was a whisper.

"Everywhere," said Zelda quietly. "The faefolk number the greatest. They hide in flowers and trees and bushes all around the world. They just usually prefer to sleep."

Leopold made a quick turn, and my shoulder slammed into the window. "That's why it only makes sense Minnie made this deal with them. I wouldn't want an army of that size as an enemy. Not until they absolutely had to be."

Well, once the merfolk surrendered, Dean and I would

have a *very* short window of time to get Autumn to agree to surrender, too. Otherwise...

The car screeched to a stop—at least several hundred feet from the bed and breakfast. The road in front of us was cluttered with other sleek vehicles, many of which were vintage—particularly Minnie's shiny, red number closest to the inn up ahead.

"Oh, here's your phone," said Zelda, grabbing the phone from where she must have tossed it on the seat beside her before my experiment in the lake.

"Thanks."

I hesitated as Leopold cut the engine. I could call the police—the army. It'd be international news if all these creatures were proven to exist, but this was high stakes. If a teenager couldn't sit back and just rely on the adults who were supposed to know what to do to *do something* in a situation like this...

"Ive?" asked Dean, shortening my already short name into something soft and sweet.

I looked up and smiled at him just as my phone buzzed with a message. The screen showed the first few lines of a message from Paisley, checking in.

So how was the college visit? It feels like I haven't seen you in forever, she wrote. *Lyric and—*

I opened the message, needing to know Lyric was safe, that she hadn't gone after her ex and gotten even more tangled up in this.

Leopold let out a cry like he was cheering on a football team. "I smell blood!" He opened the car door and was out, his form getting lost somewhere in the darkness toward the bed and breakfast.

His words added an extra layer of panic to my already tingling limbs.

"Ivy?" asked Zelda, but I was focused on the message.

Lyric and I are having a sleepover after all that shopping. Alan is driving us nuts. He hid in my closet for forty minutes and popped out to

"It's fine," I said, placing the phone down on the seat
between Zelda and me. No one else was going to save us. I
looked up and met Zelda's and Dean's eyes in turn. "Let's do
this."

———

Though Leopold marched ahead of us like a rock star about to
descend upon a packed amphitheater, Dean gestured silently
for Zelda and me to take a more stealthy approach.

The plan *was* to betray what the vampires wanted in the
end, anyway. They'd have to be thankful they got a second
chance at an actual life—and be content with it.

We ducked behind vehicles, aiming for a set of bushes
framing the house. At the back of the house was a garden,
largely in hibernation now that it was late fall. More bushes
framed the garden in a long green rectangle, but white foam
domes lined the walkways inside the garden, the overhead trel-
lises bare.

The windows of the bed and breakfast were dimly lit, not
betraying much of anything inside. The sole light came from
the direction of what I thought might be the kitchen.

Muffled voices carried through the glass, the unmistakable
smug tone of Leopold announcing his presence. Zelda winced
beside me, but since there were pretty much all the vampires
in there, he was in no danger.

We were still in an alliance with the faefolk.

"Over there," whispered Dean, pointing past the sleeping
garden. The yard naturally dipped into a rock-covered gentle
slope, which led straight to Lake Fowles.

"The merfolk," I said, aghast.

The perfect place for them to march right up and to the

house, and yet everyone was just waiting inside, no one bothering to guard the inn from behind.

A small gust of wind brushed past, and I shivered, almost as if just now remembering I was still soaked to the bone.

Without a word, Dean stood straighter, unbuttoning his suit coat and draping it around my shoulders.

"Thanks," I whispered. The coat shouldn't have had any scent—dead flesh didn't soak up musk and sweetness—but as I inhaled, there was something in the air that soothed me.

"So what's the plan?" asked Zelda. "We should let them know they're leaving themselves wide open."

Dean put a finger to his lips and pointed up. As if on cue, out from a chimney at the top of the roof swarmed a mass of green light, the noise closer to that of bats now than bees or hummingbirds.

But beyond the twittering twitch of their wings, there was something else. Like a hum. A calling.

We hadn't beaten them here. But they were retreating—coming out. Headed straight for the opening that led to Lake Fowles.

With a melodious screech, a mermaid—Laguna, I thought—flew out of the water, high enough that I could see her past the short cliff. She was singing, calling...

Dean's hand wrapped around my wrist and the world went still.

"Don't listen," he said pointedly. I looked at what was happening. Laguna was almost back under the lake's surface, other merfolk's heads bobbing beside her. Their mouths were all open in song.

The swarm of faeries was headed straight for them—to attack them, I'd thought at first, but now I wasn't so sure.

Even Zelda looked a little drowsy beside us, frozen in a single moment.

"Vampires *can* resist the siren call," explained Dean. "But they have to be alert. Ready."

I nodded. I'd done it before. I could do it again.

But then that sense of calm and ease turned to dread. "What's the plan, Dean?" I asked, knowing that for this one moment, lost in time, no one else could hear us.

Zelda would help, but there wasn't anyone else we could count on.

"Get in there. Get them to surrender." His grip tightened on mine. "If you want your life back, we have to—"

"But what kind of life will you have after? How will you adjust?"

"That doesn't matter." He looked down. "I've had my life—and then some. I've stolen from time time and again. Just make the wish, Ive." He smiled at me. "I believe in you."

Time snapped back, a sudden, ear-splitting noise bursting into a vacuum of silence.

"Come on!" I grabbed Zelda by the wrist before she could follow the fleeting faeries out into the water.

She shook her head, blinking, but stumbled after me, Dean leading the way back to the front of the house, away from this mess.

The back door burst open, familiar voices ringing out in a battle cry as a number of the vampires made their way out into the garden and the cliff's edge. But we kept moving forward, making a sharp turn to climb up the side of the front porch. No time to waste even bothering to run to the steps.

I launched myself over the railing, my feet slapping against the whitewashed wood. Dean and I helped Zelda up after us. She flung a chunk of hair over her shoulder. "This is familiar, huh, Dean? Only in reverse? Breaking in instead of busting out?"

The corner of his mouth quirked. I didn't have time to ask.

Rushing for the door, I stopped when a vehicle came to a screeching halt on the road, my instincts compelling me to look. A plain brown sedan that looked vaguely familiar parked in the middle of the road, the front doors flying open even as the car kept running.

I'd seen that car in my dad and Noelle's driveway on occasion.

Journey Slowe popped out of the driver's seat, her cousin, Dante, out from the front.

"No," I whispered under my breath.

They'd both been bitten, so they'd both known about the vampire coven. But they'd stayed away the past week or so. What were they doing here now?

"Stay back!" I shouted, running down the front steps after all.

But both just ran toward me.

So fast, I actually started backing up.

If I remembered right, Dante had been on the football team the year before.

"Ivy!" Dean's voice was somewhere close behind me, and then in one blink and another, he stood between me and the approaching linebacker, crossing his arms in front of him to block his approach.

But Journey just slipped right past them both, straight toward me.

"Where's Ember?" she shouted. "She promised to check in with me every hour—it's been hours since I've heard from her!"

Zelda was there beside us, her sputtering attempts at pausing time somehow more noticeable than Dean's, her form almost fluttering in and out as she managed to tackle my classmate. But Journey quickly turned her around, summoning some kind of strength I hadn't thought she'd had.

The blonde vampire hissed, baring her fangs at Journey, her mouth inching toward the girl's wrist.

"Stop!" I shouted, to Zelda, to Journey—to all of them. "What are you doing here?"

Journey eyed Zelda cautiously, but Zelda sealed her lips and Journey rolled off her. There were leaves stuck to her thick hair. "Ember isn't stupid. She knew you'd be planning something. She wanted us to stay out of it, but when she didn't answer my texts or calls, I texted Devam, who managed to actually talk to me for once to brag about 'putting an end to things.' What were we supposed to think?"

Dante slipped out from Dean's grasp and helped his cousin up. "Auntie's going to be pissed we took her car."

"She'll understand when we tell her Ember needed us."

The two cousins stood warily side by side, Journey a full head shorter than her cousin, but no less determined to get to the bottom of this.

"I don't know if she's okay," I admitted. Journey's lip trembled. I pointed to the bed and breakfast quickly before she could say more. "But she's in there most likely—and we need to get there *now* to stop whatever is it the faefolk have planned."

"They're *your* allies," said Journey.

"Yes, but..." I shook my head. We were wasting time. "I'll explain later. I don't want to hurt anyone, okay? I just want to make sure Autumn is safe."

I started jogging back toward the front door, and this time neither tried to stop me. Dean and Zelda moved swiftly to join me. "You two stay here!" I called over my shoulder. "Get back in your car and go—I'll try to save her. I promise."

Dante and Journey looked at one another, some kind of silent conference going on between them. But I couldn't wait to see what they decided.

I'd warned them.

I didn't want anyone to get hurt.

But my entire family was in there. And they—and the fate of the world—would have to come first.

No matter what foolish things Ember and her friends decided to do.

CHAPTER TWENTY-SIX

EMBER

A choking, gurgling sound caused my eyes to snap open. I wasn't feeling pain at all like I'd expected.

In front of me, Calder blocked the path of Autumn's winding vines. It had split off into multiple tendrils, two of which were squeezing his wrists until they started turning bright red and purple. The other tendrils slowly wound around him, heading for Bay and Llyr, for me...

"Enough!" I screamed, crawling forward to get around Calder and yank at the thin, twisting plant life choking the blood out of him.

The basement filled with the laughter of the faeries as footfalls pounded overhead. It sounded like far more than just Ivy and Autumn's parents and my mom, but I didn't have time to think about it. If it wasn't the merfolk coming down to help us, it was just another obstacle in my way.

But seeing Calder's face strain, the perspiration at his brow —I was going to fight through every single obstacle until someone took me out of this battle once and for all.

Because that little witch of a step-sister was not going to be the one to end this.

"Ember, go." Calder's words were strained between his lips as he struggled to pull his purpling arms back.

Without even breaking skin, the scent of blood was in the air, and it was enough. The hunger hit my throat and my incisors were on the vines gripping his arms, ripping, tearing them apart as if they were the sweetest flesh.

Autumn screamed from over by the staircase, and the vines went still, small pieces still dangling from Calder's forearms as he took a deep breath. Something sweet tingled from the corner of my mouth. I put a finger there and pulled it back. It was blue, but thick and burning on my flesh—like venom.

The venom that had created the vampires maybe.

Titania spoke. "Continue, child! They're weakened."

My gaze sought the traitorous Orin, but he was gone. The door leading overhead was open, only the faintest, dimmest light tricking down from the house above.

A lock of Autumn's hair hung wildly over her face as she stared at her green, glowing hand. Had me biting the vine she'd been controlling somehow hurt her directly?

Titania seemed irritated, and she brushed past Autumn, nearly toppling her over, charging up the stairs. "Come!" she shouted, louder than necessary if speaking to whoever it was up the stairs. "Attack and let this be the end of it!"

With a sputter, Autumn held her hands out, a burst of wind flattening us back against the wall for a moment until it stopped. She stared at her hands again.

Calder gripped me against his side, his chin resting atop my head as Bay and Llyr tossed aside the vestiges of the vines they'd been fighting and flanked us as closely as possible once more.

"We're sitting ducks," murmured Llyr, the words clearly painful between breaths.

"Grow legs and get out of here?" asked Bay. His voice was quiet, almost murmured as he took in the remaining faeries all around us. Paling, he caught sight of the bed and breakfast owners' corpses. "We need help. The others should be in the lake by now. It's not that far."

"No," I said, patting Calder's chest just once. Firmly but

lovingly. I closed my eyes and focused. I was wet, but I didn't need to have a tail just now. "We can get her to surrender now."

Oberon's eyes narrowed as he blocked the bottom of the staircase.

"Ember, what are you—"

But my heart had gone cold, quiet inside my body. My tail was splitting, my fins morphing back into feet.

The inn above shrieked with the humming and buzzing of flapping wings, and Titania reappeared at the stop of the stairs. Her hand extended downward at us, the swarm of green lights bobbing behind her.

"Ember, watch out!" cried Calder. He struggled, dragging himself on his forearms toward me. I had legs, albeit covered in scales. Feet, though they were translucent like my fins.

Flesh as cold as the undead's.

Eyes that focused in on the darkness and saw every detail.

The swarm descended and then it froze.

Everything around me froze, the shrieking cut short and replaced with almost unbearable silence.

But I didn't hesitate. I crossed the room, splashing through the stiff puddle at my feet that felt more like gelatin beneath me.

I maneuvered past the frozen Oberon and came to Autumn's side.

Then, without even waiting to think about it, I sunk my fangs into her neck and dumped out every bit of venom I could muster.

The world snapped back partway through my feeding—if you could call it that, as I was giving her venom rather than taking her blood.

Autumn started moving and screaming after an extra beat, as if she hadn't even had time to register what was happening before she felt it.

I kept injecting.

And then the swarm descended straight at me, poking me,

swift, clean, but painful cuts crisscrossing all over my exposed flesh.

"Ember!" Calder screamed somewhere behind me.

My scaly knees buckled, but I held on.

"Surrender." My voice came out muffled through the flesh in my mouth.

Autumn's only response was to scream louder, harsher, the sound a needle in my ears.

A sharp, large stick pierced my shoulder from behind me and I gasped, my teeth pulling out of Autumn's neck with a suctioning snap.

My nails still dug into her clavicle as I fell back against the wall behind the basement staircase, whatever it was in my back bouncing against the concrete.

Oberon was behind me, his hand devoid of the long, sharp stick he'd fashioned into a weapon of sorts. But was it poisoned this time?

No matter. He wasn't important. That wasn't important. The child still in my grip was. A burning sensation pumping through my veins, I growled as I looked at Autumn and pulled her down to slink down against the step with me.

My heart was trying to beat, but it was slow, too slow. The corners of my vision were darkening.

Without meaning to, my mind became consumed with a question. *Why? Why fight for them? You stupid kid...*

Inside Autumn's mind, I saw.

Orin like a cool older brother, doing magic tricks with flowers in the palm of his hand.

Ivy, beloved sister, always gone, always busy with friends.

A new step-mom, a snooty new step-sister... A baby on the way, meaning I—Autumn—wouldn't be the youngest anymore. Dad wouldn't care as much.

Mom—Autumn's mom—always just a little sad. Too flustered. Too stressed. Always on the edge of nodding off to sleep.

I liked being alone, but I wanted friends, too. I wanted to be special.

With a start, I came back to myself, my grip on Autumn's clavicle loosening, a little trail of blood left behind by my scratch.

Of course. I'd known that, but I'd let my anger get the best of me.

This kid didn't know what she was doing.

And she was my sister.

"Autumn," I croaked, ignoring the fluttering sounds all around me, the sharp sting of little weapons on my flesh. "Autumn, they're evil. They want to kill everyone. Your family. *Our* family. Your friends. The entire world." I saw more darkness than anything now. Calder's voice was calling my name beyond the clash of little weaponized sticks. Tails whapped against the concrete. "Save us," I whispered. I pointed to the corner of the basement, where the bodies of the innocent bed and breakfast owners were. With the mermen doing their best to hold their own against the remaining faeries, you could see them now. Autumn trembled as if she'd seen a ghost. "Your family loves you..." I said. "My mom... I... love you..."

Then it went all went black, Autumn's shrill cry the last thing in my ears.

CHAPTER TWENTY-SEVEN

IVY

The sharp screech carrying over all the buzzing in the air just as I reached the open front door was familiar. It immediately kicked my big sister instincts into gear.

"Autumn!"

But waiting inside the quaintly decorated foyer of the bed and breakfast was a handful of vampires and my mom and dad —their backs against the bannister of the stairs, standing there like zombies.

Minnie put a hand on her hip, her lips pursed. "'Bout time you all got here." She nodded at Zelda. "Leopold went with Ernesto and Herbert to the back. Seems some little species of flying troublemakers can't do it without their vampire offspring after all." Her gaze turned on a form at the back of the room. Orin leaned against the bannister beside my mom and dad, their eyes dull and glazed-over. I brushed past the throng of pallid, cold flesh, sparing a quick glance at my parents to make sure they were both in one piece, and settled in front of Orin. He didn't acknowledge me. There was a faint glow of muddied light coming from the inside of a pouch at his waist and I wondered briefly if he had a little faery tucked away in there. "Where's Autumn?"

Behind me, Journey's voice carried across the open space. "Devam..."

"Raelynn Kelly?" added Dante.

So they'd come inside, after all. Just what I needed. Four students from Union instead of just my family to worry about.

And Ember's father—he was supposed to be a bloodbag, but he looked like a full-fledged vampire now to me, complete with slicked-back thinning blond hair and a pallid tone to his once-tanned skin. He kind of looked at home in the 1940s suit, only he came across as just a touch more mobster sleazy than classy like most of the others of his kind.

The rest of the vampires must have gone outside, as only the fledgling ones flanked Minnie.

Fledgling vampires—murdered humans living a half-life now.

Not that there was much I could do for Devam and Raelynn and Ember's dad besides win this thing and *make that wish*.

"Oh, my dears," crooned Minnie to Journey and Dante. Mr. Goodwin gazed at her as if she were Venus herself descended among humans. "You've come to join us on this most special of days. Welcome, welcome. I knew you'd gotten a taste for our *way of life*..."

I swallowed back bile. Lyric had been one step away from joining them. If it weren't for Paisley keeping her grounded back home, she could have been here. Could have been one of them.

"*Where is she?*" I repeated. I didn't sense Dean right behind me until his cold, comforting hand touched my shoulder through the still-damp dress.

Orin, his hands shoved into his pockets, just nodded his chin down the hall.

Another familiar scream rang out from there.

My parents—brainwashed to do what, exactly, I couldn't say, though it was just as well—didn't even flinch at the sound of their youngest child's clear pain.

But I was down the hall at the open door, my feet having carried me before I even realized, the faint trickle of water reaching my ears before something slammed into my chest.

Letting out a grunt, I tumbled backward into Dean's waiting arms, my grip on the form in front of me to keep it from barreling right past me.

"Autumn!" I just barely held on to her by the arm.

Panting visibly, she stared up at me, her brown eyes wide, her hair a frizzy mess that hung over her face.

Though a bit worse for wear, she didn't look hurt.

"Iv-Ivy..." She could barely get out the words.

"What happened?" I looked over my shoulder at the open doorway. It was dark down there, but there was that telltale green glow. Faeries still lingered, even if so many of them had been summoned outside by the siren call.

Titania burst through the doorway, Oberon on her heels and then a half dozen more human-sized faeries. All were still in their woodland attire, except for Titania, who'd changed into a hippie, Earth-child outfit she must have stolen from the bed and breakfast owner, who was... Wherever they put their brainwashed zombies besides my parents. And where were Ember and her mom?

Titania practically shoved us aside to get to Orin. "Where is it?"

Orin looked startled to be addressed. "What is 'it' exactly?"

"You know bloody well what." Her nose wrinkled. "The orb —bathed in the magic of consummate lands."

Orin fumbled and withdrew the glowing stone from the pouch at his side. It shone red and green and... Faintly, ever so faintly, it shone blue.

But the blue was fading.

Titania cursed and swirled on us—on Autumn specifically. "It has to be *you*!" she shouted. "You're our champion. Finish her off! Now! While she's weak!"

Finish her... off?

Journey let out a cry and barreled toward us. Zelda caught her by the arm and held her back.

She seemed to understand what that meant before I had. *Ember.*

Titania regarded Journey as if she'd just spotted a new toy. "Well, what have we here?"

Minnie stepped forward. "A potential new vampire—after we win, of course."

The two women stared one another down, the sound of water splashing, of grunting and fighting, and the soft hum of song carried into the house from the backyard.

"We're moments away from eliminating the merfolk," said Titania, her head stiff and erect like a true regal queen. "So I would say the chances of this new child becoming one of yours is pretty slim."

"Oh?" asked Minnie.

"I wouldn't join either of you if my life depended on it!" barked Journey, yanking her arm from Zelda's grip. Dante and Devam saddled up beside her, Devam studying his ex-girlfriend with a frown.

"I wasn't asking you to *join* us, my sweet," said Titania.

"Ivy," Autumn whispered, tugging on the front of my wrinkly dress. "Ivy, they killed the people who owned this place—they drank them dry."

Something went cold inside me.

"And Ember—she's hurt. I—"

I patted her and nudged her toward Dean, who took Autumn by the shoulder as the faery queen bickered with the vampire queen and the sound of a battle carried on the air outside.

"It won't matter how many vampires you add to your coven or when," said Titania brusquely. "You have never been anything but an offshoot of our kind. We made you. We will unmake you."

"Then we don't have to wait to change them, do we?"

sneered Minnie. "What good is this alliance with threats like that?"

With a hiss that broke through the sounds of bickering, Raelynn turned everyone's heads as she latched on to Dante's neck, drinking blood, Ember's dad letting out a second hiss and drinking Dante's blood from the poor guy's other side.

Journey screamed and started pelting Raelynn with her fists, but Devam pounced on her in a flash, pulling her back and sinking his teeth into her own flesh.

A string of explicatives shot through my brain. Minnie was laughing. "Save them!" I said to Dean.

Zelda moved quicker, flitting in and out of time to get between the freshly turned vampires and their prey.

"Ive." Dean grabbed me by the hand and the world went still, silent. "If they turn, we can save them with our wish. But now's the time—get the other girls to surrender."

Autumn blinked. She *blinked in the frozen world*, and I realized Dean gripped her by the shoulder. She went to take a step forward, but he yanked her back. "Stay still," Dean said, the muscles on his brow starting to become a bit strained. "You won't stay with us if I stop touching you."

Right. With time stopped, he'd bought Journey and Dante some time anyway.

"Autumn," I said, doing my best to lean on one knee while Dean still held on to my wrist. I could pause time, too, but if we broke apart, I'd lose this one moment—lose this chance. "Autumn, please. Tell me you surrender to me."

Autumn's eyes watered, a single tear spilling down her cheek before she reached out and grabbed me.

"I'm sorry," she croaked, burying her face against my shoulder. "I'm sorry. I didn't understand—"

"I know," I whispered soothingly, patting her back with my free hand. "I know. But you need to surrender to me."

"I—" She stepped back, her legs wobbly, her mouth dry. Her jaw hung open, her mouth wide.

I turned around to see what she was looking at. Two of the

faeries stood on either side of our parents, their sharpened stick weapons snug against their larynxes.

How could I have missed that?

"I can't," said Autumn, and she stepped sideways, slipping from Dean's grasp.

He swore and then the world popped back into movement, Autumn not hesitating a moment as she ran toward our parents.

"Come, child," said Titania, dragging her by the arm just before Autumn could reach Mom and Dad. "If you don't want us to drain them dry next, you'll finish what we've started for you." She smiled, but there was something sharp and primal in her beautiful eyes.

"Ivy." Dean tilted his head toward the open door.

Ember first then.

We bolted for the door just as Calder stepped up it, naked from the waist down, a lifeless Ember in his arms. Dark red stained her shoulder. Her robe slung half open, a swimsuit top on her upper half and... red fish scales on her legs.

Calder took one look at me and swallowed. He looked sickly.

I tried to fight the sudden squeeze of my heart at the scent of dried blood in the air, stronger here than the blood being drained behind me.

Remembering Journey and Dante, I turned. Both were slumped on the ground, Zelda blocking the fledgling vampires from reaching them again, but she shook her head when I caught her eye, the droop of her features telling me all.

Too late for them, too.

"Darling, bring our last guest here, would you?" Titania spoke to Orin, whom I'd almost forgotten about. "Give that to your father."

It seemed like he'd almost forgotten where he was, too. Startled, he put the orb in Oberon's outstretched hand and then in a flash, he disappeared, replaced by a flying green light that soared up over the banister and up the staircase.

Titania shoved Autumn toward Dean, Calder, Ember, and me, but she didn't let go.

"Finish it, child," she said. She pointed to our parents and then to the stairs. "Or we'll finish every last member of your family, down to the twins forming inside your step-mother's womb."

Twins? I shook my head. Now wasn't the time.

Autumn flushed and coughed, looking up at me sheepishly. "Just... Just surrender," she said.

"Autumn, I can't," I whispered under my hushed breath. Outside, the siren call grew louder, a vibrant chorus, and I—along with Autumn and the faeries nearby—trembled. Like a light switch, I turned on as much venom as I could, sending it rippling through my veins, to stop the song from impacting me.

"*Now!*" shouted Titania, a growl on her voice. "Now, you foolish child—" She grabbed a pointed stick from the nearest faery and forced Autumn's free hand to wrap around it. "Kill them! You don't need them—you'll have us! And your new siblings. I'll allow them to live with us."

Autumn sobbed.

I hissed, the blood in the air so much stronger now, so tempting.

Autumn raised the pointed weapon with a shaky arm, so weak that even if she hit me with it, it probably wouldn't do more than nudge at my skin.

Minnie hissed behind Titania. "The traitorous champion of water first," she snapped. "Or our truce is off once and for all while you still need us." She laughed. "The siren call isn't so tempting to our kind."

"That's because you're *dead* and forget what it is to be a living being," snapped Titania. But she conceded, dragging Autumn closer to Ember in Calder's arms. She scoffed at the merman prince. "Do you plan on putting up a fight? You'll have to drop your princess first."

"No," said Calder softly.

"But I do!" said Ember, popping to life in Calder's arms. Her eyes were sparkling, piercing blue, her upper incisors protruding long and sharp from between her open lips. No one had time to react before her hand grabbed my wrist and time paused around us.

CHAPTER TWENTY-EIGHT

EMBER

Ivy's jaw was stuck in an open position as I slid out of Calder's arms and put my feet on the ground. He held tightly to my elbow as we'd planned, so he was the only other thing moving inside this frozen bubble of time.

He looked around. "Whoa. No wonder they're so fast."

I smiled at him. Though a number of the faefolk still fought Bay and Llyr in the basement, most were gone—summoned by Calder's family's siren call outside.

None had thought to brainwash my boyfriend again.

Despite her shock, Ivy adjusted to the change fairly quickly. "Autumn said you were..."

I tilted my head toward my shoulder. "I got impaled there with the faery king's weapon. But he missed any vital spots—probably because the champion is the one who's supposed to *end* me. The stick must not have been poisoned for the same reason. Once they were all distracted, it was just a matter of summoning my vampire venom to heal it."

Ivy took in my form, red scales on my legs, vintage red-and-white swimsuit top. "You're a mermaid vampire," she said.

"A vampire mermaid." As I said the words, Calder squeezed my elbow. I didn't know why the order mattered, but it did.

"Yeah, well, I learned a few tricks in that vein, too." Ivy

frowned. "Autumn's still in this. I won't even think of surrendering." She gazed over her shoulder at her parents, still hostages. Up the stairs somewhere, Orin was supposed to be fetching my own mother.

The venom tingled in my veins. I felt stronger this way than I ever had—with the scales against my flesh, the venom in my blood. But still, I'd never held a time pause this long.

"I don't want to hurt her," I said, injecting strength into the raspy quality of my voice. "But, Ivy, if she wins, all of humanity is doomed."

Ivy's brows drew close together. "And if you win?" She stared at Calder. "The world is also doomed."

"No," said Calder and I at the same time. I locked eyes with him over my shoulder and nodded.

"The other merfolk think that's what I'll wish for if I win— but instead, I'll wish for the vampires to come back to life. To be human again. It's the only way to make up for what I've done."

Ivy's jaw dropped. "How can I trust you?"

My eyes narrowed. "I could ask you the same thing. If vampires win—"

"They've never wished for the eradication of humanity," she said, her tone sharp. "But even so... Dean and I—we plan to wish for the same thing. No more supernatural creatures. No vampires. No mermaids. No faeries."

"That's not the same thing at all." Calder's face grew red, his lips curling. "You just hate me—"

"Excuse me?" said Ivy. "This isn't about *you*, and oh, yeah, while you brought it up, you mean I might hate you because you tricked me into trying to destroy the world?"

"You—" But Calder froze, his hand hovering just below my elbow. He'd never time paused before, so he didn't have the practice of holding on to the person causing it.

I used the opportunity to grab Ivy by both wrists. "Listen to me," I said. "I can't wish for that. I don't want to flood the world—believe me, you know I love my mom and Journey and… and… Well, I just wouldn't. But I can't take Calder's identity away from him."

Ivy scoffed. "Why not? I'd say they deserve it. They all do —and frankly, that's getting off light. If we don't make the wish fast after you and Autumn surrender, the faeries and merfolk will *cease to exist*, remember?"

She had a point. Then a wave of nausea flooded my senses. "Maybe the faefolk can disappear. They murdered the owners of this place. Or did you already know that?"

Judging by the way Ivy's pale face went paler, I'd say not. But she nodded, biting her lip. Maybe Autumn had told her. I didn't think she'd have agreed to it.

"Fine," she said. "Not like Orin proved much of a friend anyway. We get Autumn to surrender first, take out the faeries, and then you surrender to me so I can save your boyfriend's butt by letting him be human before all of merfolk kind fades away."

"No." I squeezed her hand. I was right about this. "My way brings Raelynn and Devam back to their human life—*and* lets Calder and his family stay their true selves."

"Don't forget about Journey and Dante." Ivy jutted her chin down the hall.

"Journey and…?"

Growing disoriented, I focused my sharp vampire eyes down the hall, past the frozen forms to Zelda on the ground beside…

Beside Journey and Dante. What were they *doing* here? I'd told them to stay away.

Shrieking, I felt the venom fluctuating within my system, my grip on this piece of space and time slipping. "*You* did this!" I shouted. "You turned my friends into hostages!"

"No," started Ivy. "It wasn't me or Dean. Or even Zelda. I tried to—"

But the world slipped back into action, my grip on the time pause gone entirely.

"Ember." Calder caught me as I stumbled backward, Ivy's

wrists slipping from my grip. For a second there, probably from Ivy's mind, I'd had flashes of Minnie ordering vampires to attack my friends—ordering *my father to*. He'd turned too.

Hissing, I bolted down the hallway before anyone else could react and launched myself at my dad, whom I hadn't even realized was there until that moment. Of course he was, the besotted idiot.

We fell to the ground. Dad squirmed beneath me, trying to shove me off, then laughed. "Ember?" He stared up at my lips, at the incisors I knew protruded out of my mouth at the moment. "Thanks, kid, but you're too late. I've asked you to turn me for weeks now, but Minnie finally obliged."

"You turned new vampires before you got here?" Orin was halfway down the stairs, my unconscious or sleeping mother slung over his shoulder like a sack of potatoes.

I hissed up at him.

Minnie's annoying, mouse-like laugh echoed from down the hallway. "Only within the past few hours. Surely, you can understand we needed all the help we could get." She approached Journey and Dante on the floor, ignoring Zelda as she leaned down with careful movements so as not to disturb her tight skirt. She ran a palm over both of their foreheads. "Yes, they're coming along nicely. Should be ready once this is all done." She smiled broadly at Raelynn and Devam as she stood back up. "The first of a new generation to inject some beauty and freshness to a sadly stale coven." Flicking her head, she pulled out a hair pin and let her red hair go tumbling down. "I'm growing quite bored of 1940s." She sashayed past Zelda, likely purposely slamming into her.

She stared down at my dad on the floor and her nose wrinkled before turning up in the air. "He was an exception. Too old for my tastes, really, but I thought having him turned might add a little more chaos to the mix."

Grinding my teeth, I shoved those incisors back into my gums and squeezed my scaled legs together. Even without a new source of water, they merged quickly into a tail and I used those powerful muscles to slam against Dad's chest, knocking him harder to the ground and making him pass out. He'd have a bruise for a bit, but he was a vampire now—he could heal once he got used to it.

"This changes nothing," I said. "You're still going to pay for everything."

Minnie's eyes widened. "Well. This is fascinating."

The others in the room hadn't taken this little segue lying down as there was a scream back from near the basement, Dean grabbing hold of a faery's stick with both hands as Ivy slipped around the tall, handsome faery woman to drag her zombie-like mother away.

"Enough!" shouted Titania. "Now." She nodded to the other faery with his stick pointed at Easton's throat.

"Daddy!" Autumn screamed as the stick drew blood.

Before it could do more than pierce the flesh, the scent of fresh blood mingled with the coppery tinge already in the air and venom flooded my system, snapping my tail back into scaled legs once more.

With a flickering jump in and out of paused time, I was at Easton's side at the same time Ivy was, her own teeth bared. Without conferring with one another, the two of us took hold of the faery and yanked, pulling him back from Easton and tossing him to the wall opposite.

Ivy glanced at me as we both stood there, heaving for breath, our incisors halfway out so we shouldn't have even *needed* breath. But neither of us was a whole vampire at present.

"Thanks," she said quietly.

Dean was corralling Ivy's parents toward Journey and Dante on the floor. Zelda stood, ready to join Dean in guarding all four of them.

I didn't understand why she was helping.

Maybe... Maybe Ivy was serious about her quest to turn them all human. And she'd gotten Dean's and Zelda's consent.

Neither had ever felt close enough to me to share such a desire, a desire to be human again.

I'd only been one of them superficially.

But I strangely found that I didn't even care.

"They're my family, too," I said softly.

"Ember!" Calder was at my side once more.

Ivy took a few wary steps back toward Dean and Zelda, her eyes trained almost entirely on Autumn still held tightly by the arm by Titania, Oberon flanking her on the other side to keep her from escaping.

"Autumn," said Ivy softly. "They're safe. Just please surrender—"

Titania laughed and gestured to her son at the foot of the stairs.

Her son with my mom tossed over her shoulder, Minnie leaning casually in the corner of the room just a few feet from him.

"Her family is still in danger," she said. "Whatever she thinks of her second mother, there are the twins at stake."

Twins? Right. Titania had said that before, as if she had some kind of faery ultrasound sense.

Did Mom *know* that?

My blood ran cold, the venom retreating, the fire in my heart replaced with panic. Mom and the baby—*babies*.

I started to move toward them.

"Wait," said Calder in my ear. "It's not safe."

He nodded toward Raelynn and Devam, who'd somehow slipped into perfect positions along my path toward Orin, more to protect Minnie than anything.

Ready to jump in if I so much as put a foot in that direction.

Letting out a great sigh, Orin lowered himself enough to let my mom roll onto the stairs behind me. "She's barely pregnant, but she's heavier than she looks." He stood, stretching and rolling his shoulders.

"Now, Autumn!" Titania shrieked. "Attack!"

I slipped my hand out of Calder's and summoned that venom. I struggled to hold on to it, but I managed to flicker and pop in and out of existence, slipping past Raelynn and then Devam and then—

Minnie jumped into the same piece of frozen time I occupied, her hand at my throat, lifting me up into the air with one arm with a strength I hadn't realized she'd possessed.

Her ruby red smile was somehow both enticing and frightening at the same time.

"Clever little trick you've got there, still relying on vampire venom to skip through time."

I wanted to respond, but I couldn't breathe. I shouldn't have needed to, but my body wasn't flooded enough with the venom to keep me going. My grip on time space flickered, losing it entirely, but with a loud crack, we snapped back into the stillness, Minnie clearly the one in charge now.

I sputtered, my scaled legs struggling to fuse together to give me that tail strength. This was the second time I'd been choked in too short a while, and my body didn't seem to know what to do, my gills struggling to form from my flesh beneath the cold, cold iciness of her fingers, the gills finding no water to breathe even when they did manage to flap.

"Surrender to my champion," Minnie hissed.

I struggled to shake my head.

"Your father is mine," she added.

My face must have betrayed nothing. Nothing regarding that. But I did look... As the edges of my vision went black, I looked for my loved ones, the only one I could see just then unconscious on the stairs behind a frozen Orin.

Minnie's bright blue eyes flicked to my mother's prone body.

She dropped me and the chaos around me flickered back to life.

Minnie was already behind Orin, a vicious hiss escaping her lips, her teeth sinking into my mother's throat.

CHAPTER TWENTY-NINE

IVY

"Stop! I'll surrender!" Autumn screamed. I was halfway toward Noelle—Ember was hovering one second, falling back to her feet the next, as if she'd been leaping up in the air or someone had held her up.

And then the bloodcurdling sound of Minnie's hiss brought my gaze to the stairs, where she was biting Noelle's neck.

"Foolish child, the vampire is on our side—get the champion of water now and she'll stop!" Titania was shaking Autumn as my sister struggled to be free of her.

With a silent apology toward Ember and my step-mom, I shifted direction toward Autumn. She'd said the words. Maybe she needed to say them *to* me.

This was the best chance we had.

"Autumn, say it again—to me!" I turned.

But Ember was already in front of my sister, popping back into existence after cheating her way to her.

"Autumn!" she said, grabbing her by the shoulders. She looked about to cry herself.

"Wait—" I started.

"I surrender to you," said Autumn, soft enough that I shouldn't have been able to hear her, but with my venomous heart pumping so hard, my sight so focused, I read the words from her lips before I knew them to be true.

A shockwave spread out from right beside Autumn, the force towering over her head. Ember herself dodged it just in time, shielding Autumn in her arms. It sent Oberon flying, knocked Titania against the wall and then headed straight toward me.

With a *pop*, the world paused and Dean's arm was wrapped around my chest from behind, dragging me downward.

"What—?" I started.

"We have to get down," Dean said, tucking us both into a roll.

We banged up against the bottom step, Dean shielding my body from the impact.

"The orb is in the faery king's possession," Dean explained. Time flickered back into existence for a moment, the sound deafening.

I screamed, which echoed into the stillness of the time.

"The kid surrendered to a champion. This marks the magic acknowledging the transaction."

Ember and Autumn were safely below the arc's wave now, Calder crouched just behind them.

Oberon the faery king's facial features were twisted, the cause of the pain emanating from the glowing orb in his hand, the green part of the orb responsible for this sharp arc of green light no longer aglow.

"They'll disappear?" I asked hopefully.

"No, I don't think so," said Dean. "Not until two out of three are defeated."

I cursed and scanned the room.

In front of me, Zelda was frozen shielding my mom and dad, getting them toward the ground. Journey and Dante were safely passed out—Devam, Raelynn, and Ember's dad flying backward already from the impact.

I scrambled up, careful to keep Dean's arm in contact with me. "Noelle?"

Minnie was flying backward, no longer biting my stepmother. Orin was at first nowhere to be found—but then I spotted the little green ball of light hovering far above the arc's path.

"So now we just need Ember to surrender."

Most of the merfolk were outside, far from us. There were enough vampires here that—

With a shrieking hiss, Minnie's midflight frozen form came to life in the stillness, her blue eyes flashing red.

"What the—?" I started, but Minnie jumped down to the ground, her incisors so long, they were practically glistening.

She soared across the frozen time space, ignoring Dean's cry of her name, and positioned herself in front of the flung-back faery queen.

"She's traveling through my paused time space," said Dean, his hand clutching my shoulder tight. "As the oldest of us, she can control time better than any of us, but I've never seen her do *this*."

That was great to know. But so long as she didn't divine Dean's and my intentions with our wish, at least she was on our side.

For now.

Time flickered back with a roar, the shockwave finishing its movement, a gust of wind whapping through my cold dress and my hair.

When the sound faded, the only noises left were the distant sound of the siren call, the hiss of fangs outside.

And the gulp, gulp, gulp of Minnie drinking blood.

I scrambled to my knees and then to my feet, Dean offering me support along the way.

Minnie was perched atop Titania now, drinking her blood.

The faery queen was still—the faery king had a green, oozing hole burned into his side, his face pallid and lifeless.

This was the effect of the shockwave?

Minnie peeled away from Titania's throat, the sweet trickle

of venomous green blood assaulting the air as it dripped down her chin.

"Guess we saw *who* unmade *whom*." She laughed. Her mobster moll laugh was always unsettling, but it was particularly shiver-inducing with her cleaning her chin with her finger, sucking the green blood off the manicured fingertip.

"Ivy!" cried Autumn. She shivered in Ember's arms, pushing her away. Ember let her go and my little sister limped across the room into my waiting arms.

She buried her face into my skirt, and I patted her back. She was safe now.

"Come, children," said Minnie, standing to her feet. She gestured to Devam and Raelynn, who seemed a little worse for wear but were getting to their feet nonetheless, smoothing out their vintage attire. "Partake in a faery blood feast and we will grow *stronger*."

Neither the king nor queen moved.

But a flickering green light above my head shot upward.

"Not so fast!" said Minnie, passing by Devam and Raelynn as the latter two eagerly clamped their teeth on the necks of the closest two faery guards. "Come back, little referee prince!"

With a blink and a flash, Minnie was at the top of the stairs, closing the distance between her and Orin.

"Don't let her hurt him," said Autumn, pulling back. Her eyes were puffy now. "He's nicer than the rest of them—"

I pushed her back against my chest. Orin was not my concern right now, particularly not after he'd dragged her into this mess to begin with.

My focus was entirely on Ember.

She stood, a half-nude Calder helping her to her feet, her legs still spotted with red scales. One of her hands clutched Calder's as she leaned back against the damp gray T-shirt over his chest, his other arm wrapped around her shoulder.

Dean slipped in behind me, offering me support with one arm across my back.

Ember's dad stumbled to his feet beside me, and Ember flinched, but she didn't move.

"Ember, we want the same thing," I said. The orb sparkled behind her atop the faery king's corpse. Blue and red and black now.

"No, we don't," she said flatly. No room for debate.

I squeezed Autumn tighter. "We both want to save them." I tilted my head toward her dad—toward Journey and Dante, Devam and Raelynn. The latter two looked so unlike what they once had, so inhuman.

And Journey and Dante—they stirred. Together. Shifting upward, their eyes were blinking, their irises' dark color replaced with unnaturally bright blue.

They sniffed the air, the smell of blood no doubt outweighing their confusion, giving them focus in their new lives among the undead.

Ember leaned against Calder. "I can save them all."

"You can't," I said. I looked to Dean for emphasis and he nodded. "If I surrendered, that would be it. The vampires would start disappearing and then you wouldn't be able to save any of them."

Her expression grew pinched, her cheeks red. "But if *you* win, Calder and his family—"

"Yes," I said, daring Calder to say anything. He looked away, not meeting my eyes, staring down at Ember in his arms. "But the people you love—*these* people will be safe." I didn't get why she couldn't see that. If she won, the vampires would begin disappearing and then there'd be no one to wish back to a normal existence. No one besides Calder.

I guessed that was reason enough for her hesitation.
Still...

As if on cue, Journey and Dante each let out a hiss, joining Devam and Raelynn on either side of their chosen faery snacks, drinking blood from the already lifeless creatures.

I looked away, the blood scent in the air now more sickening than inviting.

"Journey!" said Ember, her voice shaking. Tears streamed down her cheeks as she buried her face against Calder's chest.

He took her chin in his hands and tilted it up. "It's all right, Em. It's all right. I..." He swallowed visibly. "I'll be all right."

Was he *condoning* her surrendering to me? Triumphant, I seized on the opportunity. "Well, you're outmatched," I pointed out. "So you don't have to feel guilty about it. You really have no choice."

"Ive," said Dean in a quiet tone. Right. Don't poke the bear.

Too late. Ember tore away from Calder, her nostrils flaring. "Don't act as if this is no big deal!" she screamed. "You know *nothing—*"

A green light rushed down the stairs and floated between Ember and me, and with a *pop*, Orin appeared full-size, his chest heaving, his brow dotted with sweat.

"You're all... free... of my control." He spoke stiltedly.

"Dean, take Autumn—get Noelle," I said quickly, shoving my sister behind me.

Dean hesitated but took hold of Autumn's hand, popping in and out of existence first to grab Noelle from the stairs and sling her over his shoulder, then to deposit them both behind Zelda along with my parents. My parents, who were blinking hard, taking in the sights around them.

"Autumn?" Mom said first, grabbing her daughter and cradling her to her chest. "What's going on—?"

"Noelle!" Easton dove forward to take my comatose step-mom from Dean's shoulder. A bit of dried blood was caked in two streams down her neck.

I didn't have time to deal with them. "Get out of the way," I said to Orin, my right fist glowing red, the slightest tinge of violet ice sparkling among the fire I called to my fist.

"Ivy...?" said Mom from behind me. I couldn't look. I had to trust Zelda and Dean to keep them safe.

"Step aside," Ember said from behind Orin, the bluish

purple of her own fist bright enough to see clearly on the other side of him.

"Wait," said Orin, holding out an arm in both directions toward each of us. "You can both get what you want—"

I pelted him with a fireball, and he brought up a gust of wind only just in time, redirecting it toward the wall, though it singed the tips of his hair. With a grunt, he had to shoot another bit of wind at that to put it out.

"*Ivy!*" shouted Ember, as if I'd done something wrong.

I trusted this faery's silver tongue about as far as I could throw him.

"Oh, pretty prince." Minnie's voice was singsong as she descended the stairs slowly. She licked her lips. "Let's end this chase, shall we?"

It was the opening Orin needed. He took hold of my wrist. Dean shouted my name, and my heart went still. I shouldn't have let him get so close.

"Read me," he said. "I know mermaid blood still flows within you—"

My voice caught in my throat. I couldn't. I didn't know what I should ask him—I didn't *care*. He had my wrist in his fist and he was my enemy. He'd done what he'd done to my sister and—

I summoned all of the fiery flame I could to my fist, the crackling of the bits of ice forming within melting under the hot fire.

Orin let out a yelp of pain and Ember shouted my name.

The fire caught on Orin's hair once more, but still he held on.

"Ivy! Stop!" Ember cried.

And then, with a jolt, her ice-cold hand landed on my forearm, and the world went still around the two of us.

CHAPTER THIRTY

EMBER

The venom seared through my veins, threatening to bubble out of my flesh, as I poured all my effort into keeping time paused. Ivy sneered as she stood in front of me, twisting her arm away.

Orin still had her other hand by the wrist, and that was enough to drag him in with us.

"Wow," he said, staring around him. "I've always wanted to try this."

"Shut up," both Ivy and I said at once.

Ivy quickly pivoted back to me. "He's lying, Ember."

"How can we both get what we want?" I said simply to Orin, ignoring my stubborn step-sister.

Orin grinned. "Well..."

"Liar!" said Ivy. She struggled to get out of my grip.

"Hey now," said Orin. "I'll freely admit this is to save my own skin."

Ivy's lips pinched. She was ready to listen.

I knew the easiest way to see through any potential lies.

With my left hand, I took hold of his forearm and reached inside for the answers. My blood was at war with the venom within me, both needed at that moment, but Calder's life was at stake. I could keep the balance.

Flying through Orin's memories, I saw quick images pass me by.

Orin—me, from my point of view—wearing a one-shouldered outfit made of leaves in the forest, lolling about, my mind hazy as if in a dream. Mother and Father—Titania and Oberon—gorgeous but overwhelming and severe as the most majestic of mountains. A quick flash of them lecturing me, the words unclear, purposely tuned out, the pinch on Titania's face, the impassiveness on Oberon's clear enough.

A clash long ago, faeries against merfolk. An endless bounty of trees and water and plains all around us.

Fighting a handsome merman prince, his hair dark, his complexion a smooth beige, his tail whapping up with a splash from what I knew one day to be the lake in Standing Springs Park.

Stumbling through the untouched woods, bodies everywhere— little faeries splayed across bushes, green blood dripping down; larger faeries, their eyes blank, their necks twisted at the water's edge; merfolk flapping about on the shoreline beside them like beached sea life, blood pooling amidst the pebbles and bits of sand in the park.

Cries of pain in the air, a mermaid's quiet lament. My—Orin's— side hurting so much. I looked down to pull away my hand and see it covered in green, a hole the size of an apple above my hip.

The sides ceasing their battle, the scent of blood still lingering in the air. Titania and Oberon, fiercer than they ever looked with me, cutting their arms and drawing a circle with blood in a field, a red-faced, trembling woman and a man—nude, their hair still soaked, clearly the mermaid and merman queen and king—making similar cuts on their forearms and finishing the circle to meet up with the faeries' green blood. The woman's nose, the man's complexion—they both resembled the merman prince I'd fought. I looked at my hand. The green had faded but was there still, mixed with dried red stuck beneath my long fingernails. The prince's blood, I was sure.

As the circle of blood, of sorrow, came together, out from beneath the ground at the center, shooting pockets of dirt and grass up into the sky as it soared, floated a shiny, smooth stone. Perfectly round. Glowing green and blue equally.

All four leaders stared at it as the stone rose into the air—then sank back down again, hissing as if newly kilned in a fire. On the ground, the orb-like stone was black.

They inspected it. Mother spoke, something about "the blood of your enemies, the power of a champion."

I didn't ask.

I leaned my head back against a withering tree trunk, felt the life fade out of the tree and soar into the magic circle. The birth of the consummate lands, a place filled with both of our kinds' magic, a place that someday—far in the future, after our kinds had each had time to rest—would determine which kind had domain over the entire world.

Where were we? We'd traveled the world until now. Our battle had taken us someplace strange, but a beautiful land. There were very few of those humans here and they lived in such harmony with nature.

The faeries bade me to come with them, and I shook my head, simply leaning against the tree trunk. I'd been here for many rotations of the sun and moon, just sitting here. Mother and Father turned their noses at me and left.

Days and nights passed. The tree behind my back siphoned some energy from me, grew out and up into a mighty woods. When the tree branch caressed my face, at last I moved.

Mother and Father returned. I had a small dwelling in the woods that has grown out around the consummate lands. They spoke in harsh tones. Their words didn't reach me. I caressed a flower grown from one of my own vines.

Mother approached it and pricked her finger on a thorn. Laughing, she squeezed more blood onto it and ripped it from its vine, triumphantly speaking to my father about her plans. Venom in the blood. The humans. Not these ones here—the ones in that dirty, unclean place across the ocean's edge.

They came back with a pale human with hair like fire. Her eyes were unnaturally bright blue in the dark of the night. Her teeth were longer than they ought to have been, the vitality of life missing from her skin.

In Father's hands was the black orb, lit up in one third by the vivid color of red.

I stayed behind.

I didn't witness it, but I knew. I felt the clash again nearby, the vampire child fighting in our stead, her broken heart, the disturbance among the people native to her land, the sacrifice they made.

More time passed. And more time passed.

The world changed around me, but I stayed safe in my home in the woods, barely daring to peek outside. My magic kept me safe.

Until one day, chasing a butterfly, I did look out. I saw the world for what it had become. Strange, unkind—selfish, caring more for themselves than for anything the planet had to offer.

But... Books. Radio. Then movies and TV. There was so much to do. So many reasons to leave my cottage.

But then it began again, this battle for dominance. And I knew— Orin knew—it was only a matter of time before my parents woke up. I was determined to have as much fun as I could before they came to end everything that made me happy.

In a flash, the events as I—myself—had experienced them flew by in an instant, leading me like a missile directly to Orin's only thought that really mattered to me.

The only way to save more than one species. After the second champion surrendered, both the losing species would begin to fade away. One at a time, a few moments for each as they disintegrated into the ash that powered the very life force flowing through the planet's veins.

The wish had to be made before too many disintegrated. The wish could be made in time to save most.

But it would not be made in time to save them all.

With a jolt, I came back to myself, and then with a second lurch, I lost my grip on time.

The world was noisy and chaotic around us, Orin tumbling back from the both of us to put out the fire in his hair.

"What happened?" Ivy asked, not missing a beat. "What did you read in his mind?"

Ivy's parents were shouting somewhere behind us. The scent of strange, venomous blood was in the air and my heart clenched at the sight of the four Union High students drinking faery blood.

It was my fault they were like that. My fault they were... dead.

And Dad. Dad deserved a lot of the blame about what had gone wrong in his life, but the fact remained that he never would have met Minnie if it hadn't been for me.

I couldn't risk a single one vanishing before I could save them.

My mouth open, my tongue dry. I couldn't voice it. I couldn't...

"Ember!" Calder took me into his arms and kissed the top of my head.

"The blood of your enemies," I whispered, that half-heard line swimming to the tip of my tongue, like some part of me knew it was the most important thing I'd gleaned. "The power of a champion."

Calder squeezed me harder. "We can defeat them without spilling blood."

"No," I said. I didn't know why, but that didn't feel true anymore.

I would *try* to make it happen, but if push came to shove...

Calder took my chin in his grip, tilting my head to look up at him. "Then let me go, Ember. I don't deserve to live. Not after what I did to my dad."

"Don't be ridiculous!" I shouted, burying my forehead against his chest. "That wasn't your fault."

"The merfolk don't deserve—"

"Stop it," I said. All the noise was just background to my heartbeat thundering loudly in my head.

"You found something out, didn't you?" he asked. "Do it. Do what you need to do."

"No." I dug my hands into the soaked fabric stretched over his chest. "No. I can't risk it..." There was a chance Calder wouldn't go first if I surrendered, but someone he loved would. And he'd never forgive me.

And there... there was the chance he'd be first. Orin's

memory of the ancient merman prince's blood dried beneath his fingernails flashed in my head.

Minnie's giggle punctuated the air, louder even than the racing of my heart.

She moved closer, the clop of her heels on the runner rug barely muffled.

"Minnie!" There was a mighty crash as the sounds of the outside battle grew louder.

Everyone turned to the front doorway to see Leopold, his suit askew and torn, red steam rising from exposed slits of his flesh. "The little insects are weak—they dove right into the water. The fishfolk are climbing out of the lake, fighting with projectiles, spraying us with water where they can—"

"And this poses a *problem* to you?" Minnie's nose pinched. "Where are the others?"

Before he could answer, he shrieked as a steady spray of water hit him in the side, the red steam pouring off him obscuring him from sight.

Calder patted my back. "It's my mom and the others. Someone must have gone back to the RVs to get the weed sprayers they filled with water."

Ah. Right. Smart.

Bay and Llyr stumbled past us from the open basement doorway, standing between us and the remaining vampires.

Somehow, we had the advantage. We could win this.

Did... Did I want to win this?

Tittering, Minnie shot forward toward Zelda, shoving her aside, her target in Orin forgotten. "Come, my beautiful new children! Feast on this family! Bring them to our side and *both* the champions will do as I say!"

"No!" Ivy and I shouted as one.

Breaking away from Calder, I pushed past Llyr and Bay. As I passed Orin, he stepped back into the shadow, the only thing keeping him in sight the blue-and-red glow from the orb at his fallen father's side. Ivy broke away from Dean and grabbed my wrist as she and I wound up side by side. Before the world went still, Nerida herself appeared in the doorway amidst the red steam, a weed sprayer strapped to her back and its nozzle in her hand. She shot a stream of water at Leopold and he hissed, crumpling to the ground, steam as thick as fog souring into the air. Nerida stepped farther inside, singing a song that made Ivy flinch—if just for a moment.

"Now, champion!" Nerida said, her tone still musical. Minnie wasn't affected by the song, but the fledgling vampires and Ivy were, the vampires ceasing their endless quenching of their thirst, tilting their heads stiffly like inhuman monsters as they shuffled their feet toward the source of the sound.

Ivy took a step toward Nerida. I took both her hands in mine and the world went still.

She shook her head, blinking hard. "Thanks. I wasn't focused enough to block out the siren call."

We didn't have time for this. I looked over my shoulder at our family. Ivy's mom and dad shielded Autumn, but her little wide, brown eyes were unmistakable, the fear inside them banishing all sense of play she'd ever had. My mom was behind them, Easton sticking out one long arm in vain to try to shield both his daughter and his wife at once.

The fledging vampires—my classmates, my friends, my father—were frozen on their way to the mermaid queen, their bright blue eyes fierce with hunger and confusion.

There didn't seem to be a trace of Journey left.

"Whoever makes the wish to end supernatural creatures can save most of the other species," I explained. "When the second champion surrenders, the two losing species start disappearing, but one at a time and slowly—"

Realization seemed to dawn on Ivy's face. "So if you wish for no more vampires, but the vampires are disappearing—"

"The ones who change to humans before that happens won't be in danger," I said. I hoped.

Ivy swallowed. "Ember, we need to save more vampires than merfolk—"

"I know," I whispered. I looked down.

"We can't risk one of *them* going first." Ivy chewed her lip. "What if it goes by age? What if Journey and Dante, being the youngest vampires, disappear first?"

"I know!" My voice echoed in the still, empty vacuum. It was a risk I couldn't take.

I turned to Calder. His eyes were wet, dull. If the newest merfolk went first, there were children... He might not be at risk, but who could ever forgive me for being responsible for the death of *children?* The faefolk I couldn't have cared less about at this point, not to mention all were so very old, but the merfolk were just people if they lost their fins.

"Ember, *please*." Ivy's eyes were watering, and I wasn't sure why she had so much at stake in letting the vampires win. It wasn't *her* best friends on the line. I knew she and Devam and Raelynn had been in the same social circle, but just barely. It wasn't *her* dad...

I followed her gaze. To Dean.

The cords in his neck were stiff as he moved toward our family. His bright blue gaze never left Ivy.

I laughed. I'd dated him for weeks, and these two were actually in love after less than a week? Ridiculous.

She could have him, though. None of that mattered anymore. Besides, I...

I...

Calder.

I knew what it felt like to be in love now, and I hadn't even been with Calder for that much longer than Ivy had been with Dean.

I wiped my tear-stained cheek against my shoulder. We were both ridiculous.

"Okay," I said quietly. "I'll—"

With a hiss, a form went flying beside us and both Ivy and I turned. Minnie had jumped into *my* time pause, her fangs bared—at me.

Ivy shoved me aside and the time pause broke. Minnie

slammed against my step-sister, and the three of us tumbled to the ground.

Minnie's fangs drew gashes against Ivy's cheeks and Ivy let out a cry of pain.

"Fool!" hissed Minnie, her baby voice warped. She scrambled to push herself up, but Ivy bore her own fangs, the scars on her face healing fast with the venom in her veins, and with a roar, she bit into Minnie's ear, tearing it, the blue blood spurting out like a fountain.

The fledgling vampires stopped, their attention all drawn to Minnie, Nerida's song meaningless now. They sniffed the air. Journey leaped toward her first.

Ivy cursed and shoved Minnie off her.

Nerida cackled in her singsong voice nearby.

Slapping my legs together, I formed my tail again. As I had with my dad, I spun on the ground like a breakdancer and used my tail strength to flick Minnie down the hall.

Orin, in her path, stumbled back and turned into a little faery, the green light soaring up and away.

Minnie rolled near the red-and-blue glow of the orb on Oberon's corpse.

"Now, champion!" said Nerida.

I looked at Calder softly.

He swallowed and nodded.

"Ivy," I said. "I surrender to the champion of blood. I surrender the water."

"*No!*" shrieked Nerida.

The orb snapped as it had before, a blue arc of light shooting outward, slicing through Minnie and reaching toward the air.

"Everyone, down!" I screamed.

Calder leaped atop me, his bare body covering mine.

I didn't look away, making sure Zelda covered my family, who were all on the ground and out of harm's way.

Dean popped in and out, managing to sweep Ivy away and

then drop her atop our family to avoid the slam of the blue light's deafening arc.

The fledging vampires—none reacted in time, each thrown backward, slamming into walls. Dad went straight through a window, the shattered glass deafening.

"Dad!" I cried. "Journey! Dante!"

I breathed in and out, hard. Deep.

Everything was quiet, but for the crackling of glass falling out of the window pane, the crunch of footfalls on bits of plaster.

"What have you *done?*" said Nerida, stumbling her way toward me.

And then with one false step, her bare foot turned to sand.

Sand that started flying upward.

"Ivy!" I shouted. It wasn't starting with the youngest—I was simultaneously relieved and frightened. "Ivy!" My voice scratched my throat, threatened to shatter my larynx.

Ivy and Dean scrambled to their feet and held each other's hands. With a series of pops, they were across the room, the smoldering black-and-red orb now in Ivy's hands.

Nerida was collapsing, half pure sand now.

"Mom!" Calder's hands shook on my back.

"Your fault," she said through clenched teeth. "You killed your father. You killed us all!" She screeched, and then her lips were engulfed by the sand, the very top of her strikingly beautiful auburn hair sifting into sandy dust particles in the air. Around us, the air seemed coated with the fine dust, some of it shining in a verdant green.

"I wish for all supernatural creatures to become human!" shouted Ivy, her voice rushing out. She shook the orb in her hands.

A few steps in front of me, the tips of Llyr's fingers began turning to sand that shifted upward, joining the sand from Nerida, as well as the sparkly green powder I realized rose from the corpses of faefolk all around us.

"Llyr!" shouted Bay, seizing his boyfriend by the shoulders.

Tears streamed out of his eyes as he shook him, kissing his cheeks, his lips. "Don't go!"

"*Ivy!*" I said.

"It's not working!" she said. She shook the orb harder. "Dean, help!"

"We wish for all supernatural creatures to be human!" Dean shouted, his normally controlled voice wavering. Ivy joined him. They held the orb between them and repeated the vow over and over.

"*Orin!*" shouted Ivy.

But the traitorous faery prince was nowhere to be seen.

"Ember, I'm sorry for everything," said Calder. His eyes were shining with tears. He kissed me—hard. Like he knew it would be the last time.

He pulled back.

Beside us, Llyr was almost gone entirely, Bay holding on to sand and dust that seeped through his fingers.

"Calder, I'm sorry," I said, crying. "I'm so sorry." I looked around. Zelda was as pale as ever—the fledging vampires hurt or worse and every bit still vampires. This had all been for nothing. Nothing had worked out. It had all turned out terribly.

Calder sprinted down the hall and, strangely, dipped his hand in the oozing green blood of the fallen faery king. He smeared the blood on the orb between Ivy's and Dean's hands.

"What are you doing?" Ivy looked aghast.

My bare, scaled feet took too long to get me near them, my heart thundering too hard to call upon the venom to pause time.

"Maybe you need the blood of your enemies on it," he said. "Champions would work—but so could royalty."

No. I couldn't have heard him right.

Calder's left hand started breaking apart—*no!*—and that just seemed to make him more certain of everything.

He nodded at Dean and pointed to his neck.

Dean grimaced and bit my boyfriend, not like a vampire

drinking, but just enough to start the veins gushing out, just as I skidded up behind them.

Calder's blood spurted upward, showering Dean and Ivy and me—and the orb.

"Calder!"

"I've always been in love with—" he said, but his head turned to sand before my eyes, shifting downward to disintegrate the rest of his body like falling dominoes.

No.

I collapsed to my knees, slamming them painfully on the runner rug soaked in blood.

"We wish for all supernatural creatures to be human!" said Dean and Ivy at once the moment they both held on to the orb again.

The red light shot out like an arc before I could blink, the energy pushing me backward.

EPILOGUE
IVY

"I don't know if you should go." Mom hovered in the doorway of my room at her townhouse. She'd been standing there the past twenty minutes fretting, checking every few seconds to make sure Autumn was still in her room across from mine, the light brightly on in her room, the little tinny quality of one of her show's theme songs echoing out of Mom's tablet's speakers.

I puckered my lips in the little mirror I had propped up atop my dresser, then put the cap back on the lipstick. "Mom, it's been weeks."

She fidgeted some more, a lock of her dark hair falling out of her messy bun.

Closing the distance between us, I hugged her, my chin resting atop her head. "I'm fine, Mom. Better than fine. Things turned out... great." I pulled back. "As great as could be expected." The skin at the back of my neck grew itchy and I resisted the temptation to scratch it by clutching my vivid, red nails against my palm.

Things *could* have turned out better.

Orin was missing, presumed turned to dust, though I couldn't say I'd shed a tear over that.

Almost all of the faefolk had vanished before we'd successfully managed to make our wish. Perhaps because their champion had surrendered first. Some of those outside during the wish witnessed a few green balls of light pop, human-sized people falling to the ground.

By then, all the ruckus had finally carried down the road or across the lake and emergency vehicles had been on their way. The former faeries had scattered like frightened cats.

So some were still out there, but they'd have no idea how to blend in with human society. And they were powerless. If they got up to any trouble, we'd spot them.

Their king and queen were definitely dead, carted off by the police, two of many victims of a "gas explosion," they'd determined, in the bed and breakfast's basement.

As to why there had been so many strange outfits—and even half-naked people lying about—my parents had stepped up and explained it was all a theme party gone horribly wrong. That they hadn't even known everyone—that the bed and breakfast had been hosting it.

My *parents* had played along. Rather than tell the authorities what they had witnessed, what their daughters had done. Dad had kissed both Autumn and me and left us with Mom, going off with Noelle to the hospital.

Noelle and the babies—yes, twins, there went any hope of being well rested after they were due to be born in the summer, but at least that would be when I'd be on my way out the door—were fine now, too. She didn't remember any of it, but with both Mom and Dad insisting what they'd witnessed was true, with how Ember was... She seemed to believe us.

Mostly.

Ember... I'd let her down. Merfolk had definitely survived, but not all of them. Bay and Laguna had lost Llyr and Cascade and however many more of their friends and family. Young, old... Too many. Among them, of course, Calder.

The loss of Calder, especially after he'd purposely put himself in harm's way like that to make sure we succeeded— that did eat at me, no matter what had happened between us.

Especially after learning he never would have wished for the world to be flooded after all, that that had just been what his family had wanted.

Though I wasn't entirely sure being with Ember hadn't had something to do with his change of heart. If we hadn't swapped sides, maybe he never would have made that sacrifice. Maybe our family never would have gotten out of this intact if we hadn't switched. Maybe our world would be at an end.

The vampires—the *former* vampires—were fine. Every one of them but Minnie, who'd died for good when she'd turned human, unable to heal her grievous wounds in time.

Ember's dad and a few of the others had taken that hard, but mostly the vampires were ready to make the most of what time they had left.

The ones who'd turned decades ago especially understood that what they had now had an expiration date on it. This was a second chance—a *last* chance. Some had taken that better than others. Journey and Dante had barely been affected. Devam and Raelynn both were a bit sullen, withdrawn. They'd skipped a lot of school in the weeks since.

But they'd get used to it.

Ember's dad had skipped town, as far as I knew. Left Ember when she'd needed him. But all she had said on the subject was good riddance and her older brother had seen him once in the days since, so he was still out there, doing whatever it was he'd done before all of this.

My phone buzzed on my nightstand just as something soft and purry wound itself around our ankles. I scooped Blossom up and gave her a few chin tickles as my phone kept vibrating before handing our kitty to Mom, who took her in her arms almost as a reflex, for lack of something else to hold on to.

"We already celebrated your birthday," Mom said as I did one last check in the mirror. "With your father and Noelle and Autumn and Ember."

"Celebrating" my birthday two nights ago had involved ordering a pizza and huddling around Dad and Noelle's dining room table, my parents skittish at every rustle of the wind, Ember sullen and barely looking at me, Autumn lacking her usual energy.

Mom and Dad had enrolled her in therapy—I'd passed on the offer. A kid could get away with an imagination full of faeries and mermaids and vampires.

I doubted a therapist would look at my ravings about the matter as simply a way to cope with witnessing a terrible gas explosion.

So my birthday had been just another reminder of how wounded my family was. No friends had been allowed, lest they turn out to drink anyone's blood or sprout fish scales. Now it was my turn to do things *my* style.

I was going to get my life back yet. My makeup was thick, my lips a bright, unholy red, my eyeshadow a pale forest green. I smoothed down the red cable-knit sweater dress, the black, long-sleeved fishnet shirt I had on underneath poking through as it covered the backs of my hands and looped through my middle fingers. The shirt matched the black fishnet stockings I had on my legs. I was going to be a little chilly at the bonfire before we headed over to Paisley's, but I wanted to look nice.

"This isn't just for my birthday," I said. "Journey got us permission to have the bonfire at Standing Springs Park to celebrate the holidays."

Christmas was around the corner. Most of the Thanksgiving decorations were still hung up at Dad's. Mom never went all in on the holiday, though.

"I wish you would reconsider," Mom said for the dozenth time.

"So you've said." I grabbed my phone and texted Paisley back. She and her boyfriend, Grey, were waiting out front already, Lyric and a few of the guys from the baseball team already halfway to the park.

It took some effort, but I managed to squeeze past Mom. Luckily for me, she was short enough that it was impossible for her to take up the entire doorway.

"Ivy... Is *he* going to be there?" she asked quietly.

He. I didn't need to ask whom.

"I'm going with Paisley and Grey. They're waiting for me outside." My phone buzzed again and I held it up so she could see I wasn't lying.

"That's not what I asked."

Blossom let out a little tittering chirp and jumped out of Mom's grip, sashaying casually over to Autumn's open doorway.

"Mom, I'm eighteen now." I swallowed. I knew that wasn't enough. Not really.

"And that boy is... That boy is..."

"Seventeen," I finished for her.

She pinched her lips together.

"He really is! But, *okay*, it's technically eighty-something. Or ninety-something. I don't know exactly," I admitted.

"And—never mind that it's *legal*—you think it's appropriate for an eighteen-year-old and a *hundred*-year old—"

"Okay, okay." I scratched the back of my neck. She had me there. I didn't think even the biggest age difference in a relationship in history boasted eighty-ish years apart. Not even some old, decrepit billionaire and a hot, young model.

That didn't stop me from feeling a sunken lead weight in my stomach at the thought of invoking *logic* in this situation. But it had been hard enough for Mom to let me go at all. Her and Dad's houses had been about the extent of my life outside of school the past few weeks.

"I get it," I said. "I need to... I need to focus on me. On my life."

And maybe once you're a little more adult... I found myself thinking.

I shook my head. Maybe by then, I'd be over this entirely.

Mom gave me another hug, sighing even so. "Be careful," she said. "And text me every ten minutes."

"*Mom.*"

She stood back and held a finger up. "Grant me this much.

At least for a little while. You may technically be an adult, but you'll always be my baby."

I let her squeeze me one more time and then extricated myself to descend the narrow stairway to the front door.

Digging around in the cramped shoe and jacket closet, I grabbed the coat I knew would be warmest.

It smelled of Dean still. I wouldn't have thought Dean would have had a scent as a vampire, but he had—it was like a crisp, cold breeze, a hint of copper. I really ought to give it back, considering he could be affected by the cold now.

He'd fished it out of his car and draped it around me during the chaos of the bed and breakfast cleanup. We'd stolen a quiet moment, Dean putting his forehead to mine, before Mom and Dad had scurried over and yanked me away to go get changed so I wouldn't catch cold.

Dean's forehead had been warm, his skin several shades peachier.

I shivered just thinking about it.

Halfway to the parking lot of the townhouse complex and Paisley's car, I heard Autumn call me from behind.

I turned on my heel. She was carrying Blossom, and she wasn't wearing a coat. Her unicorn pajamas were flannel, but not necessarily warm enough.

Mom hovered in the doorway several steps behind her.

"Autumn, what are you doing?" I ran back over to her. "Don't bring the cat out here."

But Blossom purred hard in Autumn's grip, not interested in escaping, only in settling my sister's shaking hands.

Autumn's lip trembled, too, and I noticed the puffy redness beneath her eyes.

"I'll save Ember's boyfriend," she said. "And all those other merpeople and faeries. I don't know how. But I promise."

I tucked her head against my chest—gently, careful not to squish Blossom between us. "Don't say that," I said. "Autumn, they're gone—and it's not your fault."

"*No*," she said. "It is!" She pushed backward and Blossom growled just a little bit at the rise in Autumn's voice.

"It's not." I took her by both shoulders. "Don't you dare think that."

"I..." Her lips were trembling hard.

"You are the least to blame of anyone," I said. "Orin and his family—they *used* you. And I won't hear a word of this, okay? You just focus on being a kid—like you should have been doing all this time." I softly pinched her nose, and she tore back, swatting at me with one hand but quickly moving back to keep Blossom from falling.

"I'm not a kid," she snapped.

"You *are*, whether you like it or not." I put my hands on my hips. "Now get inside and *relax*, okay?"

Mom called her name.

She frowned but turned around, checking over her shoulder at me every few seconds until safely back inside. Mom's gaze lingered just a little at me before shutting the door.

"Ivy!" Paisley leapt on me from behind, giving me a hug. "I thought you'd never get out here."

I side-hugged her back, bumping her with my hip. "It's the birthday girl's prerogative to be a little late, right?"

"Technically, it was your birthday two days ago."

"All right, all right, you got me. I'm sorry."

"*Good*. Because I was about to wonder if I'd ever see you again at this rate."

She had no idea how intently I'd so recently thought the same about her—about all of our friends. About everyone.

Grey honked the horn on his car as Paisley slipped her arm through mine and led the way.

———

EMBER

"It can be hard to accept the loss of a loved one," my counselor told me every session. "Acceptance. That's the first turning point in the stages of grief. Don't rush to get there. You'll know when you do."

"Isn't that sweet?" Journey nudged her arm against mine just as a crackle of firewood snapped me out the blank state I'd found myself in. Across the giant bonfire that lit up the cold, December night all around us, Lyric Penham was handing Raelynn a mug of steaming hot chocolate and Raelynn, whose blank expression seemed a reflection of my own, perked up at the sight of her—just slightly. They were talking to one another and Lyric slipped in on the log beside Raelynn, who leaned her cheek against Lyric's shoulder. Lyric's usually severe expression softened, the two staring straight ahead at the flames. The firelight flickered in their eyes, and for the briefest of moments, I imagined Raelynn's eyes to be bright and blinding, the chill of blue venom still in her veins.

But I knew better. She and Devam had been "miraculously" cured of their condition with a little rest and time. Journey and Dante had never had to explain it to anyone, considering they'd turned to vampires for such a short period.

"Rae's going to be so happy!" Journey clutched on to my upper arm, and I was reminded of an echo of myself in her, excited over seeing romance unfold before her. "I know the whole... thing... messed stuff up for a while, but she really likes Lyric. Lyric's got a track and field scholarship to some school in Indiana and Raelynn has her heart set on Bradview. So they'd always planned on going to separate colleges, but I'd always thought they'd make the whole long-distance thing last. Rae tells me Lyric can be stubborn, but I know she loves her."

It must have been nice to bounce back so quick to a life where these kinds of things mattered still.

Journey leaned closer. "I'm so glad we managed to keep Lyric out of most of it at least." She chewed her lip. "Though I wonder... How much people should know."

Her gaze fell over the rest of the group gathered. Journey might have felt a sudden bond with these people after all we'd been through, but I'd still never spoken more than a handful of words to most of them.

Except for Ivy, of course.

Her laughter carried across the roaring fire, her smile stunningly vibrant as she leaned against Paisley Parr, the two of them giggling at something one of them had said.

A few feet away was an open car trunk where the insulated drink dispenser Journey had brought and filled with hot cocoa from her dad's diner was set up with an array of her dad's diner mugs. Hovering by it were Dean and Zelda, the only two possibly more out of place than I was.

Zelda gazed nervously at the fire every few seconds, her long, blonde hair down and unadorned beneath her red wool cap. She was wearing a puffy, red down coat I never would have expected her to wear, jeans poking out from underneath.

Her makeup was soft, subdued. She was still beautiful, but she didn't resemble some vintage starlet trapped in time. She sipped her mug cautiously, and the trembling of her chin stilled as a smile blossomed on her lips.

She seemed to like the taste of the drink. Vampires drank more than just blood—but I didn't remember them ever drinking hot drinks, or anything with cocoa.

But then a spark flew out of the bonfire—plenty far away from them—and Zelda let out a little cry.

Everyone turned to join me in looking at them.

Dean stood between Zelda and the fire and spoke softly to her. She settled somewhat, staring down at her mug.

"She's rather jumpy, isn't she?" Journey said. "Do you think those two are...?"

I scoffed. "Zelda's with Leopold, this chauvinistic one, and Dean..." I studied Ivy. The smile had fallen off her face as she stared after the former vampires, her brow knitting as she purposefully gazed away.

Was Dean with Zelda now?

There was no way.

Dean and Ivy had seemed so different together than he'd been with me.

Zelda took a swig of her mug and smiled nervously.

For the first time since we'd arrived, I took a good look at Dean.

Handsome, but hardly as striking as he'd been as a vampire. Despite the winter weather, his skin was looking a bit tanner than I would have expected. His dark blond hair was messy on his head, a plaid scarf around his neck, and he wore a utilitarian green winter outdoor outlet store coat above a pair of khakis. He barely resembled himself at all. Or maybe this *was* him. He sipped his hot cocoa, and the steam exiting his mouth seemed so out of place.

The only thing that *appeared* to be the same old, same old with him was the way he carried himself. Confident, calm, with a sort of wisdom the decades he was hiding had imbued into his very core.

After Zelda appeared to settle, everyone went back to their conversations. Dean gazed pointedly at Ivy and frowned when he saw how the light had gone out of her a little.

A car pulled up and got everyone's attention once more.

The headlights switched off and out stepped Dante and Joe —not a pair I'd ever seen together before a few weeks ago, but as far as Joe knew, he *had* rescued Dante from a "drug episode" shortly before Thanksgiving.

I guessed the two had hit it off. Journey tried to keep me informed about everything going on at school because even when I showed up, my heart wasn't fully in it. Mom—who seemed somewhat skeptical about what had gone on, were it not for both Easton and Glory attesting to it, she wouldn't have believed it at all, I was sure—had insisted on a grief counselor nonetheless, though the sessions felt pointless.

I couldn't explain how my boyfriend had "died," not really. He was a victim of the gas explosion a few towns over—the counselor had heard of it. That was all I could say.

That, and it had been my fault. He'd... shielded me, I'd explained. It seemed better than saying he'd sacrificed himself for me.

Dante waved at Journey and headed our way. He was dressed pretty sleek in a wool coat that practically matched his cousin's. They both seemed to exude style without trying, boosted by the glow on their cheeks from a thankfulness for life that I envied.

I'd come to the party in pink sweats, a bulky overcoat tossed on over them on my way out the door. I'd planned on spending the night lying in the dark on my bed.

Journey has insisted I'd spent enough of those.

But she didn't understand.

"Hey, Goodwin!" said Joe. He, too, was wearing sweats, but he hadn't thought to throw on a coat. Shivering, he rubbed his arms and danced in place to warm himself up. "How's it been? You haven't shown in class much."

"Calder died," I said flatly.

His lips went into a straight line. He didn't seem surprised —I was sure the news had made the rounds.

"Yeah..." He swallowed. "If you need anything, you just let me know, okay?"

I nodded numbly as he sat down on the log beside me, Dante on the other side of Journey, their conversation present but somehow distant enough that I didn't latch on to any of the words. Hugging myself, I stared blankly into the fire, the movement of the flames.

"Any plans for the holidays?" Joe asked.

I shook my head numbly.

"Right. Sorry. I don't know what to say."

"Don't," I said. "Don't say anything."

"Okay." He stared straight ahead, interlacing his fingers between his knees. We both didn't speak for a while. I couldn't say how long.

Every few minutes, I pictured Calder's face. The blood all over his neck. The way he'd said he loved...

He loved me.

We hadn't been a couple for long, but it had been long enough. My soul ached with the thought of never seeing him again.

"You know, we don't have to just be study buddies," said Joe.

That got me to tear my eyes away. I sent him a sharp look. "'Study buddies'?"

He had the decency to look sheepish. "Okay, well, I know I don't really help *you* with much, but you're smart, Goodwin. What can I possibly teach you?"

I shrugged.

He kept going, though. "What I mean is, if you want to hang out, get your mind off things..."

"Thanks, but..." I left the rest unsaid.

"Right." He let out a deep breath. "Just know that the offer stands. With or without Journey and Dante, if you need a shoulder to cry on, I'm here."

I raised an eyebrow. But I was unnerved by the way his face seemed to brighten as I looked at him.

"As friends," he said quickly. "Of course it'd be too soon to—"

"Thanks," I said. "I appreciate it."

And I did.

But he wouldn't understand.

"I... I need to head to the ladies' room," I said after a beat.

He nodded, chewing his lip, and I stood. I felt a little woozy and Journey jumped up to stabilize me. "Want me to come with you?"

"No." I put a hand on her arm firmly. "I'm fine." I tried my best to smile.

Journey hesitated, but she nodded.

She knew the truth but was willing to run with the lie if I was. If it would mean I could pretend to be okay, maybe someday I would be.

I didn't really need to go to the bathroom, but I headed in that direction anyway.

The farther I got from the fire, the colder and quieter the night air was. I tugged down on my winter hat and stopped when I heard movement in the dark a few yards away from me.

It was weird not being able to see clearly in the night like I once had been able to.

"I understand." I knew that voice. Dean's.

I'd been so caught up in my thoughts that I hadn't seen him walk away from the bonfire.

"I understand, but I won't say I'm happy..." His voice seemed to catch in his throat. There was something off about it, some sense of vitality in it, even though the words clearly caused him pain.

I blinked and shuffled closer, as quietly as I could.

One form became two as Ivy stepped back from Dean's embrace. Tears were staining her cheeks.

"Maybe someday," she said. "I can't promise my parents will ever understand, but someday... When they're a bit more relaxed about everything. Then—"

So Zelda and Dean weren't together after all.

But neither were Dean and Ivy.

"I'm only now about to really start living, but that doesn't change the fact that I'm so much older than you."

"I don't care about that. Maybe I should, but—"

"Let's live our lives," he replied. "And then, maybe once this life truly becomes my own, all the rest will just be a memory. Maybe it won't count."

"Maybe."

Dean kissed the top of Ivy's head and didn't say anything more.

I shuffled away from the direction of the restroom, down toward the sandy shore of the lake, out of sight before they noticed me.

I didn't know what I felt about what I'd witnessed. The idea of Dean with Ivy didn't fill me with jealousy anymore. I didn't take delight in the thought that Ivy was deciding to keep her distance. As long as we were both legal, age wouldn't have mattered to me, but Ivy wasn't me.

I sat down on a rock near the water's edge. It was nearly still, though the slight rustling of the water reminded me that this lake, unlike Lake Fowles, lived and breathed. Connected to the river and to Lake Michigan from there and out into the ocean. If you knew the way, you could get anywhere from this place.

I knew beneath that island in the middle of the lake there was a rocky underwater miniature palace. Calder had told me about it, though we hadn't had time to explore it together.

It would be empty—now and for the rest of time.

The surviving merfolk had left. I didn't know where they'd gone. I couldn't face them, had never bonded with them, though their loss at my hands still ate at me, despite their wicked intentions.

The sight of Calder, covered in blood, popped into my head.

"Hello."

A familiar voice made my spine go stiff.

No. Not *that* voice. He was supposed to be gone.

To prove I wasn't dreaming, Orin shuffled toward me on the sand, coming from the direction opposite of the bonfire party.

"Don't freak out, all right? Bit chock-a-block over there, so when I saw you heading off on your own, I just thought I'd see if you were up for a little talk."

Never had a cockney accent been so grating.

"*You!*" I shouted, scrambling to my feet. "*You* survived." I didn't hide the anger in my voice, the accusation. *You and not him.*

He put both hands up in surrender then shivered and seemed to think better of it, clutching his arms through a woolen coat. It looked a little worse for wear, burs and bits of little twigs stuck to its fibers, the same in his hair.

"I didn't make the rules," he said.

I barked a laugh.

"Okay, okay," he said. "I may have given off the impression that I did—"

"Shut up, Orin. Just shut up." I massaged my temples and sat back down on the rock.

Let him attack me, annoy me, whatever it was he'd come to do.

I felt too numb to cry out, to hope Dean and Ivy were still near enough to hear me.

Let them find my tattered body and wonder where they'd gone wrong.

Orin slipped in beside me on the rock, just large enough to seat two people.

I stared daggers at him, but he didn't flinch.

"Let me guess. You want something from *me* now that you have no powers," I said. "Is that why you're not attacking me?"

"Oy, not fair," he said. He tapped the side of his head. "I know you're cheesed off, but you saw inside me, didn't you? You know I'm not really dodgy like that. Not at heart."

"I'm still wondering if you *have* such a thing," I spat.

Sighing, Orin twiddled his thumbs on his lap. "Okay, I can see you're getting shirty. Any more vitriol you want to lobby at me?"

"Oh, I could go on all night."

"Then do. Get it out of your system. Because then we need to talk."

Letting out a deep breath, I didn't turn to look at him. "Lay it on me. Just ask and go away."

"I'm not *asking* you for anything," he said. "I'm here to offer you hope."

"Oh?" I asked, chuckling. The movement hurt my stomach. "Do explain."

"I *think* we can get them back," he said. "Your disappeared merfolk. My faefolk. And not my parents or Minnie—no one who was killed a different way. The ones who turned to sand and ash."

My heart seemed to grow still. Then I remembered whom I was speaking to. "I don't believe you."

"Even with the wish granted, there's still magic in the consummate lands. Blood spilled there long ago imbues the very fiber of this town."

I was ready to make a biting remark, but his memories flashed through my head. I'd seen the ritual through his eyes. Then I chuckled. "But there are no merfolk or faefolk anymore."

"Yes, but they wished for *supernatural creatures to become human*, not for all magic to cease to exist, did they not?"

True. I chewed my lip a moment. "So?"

"So... There's a chance," he said simply.

Now I shifted to face him. He didn't appear amused or anxious. But that didn't mean he wasn't lying.

"How?" I asked. Let him get his ploy out there entirely so I knew what he might get up to the moment he walked away from me.

"*Well*, though there's a chance that the champion of blood's little wish may have messed with their abilities, too, albeit unintentionally—but, you know, their magic is from a far more reliable source, so it's entirely possible—"

"*Orin*. Spit it out."

He grinned, and it didn't look like he was laughing *at* me for once. "I suggest we find the fallen angels."

"The... fallen angels?" All of my thoughts froze.

"The angels who walk amongst us," said Orin, nodding. "Though to tell the truth, I've never actually *met* one, and now I'm utterly powerless, so... finding one may take a while. Then I couldn't say for *certain* that any would help us..."

I laughed. It wasn't the reaction I'd been expecting, but I laughed, the sound carrying out across the empty, still water.

According to this untrustworthy, manipulative imp, there was a chance Calder could come back to life.

A chance that even he didn't seem that confident in.

My counselor spoke in my head. *"Don't rush to get there. You'll know when you do."*

"Orin, you let me know when you find an angel." I stood and brushed any dirt from the rock off of the back of my coat. "And if they'll be willing to bring people back from the dead."

Because he *was* dead. He was gone.

And I was no longer foolish enough to rely on a faery prince's word that he could save him.

"Oh, I will," said Orin to my retreating back. "Don't you doubt that."

I wasn't going to hold my breath.

A traumatized former faery champion. The beguiling former faery prince who manipulated her once before. A chance to correct the past mistakes that haunt her as the battle between blood, bloom, and water fades into memory.

Autumn Sheppard could once grow vines from her hands, but if she shared that with anyone, they'd think she was delusional. She's spent the past ten years suppressing the nightmare of her actions during the battle between faeries, vampires, and mermaids, even as her older sister and step-sister moved on with their lives.

When Orin, the conniving faery prince, asks for her help, she wants to run, but he's the only one who still has faith that she can make things right. Tasked with finding a fallen angel, Autumn discovers the hottest boy in school is exactly the guy she needs on her side. If only he could see past her geeky, outcast personality—and believe that magic is real.

The fifth and final book in the Blood, Bloom, & Water series takes the story ten years into the future, when the former champion of bloom is the only hope for the resurrection of lost friends and foes alike. With the help of a fallen angel, she might succeed—even if her wish comes with fatal consequences.

ABOUT THE AUTHOR

Amy McNulty is an editor and author of books that run the gamut from YA speculative fiction to contemporary romance. A lifelong fiction fanatic, she fangirls over books, anime, manga, comics, movies, games, and TV shows from her home state of Wisconsin. When not editing her clients' novels, she's busy fulfilling her dream by crafting fantastical worlds of her own.

Sign up for Amy's newsletter to receive news and exclusive information about her current and upcoming projects. Get a free YA romantic sci-fi novelette when you do!

LOOK FOR MORE YA SPECULATIVE FICTION READS FROM SNOWY WINGS PUBLISHING

BETWEEN WORLDS
MICKY O'BRADY

For sixteen-year-old Noa Keegan panic attacks are part of life, but this one is different: she wakes up in a parallel universe, Terra, where she is treated as a security risk. Her guard, a nineteen-year-old Sentinel named Avery McTighe, is easily the most serious and mesmerizing person Noa has ever met.

When anti-government rebels kidnap her and Avery, the two of them realize Terra plans to wipe out Earth's population for better access to its resources. Bound together by mutual attraction and a common goal, Noa and Avery must find a way to abort Terra's murderous schemes, but when Avery gets injured, their chances are bleak.

Hunted across universes by Terran forces and with the clock ticking down to the annihilation of the human race, Noa has one shot at saving the universe she grew up in—or the Sentinel she's falling in love with.

CRIMSON MAGE
DOROTHY DREYER

Upon the one hundredth reincarnation of the Lotus empress, the dark god Kashmeru would send out his shadow army--Pishacha--to destroy the reborn empress, which in turn would bring about the collapse of the universe.

The world changed at the time of the Eradication. The New Asian Administration outlawed mages, forbidding any use of their powers. To protect her imprisoned family, Mayhara Guatama made a deal to surrender her mage status and pledge her life to the New Order.

Years have passed, the chaos from the upheaval long since settled. Or so Mayhara believed... until she receives a mysterious message pleading for her help.

Stunned by the claim that the empress has been reincarnated, Mayhara must choose between fealty to the Lotus empire, or honoring the decree that assures her family's safety.

READ MORE FROM AMY MCNULTY

THE NEVER VEIL SERIES

"The story is fun and engaging, featuring a female protagonist who will resonate with young teens." -School Library Journal

"...A whirlwind of time-bending adventures that immerse readers in a maelstrom of plot twists and allusions to "Beauty and the Beast" and other fairy tale love stories, while Noll's understanding of gender-based social and cultural dynamics develops." -Publishers Weekly

Nobody's Goddess (Book One in The Never Veil Series), winner of The Romance Reviews Summer 2016 Readers' Choice Award for Young Adult Romance:

In a village of masked men, each man is compelled to love only one woman and to follow the commands of his "goddess" without question. A woman may reject the only man who will love her if she pleases, but she will be alone forever. A man must stay masked until his goddess returns his love—and if she can't or won't, he remains masked forever.

Seventeen-year-old Noll's childhood friends have paired off and her closest companion, Jurij, found his goddess in Noll's own sister. Desperate to find a way to break this ancient spell, Noll instead discovers why no man has ever chosen her. She is in fact the goddess of the mysterious lord of the village, a man who refuses to let Noll have her right as a woman to spurn him.

Thus begins a dangerous game between the choice of woman and the magic of man. The stakes are no less than freedom and happiness, life and death—and neither Noll nor the veiled lord is willing to lose.

The complete The Never Veil Series is out now and is free on Kindle Unlimited!

FALL FAR FROM THE TREE
DUOLOGY

Terror. Callousness. Denial. Rebellion. How the four teenage children of leaders in the duchy and the neighboring empire of Hanaobi choose to adapt to their nefarious parents' whims is a matter of survival.

Rohesia, daughter of the duke, spends her days hunting "outsiders," fugitives who've snuck onto her father's island duchy. That she lives when even children who resemble her are subject to death hardens her heart to tackle the task.

Fastello is the son of the "king" of the raiders who steal from the rich and share with the poor. When aristocrats die in the raids, Fastello questions what his peoples' increasingly wicked methods of survival have cost them.

An orphan raised by a convent of mothers, Cateline can think of no higher aim in life than to serve her religion, even if it means turning a blind eye to the suffering of other orphans under the mothers' care.

Kojiro, new heir to the Hanaobi empire, must avenge his people against the "barbarians" who live in the duchy, terrified the empress, his own mother, might rather see him die than succeed.

When the paths of these four young adults cross, they must rely on one another for survival—but the love of even a malevolent guardian is hard to leave behind.

The complete Fall Far from the Tree duology is out now and is available widely.

BALLAD OF THE BEANSTALK

A Library Journal Self-e Selection.

As her fingers move across the strings of her family's heirloom harp, sixteen-year-old Clarion can forget. She doesn't dwell on the recent passing of her beloved

father or the fact that her mother has just sold everything they owned, including that very same instrument
that gives Clarion life. She doesn't think about how her
friends treat her like a feeble, brittle thing to be
protected. She doesn't worry about how to tell the
elegant Elena, her best friend and first love, that she
doesn't want to be her sweetheart anymore. She
becomes the melody and loses herself in the song.

When Mack, a lord's dashing young son, rides into
town so his father and Elena's can arrange a marriage
between the two youth, Clarion finds herself falling in
love with a boy for the first time. Drawn to Clarion's
music, Mack puts Clarion and Elena's relationship to
the test, but he soon vanishes by climbing up a giant
beanstalk that only Clarion has seen. When even the
town witch won't help, Clarion is determined to rescue
Mack herself and prove once and for all that she doesn't
need protecting. But while she fancied herself a savior,
she couldn't have imagined the enormous world of
danger that awaits her in the kingdom of the clouds.

A prequel to the fairy tale *Jack and the Beanstalk* that
reveals the true story behind the magical singing harp.

Ballad of the Beanstalk is available now in e-book, paperback,
and audiobook.